SURVIVE

Courtney Konstantin

Copyright © 2018 by Courtney Konstantin
All rights reserved. This book or any portion thereof may not be reproduced or used in any manner whatsoever without the express written permission of the publisher except for the use of brief quotations in a book review.

Dedication

For my Grams, who has read every random word I have written, even when it was filled with zombies.
Thank you for making me believe. Love you more.

CHAPTER ONE

"We have to start Sundown, Max, do you understand?"

"Yes, but, Alex, do you really think this is as bad as it looks..." Max trailed off as a fast busy sounded in her ear. Setting down the phone slowly, she turned back to look at the news being broadcasted in Charleston, South Carolina. In a daze, Max watched as scared reporters repeated the same messages of infected people becoming violent and attacking others. Video clips from around the country played: screaming, running, and blood starring in each place.

"Mom?" Jack said, standing next to Max. She looked so much like Max. Though, Jack kept her black curls long, while Max always kept hers short and manageable. Jack inherited hazel eyes from her father, instead of Max's ice blue. Those eyes met hers now, full of worry and fear.

"Mom? What did Auntie Alex say?"

Alex, Max's older sister, called and used the one word that their father had always repeated and ingrained in their minds. Sundown. That word was more of a plan than just a term. It was what their father envisioned would happen when the world fell apart. Sundown on society and everything they knew. When Alex, Max, or their brother Rafe used that word, it meant one thing. Run.

Growing up Alex was more of a mother figure to Max at times than a big sister. Their mother had died giving birth to Max, leaving Max with no memory of the woman that smiled in the photos she grew up looking at. Alex was only four years older than Max. That didn't stop her from mothering Max whenever she felt their father wasn't handling the job correctly. As a small child, Max idolized Alex. When they were teenagers, Max rebelled against Alex. Now the two of them were not only sisters but close friends.

Max had called Alex at the start of the weekend about a news story out of Florida. At that time, it was drugs and violence. Alex had laughed off the story but, in her gut, Max thought there was something else going on. Their father, Mitch Duncan, had taught Max to always trust her gut. She had followed his lessons religiously. She knew that story was something more. She hadn't expected things to get as bad as they were.

After speaking with Alex at the start of the weekend, Max and Jack headed out of town for a small camping trip. Max enjoyed being away from the world, in nature, the way she spent much of her childhood. Just taking Jack to the forest, leaving all connections with the real world behind. They enjoyed their time away together, Max teaching Jack the things she knew from her childhood. It seemed this time she left the real world for too long. Now it was falling apart.

Driving back into Charleston, Max thought there was more traffic than normal. They drove during the early dark hours of the morning and Max hadn't noticed any of the pandemonia that was showing on the news now. Frankly, she was used to seeing some interesting events living in South Carolina. The reporter on the TV was now saying that if you came into contact with an infected, do not approach, do not try to reason with them. Just get away safely.

Jack's small hand slid into Max's as they watched the devastation. Max looked down at her again, thoughts running through her head. Sundown meant she needed to get herself and Jack to Montana. Her childhood home, later her father's compound, was near Flathead Lake. Calling it a compound was fitting as her father had created a place for safety if anything in the world should threaten them. Her brother, Rafe, had been living there since their father's death three years before.

Thinking of Rafe, Max released Jack's hand and picked up the phone again. Grateful she still had a dial tone, she punched in the numbers for Rafe's cell phone. She immediately heard Rafe's voice mail message. She left a brief message, relaying the activation of Sundown. She could only hope he received the message and wasn't off the grid somewhere with no knowledge of what was happening around the populated areas.

Max stood, drumming her fingers on the kitchen table. She knew how to survive, knew where to go and how to get there. Looking around her small apartment, Max made decisions on what they would need. Time couldn't be wasted. Charleston was a heavily populated area. With the way the infection was spreading, the city was already too dangerous to be in.

"Jack, we're going to Montana," Max said finally.

"Why?"

"Because things are going to get really bad before they get any better. Uncle Rafe's place, our family place, is the safest place for us now," Max explained.

Jack stood watching the news as Max turned into the kitchen and started emptying the cabinets of things they could take with them. The trip to Montana would be a long one with everyone fleeing the cities. She piled all the canned foods together, adding them to a box of MREs she had stored in her pantry.

The sound of running feet caused Max to freeze in place. The windows of her first-floor apartment were all covered with blinds, so she wasn't worried about someone seeing in. That wouldn't stop looters from trying to break in. Light on her feet Max ran toward the front door where they had set all of their camping gear. She pulled her tactical tomahawk from its sheath.

She went to the small window in Jack's room that had a view of the parking area. Pulling back the blinds just a bit, she peered out just in time to see a woman running by. Her face was etched with fear as she looked over her shoulder. Max leaned closer to the window and looked in the direction the woman was looking. She wasn't prepared for what she saw.

The old apartment handyman was chasing after her. Max changed her mind, he wasn't chasing as much as following. The movements of his body were strange and unnatural. Each joint seemed to pop and move the body in different directions, no longer working together with a working brain. What horrified Max the most though, was his uniform. Normally a man to be clean and crisp when he came to your apartment to fix something, he was now covered in blood. So thick in some places, it was black.

The man staggered past the window, never giving the glass a second glance. The woman was well out of sight, but the man kept going in the same general direction. As he passed, Max got a good look at his face and she gasped. His eyes were black and dead. She tried to remember what color they were before but realized she was kidding herself to think for a moment that his eyes were anywhere near that abnormal color.

Max didn't move away from the window until the infected man was gone. Turning to leave the room, she almost screamed when she ran straight into Jack who was standing behind her.

"How long have you been standing there?" Max asked, clutching her heaving chest.

"Long enough," Jack answered.

"That's what we have to avoid," Max said, gesturing toward the window.

"What happened to him? Why was he covered in blood?"

"It's this infection. It's making people hurt other people. So stay away from anything that has black eyes," Max concluded as she left the room.

Max grabbed their bug out bags, always in the hall closet. She stuffed MREs and bottled waters into them. She would try to load more food into her small truck, but they needed provisions on them in case the worst happened. Teaching Jack about bug out bags and being prepared was second nature. Max knew she didn't even need to check the bags for accuracy, they were always kept packed completely.

After moving their provisions to the front door, Max unlocked her gun safe and pulled out her 9 mm. Her father hadn't been big on holidays or gifts. When he did give things they were items associated with prepping. Alex and Max received matching 9 mm handguns from him one Christmas. It was Max's go to gun, and she strapped it to her hip. On the other side, she strapped the tomahawk sheath, another weapon that had been a gift from her father.

Mitch Duncan was never the normal father. He was all Max had known. Losing his wife had sent her father into a dark spiral. He found a conspiracy in everyday events and was obsessed with being prepared for the worst to happen. While Alex seemed to resent Mitch at times and Rafe was indifferent, Max hung on his every lesson. For her, Mitch's gruff exterior and erratic personality didn't make him less of a father.

The tactical tomahawk was a gift for her twelfth birthday. Most girls at her age would have been horrified by the brushed metal, sharp edges, and smooth leather sheath. Max, on the other hand, was overly thrilled. Even more so when Mitch taught her to throw it accurately enough to hit a tree trunk from ten feet away. He also taught her how to use it as a weapon in close combat, and that was what Max thought would be useful now.

Jack met Max at the front door, her own small knife on her belt. She looked determined and ready. For an eight-year-old girl, she was wildly insightful and not much missed her observations. She bent and picked up her bug out bag, swinging it onto her back.

"I'm ready. Are we going now?" She asked Max.

"I'm going to take these bags out first. Wait here and stay out of sight. As soon as the truck is loaded, I'll come back for you," Max replied as she loaded her hands full of bags.

Opening the front door slowly, Max peered around the walkway. Nothing seemed to move. Standing still for a moment she listened. Chaos seemed to reign in the city. Screams and shouts could be heard. The sounds of gunfire seemed to echo through the buildings, closer than Max would have liked. Gunfire meant people fighting. Whatever they were fighting, Max didn't want to see, so she hoped the healthy people were winning.

Stepping out, she motioned for Jack to close and lock the door behind her. Once she heard the click she rushed toward the parking lot. Getting to her truck, she opened the back door and loaded the food quickly, looking around constantly for any sneak attacks from the infected nearby. Max rushed two more trips to the truck with food, clothing, first aid supplies, and water. She closed the door behind her in the apartment one more time.

"The TV and phone aren't working anymore," Jack said.

"Didn't expect them to last long," Max replied. "This is what Gramps always said would happen. The world would easily fall apart."

"Do we just go?"

Max thought about that. Living on the East Coast had taken her far from her family. At the time, she was rebelling against the constraints her father put on her life. Max couldn't live in the compound, watching Jack be completely cut off from the world. Running had left them without family ties nearby. But Max couldn't help but think of some of the women she worked with at a local dentist office. Most of them were older than Max and felt it was their duty to be Max and Jack's family.

Now those connections confused Max's plans. She didn't need to care about anyone else but Jack. Leaving town immediately and getting to Montana as fast as possible should be their only goal. But here she stood, one hand on the doorknob, not sure of the decision she should make. She cursed inwardly, knowing this was the main reason she never wanted to have these relationships.

"We have to make a stop," Max said finally, a decision made. She would go to the dentist office, find the addresses of the women who had been kind. If she could help, she would. If not, they would move on quickly.

Opening the door slowly, Max checked the walkway again. She heard a door slam down the way and the noise caused her to pause. Nothing seemed to move, so she stepped out with Jack's hand in hers. They left the door unlocked, knowing they would never come back. Max figured someone else might come along that needed the shelter. When they arrived at the truck, Max helped Jack into the passenger side, keeping her bug out bag at her feet.

As Max rounded the truck to get to her door a growl sounded behind her. Jack banged on the window, causing the growling infected to turn it's attention to her. Max swung around, pulling her tomahawk as she turned. She found an infected teenager limping toward the truck. She knew she could get in the truck and get away, but that would leave the boy to possibly kill someone else.

Max whistled loudly toward the infected. His head whipped toward the sound, his body following in a grotesque manner. His unresponsive body bounced off the corner of the truck before rounding toward where Max stood. Clawed hands reached out toward her, fingers covered in blood. Snarls sounded from the throat, coming out of a mouth painted in red. The smell coming from him caused Max's stomach to convulse. Thinking about her father's lessons about close combat with the tomahawk, Max stepped into her swing, bringing the tomahawk down swiftly.

The blade sliced into the shoulder of the teenager and Max quickly yanked it free. Slamming into the back of the truck, the infected started to fall to the ground and Max felt triumph. That feeling was quickly quashed as the infected gained its footing and swung back in her direction. His arm was hanging off of his body, unnaturally flopping around as he tried to reach Max.

Disbelieving, Max watched the sick boy for another moment. The blow to the shoulder should have taken him down. At least slowed him. There was no reaction to the pain that should have come from the injury. He seemed to keep moving with only one thought in his mind. A Max Happy Meal. The absurd thought came into Max's mind and she almost laughed. Shaking her head, she cleared everything out except the fight.

The boy was on her again, his unbroken arm up again, fingers reaching to rake at her skin. Stepping to the side of his reach, Max used the tomahawk to redirect his body. She wanted to test how the infected would react to a moving target. He didn't waste time swinging back around toward Max with a snarl. Wasting no more time, Max did the only thing she could think. She raised the tomahawk again. With all of her strength, she brought the blade down with a whistling crack.

CHAPTER TWO

The feeling of the tomahawk blade crashing into the skull of the infected boy reminded Max of slicing watermelons with her father. Mitch Duncan didn't give gifts of weapons without ensuring his kids knew how to use them and care for them. Max wanted to use her tomahawk so badly. Mitch made her practice on watermelons and later logs as she improved. Watermelons cracked in half when struck by the tomahawk. That was different, so much different, than hitting what was once a human head.

As the infected boy's body fell, the tomahawk was ripped from Max's hand. Appalled at herself for losing her weapon so easily, Max quickly dislodged the deeply embedded blade. She would keep that in mind when fighting any others. She wouldn't allow her weapon to be so easily lost again.

Max jumped in the truck, quickly starting the engine. The locks clicked, and Max looked over at Jack, the little girl's finger on the lock button.

"Momma, did you just kill that kid?" Jack asked quietly.

"That kid wasn't alive anymore. It was the best thing to do for him," Max explained, throwing the truck into reverse and backing out of their parking spot.

Everywhere Max looked, blood and bodies seemed to be piled. They circled the buildings, winding their way through to the exit. The windows of the apartment office building were broken in and the clubhouse raided. Max could see hanging cords where the flat-screen televisions used to hang. She shook her head in disgust realizing in all this madness there were people that decided to steal pointless electronics.

Growing up electronics had not been a luxury the Duncan kids knew. Mitch kept a small TV in his room that had a handful of channels that were found by old rabbit ears. This was only for the end of the world. Mitch would explain that the first thing to really be unreliable would be wired cable and electricity. Every night after dinner Mitch could be found in front of his small TV watching the evening news. As Max got older, she knew her father wasn't normal. His whispers could be heard down the hall, as he jotted down confusing notes of conspiracy from the news stories he watched.

Now Max lived in a world where electronics ruled. She had all of the normal things, TV, computer, cell phone. But she also knew how to navigate by the sun and stars, could go days without turning on the TV and knew how to live without a cell phone strapped to her ear. As she pulled away from the ravaged clubhouse she took a deep breath, pulling confidence and determination from deep down. She didn't need society. She could survive without it all.

The main road outside of the apartment was clogged with vehicles trying to escape. Max quickly cut into the crowd of vehicles trying to drive in the bike lane, and she followed. As soon as she could cut through a parking lot to another road she did. Cars jumped medians, sidewalks, and other barriers just to avoid the congestion. Max watched the vehicles around her with sharp eyes, making sure no one got it into their heads to hit them.

Cutting through another parking lot, she saw a woman standing next to a building. Max slowed and watched her for a moment, not entirely sure if she was infected or not. The woman seemed frozen in place, watching as the chaos rolled around her. Max honked her horn at her, causing the woman to jump before swinging her head toward them. Cautiously Max rolled down her window.

"You need to get moving!" Max yelled out her window.

"I...I...what?" The woman stammered in reply. Max had little patience for those that couldn't handle themselves in a crisis.

"Lady, can't you see what's happening in front of you? You aren't safe just standing out here!" Max called back to her. The woman swung her gaze back to the clogged traffic. Screaming and gunshots seemed to permanently hang in the air.

"Listen, I can't hang out here with you and be besties. You need to get inside or evacuate or something. Get moving!" Max yelled. The last statement seemed to reach the woman and she disappeared around the corner of the building. Max found herself hoping the woman figured things out before she caught teeth to the throat.

The normal commute to her place of work was twenty minutes. An hour and a half of frustrating driving found them finally a street away from the dentist office. Max hopped the truck onto the small sidewalk and cut around traffic where she could. The sound of screeching brakes sounded suddenly as a loud crunch followed. Max slowed and looked around to find the accident that must have happened. As they moved forward smoke rising from the engine of a small sedan could be seen.

"Oh my god," Max said quietly.

"Momma..." Jack said, trailing off as they watched the scene unfold in front of them. The car accident had been caused by a group of infected that had wandered into the street. Max noted that some of them were wearing military fatigues and she found that odd. The infected were surrounding the small vehicle that had crashed. The windows were down and screams could be heard from inside the vehicle as the infected reached in and clawed at their meal.

"Jack, look away," Max instructed as the infected pulled a man from the car. The man continued to scream as his body fell to the ground and the infected fell atop to feast. Max stopped the truck with a clear sight of the man. Checking her surroundings, she quickly rolled her window down. She aimed her 9 mm out of the window and fired a round at the man on the ground. Her shot was true, and the man's suffering was ended. However, that didn't stop the feasting infected.

Max quickly rolled up her window and shoved her gun back into its holster. She watched for a moment as the infected ripped at the man's body, his blood pooled beneath and spread in a dark streak across the road. She quickly glanced at Jack and found her swiping furiously at tears on her face.

"I had to help him," Max said simply. Jack didn't reply.

Max concentrated on the short distance they had left to get to the dentist office. The sound of her gunshot had scared some people out of their cars and they were running with no direction. Max laid on the horn warning pedestrians that she was coming. Suddenly an infected stepped in front of the car and Jack let out a quick shriek. Having had her fill of infected in the road, Max stepped on the gas pedal and slammed into the body of the infected. What used to be a small woman bounced off the front bumper of the truck. She fell to the ground and Max felt part of the body fall under the driver's side wheels.

Looking in the rearview mirror Max could see the body she ran over. She was taken by surprise when she saw the infected arms swinging in the air as if clawing for purchase in a warm uninfected body. It didn't seem to be able to rise from the asphalt, but the extremities not smashed by the wheels of her truck were still working on their own. Max felt fear try and rise in her chest, but she tapped it down. Fear was a losing game and she had no intentions of dying.

Max started a list in her head of what she was learning from the infected. With each confrontation, the infected displayed their traits. Injuries didn't seem to stop their one-track goal of eating. Broken bones, contusions, gashes, none of these things created any sort of reaction from them. The only thing that mattered to them was the uninfected. Max had to assume a wound to the brain was the only way of stopping them, after she was able to kill the boy at her apartment.

The truck screeched to a halt in front of the glass doors of a small office building. Max sat with the truck running, watching around the parking lot for any movement. She watched as someone ran from the neighboring business. As the woman ran by, Max recognized her as the receptionist that worked next door. The receptionist didn't even glance at the running truck as she ran to a waiting car. Moments later she sped out of the parking lot, wheels screaming across the asphalt as she found a break in traffic.

"Let's go. I'm going to get the address for Denise. Check and see if she needs help out of town. Then we'll start our trip," Max explained as she killed the engine.

Jack didn't respond. She followed Max out of the truck, both of them carrying their bug out bags. Jack followed her mother's lessons of never leaving your supplies and always being prepared. Max never had to remind her. Much like Max, when she was Jack's age, growing up with Mitch. Max tried to give Jack a more rounded upbringing, but she always found herself relying on what she knew. And that was the prepping lessons she learned from Mitch.

Entering the dentist office, Max pulled her tomahawk as a precaution. The door was locked and none of the windows were broken yet. However, Max wasn't lowering her guard. She rounded the front desk and entered the hallway that led to her office. Stopping at the supply room, Max had a revelation looking at the locked case of medication. Going to the case, Max used her tomahawk to break out the front glass. She was greeted with a view of packages of limited supply prescription medications.

Motioning Jack over, Max opened both of their bug out bags. Following her mother's instructions, Jack started dumping boxes of meds into their bags. Max headed to her office to find the address she needed. In her office, she also grabbed the multi-tool she had stored in her desk for small office repairs. The tool also had a saw and flint on it, items Max knew they would need on the road.

Max found herself thinking about Mitch and the items he typically referred to as essentials. Always be able to cook, hunt, protect, and survive. Everything he taught Max and her siblings was based around that. When Max was in elementary school she was almost suspended for bringing a multi-tool to school. She didn't understand how it was a dangerous thing because she knew how to use each tool appropriately. At that age, Max hadn't realized how different her family was from her bubbly school friends. After she got caught with the tool, Mitch taught her to always hide her tools. He didn't believe in any authority telling him what to do.

Sometimes Max didn't understand why he allowed his children to attend public school. When she looked back she was thankful they were able to have that experience. And now she was convinced he only allowed them to go so he had the quiet time to work on his compound in ways he couldn't with his young children underfoot. The rest of the time he gave the kids useful tasks to contribute to their survival at home.

Out of his three children, Max was the most interested in his lessons. She had never known her mother. As Max stood at her desk she thought of the stories her father would tell of her mother. His eyes would go soft and sometimes watery when he spoke of her. She was the love of his life. Without her, he didn't know how to completely function in the real world. Without any influence from her in life, Max turned out harder than Alex or Rafe.

Alex had tried to give Max the affection of a mother. However, she was just a child herself, only knowing her mother for the early four years of her life. When their father wouldn't talk of their mother, the girls would sit around her photos and create stories about who she had been. Max would go to bed dreaming of a mother's love and female presence in her life. But when she grew up, it was easier for her to let go of those dreams. It wasn't the same for Alex.

Thinking of Alex, Max began to worry. Alex was softer, more emotional than Max. Sometimes Max envied her sister, her heart and her ability to love fully. However, it was that softness that worried Max. She found herself imagining the worst. Alex not making it to Montana and her niece Billie and nephew Henry being left alone somewhere on the road. Max brought herself back to the present and shook the dark thoughts from her mind. Alex would be in Montana waiting for her, she wouldn't doubt that again.

As Max walked up the hallway she heard someone at the front doors. She hurried into the storage room with Jack and grabbed her to move her away from the medication case. Jack's scream would have given them away, but Max covered her mouth quickly. Using hand motions she let Jack know to stay quiet. Her daughter nodded her head and squeezed back into the dark corner Max pushed her into. Just as Max turned her back on Jack and prepared for a fight, she heard the glass on the front door shatter.

"Why are we breaking into an office?" The voice of a man floated down the hallway. The sound of footsteps on broken glass indicated the intruders had entered the reception area.

"This is a dentist, I bet they have drugs." The voice of a second man answered, sounding closer than the first.

Hearing they were after drugs, Max began to feel her heart speed up with panic. Quietly Max pulled her tomahawk again, letting it hang loosely at her side. If the men headed down the hallway they would easily find the room they hid in. Waiting to be found, preparing to fight, Max stood tensely, hiding Jack with her body. The shotgun blast that sounded next echoed powerfully through the small office.

CHAPTER THREE

"They're coming!" One man's voice yelled, sounding high and shrill in his panic.

The sound of the shotgun pump action was only a moment before another loud shot. A scuffle was happening in the reception area of the office. Max listened intently, the sounds of growling reaching her ears. She realized the men weren't fighting other living people but infected that had wandered through the broken glass door.

Max knew she needed to make a decision quickly. They could escape through the back fire door, but their transportation awaited them on the other side of the building. Taking a deep breath, Max turned to Jack.

"You are to stay here, understand? I'm going to go out there, clear it out, so we can get to the truck," Max said. Jack's face was pale, her hazel eyes full of fear.

"You'll come to get me?" She asked.

"Of course. Stay hidden and quiet. Don't come out unless it's me telling you to," Max said in a hurried whisper.

Without another word, Max turned toward the door of the medical room. She hesitated at the doorway, peering slowly toward the reception area. A fight sounded like it still raged. Max could see the shadows of movement down the hall, but nothing was in the hall with her. She quietly tiptoed to the end of the hall and peeked into the reception area. What she found chilled her to the very core. Two men stood back to back in the largest part of the room. The room was filling with infected bodies.

The men seemed capable, defending themselves from the mindless attacks of the infected. Taking a chance Max stepped into the room fully and brought her tomahawk down on the nearest infected head. Anticipating the depth of the blow, Max braced as the body fell and allowed the momentum to free her blade. Now in the room, Max could hear the grunts and curses of the men fighting. Shutting them out, she fell into a fighting stance and chopped down the infected nearest to her.

The infected flowing into the office were men and women alike. Some would have seemed alive, had it not been for black eyes and growling sounds coming from their throats. The smell in the small area was enough to make Max gag. The rotten smell of decayed flesh floated around the infected bodies.

Her movements soon attracted more infected and as a tide, the nearest ones turned toward her. Max tapped her fear down and just continued to move her tomahawk. To save time, she struck out at a different body part, causing bodies to fall even if not completely dead. When space opened, she would bring her tomahawk down on a skull, a sickening crunch sounding each time.

She worked on keeping her mind focused, not thinking about the gore that was splashed across her clothing. She took a step forward and almost slipped on blood that layered the tile floor. Glancing down she grimaced at the body she stepped over. The infected that had attacked the person had picnicked on the stomach and now insides were open to Max's eyes.

Bodies seemed to pile up around Max and the men fighting. The flow from outside slowed and finally stopped. Leaving the three of them heaving in the reception area. The men eyed Max, who stood up straighter and swung her tomahawk around. She tried to look nonchalant but effectively dangerous.

"We are lucky they got caught up on the frame of the window and the dead bodies. We would have been meat. Thanks for the help," one of the men said to Max.

"You can take what you want from here. I'm just leaving," Max replied. She turned toward the hallway.

"The door is clear, where are you going?" The other man demanded. Max could easily figure he was afraid she would be getting away with his drugs.

"I worked here. I just need to get a photo from my desk. I don't want to leave it," Max lied. That seemed to satisfy the men, and they didn't comment or follow as Max rushed down the hall.

Stepping into the medical room, Max quickly grabbed her bug out bag and slung it over her shoulders. She motioned to Jack who peered around the medicine case, to grab her pack as well. Jack obeyed quickly, zipping up her pack, which hid the meds they did take. Before walking back into the hallway, Max pulled her 9 mm. The men had a shotgun, but she was sure they wouldn't risk their own lives to stop Max and Jack.

Coming into sight of the men, Max immediately leveled her gun at them. The man that had thanked her looked surprised, but the one that asked where she was going looked angry.

"That's more than a photo lady," the angry man said.

"Weird, so it is," Max replied, sarcasm dripped from her voice.

"What's in the packs?" He asked.

"Pretty sure it's full of none of your business," Max shot back. As she spoke, she walked using her peripheral vision, stepping around bodies. She knew without saying anything that Jack was following her footsteps exactly, just as she had always taught her. Her daughter knew that Max would never step somewhere unsafe, so she always was to step in the same place.

"Let's just leave them alone," the thankful man said to his companion.

"They could have cleaned out the drugs," the angry man replied.

"I guess you'll need to go see," Max replied as they reached the doorway. Angry man ran toward the hallway as she pushed Jack behind her, pulling the keys from her pocket and giving them to the girl. Max didn't want to risk taking her eyes off the men until the truck was open and started. Jack's feet could be heard running across the short distance of pavement. Moments later the engine sounded and Max backed up more.

"Bitch!" The yell came from the medical room. Max knew the man had found the smashed open case. Before turning, she looked down the site of her 9 mm at the nicer of the two men.

"You should find someone new to watch your back." With that Max turned and sprinted the short distance to the truck. As she got to the driver's door she was already swinging off her pack. She shoved the pack to Jack and jumped into the seat. Not waiting for seat belts or angry men with shotguns, Max threw the truck into reverse and squealed out of the parking spot.

An hour of traffic later, Max and Jack wound through residential streets. Without GPS, Max used her city map to find the home of Denise. The longer the drive took, the more often she thought about just abandoning her mission and leaving town. But she had already told Jack they were going to find Denise and the little girl was fond of the woman. Max again thought about her avoidance of connections. This would be so much easier if she didn't need to care about anyone else.

The homes along the quaint street looked to be part of a war zone, battles waged on their pristine green lawns. Max drove slowly, checking the addresses as they passed homes. She hit the breaks quickly when she found the house that matched the address in Denise's employee file. It was odd that she and Jack had never actually been to the house. Denise had offered and invited numerous times. But Max shied away from forming any real bond. Their relationship consisted of office lunches out and occasional dinners with Jack in tow.

Denise lived in a two-story townhouse, sandwiched between two other houses. Max sat, the truck running, as she studied the door standing ajar on Denise's home. Along all of the lawns, there were signs of infected attacks. The bodies lying haphazardly in places indicated there was a loser in those fights. Without closer inspection, Max couldn't be sure if the bodies were infected dead or human dead.

"I don't like this," Max remarked quietly.

"Do you think she's dead?" Jack asked.

"At this point, I think it's likely," Max responded. Jack didn't say anything, but her sniffle indicated that her mother's answer upset her. Max sighed inwardly. She wasn't sure how to make this all better for her daughter. The realization of the world falling apart was too much for an adult to handle, let alone an eight-year-old child. It was what they were faced with and making it softer didn't make it untrue.

"I'm going to go check. Keep the truck running. Doors locked," Max said as she pulled her tomahawk free. She was soundless as she popped open the door of the truck. Carefully she closed it as quietly as she could, not wishing to draw attention to Jack inside the truck. If the infected were to find her, they would window shop for their meal. Max couldn't allow that.

Waiting, she didn't turn toward Denise's house until she heard the click of the lock mechanism. She nodded to Jack and turned to survey the area. At the end of the street, she could see people moving, but it was impossible to tell at that distance if they were infected or not. Slowly she moved toward the open doorway. The house beyond was dark, no lights on, no shades were down. It seemed like Denise may have been hiding in her house.

Max's mind went over the different scenarios of why Denise would have opened her door during a plague outbreak like this. The woman's heart was pure gold and that would have been her downfall. Max could only guess that she probably had someone she knew come to the door and opened to help them. Human connections, again causing problems.

Entering the house, Max checked the corners of the immediate room she was in. It was once a sweetly furnished living room. Now all Max saw was a TV crashed to the ground and a couch toppled over. Blood splashed the wall behind the couch, a sickly mosaic causing Max to curse inwardly. She wanted to turn around immediately and leave. However, much like the boy at her apartment complex, she couldn't leave whatever was in the house to kill someone else.

Swinging her gaze side to side, she continued to keep her head on a swivel. She didn't believe the infected were intelligent enough to sneak up on a living being. Though, that wasn't something she was interested in testing. Deciding that following the trail of blood was the best plan, she headed toward the stairs. Stopping before she ascended, she listened for any movement, unnatural or otherwise. The house was silent as a tomb, the feeling not lost on Max.

At the top of the stairs, the blood trail seemed to accumulate into a deep puddle. The final attack seemed to happen there. Doors stood open to the right of the staircase. Max tensed when she saw legs sticking out of one of the open rooms. The legs didn't twitch or try to stand, so Max approached cautiously.

The breath came out of Max in a rush when she realized the legs didn't belong to Denise, but to an elderly man. Bile stung Max's throat as she admitted she only assumed it was a man by the clothes on the bottom of the body. The head was completely destroyed. A brick lay next to the body, clearly the weapon that battered the skull until it was the pulp laying on the bedroom floor. Max backed away fighting the urge to vomit in the hallway.

Rushing back the way she came, she entered the bathroom she had passed. Her stomach started to heave, but she swallowed it down and forced herself to toughen up. She ran some water from the sink and splashed her face, the water cool against her heated skin. The one thing she knew was the body wasn't Denise. Max stared at herself in the mirror. She was pale, her skin clammy. No amount of strength made dealing with this plague easy.

A small sound caused Max to freeze. She cocked her head to the side, listening for the sound again. A strange moan came from behind her, and Max whirled around. She faced a closed door, which she had assumed was a linen closet. Her panic when she ran into the bathroom had caused her to miss the bloody handprint on the doorknob. Again, a gurgling moan came from behind the door.

Max took a deep breath, stepping closer to the door. Tomahawk raised high over her head, she flung open the door. A body dropped out of the closet and Max yelped, jumping back in surprise.

"Denise?" Max said. The woman was covered in blood, her eyes squeezed shut. She was gripping a blood-soaked towel to her upper arm. The sound of Max's voice caused the older woman to groan quietly and she tried to curl up in a ball.

"Denise," Max said more forcefully. She crouched down next to the woman, trying to roll her back toward her. Her skin was hot, burning with fever. Taking a chance, Max checked her throat for a pulse, finding it quick and erratic.

"What happened, Denise? Can you tell me?" Max asked. She reached into the linen cabinet and grabbed a towel that wasn't completely bloody. Sliding the soft material under Denise's head, the older woman moaned quietly.

"Neighbor...fight...bite...killed him," Denise rambled quietly.

"You killed the man in the bedroom? With the brick?" Max asked. Denise's nod was barely noticeable to Max. She was incredulous. Denise was a soft-spoken, sweet woman. Max would never have imagined she had a fighting bone in her body. Self-preservation caused even the best people to change.

Max ran through scenarios in her mind. Now that she had found Denise and she was injured, Max couldn't just leave her. Thinking of her fever, Max left the bathroom and went back to the room where the dead body was. Her eyes avoided looking at the grotesque scene again. Instead, she focused on the bed and stepped around the bloody mess on the floor. Bringing a blanket back to Denise, Max draped it over her.

The bathroom floor was no place for someone with an injury, but Max doubted she could move the woman on her own. Denise seemed to be out of it and unable to help. Max rolled her onto her back, causing Denise to hiss in pain.

"I'm sorry," Max murmured. She carefully pulled the towel away from Denise's upper arm. Max was shocked to see much of Denise's flesh missing in the shape of a circular human bite.

"Shit, Denise, how did you even make it this long?" Max whispered. The flow of blood from the wound seemed to be slow, but it wasn't stopping. Denise needed real medical attention. No ambulances would be coming for the woman though.

Max grabbed a few clean square washcloths. She packed those against the wound. Then taking a longer hand towel she wrapped the towel around the washcloths, tying it tightly. Denise was deathly pale, unmoving now, even with Max's pressure and movement around her wound. Max stopped for a moment and watched for Denise to breathe. Air went in and out of the woman's lungs and Max let out the breath she had been holding.

Even the best-laid plans have wrenches thrown in, Max thought to herself. She wanted to be on the road, out of Charleston and on her way to her family in Montana. However, she just couldn't leave Denise alone on her bathroom floor. Staying the day wouldn't hurt she decided. She and Jack could sleep downstairs after Max flipped the couch the right way. And maybe they could get Denise help later.

"I'll be right back, Denise. I'm going to get Jack out of the truck. I'd say stay here, but I don't think you're moving anytime soon," Max muttered.

Max went downstairs to the living room. She decided to make it a little less shocking for Jack and flipped the couch to its feet. She couldn't do anything about the smashed TV or lamp. But the couch gave them somewhere to sit and possibly sleep. Max then went to the kitchen. The power seemed to still be on, which meant they could have a decent meal for lunch and dinner. That fact made Max feel better about staying the day.

With Jack inside Max limited her movement to just downstairs. Her daughter didn't need to see the horror that was laying in the upstairs bedroom. Max explained that Denise was injured so they would stay and try to get her help. Jack accepted that and sat on the couch with a book. Max locked the door and found a piece of splintered wood from the TV stand to shove under the door, ensuring no one was entering without their knowledge. She pulled the shades in all the windows and made sure the back door was locked and barred.

In the kitchen, Max turned on the water and wet down a towel. She scrubbed at her hands and arms, trying to get rid of the blood of the day's events. She looked down at her shirt and realized it couldn't be salvaged. She went back into the living room and retrieved a clean shirt from her bug out bag. Changing quickly, she already felt better now that she was clean.

Leaving Jack to read her book, Max headed back upstairs to check on Denise. She was surprised to find the woman sitting up and leaning against the bathroom wall. She didn't move when Max approached, just watched her through hooded eyes.

"Max, what are you doing here?" Denise asked, her voice hoarse and low.

"We came to check on you, get you out of the city maybe," Max replied. She bent to check the makeshift bandage she had on Denise's arm. It was still in place, but blood was seeping through.

"I...I think I killed my neighbor," Denise whispered.

Max went with direct, her normal setting. "Yes, you did. But I'm pretty sure it was in self-defense. I'm also pretty positive he wasn't your neighbor anymore."

"He bit me." The events of the day seemed to suddenly dawn on Denise. Tears slipped from her cheeks, making Max even more uncomfortable. She didn't do well with emotions. She grabbed a handful of toilet paper and handed it to Denise, who mopped at her face with her good arm. The motion seemed to exhaust her, and her head fell back against the wall.

"You should probably rest. You have a fever." As Max spoke Denise slumped to the side, sliding back to the towel pillow Max had created for her. Max covered her back up with the blanket and wet a washcloth with cold water to go on her forehead.

Denise had a well-stocked kitchen for being a woman that lived alone. At least Max thought she lived alone. Guilt tried to creep into Max's mind as she realized how little she knew about the woman. A woman who had tried hard to be kind to her and Jack. She pushed the feelings aside and focused on a hearty meal for Jack.

During the day Max checked on Denise in twenty-minute intervals. She changed her bandage once when she found blood was starting to slowly pool on the bathroom floor again. When she examined the wound again she was shocked to find the skin turning black in and around the bite. It was too soon for infection or something like gangrene. Max wracked her brain, trying to remember all the lessons her father taught about illness and injury. She couldn't think of a single thing that would have infected the wound so quickly.

After a dinner of cheeseburgers, strawberries, and kidney beans, Jack settled to read her book again. She had already unpacked and repacked her entire bug out bag. She then decided to do the same with Max's. Jack had an organizational streak that mostly drove Max crazy. However right now, being organized and prepared was going to help them survive. Max instructed Jack to pack any additional small food items. Whenever they were able to leave, the extra food would help provide for Denise until they got her help.

A thud from above their heads, had Max freezing as she packed food into a messenger style bag she had found. Thinking Denise had woken and tried to move on her own, Max rushed upstairs. When she got to the bathroom though, Denise was on the ground, lying still. Her legs looked to be moved, but she was still sleeping. As Max watched her, she didn't see her chest rise.

Panic flowed through Max's veins. Thinking Denise dead, she dropped down to check her pulse. It was weak but still beat slowly against Max's fingers. She lifted one of Denise's eyelids, thinking to check the reaction state of her pupils. She was met with black, no color, no white, just solid black. Max yelped quietly and quickly shuffled away from her body. She had never seen eyes like that before, at least not on the living.

CHAPTER FOUR

Growing up in Montana on a large piece of land, it was only natural to have animals. When Max was young, Mitch warned her to not name the animals. He would explain to her that they weren't pets. And by giving them names she was making the job of butchering and eating the animals that much harder.

Max didn't learn her lesson until the day her pet cow Moo was butchered for winter provisions. When Moo was taken to the room where Mitch butchered animals, Alex tried to distract Max. But she knew what was happening. Max at the young age of six tried to decide she would be a vegetarian. She would never eat the meat that came from Moo. Her phase didn't last long after Mitch put his foot down. For a week he forced Max to only eat meat to get over her silly belief.

It was such a strange memory to be thinking of now, as she fought traffic away from Denise's house the next morning. Max couldn't forget the way Denise looked when she woke as an infected. Her black eyes focused on Max immediately. Without hesitation, Max ended Denise's dead life with a bowie knife to her brain. Max had laid her body back down on the bathroom floor and covered her face with the blanket.

It had already been dark when Denise woke. Max did not want to travel at night unless it was completely necessary. Jack had curled up on the couch to sleep, but Max sat awake all night, thinking of Denise's body upstairs. When they left in the morning, Max chose to not tell Jack that Denise was dead. Rather she said she had family coming to get her, so they could get back on the road.

Her hands tightened on the steering wheel, her knuckles white, as she tried to suck down the distraught feeling she felt. Killing someone she once knew wasn't something she was prepared for. Her mind continued to wander back to the animals and the lesson Mitch was trying to teach her. Maybe he always believed the world would end up like this and she would be forced to kill people she knew. Did he expect her to never have people she loved, growing to be just like him?

Max wasn't sure she would ever forget the feeling of the knife piercing Denise's skull. Her black eyes died almost immediately, the driving force of hunger suddenly gone as if a light switch had been flipped. Even knowing Denise was truly dead before the knife even touched her, Max felt guilt and pain. She looked around her house while Jack slept and found photos of Denise smiling with people. Some that resembled her, a family that Max never knew about. Would those people know their loved one was dead in her home?

One bite. *Was that all it took?* Max sat in thought, trying to pull together what she knew. Denise was the first infected she had seen before they turned. The only thing wrong with her had been the one bite and the raging fever that seemed to come with it. No matter what aid Max provided, the blood continued to ooze from the wound, as if her body was preventing the healing process. *Maybe the infection doesn't allow the body to fix itself?* The thoughts were swirling around in her head. She wanted to slam her head into the steering wheel a few times, maybe then it would all make sense.

Sitting in traffic, Max wasn't feeling the same urgency she did the day prior. She felt weighed down, the emotions she was experiencing were confusing for her. She looked over at Jack, who sat with her eyes glued to the activity outside their vehicle. Beyond her siblings, her father, and Jack, there had only been one other person she really had loved in life. Though that time had passed, Max always found herself thinking of him. Griffin Wells. Thinking of him now made her heart beat with panic, wondering where he was.

Griffin had been her high school sweetheart. They went through all of high school together in Montana. However, right after they graduated, Griffin made the huge decision to enlist in the Army. He was shipped off to boot camp before their summer had even started. Despite all of their whispered love and promises, Max never heard from him again. Now, because Rafe still lived in Montana, Max knew through family connections that Griffin was in North Carolina. He had been stationed there and had decided to stay after serving his eight years.

Max was lost in thought. She was absently watching the traffic, looking for openings to jump into. However, she didn't see the man creeping up on her side of the truck. When her window shattered, and glass rained down on her, she didn't even have time to reach for her gun.

"Get out of the truck," the man behind the rifle said. The rifle that was now pointed at Max's face. Max kept her hands visible, meeting the man's eyes. He looked to be an ordinary guy, wearing a shirt from a local bar and jeans.

"Mom!" Jack exclaimed from the passenger seat. Swinging her gaze to her daughter, Max saw a woman at her window, pointing a handgun toward Max from the other side. The woman didn't meet Max's gaze, her eyes seemingly down in regret and doubt. Max turned her attention back to the man who seemed to be in charge.

"Listen, man, we're all having a shit time right now," she started.

"I don't care about what time you're having. I want your truck," the man said curtly, cutting off Max.

"Ok, I get it. But I have my daughter in here," Max said, motioning behind her. She had turned her body, her rib cage pushing against the steering wheel, effectively blocking the man's aim at Jack.

"Just get out of the damn truck!" Rifleman yelled at Max. She could see he was nervous and she didn't like his finger on the trigger while he was feeling that way. She ran scenarios through her mind. She couldn't challenge the guy and have him let off a shot at her, or god forbid Jack. Her daughter couldn't be left alone in this chaos. Decision made, Max motioned to Jack to grab their go bags. Slowly Max slung the messenger bag of food over her shoulder. She motioned to the man that she was going to open her door.

"Ok. You can have the truck. But my daughter needs to get out of the truck first. Once I see she's out and away, I'll get out and leave the keys inside," Max explained. The man seemed to think over her offer quickly and then nodded his head.

"Jack, get out of the truck. Take our bags. Walk to the sidewalk," Max said over her shoulder.

"But, Momma," Jack started.

"No, Jacklyn. Please just do it. I'm right behind you. We'll figure this out," Max said quickly. She used her daughter's full first name, typically shortened to the nickname in a tradition started by Mitch Duncan. Using her real first name was a sign to Jack that Max wanted her to obey no question.

She heard Jack pop open her door. As she passed the woman with the gun, the woman whispered she was sorry. Jack didn't answer, just continued walking away from the truck.

With her daughter away, Max opened the driver's side door and stepped from the truck. Rifleman followed her, keeping her in his sights. Max understood the panic. She understood survival. What she couldn't understand was hurting others for your own survival over theirs.

"By the way, we would have taken you anywhere you wanted, if you had just asked," Max said to the man. With that, she turned her back on the man, no longer worried he would shoot her.

Meeting Jack on the sidewalk, Max gave her a quick hug and slung her own go back over her shoulders.

"Carjacked...I wouldn't have even thought it," Max muttered.

"People are scared," Jack replied, obviously not blaming the people for their stupid behavior.

"Everyone is. But you don't put others in danger because you think you deserve more than them," Max responded. As she spoke she took in their surroundings, trying to make a plan. She would not be jacking someone else, so they needed a better plan than stealing from someone.

They were too exposed standing by the side of a busy main street. Cars were jumping the curbs wherever they could. Horns blared as near misses happened. People yelled from cracked car windows. Max took Jack's arm and lead her away from the chaos. They were in the parking lot of a Mexican restaurant. She led them over to the wall, something to keep anyone from sneaking up on them. It was still fairly early in the day, however without a vehicle they were not going to cover much ground.

A feeling of claustrophobic panic struck Max. There were too many people in the city. They wouldn't be safe until they were beyond the state border and headed to Montana. Standing there near the wall and in the shade of a tree, Max watched the panic around them. People ran between cars, as those cars struggled through traffic trying to reach their destinations.

An idea began to form in Max's mind. Even with a vehicle, people weren't going anywhere. Looking back into the traffic, Max could even still see her truck sitting right where they had left it. She could see the man in the driver's seat, banging the steering wheel and laying on the horn like the rest of the drivers. He wasn't going to get anywhere in his stolen vehicle. Wait it out. It wasn't Max's way, she was always ready to go. However, the mayhem raging in the city was inescapable.

Suddenly the tempo of the moving crowd changed. People started screaming, dropping their items and running in panic. Max tensed, immediately sensing danger. She motioned to Jack to follow and they slowly crept toward the street to see what people were fleeing from.

"Oh my god," Max breathed. She heard Jack's shocked inhale behind her, but her daughter knew better than to make too much noise.

What mother and daughter saw was a mob. Not of healthy people fleeing, but of the infected. Even at a distance, their strange uncoordinated movements gave them away, looking like puppets on strings that weren't being controlled. The mob spanned the entire road, bumping into each other, running into cars, but slowly making their way forward. Max knew they had to move.

"We need to run," Max said to Jack. All the girl did was nod and tighten the straps on her pack.

Turning away from the road, Max quickly decided to cut through buildings, to avoid the main pack of infected. As well as avoiding any more panicked people that wanted to do something stupid. With Jack on her heels, the two of them entered the alley that was behind the Mexican restaurant. The back door of the building swung open as they ran and Max had her gun out and aimed before she thought. A man weighed down with bags of what Max assumed was food screamed when he saw Max pointing her 9 mm at his face.

"Sorry," Max said simply, holstering the gun. The man didn't answer or look back as he ran down the alley.

As they exited the third alley they went through, they met a dead end and had to join the road again. The screams of frightened people had followed them, an orchestra of the terror. Max and Jack slowly approached the congested road again. They had come to a large intersection. A vehicle accident in the middle had stopped people from driving through clearly. Now the intersection was full of the infected, the remaining living fighting off the attacks.

Max spun her tomahawk that she had been carrying while they ran. She itched to stay and fight, but she couldn't see a safe hiding place for Jack. Leaving Jack unprotected wasn't an option for her. However, they would have to enter the intersection to continue their travel on foot.

Standing in the mouth of the alley they caught the attention of the two nearest infected. Max pushed Jack back into the alley slightly. Looking back where they had come from, Max didn't see any immediate dangers.

"Stay here. I'm going to handle these two, then we'll keep going." Max said. Jack just nodded and pressed against the wall.

Without hesitation, Max met the infected head on. Her tomahawk sliced into the first infected's leg and as she yanked the blade back the infected lost its balance and fell to the asphalt. With the first infected down, Max stepped toward the second, slamming the tomahawk into its skull. She rounded just as the first infected was gaining its footing, half crawling to reach her.

A wave of anger swept through Max. This sickness was stealing people's lives. She saw the infected as the sickness itself, no longer the living people the bodies once were. Now, these snarling, grotesque beings were the host of this illness that was killing everyone around her.

Without thinking, Max struck out with one booted foot, catching the infected under the chin, toppling it backward. The anger she was feeling fueled her movements. Standing over the infected, she stepped down on its neck with one booted foot. The infected tried to claw into her jeans but couldn't find purchase. With a cry, Max swung her tomahawk down and crushed the skull of the sick body.

She took a deep breath, calming her inner turmoil. Looking around, she saw fights being waged and lost all around her. She knew she couldn't just walk away without doing something. Even if she didn't feel the need to help these living people, she didn't want to leave more infected to wander the city.

A cry near her had Max pulling her gun and spinning quickly. She saw a woman fighting off an infected man twice her size. Max groaned and quickly ran toward the pair. When she was close enough she pressed the gun point blank to the infected man's head and pulled the trigger. He never saw Max coming and his attention was purely on the meal at hand.

The woman screamed as the bullet tore through the infected. His body limply collapsed and Max looked over at the woman.

"Are you alright?"

"I...you shot him," the woman answered.

"Yeah. He was trying to eat you, right?" Max replied sarcastically.

"I think so. I don't even know. He worked at the gas station. I remember him," the woman rambled.

"He was dead before I ever shot him. You should go now. Run," Max said, motioning around them.

"Thank you," the woman said, before turning and fleeing.

"You're welcome," Max mumbled as she turned back toward the nearest fight.

She couldn't be sure but it felt like the amount of infected was increasing in the intersection. The noises of fighting, shots, and screams were drawing the ill to the living, to feast. Max continued to fight as she headed back to where she left Jack. She had lost count of the number of infected she herself had put down, but by the time she reached Jack she was popping her 9mm magazine and shoving it into her pocket. She found her spare and slapped it into the gun.

Jack's face was pale and full of fear. She had a perfect vantage point of the intersection hiding in the shadows of the alley. It was a war zone with one side clearly losing far more than the other. The living were dwindling in the area and Max feared they would be the next targets if they didn't move quickly. There were too many infected in the city to keep walking in the open.

A large parking lot opened at one end of the intersection and Max recognized the mall buildings beyond that. The mall was large, but if it were never opened that morning due to the emergency, they may be able to lock themselves safely inside one of the smaller stores. It wasn't the prime choice, but it would be harder for anyone to sneak up on them. Additionally, it happened to be the one side of the intersection not crawling with the infected.

"The mall over there," Max told Jack, pointing to the buildings.

"You hate the mall," Jack remarked.

"Well, that's true. But we aren't shopping. We're breaking in," Max stated.

"Totally different," Jack agreed.

"Stay right with me. If we are approached by an infected, stay away from my right arm so I can shoot or fight," Max instructed.

They stepped into the intersection, Jack on Max's left side. The two of them carefully navigated around the abandoned cars. Some were covered in blood spray, bodies against them or dead inside. Others were clean and it helped Max to imagine those people had abandoned the cars earlier and got away without harm. Jack pressed closely to Max's side, almost causing her to trip. She put her arm around her daughter and hugged her to her side. The death and carnage were a lot, even for Max.

Suddenly Jack was yanked back a step, causing Max to spin with her. She found herself face to face with an infected that had latched onto Jack's go bag. Jack let out a high-pitched shriek that only caused the infected to hiss and become more frantic. Max grabbed the front of Jack's shirt and yanked her body toward her. At the same time, she lifted her 9mm and shot the infected directly in the eye.

Holding onto Jack kept her from being dragged to the ground with the infected body. When the hands were yanked off her pack, Jack fell into her. Small sobs shook her body. Max took her shoulders and held her back from her so she could look her in the face.

"Jack, you're fine. I've got you," Max said briskly. She was never very good with emotions that caused anyone to cry. Her own heart was roaring with fear. One bite. She was sure that's all it took. The infected got too close to Jack for comfort.

"It's all so scary, Momma," Jack hiccupped.

"Yeah, it's not great. But it's our job to make it through this. And I need you to be strong. We are partners, just like we've always been. Got it?" Max said confidently. Jack nodded her head and swiped the tears from her face using her shirt sleeve.

Turning back toward the mall side of the intersection Max cursed inwardly to see that their run-in with the infected had attracted some additional attention.

"On my left side again, Jack," Max said sternly. She held her gun up and walked directly to what she hoped would be a safe haven. She circled, keeping an eye on the approaching infected. She didn't have enough bullets in her gun to protect them.

"We have to run, stay close, Jack," Max said, the urgency in her tone made Jack pay close attention.

Concentrating her fire ahead of them, Max took down three infected that were between them and the mall. She grabbed Jack's hand with her left and took off for the parking lot. Halfway to the entrance of the lot, Max brought them up short as additional infected wandered into their path.

"Damn it," Max breathed. She pulled her 9mm again and fired, missing the first infected with her first shot. She readjusted and held her breath and fired again. Realizing she didn't have enough ammo to keep firing, she holstered her gun and pulled out her tomahawk again. All she needed was to get to the doors of the mall and hopefully find a place to hide inside.

Max estimated five infected before the parking lot. There was no way to know what would be there once they reached it. *One problem at a time.* Grabbing Jack's hand again, Max started off at a fast pace. She didn't concentrate on killing infected, just stopping them from reaching her or Jack. Using her tomahawk, she sliced at arms and legs, keeping a hold of Jack's hand all the while.

When they reached the clearing of the parking lot, Max picked up speed and the pair ran for the nearest part of the building. Jack lagged, gasping for Max to slow down. However, a backward glance told Max they weren't in the clear as infected began to pour into the parking lot. *Where did they all come from?*

They reached an automatic glass door entrance but the doors didn't budge. Max had anticipated that no power and no employees since the mall never opened once the infection began to spread.

"Momma," Jack gasped, looking behind them at the infected that were approaching.

"I know, I know," Max replied. She didn't want to break out a door. If she did, the mall was no longer the safe haven she was hoping for. She crouched down looking at the locks and wished she knew how to actually pick a lock. Even if she did, a glance above showed a second locking mechanism that she had no idea what to do with.

Brain whirling with alternative ideas, Max was about to turn away from the door when she saw a flash of light inside the dark mall interior. She pressed her face against the glass and used her hands to shield out the sunlight. She could see people moving inside the mall. From their movements and the fact someone had a flashlight, Max knew they were healthy people.

Her panicked banging on the glass drove the infected more in their direction. The people in the mall stood off from the door but Max could tell they watched her.

"Please! Let us in. We aren't bitten!" Max exclaimed. She wasn't sure the people heard her, but they seemed to be talking among themselves. Max pulled Jack closer, so the people could see. Maybe they could turn away a lone woman but there was no way they would ignore a child.

"My daughter, she's only eight-years-old. Please let us in!" Max cried out again.

A woman stepped closer to the door and Max could tell she was arguing with the other occupants. Max looked back and realized the infected were closing in. Looking from side to side, she began to decide which side had fewer infected. She pulled her tomahawk preparing to fight their way out. One infected got within her swinging range and she embedded her tomahawk in his head.

Behind her, she could hear the click of locks on one of the side glass doors. Jack was at the door, pressing against it in fear. Max backed up to Jack, staying between her and the infected. Two infected came at them, arms reaching, fingers raking at the air in front of Max's face. She leaned back to avoid the nearest, using her tomahawk to shove the small framed woman back from her. As the infected stumbled, Max brought her blade down on the next infected's head. He crumpled quickly at the feet of the woman infected. Max didn't waste anytime cutting down the second infected, buying them a few more moments before being overran.

As she pulled the tomahawk from the second skull, the door behind them was pulled open. The woman that unlocked the door grabbed Jack by her pack and yanked her inside. Max took two fast strides and followed closely behind. The door locked behind them just as infected began to bounce into it, realizing their meal had escaped their grasp.

Max stood and watched the infected for a moment. They had no fine motor skills, no mental capacity to break windows or pick locks. Mindless beings just bouncing off the glass.

"You should step back. They will probably go away if they can't see us," a man spoke up from further inside the mall. Max turned to study the group of mall refugees. A mall wouldn't have been her first choice. However, at the moment, it had been the clearest place she could run with Jack. Now she stood, sizing up the group while being sized up herself.

It wasn't in Max's natural behavior to befriend people. She also never relied on anyone else to provide for her or Jack. The mall wasn't their place and she knew she would need to curb some of her base instincts to take over. Be cool. She wasn't sure she knew how to do that. Nevertheless, she would try to think like her sister Alex. Max tried to put a soft smile on her face.

"Hi. Thanks for letting us in," she said evenly. She led Jack further into the mall, silently agreeing with the man that the infected would lose interest as soon as they couldn't see the living.

"Where are you from?"

"Do you know what's happening?"

"Did you see the police?"

"Is help coming?"

Questions were shot from all directions. Max counted the group, finding 12 people huddling together away from the doors they entered in. Her patience already on the thin side, she held up her hands for silence.

"We are from here, Charleston. No, we didn't see police or any first responders in general. I have no idea if there is help coming. What's happening? Well, you can see for yourself," she finished, motioning toward the doors where they could still see the infected hitting the doors.

"What are they?"

"As far as I can tell, they're dead. And they eat the people that aren't. The news said it was a plague. Haven't you seen any news reports? Heard any radio?" Max demanded.

"No, we've been hiding in here the whole time."

CHAPTER FIVE

Max hated malls. She hated the smells and the crowds. She never felt comfortable with so many people in one building. She despised people trying to sell her things from little kiosks in the middle of the mall. And the women spraying perfume at her in the department stores. That was enough to keep her only stepping foot in the mall once a year to Christmas shop.

Despite the plague raging outside, Jack was able to find some humor in the fact that they were trapped inside the one place Max would rather burn to the ground. The people already seeking refuge there were workers who had come to work early the morning the plague broke out. From the stories they heard Max gathered there were more originally. However, in the news of the infected attacks, some of the employees attempted to get home to their families.

The ones that stayed were those that had no one else to worry about. Max quickly realized they had the belief that a rescue would be on its way. Though none of them could clearly determine if someone was looking for them. Max worked hard to not allow her frustration to show. The lack of leadership or organization was enough to push her over the edge of sanity.

The group explained that everyone had found a place to sleep. They were eating meals together in the food court, utilizing what power and gas they still had. One woman named Jules asked Max if she'd like to see the showers. When Max looked at her blankly, Jules had motioned down the length of Max, causing her to look down at herself. She was only slightly surprised to see blood splashed across her clothing.

Jules showed Max and Jack to a small spa like store. Its signs promised relaxation and beauty. All Max really cared about was hot water. Turned out they had one small shower in a back room, assuredly for guests before or after treatments.

From a young age, Jack had been taught how to take a fast shower. Max was a utilitarian by nature and wanted everything to be practical. When at home they didn't practice speed showers. However, when they camped and only had their solar camp shower, they only had time for the necessities.

Jack and Max took their turns taking fast showers. They both had changes of clean clothes in their bug out bags. The dirty ones Max decided could be trashed. There was no way of knowing when washing clothes would be possible. And if they were going to be in a mall, the options of clothes would be abundant.

When they exited the massage store another of the mall group was waiting for them.

"We are getting ready to have lunch. Are you hungry?" The small man asked.

"Sure. I know everyone introduced themselves, but I'm not good at remembering names. What was yours again?" Max asked.

"Scott," Jack offered.

"Yes, Scott," the man said smiling at Jack.

"Well, we are hungry, Scott. So, if you're offering lunch, we would accept," Max said, her smile a little more genuine that time.

They followed Scott through the mall and up a set of stairs. The food court was located centrally on the second floor. Interestingly enough there were windows to the outside here and Max stood looking out for a long time. The parking lot they had come through was off to the right of the windows. The infected milled around the area, still thickly grouped by the door they had come through.

"They seem to move in packs. And tend to lose interest after a day," Scott said, approaching from behind Max.

"You've seen this many here already?"

"Not quite this many. But the morning I got here for work, it was still dark. I parked my car, came in like I do every day. When we started getting phone calls about the chaos I came here to look outside, to see what I could see, ya know?" Max nodded her understanding and motioned for him to continue.

"Well, it was hard to tell which were those sick ones and which weren't. But while I was up here a group of employees decided to make a run for it to get home to their families. The noise of their cars drew the attention of those that were already dead. Maybe half as many," Scott said motioning below them. "I watched them for most of that first day. By the next morning, most of them had wandered off. We could see the cars out on the main road and could tell there were attacks happening constantly. We decided if we stayed inside, we'd be safe until the police arrived."

"I don't know if the police are coming," Max said softly.

"Why do you say that?"

"My father, though a little crazy by popular standards I guess, always talked about a society breakdown like this. One of the things he always stressed was that the government would fall apart. There would be no immediate services and even after some time, nothing would be the same. This feels like that," Max said solemnly.

Mitch Duncan had a lot of predictions about the end of civilization. His favorite was to talk about the world coming to an end because of an EMP. He was disgusted by the way humans were becoming dependent on electronics. He used to say that one electromagnetic pulse would end life as they knew it. He assumed it would be a war that caused it, one superpower attacking another. Max felt like this was so much worse.

"I didn't see any cops or government presence while I was on the road the last few days," Max continued. She had been so concerned with their survival, she hadn't noticed the missing sounds of sirens.

"You would think they would all be out there, trying to stop this...whatever it is," Scott said sadly.

"My guess is no one was prepared or knew what to do when the plague broke out. The news was all panic when it started yesterday." It was hard for Max to imagine the government, federal or local, having a game plan for the end of the world.

Lunch consisted of salads, fruit, and sandwiches. Max held her tongue and fought her base instincts as she watched people throw away their unfinished foods. Jack knew to finish every bite. In a situation where normal life was falling apart, you could never count on where your next meal would come from. The group in the mall were living under the impression they would be saved before supplies ran out.

A full stomach gave Max the feeling of heaviness and she decided to walk the mall. She found paper and a pen at one of the food court restaurants. As she walked she took note of all the glass doors, which she considered soft points. Easily breached for anyone living that wanted to break in. She also noted all of the emergency exits, typically down hallways between stores, that would lead out as well.

While they walked, Max and Jack took note of the places people had decided to sleep. Some people were sleeping in a small store that sold large beanbag chairs. Chairs were pushed together, sheets and blankets used to create beds. There were also beds in a shoe store that had couches for people to sit and try on the merchandise.

At the end of the mall, they came to a sporting goods store. Max smiled at Jack when they quickly realized no one had come into that store yet. Though her first instinct was to keep moving, Max knew it was safer to wait out the horde inside the mall. For now, it was a secure location. From the lunch conversation, she believed the group would not let anyone else in. They didn't even want to let Max in, but they couldn't leave Jack to be killed.

The sporting goods store was the most useful in Max's mind, next to the food court. She found ammunition for her 9mm and additional magazines. She loaded them all and packed them into her bag. Jack got excited about pitching tents inside the store and camping inside a mall. Max had never really understood the saying "It's the little things," but she assumed that's what this meant. Her eight-year-old daughter was delighted to be mall camping.

Max picked a relatively clear spot between the emergency exit and glass entrance doors. It was near the back of the store, giving them privacy from the rest of the group. Also, the doors provided quick escape, should the need arise. Together they pitched a six man tent. It was larger than anything they took camping, but Max figured why not? It was the apocalypse after all.

Jack created comfortable beds inside, making beds for each of them with double self-inflating mattresses, sleeping bags and camp pillows. Assuming they would keep the lights off at night to not attract attention they also appropriated a couple of lanterns and flashlights. Jack also found a string of battery operated twinkle lights. She took great pleasure in hanging them outside of their tent.

The sporting goods store housed quite a bit of camping and hunting gear. This type of store was right up Max's alley and she would have been happy to just not leave it. She found additional meals, ready to eat, also called MRE's. She packed a few in both of their packs. The store also boasted a large amount of hunting clothing, so both of them were able to acquire additional sets of clean clothing to pack away.

As they were repacking their bags, Jules came into their camp area. She smiled warmly at them both as she approached.

"You have made yourself quite the camp."

"Jack was having fun," Max said with a shrug.

"Scott mentioned to me that you don't believe the police are coming," Jules stated, revealing her intentions for coming to find them.

"I didn't see any police response the last few days. I'm not sure where they are or if they are coming," Max replied.

"Have you been outside a lot since this started?"

"Just enough to drive from place to place. Well and to run here," Max said.

"Where were you headed?" Jules asked. Max felt like she sure had a lot of questions for someone she just met.

"Headed out of town. Until we were carjacked." Max looked up from her pack when she said it and almost laughed out loud at the shock on Jules' face. "Right? Carjacked. Like it was the last thing I would have worried about. But there we were, glass all over the truck from the dude breaking in my window. And two guns pointed at us."

"That's horrible," Jules replied.

"Everything is horrible right now," Jack chimed in.

"Scott also said something about your father. That he knew about times like this or something?" Jules asked.

"Yeah. My dad was a prepper. Once we can get out of town, we're heading to my childhood home. That home is now also a compound my father built for exactly this situation."

"Prepper. I've heard that before. Like those shows about people hoarding?"

Max had to force herself not to roll her eyes. She had often dealt with the misconception of what exactly her father did and why. As an adult, Max was aware her father wasn't completely sane when it came to his prepping. But he always provided for them as children, made sure they had educations and taught them all they needed to know about being prepared and surviving on their own. Even in the civilized world, Max had been able to apply survival techniques to make it from day to day.

"No, not a hoarder. Growing up we lived on a large piece of land. At the time it was largely unused. As I grew up, so did the compound my father built. There's now the large house that I grew up in, a bunker for living in, in case of attack, and other outdoor buildings. It's completely self-sustaining, which will be necessary with services like power going out," Max explained. Jules stood, raptly listening to everything Max said.

"The power is still on," she commented.

"For now," Max replied simply. There was no way of knowing when the power would fail. Without healthy humans to do the work to maintain the grids, it wouldn't take long. Phone service didn't last under the weight of usage during the beginning of the outbreak.

"So, you're just going, alone?" Jules asked.

"Yes. We're meeting my family there."

"My Auntie Alex is coming too. And Uncle Rafe lives there now," Jack added. Jules smiled at the girl.

"What does Jack stand for?" Jules asked.

"Jacklyn," Jack answered.

"It was a thing my father started. He wanted boys when my sister Alex was born. So my mother made him a deal, she would choose a female name he could shorten into a boy nickname. Growing up we were never called by our full names, only the nickname he gave us," Max explained.

"So Max...for Maxine?" Jules filled in. Max nodded.

The story made Max think back to her childhood. There were prepper chores every day. Alex hated them but Max relished the knowledge her father would give her. In their teen years, even with Rafe being bigger and stronger, Mitch always picked Max for new projects. He would never have admitted having a favorite, he loved all three of them. However, Max was the one that wanted his lessons. Being a girl didn't mean anything to him then.

The mall was eerily quiet as Max and Jack wandered around the stores. The group had opened most of the rolling gates with the main keys they had. Jack spent a good amount of her time in the bookstore choosing which books she wanted to take with them to Montana. Max didn't understand wasting the space in her pack for them, but Jack always enjoyed having her nose in a book.

Besides the sporting goods store, Max didn't find much of interest in the mall. She wandered into the food court, looking at the food items that were left. These people had enough food to last them a month, maybe more, if they let no one else in. Looting was just a matter of time and Max tried to tell people that in conversation. But it seemed none were that worried about long-term.

As evening rolled around, so did dark storm clouds. South Carolina was notorious for random storms that no one saw coming. The lightning lit up the dark sky, creating weird shadows throughout the food court where everyone had gathered for dinner. A few of the mall group had worked together to fry up some chicken at an Asian restaurant and the meal was delicious. Max savored every bite, knowing this food tasted much better than MRE dinners.

The mood was a little more somber at dinner. Maybe it was all of the information Max was passing around. Or maybe a second night locked in the mall wasn't what this group was expecting. From their second story view, they could see infected all over the parking lot and street beyond. The storm didn't seem to deter them at all. It had Max wondering if they could tell the difference in human noise and weather-related noise. Lightning shed light on the crowd below often enough for her to tell that the group wasn't dissipating quickly.

As dinner ended, people began to take their leave. Jack begged Max for ice cream, so the two of them dug out some from the freezer of a dessert shop. They sat near their tent, the light of their lanterns brightening their area, and ate ice cream. If they weren't camping in the mall, the moment may have felt like a normal evening of bonding and eating ice cream. Jack smiled and talked constantly between bites, while Max sat contemplating their situation and halfway listening to Jack jabber along.

The quiet was all-enveloping, which made Max feel like she was lying in a black hole, not a tent. Jack had quickly fallen asleep on her camp pads, arms slung over her head in her typical fashion. Max laid there, watching her in the dim light of a lowered lantern. Her lips pursed as she dreamt, and her eyebrows creased together as if she were in deep thought. What did an eight-year-old dream about that caused such concentration?

In the dark, in a safe place, Max allowed herself to feel real fear for the first time in two days. When the carjacker pointed a gun at her face, she hadn't felt fear. The moment was only a bump in the road that needed to be handled. Somehow, she felt sure the man wasn't going to pull the trigger. Looking back, Max realized she was damn lucky to not have pushed any of his buttons.

Max hadn't felt fear when they were running for the mall either. She felt capable of protecting them as they made their way through the infected. When Jack's hand was ripped from her own though, panic had tried to push its way through. Seeing an infected with its claws in her pack was almost enough to send Max over some edge she didn't know she had.

She loved her daughter, there was no question in that. Growing up without a real mother had caused Max to miss out on what a mother-daughter relationship should be. She found herself raising Jack the same way she was raised.

In a very utilitarian style. Emotions didn't enter many decisions. Choices and plans were made in a practical fashion.

Looking at Jack now, in the middle of a plague, Max allowed herself to evaluate the feelings she was experiencing. Her heart swelled with love and affection for her little girl. It had always been the two of them against the world. Max wouldn't have had it any other way. She leaned over slightly and kissed her daughter on the forehead, right where her eyebrows seemed to gather. Jack let out a small sigh and sunk into an undisturbed sleep.

The next morning, they woke to a torrential downpour. Max cursed silently to herself, knowing this would keep them from leaving again. Visibility in a vehicle would be near nothing, a risk she wasn't willing to take. Adding to the need of stealing a vehicle, which would be much harder in the rain. Beyond all of those concerns, she also wasn't comfortable with the number of infected still gathered around the entrances to the mall.

Jack was thrilled to be staying at the mall for another day. After the breakfast meal of pancakes from McDonald's, she convinced Max to hang out in the bookstore with her. While Jack curled up in one of the chairs the store boasted, Max perused the maps and atlases the store had. Finding a large atlas with maps of all major freeways across the country, Max settled by Jack's feet and started reviewing some sort of plan of action for them.

As she studied the map of South Carolina, tracing where they should leave the state, she stopped and stared at North Carolina. Griffin was supposed to be there. Was he alive? Did he need her help? After all these years she wasn't sure how to handle the situation of him. If he was alive, she wasn't sure how they would even find him.

Max looked over at Jack. Her daughter had her dark hair, but her eyes were all her father's. When she stared into them, Max could get lost in memories. Now Max felt an obligation to her daughter. Her daughter who had never known who her father really was. And Griffin, who never knew he had a daughter in this world.

CHAPTER SIX

At seventeen, no daughter wants to admit to her father that she's pregnant. The day after Griffin left for boot camp, Alex had convinced Max to get a pregnancy test. Alex had already left for college a few years before, but over the phone, Max had told her how she had been feeling ill. Alex was the only one that knew Max and Griffin had slept together. She immediately worried about pregnancy.

When the little blue line showed up on the test, Max thought she would pass out. Griffin was gone, at Army boot camp where he would be unreachable at first. He had told Max he would write as soon as he was allowed. He had kissed her hard, telling her he wouldn't forget her, that they were going to make it for the long run. He swore that once he was done with boot camp and stationed somewhere, he would send for her. Max had promised to write him as soon as he sent her his address. And she had promised to wait.

Being pregnant was scary by itself. Once Max realized she was alone with her father, she was even more terrified. She knew Mitch Duncan would be severely disappointed in her lack of judgment. Not to mention just not being prepared for the worst outcome. He expected more from his children when it came to the mere basic things like hormones or making the right decisions about sex.

The conversation had been a fast one. Max had expected screaming and anger from Mitch. Instead, he sat in his favorite chair and stared at her. Minutes passed with Max standing in front of her father and him staring directly into her eyes.

"Who's is it?" He had finally asked.

"Griffin. I haven't had any other boyfriends, Dad, you know that," she had replied. He went silent again, this time looking down at his hands. Max wondered if he was picturing strangling Griffin with his bare hands at that moment.

"The boy left for the Army, right?"

"Yes. He's going to write as soon as he can," Max had said.

Days passed. Then weeks. Those weeks turned into months. In the beginning, Max would run out to the mailbox daily to check for letters. Nothing ever came. After a few months, she finally resigned herself to the fact that he wasn't going to write. He had said all the right things before he left and she had believed him. But now, with her heart broken, she realized he just said what he needed to so he could go.

Max's body began to change. She rarely left the compound, in fear of seeing someone she knew. She didn't want anyone in the nearby cities to know she was pregnant. Griffin had no idea he had a baby on the way and she didn't intend for him to find out from someone he was in contact with. Part of Max was empty and bitter. That part wanted Griffin to suffer and never know he had fathered a child.

Mitch would drive her two towns away to a doctor for her prenatal care. His initial shock and disappointment faded and he was a different man. The concept of a grandchild was one he embraced wholeheartedly. Max had never seen him do that with anything beyond his prepping. She had only seen him baby a garden or even their livestock. His demeanor just seemed to soften when they would hear her baby's heartbeat on a monitor.

Alex came home to Montana for the birth of Jack. Mitch paced the halls outside the delivery room according to the nurses that attended Max. Alex would leave only to reassure Mitch that she was fine, and the baby was doing fine. As far as Max had been concerned she was dying. The pain would never end and the baby she carried for so long hated her and wanted to cause her death.

When the cry of Jack echoed in the delivery room, Max's world shifted on its axis. Suddenly life had a different meaning beyond her father's crazy all-consuming conspiracies. There was a small human she was responsible for. The doctor laid the little purple baby on Max's chest, giving them instant skin to skin contact. When Max looked up at Alex she wasn't surprised to see the tears rolling down her face. But when she looked back down at the baby, she was shocked by the wetness on her own face.

A nurse let in the waiting Mitch, who burst in like someone had lit him on fire. Alex slowed him down, reassuring him again that Max was perfectly fine. He hugged Alex, her surprise at the gesture causing her to be stiff in his arms for a moment, before hugging him back. He then slowly approached Max and the baby.

"All ten toes and fingers?" He asked gruffly. Max just smiled at the baby and nodded.

"I'm going to name her Jacklyn. You can call her Jack," Max told him, looking up at her father. His eyes almost seemed to be full of tears. Max didn't forget the agreement he made with her mother before she died. He wasn't sure what to do with daughters. They fought over the names because he hated all things girlie. They had come to an agreement that her mother could name the girls whatever she wanted, as long as the names could be shortened to boy nicknames. Max had never heard her father utter her full name of Maxine. She wanted to give him the same for his first granddaughter.

"Well hiya, Jack," Mitch whispered as his finger softly touched her little hand.

Once Max brought Jack home to the Montana compound life drastically changed. Mitch was even more paranoid than before. He questioned the special formula Max had to buy for her since she couldn't seem to handle normal types. Before he allowed her to feed Jack anything, he would test it the day before and make sure it didn't poison him. His newest paranoid idea was poisoning baby food would be the fastest way to put an end to the human species.

Max started to feel suffocated with Jack. After the first year of her daughter's life, she realized they had to leave and take control of their own fate. Max knew she couldn't stay in Montana. There were too many relations with Griffin in the nearby towns. They would see Jack and know by her age that she must be Griffin's. If he hadn't wanted Max without a baby, she didn't want him rushing back to her out of obligation. She came to the conclusion she was going at the parenting thing alone.

Her first decision was the leave Montana. Mitch had been furious. Max had seen him angry at her and her siblings before. However, it was always typical parent anger. This vexation was beyond anything Max knew Mitch was capable of. According to him, Max was abandoning all of her education and understanding of the world by moving away from the compound. She tried to make him understand that he had prepared her better than anyone could have. In the end, she knew the real thing he was panicked about was losing Jack.

Part of Max was heartbroken to leave her father. She knew nothing of living away from the compound and the work that came with being prepared for anything. But she couldn't allow Mitch to suffocate them. She tried to picture Jack growing up and eventually being school age. She could easily see Mitch not allowing her to leave for her schooling. Max couldn't allow that to happen with her daughter, so leaving was the only option.

South Carolina was her choice because it was far away but also because she had a distant cousin living there at the time. As a child, Max knew very little about her mother or the family she came from. When she made the decision to leave she asked for Alex's assistance in finding the family they didn't really know. Sadly many had passed away already from old age and illness. However, Alex found cousins from their grandmother's sister's children. They were eager to meet and learn about the family that came from Montana.

Max never forgot about Griffin. Over the years she thought about dating, but it was a non-starter for her. She was a single mother, with a prepping complex, who was looking for a man that was her equal. No matter who she met she could never find a man that understood why it was important to be prepared. Not understanding and not caring were the first reasons for her to toss a date out on his behind. No one could compare to Griffin and she had a daily reminder of that in her daughter's face.

Now sitting in a mostly empty mall in South Carolina, with the infected crawling around outside, Max watched Jack read. She did feel guilty for not telling Jack the truth about her father. It took her a few years at school before she realized she was different by only having a mommy at home. Max cringed inwardly thinking about the day she came home from first grade asking where her daddy was. Max didn't really have an answer planned, so she just said he was gone and they were on their own.

When she had heard Griffin was in North Carolina and was staying after his time in the Army, Max almost thought it was a sign. Something she typically didn't believe in. Her mind would wander and she would think about calling him or writing to him. But she would then remember that he had left her alone, never writing like he promised. The sadness and anger would come back and she would regret even entertaining the idea of reaching out to him. He didn't deserve Jack. And Jack deserved something so much better, that it probably didn't really exist.

"What are you reading, Momma?" Jack's little voice came from behind her. The sound startled Max out of the musings she was having. Right then, stuck in the mall while the rain came down in torrential buckets, there was nothing she could truly do about Griffin.

"I was looking at the road atlas," Max replied, holding up the map to show her daughter. She looked back to the route she was planning on taking.

"It's a long way," Jack stated.

"Yeah. But we'll make it happen."

"How?" Jack asked. The girl had learned the words why and how early on in her talking days. She was inquisitive, which Max had always supported. Right now though, the questions would get old, with no answers to really give in return.

"Well, my idea is to find a car that I can hot-wire. That will have to be how we get to Montana. We'll have to collect fuel as we go. Hopefully, since it's early on, we may find gas stations with power still. Gramps taught me to siphon from other vehicles too," Max explained.

"Hot-wire? You know how to do that?" Jack seemed incredulous. It made Max smile. There were many skills Max had obtained over the years that Jack would never need to know about. The more illegal things like hot-wiring cars, stealing electricity, and siphoning gas were just a few that her father had made sure she knew. All before she was even old enough to legally drive the cars she was learning to steal. Mitch didn't teach her things so she could be a criminal, but so when the time came, and he knew it would, she could fend for herself.

By midday, Max was starting to feel despair with the amount of rain that was flowing. She thought for sure it would stop quickly. The Carolina states liked their fast storms. However, this one wasn't waning yet. March was showing the end of winter and it was bad timing.

She took Jack through some of the clothing stores, searching for changes of clothes they could take with them. They collected undergarments, warm sweaters, additional pairs of jeans and new boots for Jack. Max acquired an additional duffel bag she could sling over her shoulder and packed it full of the additional items they decided to take. She wanted them ready to go the moment the rain stopped.

They ate lunch alone behind the counter of a fast food kiosk. Max was determined to ensure that Jack ate well, while they had the supplies to do so. While the rest of the group felt that the illness and the chaos happening outside was not long term, Max felt differently. She felt deep in her gut that this was the end her father had always prepared her for.

That night sleep came easier to Max. The sense of safety was infectious. She knew by instinct that safety wasn't this easy. But after a day and a half with no incident, her body decided it needed to shut down a bit. Curled in their sleeping bags, Max and Jack slept soundly under the little lights Jack had set up.

The noise of breaking glass didn't wake her. The sound was far down the length of the mall, not echoing far enough to reach the Duncans in their tent. The crunch of the glass under feet was quiet, as the living decided to come in through the locked doors. The sound of breaking glass was louder than the sound of the falling rain, and it attracted the dead.

CHAPTER SEVEN

Shouts reverberated through the empty mall. Max sat straight up in the tent, shushing Jack as she started to call out to her mother. Listening carefully, Max tried to determine if the shouts were the living fighting the living or if it was a different nightmare. Pounding feet could be heard near the entrance to the store, indicating the living.

Max quickly shut off the lights, plunging them into total darkness. Her eyes started to slowly adjust. She grabbed her jeans and pulled them over her pajama pants, her button up shirt over her pajama shirt. Jack quickly followed her mother's lead. In less than three minutes they were dressed for whatever was in the mall.

"I need to find out what's going on," Max whispered. Jack nodded her understanding, knowing the need for silence.

As quietly as possible Max unzipped the tent door. She paused when she could peer out and glanced around the front of the tent. She was thankful for their set up, being able to see all entrances to the store they were sleeping in. She also realized that unless someone knew they were sleeping there or saw their lights, they wouldn't realize the tents weren't just displays.

Max didn't see anyone moving and she slowly unzipped the rest of the door. She equipped herself with her gun and tomahawk. She still wasn't positive what she would find, but she needed to be prepared for anything. She motioned to Jack to stay in the tent and zip it up. If there were infected they wouldn't see her and the darkness would keep any living from finding her easily.

She tiptoed away from the tent, feeling a tightness in her chest she wasn't used to. Leaving Jack behind was hard on her. However, she knew she was safer in the tent than in the mall with the unknown. Max found the opening to the mall and crouched behind a display, trying to watch what was happening.

The rain had decided to stop during the night and the moon's light illuminated the center of the mall through skylights. She could see living people running and some hiding. But she also could see uncoordinated movements, movements that didn't belong to anything still breathing. She could pick out the infected by their shadows. They seemed to chase those that ran, but their pace was much slower.

Max did not want to be locked inside the mall with the infected. There was no way there was a positive outcome in that situation. She thought about the unarmed people hiding throughout the mall. None of them had weapons. None were fighters from what she could tell. They were hiding, waiting for someone to save them. Max cursed, wondering if she was the one that had to do that very thing.

From her hiding spot, she saw a small man running in the distance. By his height and movements, she guessed it was Scott. She wanted to call out to him and tell him he needed to hide, but she knew her voice would attract unwanted attention. Her mind raced through alternatives, but nothing came to her. The only option she had was to find out what was going on in the building.

Staying low, Max ran toward the advertisement stand that stood in front of the sporting goods store. She pressed herself against it, evaluating her surroundings again.

The mall was a large open space in the middle and she knew once she ran that direction she would be exposed. She decided to hug the wall of stores and try to avoid the light of the moon reflecting in the middle.

Light on her feet, Max quickly reached the nearest store. It was pitch black inside, the security gate still pulled down. She assumed that was safe and leaned against it for a moment to allow her pounding heart to slow. When she moved again she heard shouting from further into the mall. She ran toward the sound now, trying to distinguish what was happening.

When she found the location of the conflict it wasn't the living fighting the infected. Instead, it was the living fighting the living. Max realized then she hadn't thought through how the infected had gotten into the mall. For two days they didn't seem to have the mental capacity to break the glass doors, thus creating a safe place inside the mall. Now that she saw new people fighting the people that had hid in the mall, she realized it was the living that had threatened their safe haven.

The realization brought anger into Max's mind. And that anger immediately became action as she approached the first fight and found a man punching Scott in the stomach. She didn't want to kill anyone living, but her self-defense and Muay Thai trainer had given her plenty of tactics to use in such scenarios. She left her weapons in their holsters and struck out at the strange man with a sharp blow to his kidney. As the man pivoted toward the pain, she struck him with a blow to the temple, knocking the man to the ground.

She waited above the downed man, adrenaline coursing through her, waiting for the fight to continue. Instead, the man stayed where he was. Max stepped over him to Scott, who was lying in a fetal position on the ground. She touched his shoulder, causing him to jump and cry out. When he looked and realized it was her he calmed slightly, but the fear was evident in his eyes as he looked around at the chaos.

"What happened?" Max asked.

"They broke in. The dead followed. I was trying to hide from the dead, but that guy found me," Scott said, his voice wheezing.

"How many living came in?"

"Don't know. I've seen a few different, but I've hidden. They don't have flashlights, which seems odd."

"Not odd. They were sneaking to get passed the dead. But I guess they didn't think about the noise they were making to get in here," Max surmised.

Scott didn't answer, just nodded in the dark. Max helped him to his feet and shuffled him to a nearby open store. After checking around, she determined it was empty except for them. She walked back to the entrance and from the shadow of the store, she watched another intruder sneak through the moonlight. Not bright, Max thought.

"What are you doing?" Scott's voice at her shoulder caused Max to jump and curse softly. She glared at him and he looked at her sheepishly.

"Going to handle the intruders. Then going to get Jack out of here at daybreak," Max whispered.

"Handle them?"

"Do what I have to. Lock yourself inside here. I'm going to go move the last guy into a store and lock him in. At least then I won't have to try and feel bad if an infected dines on him," Max said sarcastically. She held her hand out and Scott gave her the security keys he held for the mall.

Walking out, she looked around and didn't find any immediate threat. She pulled down the metal gate, the rolling noise echoing through the mall.

With that, Max disappeared into the darkness of the mall. She tiptoed, keeping her noise to a whisper. She found the first intruder exactly where she had left him, knocked out on the tile. Looking around she determined which store was closest and drug his body to it. The noise of the dragging attracted attention, causing Max to move with urgency.

Pushing the guy to the side of the store, Max yanked down the security gate and locked it quickly. She turned just in time to pull her tomahawk as an infected rambled at her. Fingers were bent like claws coming at her, the average looking woman wouldn't have looked sick if it weren't for the black balls for eyes she had. As Max cut her down, she assumed her injury was somewhere she couldn't see, but she took no time to check.

Max moved further into the mall, and further away from Jack. For the first time since Jack was an infant, Max found herself wishing there was someone she trusted around. Someone she could leave Jack with when she had to handle other things. But there was no one. Max had to hope that Jack stayed silent, and no intruders thought to open tent displays in the sporting goods store.

The sound of crying slowed Max's steps near a clothing store. The store was pitch black and even with Max's eyes becoming accustomed to nothing but moonlight, she couldn't make out who was in the store. She entered slowly, preparing for an attack to come from the darkness. When one didn't, she approached the crying noise.

"Who's there?" Max whispered.

"Max?" A wobbly voice answered from behind the checkout desk of the store.

"Jules? Are you hurt?"

Max rounded the counter and crouched down in front of the woman. Max brushed against her side and Jules hissed in pain. Squinting Max tried to see what was wrong. Deciding it was worth the risk, Max pulled out a small pocket flashlight she carried. She covered the light with her hand and switched it on.

In the dim light, Max could see Jules' pale face, streaked with blood. Proceeding down the side of her body, Max was able to find the source of her pain. The side of her shirt was ripped and soaked with blood. Carefully Max pulled it away from the wound and tried to inspect it. The telltale teeth marks made Max gasp and pull back quickly.

"I know," Jules whispered.

"How?" Max asked.

"I was hiding and suddenly one of the sick ones was on me, biting into my side. I fell, but instead of it following me, it caught sight of one of the looters I think."

"I'm....sorry," Max said, not knowing what suitable words were for a person that had been sentenced to death.

"Maybe I'll be fine," Jules sniffed.

"I don't really know," Max said. She was unable to just tell the woman the truth of it in her normal no-nonsense manner. Jules was a sweet woman, it was apparent just from being around her for a short time.

"It's ok. Even if I'm not, I don't have children or family to leave behind. You need to go, Max. Get Jack, run," Jules whispered urgently, grabbing Max's hand with hers. Max wanted to pull back from the gesture, the stickiness of Jules' blood causing Max to swallow down bile.

"I'm going to take care of the looters first," Max said, venom in her voice. This sweet woman wouldn't be dying of an unknown illness if the intruders hadn't broken in.

"Be careful," Jules said, her voice cracking with a cough that she tried to muffle with her arm.

Suddenly voices could be heard near the entrance to the store. Max quickly switched off the small light, darkness taking over again.

"I know I heard something," a voice said.

"There are walkers in here, it was probably one of them. You shouldn't have broken the damn door, now we can't stay here," a second voice answered.

"No shit," Max mumbled to herself. Jules squeezed her arm, trying to keep her from approaching the intruders. But Max didn't have any patience for what was happening. She wanted to handle the situation and move on. Dealing with the people behind the voices was her best bet.

Max removed Jules' hand from her arm. She squeezed the woman's fingers, a gesture unlike her. But she had a feeling that was the last moment she would see the kind woman alive. Jules' answering squeeze told her she knew that was likely as well. Max laid Jules' hand on her leg slowly, careful to not cause the woman any additional pain. With that, she started toward the store entrance.

Max stayed low, keeping her body behind the displays of clothing as she moved. The darkness did the rest. When she got close enough to the store entrance she was able to make out one figure by moonlight. He seemed to be waiting for something or acting as a lookout. Max waited. She knew the men had heard Jules cough and they would be looking for someone.

The man was an average height and skinny. Max sized him up in her mind, quickly deciding he would be an easy fight. The question was where the other man was. She listened and the silence was all that answered her. Waiting was wasting her time, the dark wouldn't last. And the dark was her friend with the intruders in the store.

As she watched the man a growl sounded from behind him, out of Max's line of sight. She didn't need to see to know it was an infected that had found the man in the middle of the mall concourse. The man swung around and Max got a good look at the crowbar he was wielding. He didn't pull any additional weapons and Max noted that she hadn't heard any gunshots since the break-in happened.

The man moved out of her line of sight, so Max moved over to a nearby display and watched as he swung the crowbar at the infected. He first struck it in the arm that was reaching out to grab him. He then swung and hit the shoulder, swinging the infected to the side. With the infected turned away, he took the opportunity to strike at the knees and the infected collapsed to the ground.

While the man was absorbed in beating the infected, Max disassembled the clothing rack nearest to her. She slid the hangers off quietly and pulled the wood pole from the rack. She hefted it like a bat and decided it would do decent damage.

As Max worked, she watched the intruder beat the infected. It was like he purposely ignored striking the head of the infected. The sound of crunching bones could be heard in the store Max stood in. All the while the infected hissed and growled at the living man that it wished to feast on. Max could understand fighting with anger, but the intruder seemed to enjoy the violence and destruction of the infected.

The man's back was to Max as she quietly approached. Right as she got into swinging rang she let out a low whistle, causing the man to start and turn. Just as she saw his eyes, she swung the pole and struck him on the side of the head. She watched as his eyes rolled back and he crumpled. He fell near the infected, but with the broken body, the infected wasn't able to reach its meal.

For a split second, Max contemplated leaving the man where he fell. His desire to beat the infected to a pulp instead of just finishing it made her wonder about his true intentions. They broke into the mall for safety she thought, but a person with rage was someone that could easily do the damage that man had just done. She sighed to herself, knowing she couldn't just leave the man to be eaten.

First Max used her knife and ended the growling of the infected. As soon as the blade pierced the brain, the sound and movements stopped. The body now truly dead in the middle of a mall. Glancing down at the man, she realized she was too far from the store she locked the first man. She couldn't move this man that far. Deciding to just hide him, she grabbed him by the arms and started dragging.

A nearby kiosk provided enough cover with its small opening that was meant for one worker. She opened the door and dragged the man in. If he woke up before she was gone she would have to deal with him again, but she had other things to worry about. She crouched down giving herself time to catch her breath.

From her crouched position she heard hurried footsteps causing her to brace and prepare for an attack. But instead, one of the original mall inhabitants ran directly by her, never noticing her next to the kiosk. She recognized the girl and remembered she had a boyfriend that was in the mall with her. Max found herself wondering where he was and why the girl was running by herself.

"Little girl!" A loud bellow came from the direction the girl had come. Max quickly duck walked to the other side of the kiosk, giving herself more cover. Peering around she saw a man with a large wrench coming out of a shop. Max suddenly realized that was the shop the girl and her boyfriend had been sleeping in that night. She had a sickening feeling that the man after the girl had done something to the boyfriend.

The idea of needless killing angered Max. It went against everything Mitch had ever taught her and her siblings. When the world fell apart, leaders would be needed. Her father had taught them to be those leaders. He taught them to know how to care for others and guide them in survival. Max wasn't always great at the idea of guiding or caring, but killing for sport went against the fiber of her very being.

This man approaching the kiosk was also not very large, but Max couldn't be sure of his skills as an opponent. Once he passed her hiding spot, Max made the quick decision to attack from behind. Using the wood pole she had acquired, she swung with her full strength at the side of the man's knee. The sound of the wood striking bone and muscle was a meaty thud. His leg quickly buckled under his weight.

Catching his fall with his arm, the man's wrench slid across the tiled floor of the mall. The man's head swung around and a hatred filled stare hit Max. In the moonlight, she could see his eyes narrow at the sight of a small woman that had taken him down. He attempted to put weight back on his knee, but the pain was too great, and he collapsed again.

Max moved around the man, staying out of arm's reach. She wasn't quite sure what to do with him at that point. He watched her around him, his eyes never leaving her. A caged animal suddenly popped into Max's mind and she realized this was exactly what the man looked like.

"You shouldn't have broken in here," Max stated simply.

"You don't own this," the man spat out.

"No. But it was also safe until you idiots broke in. Smart letting in the infected."

"What? Those things. They are easy to kill," the man said with a sneer. Max almost laughed. The man had obviously not encountered more than a few of the infected, and possibly never more than one at a time.

"Well, you can stay here and wait for one of them to get you." Just as Max finished her sentence, she sensed someone behind her. As she swung to defend herself, she caught the look of panic on the man's face and she assumed she would be facing an infected. Instead, when she turned she found the girl that had been running from him. Hanging from her hand was the large wrench the man had been holding.

"He killed Kevin," the girl whispered.

"What?" Max demanded, suddenly on alert.

Without another word, the girl took two fast strides at the man and swung the large wrench at his head. The man dodged at first and tried to grab her, but without his arm to handle his weight he fell to one side. The girl lifted the wrench again and slammed it into his skull with a sickening crack. She dropped the wrench on the body and stood straight, staring down at him.

"He killed Kevin," she said again.

Max stood stunned. She assumed Kevin was the girl's boyfriend. And it appeared the intruder had killed him. Watching her, Max waited to see how she would react to possibly killing the intruder. The girl stood motionless, staring as if waiting for him to wake up. Max walked slowly to the body, her hands held up in a non-threatening manner. As she entered the girl's eye line, her eyes didn't fix on Max.

Moving to the bleeding man, Max crouched down and pressed her fingers to his neck. Finding a thready pulse, she wasn't sure if she was relieved that the girl hadn't just murdered someone or feel bad that the intruder didn't get what was due to him. She stood again and faced the girl. The young girl's eyes hadn't moved from their fixed spot and Max started to think she had gone into shock.

Slowly Max moved to her and placed her hands on her shoulders. The girl jumped slightly at the touch and her whole body was tense. Max shook her softly, trying to get her attention, but the girl's gaze was vacant. *Well hell*, Max thought to herself. The girl was not going to be able to protect herself in this state.

"Hey," Max said, shaking the girl a little harder. That brought the girl's face up, her eyes looking through Max.

"I need to get you somewhere safe. Can you walk with me?" Max said as she coaxed the girl forward.

She pulled the girl to the shadows, away from the moonlit concourse area. Keeping her eyes swinging around, she guided her toward the sporting goods store. Max didn't want anyone to follow her straight to Jack. She couldn't think of a safer place for the shocked girl.

When she approached the tent Max let out a low bird-like whistle. The tent door began to unzip in answer to her signal. Max could barely make out Jack's face when she stuck her head out to find her mother. Cajoling the girl into the tent was another feat, but once she was in, she curled into a ball in the corner. Jack looked questioning at the girl and back at her mother.

"She saw her boyfriend killed," Max whispered.

"Oh no, are the sick ones inside?"

"Yes, but he was killed by one of the living intruders," Max answered.

"How sad," Jack said quietly. She moved to sit next to the girl and softly pet her head.

Preparing to leave the tent, Max double checked her weapons and flashlight. There was no way of knowing how many additional intruders there were. So far Max knew of three that had been dealt with. There was still the second mystery voice she had heard. There could be additional unknowns. She also didn't know if there were more infected inside.

The sun was just beginning to break the horizon as a brighter gray light was filtering into the mall windows. Max knew her time was limited to figure out what her next step was inside the mall. She didn't want to keep Jack there any longer than it took for the sun to rise in the sky. She zipped up the tent and a gunshot sounded in the mall concourse. It was like the dinner bell being rung and Max's decision was made for her.

CHAPTER EIGHT

The sound was no longer her concern as Max pulled open the tent door again. Jack was already moving inside, realizing what the gunshot meant. Someone else was armed inside the mall. And they weren't worried about attracting a crowd. Max quickly crouched down inside the tent. *What's the plan, Max?*

She unzipped one of the tent windows and peeked one eye out. She watched the entrance to the sporting goods store for any sign of movement. The mall was an echo chamber, meaning the gunshot could have been anywhere. It didn't sound close, but that didn't necessarily mean it wasn't. And was the person with the gun on the move, running from the infected already?

Max glanced over at the girl that was still laying in a ball in their tent. She was a liability. However, something about her actions with the intruder, her need for justice and vengeance for her boyfriend struck a chord with Max. Not that Max had brought herself to killing a living person, she could understand the need for action after seeing something so horrific. That cord in Max was what made her decide the girl had to come with them.

"Hey," Max said to the girl. When she didn't get a response, she crawled over to her and got right in her face. Smacking her cheek a few times got the girl to look at Max.

"Hey, you in there?" Max asked.

"What? What do you want?" The girl asked in a nasty voice. Max was slightly taken aback by her attitude.

For a moment she felt her own defense swell to the surface. However, a moment was all it took for her to remember the girl had just seen her boyfriend murdered and in turn had murdered the man that had struck the death blow. There was no telling where the girl's mind was at.

"Hi. Do you remember us? I'm Max. What's your name?" Max asked softly.

"Blair, my name is Blair. Yeah, I remember you and your daughter," Blair replied, motioning slightly toward Jack.

"Ok, Blair, listen. The sun is starting to rise. Once the mall is lit, we won't be safe from the infected or any other intruders left. We need to get out of the mall," Max said quickly. Blair watched her warily. But she didn't say anything.

"Do you understand?" Max asked, expectantly. Blair just nodded slowly, seeming to understand but not really comprehending what was needed to make the plan happen.

"Ok....well, do you want to come with Jack and me? We are getting out of the city. Do you have people anywhere we could take you to?"

"Kevin was my person. And he's gone. There's no one else," Blair said quietly. She sniffed and suddenly tears were streaming down her face. She began to rock in place and Max sat dumbfounded.

Jack realized her mother had no idea how to handle the crying girl, so she crawled over and sat next to Blair. She took her hand in hers and whispered soft words. Condolences, understanding, and encouragement to come with them out of the unsafe location. Blair seemed to respond better to Jack, so Max went back to the tent window and peered out to see if anyone was around.

A dark figure moved throughout the sporting goods store. It was one of the intruders, looking through the items in the store. He was packing his things into a shopping bag. Max wanted to curse, feeling negligent in her lookout. The man had entered without her even noticing him. If he continued his current path up and down the aisles, he would end up right next to their tent.

Max turned and put her finger to her lips. Jack saw her and immediately quieted. She turned to Blair and signaled her the same way. Blair quieted as much as her sorrow would allow. Max turned to look out the window again and almost yelped when she saw the man much closer and staring straight at her.

"I can see you," the man's deep voice floated into the tent.

"Shit," Max muttered.

"Lady, you might as well come out of hiding." The man placed his shopping bag on the ground and pulled a gun from the back of his pants. Max cursed again. He was the armed intruder, the one that had shot inside the mall earlier. Max found herself wondering how good of a shot could the man really be. It was a blessing that he didn't know Jack or Blair were also hiding inside the tent.

Taking her 9mm out of the holster, she went to the tent door. Confronting him was her only option. The men that broke into the mall were impulsive and she didn't believe he wouldn't shoot blindly into the tent just to kill her. Her tomahawk was at her hip as well, in case he came at her for a closer fight.

Max may have shied away from killing the men in the mall concourse. However, this man was different. This man was coming too close to her daughter. Jack was her main priority and she wasn't going to let a stray bullet strike her. Thinking of Jack she looked at her daughter before ducking out of the tent. Her small face was tight with worry. Max just winked at her.

Immediately aiming her weapon directly at the man's chest, she stood away from the cover of the tent. He looked surprised, but he didn't raise his weapon. If he didn't try to use it on her, maybe it was because he didn't really know how to use it. Unlucky for him, Max knew how to use hers.

"Take what you need and move on," Max ordered. The man sneered at her.

"That's the plan. But what I need is this mall to myself. I could live out this plague here," the man replied, patting the nearby display of clothing.

"Other's will come, just like you did. You can't defend the mall alone," Max said.

"Oh, I'm sure I'll do just fine. Everyone will be one of those infected dead soon. There will only be a few left."

"That will take quite some time. How lucky do you think you are to be one of the few left? You've already let in the dead," Max said, motioning toward the mall concourse. In the far-off distance of the mall, the movements of the infected could be seen. Their unusual joint movements giving them away even as shadows.

"You basically told them you were in here by using that gun," Max continued. "Who or what did you shoot with it?"

"Some woman tried to bite me. She was already inside though, so you guys had your own problems," the man replied. His answer made Max's stomach drop. He could only be referring to Jules. When she left her she didn't think she would die and turn so quickly. Now she knew she was truly dead. Max felt saddened that such a nice woman had to be taken down by the likes of this man.

"Ok fine. You want the mall. Take it. I was only passing through. Let me get my gear and I'll be on my way," Max said, changing tactics. If she could get the guy to leave the store, she would take Jack and Blair through one of the doors that led directly outside.

"Your gear? Anything inside this mall is officially mine now," the man replied. Max sized the man up. She could easily take him. But if he got off a wild shot, Jack and Blair could be the mistaken target.

"I'm only taking what I brought in. What I can carry," Max lied. He would never know what she had brought in or had taken off the shelves. The man seemed to weigh his options. He eyed her gun and seemed to notice her relaxed stance with it.

"Only what you can carry," the man said slowly. But Max could see his hand twitch. He had no intention of letting her go, at least not alive. She waited and watched him. His eyes momentarily left her face and he glanced around. Max knew he was alone, no one had entered the store since they started their standoff. What he didn't know was if she was truly alone.

The moment his decision was made, Max saw it in his eyes first. They locked back on Max, narrowed and hardened. The movement of his gun hand was next and that was all it took for Max to fire her shot. Her aim was slightly off but still, the man collapsed back. He cried out from the ground, hand grasping at his shoulder where the bullet had entered.

Max rushed the man, gun aimed at him all the while. When she got to him she bent and grabbed the gun he had dropped. Easily switching the safety on, she shoved the gun into her waistband for safe keeping. The man's face had gone pale. He looked up at her desperately.

"Help me," he cracked.

"I think not. I'll be on my way," Max replied. She looked up and saw that her shot had attracted the infected and they were now making their way further into the mall. She had to move with her party.

"I'm dying," the man said.

"Oh please. It's a flesh wound. You will be if you don't figure out what to do next," Max replied, motioning toward the mall. She felt little guilt for taking down the man. She had no doubts he was going to shoot her and take everything she had. And that would have included Jack. There was nothing to stop Max from protecting her daughter.

Turning away from the man, Max ran to the tent. Jack was already exiting with Blair on her heels. Jack handed Max her bug out bag and she slung her own over her shoulders. Blair was wearing the extra bag they had packed since being in the sports store. The extra body would be helpful for carrying their supplies until they could obtain a vehicle.

"Ready to go," Jack stated motioning toward the door.

"Ok. Let's grab a few more camping meals on our way out. Need to make sure we have enough food for Blair as well," Max said. She ran back to where the man had put down the shopping bag and grabbed it. As she went back to Jack she checked the contents. Mostly the man had picked up decent items. Turning Blair around, she dumped the additional things into her pack.

As they passed the food section, Max packed as many food items she could into their packs. With that, they made their way to the glass doors. Standing at the doors, looking out at the parking lot with the soft light of dawn breaking through, Max counted the infected she could see. She stopped at ten. They were wandering aimlessly at the moment, spread out around the parking lot.

"They're far apart. One is easy to handle," Max said as she pulled her tomahawk. She could easily take care of single walkers with her tomahawk and there would be no gunfire to attract additional ones from other areas.

"What do I do?" Blair asked. Max was almost startled by the girl's voice. She stayed silent so long it was easy to forget she was there.

"Follow Jack, do what she does. Jack knows what to do when we are in dangerous situations," Max replied. As she spoke Jack nodded and smiled slightly at Blair, who didn't smile back.

Though she had the keys to the mall in the tent, Max didn't waste time trying to figure out which key went to the door. Instead, using the butt of her large flashlight, Max struck the glass three times before it finally shattered outward. The sound drew the nearest infected their way. Max stepped outside quickly and raised her tomahawk in preparation for a fight. She heard the glass crunch as Jack and Blair stepped out to follow.

"Jack, stay on my left," Max said quickly, knowing without looking that her daughter would obey and move to watch for her mother's swings.

The first infected met Max head-on. She wasted no time and ended the infected quickly with a blow to the temple. She pivoted to strike the next as it stepped up behind the first. As she moved she could see Jack and Blair in her peripheral vision, just the way she wanted it. The infected attacking required the majority of her attention. She couldn't worry about Blair wandering off and getting herself killed, not in front of Jack.

Max stepped into her fighting stance with aggression. All of her defense mechanisms seemed to fire at once. Two infected came toward her at the same time. She acted quickly out of instinct, slamming the sole of her foot into the chest of the small woman, causing the infected to fall backward. The second was a taller man and Max had no patience for him. She pivoted to one side and as his uncoordinated movements tried to follow she struck him down with her tomahawk.

When Max went to finish the woman she had knocked down, she stopped short, finding Blair with a knife in hand. The knife was covered in the gross black ooze that seemed to replace blood in the infected. Max walked over to her quickly, taking the knife she wiped it off on the infected's clothing. She handed it back to Blair and nodded her approval.

Glancing around the parking lot, there were no cars on this side, adding to Max's aggravation. She didn't want to just wander around the mall parking lot looking for just any vehicle. Blair stepped up to her side, seeming to know she was looking for a direction.

"There's a car dealership on the other side of that building," she said, pointing toward a bank sitting in the mall parking lot.

"Perfect. We can steal a car from there," Max replied. Motioning to Jack to keep up, she began to sprint across the parking lot. Luckily it seemed Blair could run, and she easily kept up with the Duncans, her feet pounding directly behind Jack's.

Max picked a direct route to the next buildings in the parking lot. She maneuvered away from the infected as she went. Faster was her goal and if she stopped and took down each infected that moved their way, they wouldn't leave the parking lot until dark again. As she ran, she heard shouts and gunshots from the mall. Max wasn't sure who was shooting, but she didn't think they should stick around to find out. She slowed and ran lower, afraid shots were coming in their direction.

They reached the building quickly. Max led Jack and Blair around the corner. She peered back around, toward the mall and the broken outdoor they had left behind them. The gunshots and loud shouting were attracting the infected from the parking lot. She could see some of the infected tripping through the door, not having the thoughts to pick up their feet and step through the door frame. That didn't stop them from stumbling through and picking themselves up on the other side.

Additional shots sounded, feeding the frenzy of infected. Max imagined the man who decided the mall was all his was being surprised by the infected that had decided to join him. Or possibly he was taken down by the other mall survivors. Max could only hope someone on the inside had trapped the man inside the sporting goods store.

As if her thoughts created the moment, the intruder threw himself through the open door moments later. Max held her breath, as she watched him swing a new gun around at the infected closing in on him. Absently, Max wondered where the man found the second gun. From the distance they were at, Max couldn't tell if he had been bitten already. However, he still had a strong fight in him. That fight wasn't going to save him, Max realized, as the infected seemed to collapse on top of him. The last noise he made was a scream that echoed throughout the empty parking lot.

Feeling a touch on her arm, Max jumped, turning quickly to face Jack. Her quizzical look made Max realize how long she had been standing there watching the scene unfold. She just shook her head at her daughter, not feeling up to explaining what had just happened. Blair stood guard at the opposite end of the building and she looked over her shoulder at the Duncans expectantly.

Max moved to Blair's side and surveyed the street they had to cross. There were cars bumper to bumper in places, accidents blocking the way for vehicles to get through. Open doors stood, blood splashed inside vehicles and on the ground nearby. Debris littered the area, from people fleeing as fast as they could. The horde that chased Max and Jack into the mall had swept this area as well.

"We'll need to move quickly, to avoid the infected," Max whispered, nodding toward the street. The infected seemed to wander through the cars, still looking for a meal. The moment they stepped into the open, they would be on display. Blair and Jack nodded their understanding.

Max hitched up her pack, tightening the straps. Spinning her tomahawk, she made sure she was prepared for any unsuspected attacks. With one last deep breath, she took off for the street. She looked back once to ensure Jack and Blair were following and was pleased to see Jack on her heels. Blair wasn't far behind, her hair whipping around her face as she raced to keep up.

The group zigzagged through cars. Max wanted to take a direct route across, but there were too many infected. As she rounded a van, an infected stepped in front of her. Max had to slide to a stop before colliding with the body. Jack and Blair crashed into each other behind Max. Without waiting, Max swung her tomahawk at the arms that were reaching out to her and then stepped in to end the infected.

Reaching the car lot wasn't the hardest part of their escape. Now that they were in the open, the infected followed. The car lot had been looted, glass littered the ground around the building. There was no safe haven there. Max took one moment to decide and ran to the building. Once inside she slowed and motioned for the girls to stay close.

Max could hot-wire a vehicle if she had the time. But time was short now. She needed to find the keys that the dealership would have stored somewhere accessible to their salesmen. She ran for the office that was all glass walls, imagining a busy sales day and a manager sitting there to boss around his employees. The glass door had been shattered in and the office was in disarray. And there on the ground behind the desk were keys tumbled across the floor from a safe that had been pried open.

Sorting through the keys, she wasn't sure exactly what she was looking for. When they had run in she had seen a few trucks and SUV vehicles, which would be her first choices. But there was no way of knowing which keys went to those specifically. Grabbing a handful, she shoved them at Blair, and then another handful at Jack. Grabbing some in her hands, she stood to leave the office.

Outside the office, ambling into the building was a group of infected. *Son of a...*Max thought to herself. Quickly looking around, she realized she had broken one of her own rules, always know all the exits. She found another window broken out on the other side of the building and decided that was their best exit. However, to get there, they were going to have to handle the infected that had now spotted them.

"At some point, we will get a break, right?" Max said as she stepped toward the door of the office. As she decided on her battle plan a loud alarm began going off outside.

CHAPTER NINE

Blinking lights and alarms blared from the car dealership parking lot. Max stood frozen, confused for a moment. The noise was enough to draw the attention of the infected, who had turned toward the parking lot and open door they had come in. The sound of jingling keys caught Max's attention and she turned to a smiling Jack.

"That worked better than I thought," Jack said. She held up keys and fobs where she had pushed the alarm buttons.

"Now we know the keys match something," Blair added.

"Nice thinking, hon'," Max praised. Looking out the window she saw the infected circling the car, looking for what they assumed was an easy loud meal.

"I don't think it will take them long to come back this way though. Let's see if any of those open those bigger vehicles over there," Max said, pointing toward the trucks and SUVs.

After a few fob clicks, they were able to flash the lights on a smaller SUV. Max was happy with that and was ready to get into a vehicle and move. The group moved through the building carefully, keeping silent to keep from attracting too much attention. When they got to the side door, they ran for the small SUV, jumping into it and locking themselves in just as the infected were realizing they were missing their moving meal.

Max behind the wheel started to feel back in control of their fate. She had struggled to stay in one place and to move on foot wasn't a favorable option. Now that they were moving again, she felt more prepared and strong. As she turned the key in the ignition she wanted to cheer as the engine purred to life. She was only slightly disappointed to see only a half tank of gas, but she could handle that later.

The SUV tires peeled from the parking lot as Max stepped on the gas. The girls struggled to get their seat belts on as Max threw the wheel and landed them on the main road. She swerved, avoiding collisions. Max almost laughed out loud when she heard Blair curse in the back seat and grab the handle above her head. Max loved to drive, and she was just glad to be back on the road.

Over an hour later, the SUV's gas gauge was falling and they were nearing the end of town. Max had the basic needs in her bug out bag for siphoning gas. But she needed more gas cans to take some with them. The girls were hungry, and Max could also use a break for a meal. She drove into a small strip mall that shared its parking lot with a gas station.

Keeping the vehicle running, Max sat and waited for something to move. Since they had left the car dealership they had seen many living people. Most just avoiding each other, working to get where they felt safest. The number of infected was more than the living and that saddened and angered Max. The numbers told her that the living were losing.

Now sitting outside the gas station she wondered about power and she wondered why there weren't more people there trying to get gas. Thinking back to the dealership, Max laid on the horn of the SUV.

"Momma!" Jack exclaimed.

"I need to know if any of those things are here," Max said, hitting the horn again.

A movement in the gas station caught her eye. It wasn't the movement of an infected. More someone watching them as they sat outside. Max didn't want to take what anyone else needed. However, they would have to share to continue surviving. The question was, did the people inside the gas station agree with that sentiment.

"Jack, pull out some of the jerky we have packed. I'm going to try to trade to get into the gas station. There are people in there," Max explained.

"You think they will let you in for some jerky?" Blair asked from the backseat.

"Smart people know that food is going to be scarce unless you are growing, killing, or gathering it yourself," Max said.

"And if they aren't smart?" Blair continued.

Max thought for a moment before answering, "Then I'll make the decision for them."

She didn't take off her weapons, on the chance the people inside weren't friendly. However, she held her hands out in the open as she exited the SUV. Holding the beef jerky above her head, she waved toward the gas station. A single face could be seen peering out at Max. *Doesn't mean he's alone,* Max thought to herself as she slowly walked toward the gas station doors.

"Hello?" Max called out when she reached the doors. She tried them once and as expected they were barricaded.

"Go away!" A woman shouted from inside.

"My daughter and I just need some gas cans. We don't want to take anything else you have," Max called back.

"Just go away. I'm not letting anyone in!"

"I have beef jerky here. A trade for some gas cans," Max replied, not giving up. She would bust out a window if she had to. The SUV was their way to get to Montana and she would do what she needed to keep it moving.

"I don't need beef jerky," the woman called through the window.

"Ok. What do you need?" Max asked.

There was a pause on the other side of the glass. Max thought the woman had walked away, but suddenly she appeared in front of Max at the glass doors. She was middle-aged in an employee shirt for the gas station. Her hair was wild and blood stained one of her pants legs. Max studied her through the glass, trying to determine if she was bitten.

"The attendant," she said, motioning to her leg. "He was attacked. I tried to save him. But he died."

"Died? Or...." Max asked, trailing off.

"He wasn't attacked by those things. He was attacked by healthy people battling over gas. Well, now we're out of gas. So, they left."

"Jesus. He was attacked by people getting gas?" Max repeated disbelievingly. Instinctively, Max knew the living could do much worse. But being faced with the terrible didn't make it easier to understand or accept. The woman didn't say anything, just nodded at Max's comment.

"So, what do you need?" Max asked again.

"A ride."

"A ride? To where?" Max asked. She wasn't starting up a taxi service. A part of her though felt if she could help the woman get to where she was going, she should try.

"About twenty minutes out of town. My parents live on a farm. I want to go there," she replied.

"Are they still alive?" Max asked. The question hit the woman like a blow. The terror showed on her face and Max felt a little guilty for not having the social etiquette to make it less upsetting.

"Yes. I talked to them yesterday before the phones went out. They were going to lock themselves up in the farmhouse. I was going to try and leave, but someone stole my car. And then the other employee...well, I couldn't leave."

"Ok. Well, we're heading out of town. Going....North," Max said, deciding at the last minute. The question had rolled around in her mind since she began studying the road atlas the day before. Was Griffin alive in North Carolina? Could she just leave the East Coast without checking? She hadn't realized the decision was made until she said North to the woman.

"Perfect. That's the way the farm is. So, will you drop me?" The woman asked her hand on the door. Max just nodded, and she opened the locks and removed the bar that was barricading the door from the inside.

Inside the station, the store section looked ransacked. Products were haphazardly tossed about. Except in one corner where souvenir blankets had been thrown. The woman's bed for the last two nights Max assumed. Survivors had swept through much of the food, medical and tobacco products. Max spied a few items left behind and bagged them in a souvenir reusable bag.

The gas station employee followed Max around as if she thought Max would run out the door and not fulfill her end of the bargain. It was like having a noisy shadow. As Max watched where she put her feet, never stepping on anything other than the floor, the woman slogged through all of the spilled items. The noise grated on Max's nerves and she had to rein in a smart-ass comment to the woman.

"What's your name?" Max asked instead.

"Ruth."

"I'm Max."

"Nice to meet ya, Max," Ruth replied.

Falling back into silence Max found herself in the small aisle that held car items. She found herself quite surprised by what people decided to take and not take. Tobacco products seemed to rate higher than batteries, chargers, jumper cables, or gas cans. *Better for us,* Max figured as she grabbed two ten-gallon cans. She also packed batteries with the food items she had in her bag. She could find a use for most items in the store, but they were on limited time. And once they reached Montana they would have everything they needed.

Thinking about Montana, and her home, made Max anxious. She wanted to hear from Alex, to know they were on their way and safe. She wanted to talk to Rafe and know that the compound was still secure as they had always planned. None of them had strayed so far from their upbringing that plan Sundown wasn't still in place. They all knew what it meant. If Rafe was safe, the compound would be ready for them when they got there.

"So, you said you're out of gas? Completely? Or did you shut it down?" Max asked. She knew there would be some sort of master switch to stop gas from flowing to the pumps. Ruth fidgeted slightly, giving all the answer Max needed.

"I want to fill up at least three of these ten-gallon cans. Can we do that?" Max coaxed. Ruth nodded and turned back toward the front of the store.

"When they started attacking poor Ernie, I hit the emergency shut off. Those bastards were hurting an unarmed sweet man, all for gas," Ruth said over her shoulder as she went to the control panel near the cash register. She used a key from her pocket to open a keypad and punched in a code. A beeping sound went off and then she hit a green button next to the emergency shut off button.

"The gas should flow again. We still have power. I'll activate pump one for you," Ruth said with a small smile.

Max ran out to pump one with three gas cans. She motioned to Blair to pull the SUV closer and once it was next to the pump, Max directly filled the vehicle first. Keeping her gaze swinging around the parking lot, she kept watching for the infected, but also any living that might get the idea to come and steal what they were pumping.

She had two cans filled when she heard a low growl from the opposite side of the SUV. Max pulled her tomahawk as she walked around the side of the SUV. The infected was making its way toward the gas station open door. Max hadn't heard her, but she assumed Ruth made some sort of noise inside to attract the infected's attention. Without preamble, Max approached and slashed down the infected with a blow to its head. She stooped to wipe off her blade and when she stood Ruth was standing in front of her, white as a ghost.

"You...you carry an ax?" Ruth asked.

"It's a tactical tomahawk," Max replied.

The name of the weapon didn't seem to satisfy Ruth and she continued to eye Max warily. Max shrugged it off and went back to filling gas cans. She wasn't concerned with how Ruth felt about her. The promise of a ride out of town got her the gas she needed. And without siphoning anything.

Max could handle some strange looks from a stranger for that.

"Ummm, Momma?" Jack's voice came from the backseat. Max looked up and Jack pointed behind her.

"Crap," mumbled Max. The infected had found them and slowly ambled toward the gas station. Max topped off the third gas can and placed it in the back of the SUV. She ran back to the open window of the SUV. Blair sat in the driver's seat looking at her expectantly.

"Fire the truck up. Keep it running. I left a bag of stuff inside. I'm going to grab it and that woman, and we'll be ready to go," Max said. She took off running. Moments later the engine purred to life and Max felt relief for the reliable transportation.

Entering the store, Max immediately grabbed the bag she had left near the cash register. She ran to the corner where Ruth had been living, but the woman wasn't there. She ran back to the front of the store expecting to find Ruth waiting there. The store was empty.

"Ruth," Max called in a low-pitched hiss. *Where in the hell did she go?*

Not willing to wait much longer, Max ran the bag out to the SUV and judged by the distance covered by the infected that they would be upon the SUV in less than three minutes. She shoved the bag into the truck and slammed the back closed. She went to Jack's open window again, looking inside.

"Where in the hell did that woman go?" Max exclaimed.

"I didn't see her leave," Blair replied.

"Ruth!" Max yelled. The infected knew they were at the station, her additional noise wasn't going to change that.

She didn't owe the woman much more than a twenty-minute drive in exchange for gas. However, she made the agreement and wouldn't just leave without fulfilling her obligation.

"Ruth! Where in the hell did you go?" Max yelled again.

"I'm here, jeez, what's the big..." Ruth's voice came from behind the station store and trailed off when she realized they were being set upon by the infected. A cigarette hung from her lips.

Without hesitation, Ruth ran behind the store. Max could tell some of the infected were splitting off toward Ruth's area and would soon split them apart.

"Ruth! Don't run that way! Shit!" Max yelled. She raced after the woman, tomahawk out of her case. She caught the first infected she ran by in the shoulder, spinning it away from its meal. She ran around the edge of the store, expecting to find Ruth hiding there. But she was gone.

"Damn it, Ruth, where in the hell are you going?" Max cursed to herself.

Max ran along the back of the building, finding the backdoor slight ajar halfway down. Running back inside the store again, she slammed the door shut behind her. Spinning she found herself in a small storeroom. She ran back into the store searching for Ruth. Max suddenly slid to a halt in the middle of the store. She could clearly see through the front windows. Shit, she cursed to herself. While she was trying to chase Ruth down, the infected had split between the front and back of the store. The path to the SUV was now full of infected.

"Ruth, girl you better come the hell out of wherever you are hiding right now!" Max growled.

"I'm here," Ruth called from her corner. She was curled into a ball on the pile of blankets when Max approached.

"What in the living hell are you doing right now?" Max asked, almost laughing at her own choice of words. Living hell. The was what she felt like she was living in right now. Her concern for other people was beginning to be a wholehearted pain in her ass.

"I'm hiding," Ruth replied. Her tone was so calm Max was surprised she didn't add a "duh" at the end. Because apparently hiding in the corner of the gas station store was complete common sense.

"Yeah, that's not going to happen. If you want a ride out of town, we are leaving."

"With those things out there? Nope," Ruth said, shaking her head, and shrinking further into the blankets.

"Well suit yourself. I've seen how these hordes behave. They won't leave until a better meal presents itself. I won't be that meal," Max replied. She pulled her 9mm from her hip and checked the magazine before slapping it back into the gun. Ten rounds were all she had on her and she planned on using them to their best ability.

"You're going to leave me here?" Ruth asked incredulously.

"Ruth, take this as you will, but yeah, I'm leaving you here. Unless you want to get your ass out of the corner and come with us," Max said. Before waiting for an answer she started toward the front of the store. She could hear Ruth scrambling to her feet behind her.

Getting to the front of the store, Max began to make some sort of attack plan in her mind. She looked over her shoulder at Ruth and knew without saying a word the woman would be useless in a fight. Max focused on Blair's face, who she could see peering through the passenger side window at them. Both she and Jack had the brains to duck down where the infected couldn't see them. The SUV was quiet enough while running that the infected weren't overly attracted to it.

"We are going straight to the truck, got it? You need to stay to my left. Do not run or go faster than I do. I can't protect you if you do that, understand?" Max explained. She looked over at Ruth as she finished and found her staring at Max with a mouth that strangely resembled a fish out of water.

"Ruth, close your mouth," Max said dryly. The woman slammed her lips together and continued to stare at her. Max just raised an eyebrow at her and Ruth nodded quickly.

"Ok, here we go. Straight line unless I say otherwise. Stay close," Max said and she swung open the door to her very own living hell.

CHAPTER TEN

Close contact fighting was something Max excelled at. The infected between her and her daughter were uncoordinated and unintelligent. But as a group they were dangerous. Max spun, keeping Ruth in her peripheral vision as she cut down infected. She only worried about ending the ones closest to them. When she had a moment of a break, she took down two approaching infected with her 9mm, cursing at herself for missing with the first shot.

Ruth couldn't seem to keep quiet, letting out screams and yelps as they moved. Max would jump when her shrill scream would sound, assuming it was because an infected had a hold of her. Instead, it was just the sight of infected close by that was scaring her. It took everything Max had to not scream at the woman to just shut her trap.

As Max fought two infected, Ruth stood off to the side watching the scene unfold. She would glance around at the crowds of infected, but she stayed close the way Max told her. Suddenly Max lost the upper hand with the last infected in her fight. The tall, lanky infected man swiped at Max, catching her on the shoulder. As Max stumbled, she thought about the strength the infected seemed to have.

Tall and lanky was on Max a moment later, looking to sink his teeth into something. She shoved up her tomahawk handle just in time. However, while she struggled with her own threat, she realized Ruth wasn't to her left. Risking a glance, Max could see her backing toward the store a look of panic on her face. Seeing Max at a slight disadvantage was making her panic and she was about to run right into unspeakable horrors.

"Ruth! No!" Max grated out, as the woman spun on her heel to run back to the store. She didn't make it three steps before she ran into an infected that had been heading her way. Max had seen it coming. In Ruth's panic, she saw nothing but the salvation of her pile of blankets.

"No!!!" Max screamed as Ruth was pulled to the ground by the attacking infected. As rage boiled to the surface, Max stepped back from tall and lanky. She pulled her tomahawk from his jaws so roughly his teeth clattered together causing goosebumps to rise on Max's arms. Fueled by anger and the discomfort of feeling like she had failed Ruth, Max's swing of the tomahawk cracked tall and lanky's skull wide open.

By the time Max reached the infected that were on Ruth, a dinner buffet had started. Ruth's screams had been short-lived, but they echoed in Max's ears. Max focused on ending the infected that had their teeth in Ruth's flesh. A lull in the attacking infected came and Max found herself looking down at Ruth's mutilated body. She didn't really know the woman except for the hour they had conversed and Max had collected gas. But Max was weighed down by immense guilt for the woman dying under her watch.

The nearby growling of infected indicated to Max that her time was up. Pulling her knife, Max sliced into Ruth's temple. The best she could do for the woman now is make sure she didn't turn into an undead being. Leaving her on the ground outside her beloved gas station store felt wrong, but there was no choice. The infected were clustering to attack Max and she needed to get to the SUV.

With one last glance at Ruth, Max spun toward the SUV and began making her way to the front seat. She could see Blair switching from the driver's seat to the front passenger seat. Max aimed her path toward that side of the SUV. She again didn't take the time to end every infected that came close to her. Slices to arms and bodies could redirect the infected long enough for her to get past.

Jumping into the SUV, Max stepped down on the gas pedal and the SUV leaped forward. Infected tried to fight their way to the SUV, but it was much bigger and powerful. Max took care in plunging through the thick group of infected that were wandering into the entrance of the parking lot. Once they were clear, she took off quickly, leaving the mess of infected and Ruth's body behind.

"Momma?" Jack said from the backseat sometime later.

"Yeah?"

"You're sort of a mess," Jack whispered.

"Shit," Max muttered. Jack was right. The fighting with the infected had splashed blood and black ooze on Max's clothing. She was thankful she was wearing a long-sleeved shirt even though the day was unseasonably warm and humid.

Pulling over on a rural road Max had picked to avoid any of the interstate congestion, she climbed out of the SUV. Jack opened the back door and handed Max clothes to change into.

"Thanks, hon," Max said.

"I think you should just burn those," Jack said sarcastically, something she definitely inherited from Max. Her comment made Max snort, and then she made a big show of tossing her button up shirt on the side of the road.

"We're going North," Blair said, coming around the SUV.

"Yeah," Max replied simply. She had unconsciously made the choice to find Griffin. Something in her knew he was alive. Looking at her daughter, their daughter, she felt she owed it to Jack to find her father and bring him to the compound. If she left him to die, Jack would know someday, and Max knew she would never forgive her. She wasn't sure yet if Jack would forgive her hiding the truth of his identity for eight years.

"I thought you were going to Montana?" Blair asked. Her voice was high and demanding. Max pulled a clean shirt over her head and looked at Blair with a raised eyebrow. The look had intimidated a many people and it didn't fail to cause Blair to wilt just slightly.

"We are. I have someone to get in North Carolina first. If you aren't ok with that, I can drop you anywhere you'd like on the way," Max replied, a little sting in her words. She didn't have to bring this girl with her anywhere. If she proved to be more trouble than she was worth, Max had half the mind to just leave her.

"No," Blair said, visibly deflating. "I have nowhere else to go." Max felt slightly guilty for making the girl feel dejected. She awkwardly patted her arm.

"It's alright. This is one very stressful situation. I'm sure we'll all have reason to be snippy," Max said. Blair smiled slightly before heading back to her seat.

Sitting back in the SUV, Max pulled out the road atlas and studied the smaller roads that lead from Charleston to Raleigh, North Carolina. A trip she had made before, typically took just over four hours to drive. Max expected it to take at least double that, with avoiding the main freeways. If they had to cut back to the freeway, Max had a good idea they would be packed and it would take time to maneuver around. She showed Blair the next few turns she wanted to make and asked her to co-pilot. The girl seemed satisfied to have a job, a purpose in the group.

The rural area was full of farms and periods of nothing but trees. The air was humid but clean. Windows were rolled down to clear out some of the gas smell that was coming from the gas cans in the back. The smell reminded Max of Ruth, which was odd for her to think. She had a feeling the image of the woman's body, feasted on by the infected, wouldn't leave her for some time.

It was getting close to twilight when they reached the edge of Raleigh city limits. During their drive, they saw very few living people. A few cars sped down the same roads they traveled, but no one signaled or stopped. Everyone had the same feeling of foreboding and finding safety was their first priority. Sitting in the SUV stopped at a blinking stoplight, Max could see infected in the distance. Smoke rose like beacons of the fight between the living and the dead.

"So where does this person live?" Blair asked.

"What person are we looking for, Momma?" Jack asked from the backseat.

"Griffin, his name is Griffin." Max didn't know what else to say about him. She couldn't explain to Jack that he had been the only real love in her life She also couldn't explain how things had ended or why she felt the obligation to come and find him.

"Do we know where this Griffin lives?" Blair asked.

"Not exactly," Max replied. That was a lie. Max had no idea in hell where Griffin lived before the plague, only that he lived in Raleigh. And Raleigh wasn't exactly small.

She looked over at Blair, who looked at her in a way that made Max want to slap the sarcasm out of her.

"Ok, I know this isn't well thought out," Max began slowly. "My first guess is he will be where the military is. He served in the Army."

"Didn't you say no one was coming to help?"

"Yeah, but I imagine the military or local law enforcement have something set up. Maybe a communications center?"

"How do we find that?" Blair asked.

Max turned on the car radio. Static filled the SUV. She began to search through the stations, allowing the auto find to just slide through the broadcast signals. She moved the SUV further into town, hoping to catch some sort of emergency signal. As she drove she kept an eye out for somewhere to sleep that night, in the chance she was completely wrong, and they couldn't find Griffin.

Turning into s neighborhood, Max surveyed the homes in the area. There was debris littering a driveway to her left, clothing spilled from a suitcase and the front door stood open. Blood splashed the sidewalk at the end of the driveway, giving a clear picture of what had happened. As they continued to drive similar stories were told. Some of the homes looked to be locked up tight. One was boarded up completely and Max approved of the household being prepared to wait out the apocalypse.

Max pulled the SUV into a driveway. One that seemed to be empty, the garage stood wide open. No vehicles were in the area. Darkness was falling and Max didn't want to travel at night. The infected weren't slowed down by the dark, as they followed their senses of smell and hearing. Max didn't like being at any sort of disadvantage.

Suddenly a piercing sound came from the SUV speakers. Max jumped on the brake to stay right where the signal was catching the antenna.

"This is an emergency broadcast. This is not a test. If you are hearing this, please proceed to the nearest shelter immediately. If you are injured, please proceed to the nearest hospital immediately. Military personnel will be available to assist you. Shelters are at the following locations. This message will repeat..." Addresses were rattled off and Max fished through her pack for paper and pen. By the time the message repeated she was ready to write down the addresses.

"Which one do you think we should try?" Blair asked.

"The nearest to start with. But we're going to wait until first light," Max said, gesturing toward the open garage.

"We're going to sleep here?" Jack asked in a small voice from the backseat.

"Well I guess we could just sleep in the SUV, but that will be uncomfortable. I figure we should sleep indoors when we have the chance," Max explained. She pulled the SUV into the garage. After getting out and checking the space she maneuvered for it to barely fit. The garage door pulled down, shutting them in.

"Being inside the garage will make it easier for us to get in and out of the vehicle when we leave," Max said as she got out of the truck.

The three got into the house and started checking all of the rooms. A small family had lived there. Husband, wife and two kids from what they could tell in photos on the walls. There was no blood in the house. However, dresser drawers were dropped and clothing was strewn. Cabinets seemed to be partially emptied with some food still gathered on the kitchen table. The family had evacuated. Max hoped they had actually made it somewhere safe and had not fallen prey to the dead.

Once it was confirmed they were alone in the house, Max checked every door and window. She pulled the shades on windows that were open and locked everything tight. Somehow the house still had power, the Raleigh grid not falling in that area yet. Going into the kitchen, Max opened the freezer and found a quart of cookie dough ice cream.

"Score!" She called to Jack and Blair.

Both came running into the kitchen. After dropping their bags in the living room, the three grabbed spoons and dug into the ice cream container together. Without speaking, they all realized how long it would be before they tasted something like ice cream again. Max let the bites melt in her mouth, savoring each taste. Jack seemed to be eating with her eyes closed. As usual, Blair seemed to not care about anything on the outside. But when she made sure to scoop every last bit from the container, Max knew it affected her more than she let on.

"With the power on, we could cook a nice meal from whatever is left. I think I saw some meat in the freezer. When the family left, they obviously couldn't take all that with them," Max said, going back to the fridge to evaluate the contents.

While Max decided on dinner, Jack pulled out the sofa bed and put the mattress on the ground. She then used the sofa cushions to make herself a makeshift bed. Blair insisted she could sleep on the ground on a sleeping bag. However, Jack raided the linen closet and piled blankets under the sleeping bag so she wasn't directly on the hard surface. Jack hummed a little under her breath as she handled the domestic tasks, feeling a little lighter being back in an actual house.

Max wasn't a master chef, but she could whip up Hamburger Helper and she was glad when she found the meat and the box meal in the house. She was also surprised to find fresh strawberries and apples in the fridge. They left in a hurry Max figured to herself. Fruit could have been packed and taken. Maybe the family didn't expect to be traveling far. Max hoped for their sake their plans worked out.

Sitting down at a kitchen table for dinner felt oddly normal. They ate in silence, each absorbing the events of the night before and the day that led them to the house they were in. Max knew Blair's mind was probably back on her boyfriend and the man she killed in the mall. She felt sad for the girl, being so young and having to handle such an emotional burden. Not that Max had any advice for her on how to make that better. But she had expected more emotions from Blair during the day they traveled. All the girl did was stare out the passenger window unless someone spoke to her.

When they laid down to sleep, Max could feel the exhaustion of the events weighing down her body. Visions of Griffin were on her mind as she fell asleep. Her dreams were fitful. She first dreamed that she found Griffin, but he was an infected dead trying to eat Jack, his own daughter. The next dream she had, Griffin was alive, but he was trying to kill her when he found out about Jack being his daughter.

"Momma," Jack's voice came through the haze of sleep. Max could feel her shoulder being shaken. Opening her eyes, she rolled to face Jack on her couch cushion bed.

"You were dreaming. Kept saying my name," Jack whispered. Max tucked a piece of her long black curly hair behind her ear.

"Just dreams, honey. Go back to sleep, I'm sorry I woke you."

"Was it bad dreams?" Jack asked. She grabbed Max's hand and held it to her cheek. It was an odd sentimental gesture for the two of them. Max typically didn't show her love in physically affectionate ways.

"Partially. But it's ok. We've seen enough nightmares the last few days to last my lifetime. I hope you aren't dreaming," Max whispered in answer.

"No. I mean it's hard to fall asleep. I keep thinking they're gonna find us, ya know?" Jack asked. Max nodded her head in understanding.

"Well from what we've seen, they can't open doors. So we are safe here. Sleep ok? Tomorrow will probably prove to be another long day," Max said. She patted Jack's cheek before pulling her hand away. Jack nodded and then yawned widely.

It took Max some time to fall asleep after that. She thought about her dreams, wondering if they were telling her something. Telling her to give up the foolish search for Griffin. Or telling her she was wrong to keep this secret for so long. Watching Jack sleep, it was hard for Max to not see Griffin right there in their daughter. No, she wouldn't give up the search. Even if Griffin found out and was furious with her, finding him was more about Jack than it was about him.

CHAPTER ELEVEN

"This is the third location we've come to. None of them have living people, maybe none of them will," Blair said, sitting in the front seat of the SUV. She held the roadmap of Raleigh that Max found at a local gas station. She sat and found the locations listed during the emergency broadcast. Once they had them all labeled, they started with the nearest one to them and started searching.

Max got out of the SUV, leaving the engine running. There would be no need to stay long. The so-called shelter was a ghost town, similar to the two before. As she walked into a nearby tent that had been erected, Max gasped at the amount of blood she found. The copper smell of blood tinged the air, but she could tell there was something else. The smell of gun smoke hit her nose and she would know it anywhere. There was a fight, but there were living fighting back with a lot of firepower.

Coming out of the tent, Max squinted in the sun. A single infected had spotted her and was making its way to her. It was sad to see old people, already frail and declining in health, changed to the infected. Their old bodies could barely handle the intense hunt that their minds seemed to demand. Instead of waiting for the old man to reach her, Max strode forward, knife in hand. She felt it was putting the poor man out of misery by sliding the blade into his skull and ending his dead walking life.

She stood in the center of what was called an emergency shelter. It was really just a large area, where chain link fences had been erected. Concrete jersey barriers were pushed to either side, to prevent the fence from easily being pushed down. Inside the fence were military tents in two lines. Those two lines were separated by another fence. Max found that set up strange and decided to investigate further.

The side she was on, with the drenched tent, seemed to have its own entrance. She circled back to the entrance where the SUV was waiting. On the ground, she found a large piece of cloth that was partially attached to the outside fence. It had seen better days and was now ripped and bloody. Carefully she pulled the cloth open and read the words that were hastily painted on it. "Sick on Left. Healthy on Right." Dropping the cloth Max turned to look at the camp as a whole. They separated the sick and healthy. That was smart. But the story told was one of overwhelming sick.

Max had seen enough. Chain link fences between the healthy and the sick weren't going to stop the infected dead from getting to their meals. The smell of gun smoke had been so strong in the bloody tent, Max was sure the infected had gotten out of hand and the military had to intervene. But where did the bodies go? Where did the living that were fighting go?

She sat in the SUV, contemplating, letting the events unfold in her mind. The military was nearby and when the plague broke out they set up multiple shelters for the residents of the nearby cities. What bothered Max about that was they didn't seem to realize how the illness worked, or what the dead did. Or they wouldn't have had the healthy separated by only a fence. Many would be looking to the military and the government to solve this for them, heal them, inoculate against whatever the illness was.

"Momma?" Jack said from the backseat.

"Hmm?" Max answered absently, completely lost in her own thoughts.

"What are we doing?" Jack asked.

Max sighed. That was the question. She didn't see enough bodies in the shelter to make up for the number of people that had to come through. That meant someone alive had cleaned up and moved what was here. They didn't take the time to take down the shelter. That told Max they had shelter somewhere else to flee to. One of the other emergency shelters in town.

"I think we keep looking. There have to be people alive still somewhere in town," Max responded. The likelihood of those people knowing Griffin or him being there was slim. Her belief was he would be associated with the military in some way. She just needed someone to tell her he was gone, and she could move on.

The fifth shelter proved to be something more than an empty shell. As they pulled the SUV onto the street the shelter was on, military men stood in front of the car pointing automatic rifles at them through the windshield. Max flashed her empty hands immediately and Blair copied her. The men started yelling at them through the window and Max indicated she wanted to roll the window down. One of the men approached her door and pointed to the locks.

"Jack, no matter what, you stay in this car until I tell you otherwise," Max said. She unlocked the door and as she suspected the man pulled it open and yanked her from the car. He immediately pushed her up against the hood of the truck and started searching her.

"You're going to find a gun, a tomahawk, and a knife. None of which I planned on using here," Max said as he roughly grabbed her hips, checking her belt.

"Are you sick?" The man asked. Max changed her perception of him though, he was much closer to a boy than a man.

"No. And none of us are bit," Max replied.

"Why are you here?"

"I thought this was an emergency shelter? We heard about it on the radio," Max said. The boy stepped back and allowed her to turn. The other men approached slowly, keeping their weapons at the ready.

"It is. We are just being careful."

"Yeah, I would guess it's time for that. We saw the other shelters. The infected took over I guess," Max said. She let her hands hang loosely at her sides. She couldn't take men with automatic rifles. But if she had to defend herself, she was ready. None of the men said anything, just watched her. Max's felt her patience slipping.

"Listen, can we come in or what? We're looking for someone," she asked.

"Why do you think this person is here?" One of the men asked.

"He was in the Army. I was thinking he would stick with the military. I may be wrong," Max replied shrugging. "I figured being around some living people would be a good change of pace."

"Name?"

"Max."

"Who's in the car?" The man continued.

"My daughter Jack and friend Blair."

"The car stays outside. You can park it somewhere nearby. Then you three can come in. Come through the healthy side," the man said, motioning toward the shelter area.

"You seriously have sick people here?" Max demanded, taking a step toward the driver's door. Griffin or not, she wasn't taking Jack into an infected shelter.

"No, not anymore," the man replied quietly. Max left it alone. She wasn't sure she wanted to know what happened.

She climbed back into the SUV. Without waiting for direction, she put the vehicle in reverse and moved away from the shelter entrance. She found a parking spot one block away. She turned to Blair and Jack.

"I'm not so sure about this place. They are really jumpy. We need to stay close," she said. Jack nodded, but Blair looked incredulous.

"It's the military. The government. They know what they're doing," Blair argued.

"The government doesn't always know what it's doing," Max countered.

"That's easy for you to say. You have somewhere to go. For people like me, they take care of us," Blair replied. Max thought for a moment. She could imagine what it would feel like to not have her family compound to go to. But with her childhood, she knew deep down, she would survive on her own with Jack. She would do whatever was necessary.

"Blair, you could come with us," Max quietly said. Knowing Alex was a bleeding heart, Max knew it wouldn't be a problem for her to bring someone to Montana with them. Hell, she knew Alex would gladly open the doors to everyone if she could.

"I don't think....no....I'd like to see what the government is planning on doing to fix this," Blair replied.

"Well let's get into the shelter first and you can see for yourself. It seems chaotic."

"Of course, it's chaos. There are dead people walking around," Blair replied, sarcasm tinting her words.

Max wasn't going to argue with the girl. She couldn't make the decision for Blair. If she chose to trust the government and stay in the shelter, that was her business. Jack was Max's only priority, the only person she was attached to and needed to provide for. She could only express her concern and offer Blair a different option.

The three got out of the SUV, slinging their packs over their backs. Max locked the vehicle and packed the keys away. She wanted to know the truck would be there if they needed a quick escape. The one block walk seemed to take forever. Max felt like her heart would explode out of her chest before she was able to ask about Griffin. As they walked, she heard an all familiar growling.

They were within sight of the shelter, but Max didn't want to leave the infected to try and attack someone else. Motioning Jack and Blair to go ahead of her, she pulled her tomahawk and turned toward the noise. Two infected came from a small alley behind a nearby business building. They must have heard the girls talking as they walked. They were focused on Max, looking for a warm meal. While waiting for them to get closer and in the open Max found herself wondering what they saw when looking at a living person.

She heard one of the military guys call out to her, but she just waved her tomahawk at him. Stepping forward toward the infected, she lifted her tomahawk and bent low to strike the first at the knee, causing it to fall to the side. While that infected struggled on the ground, Max pivoted and spun to the side of the second infected. It wasn't quite fast enough to follow her movements and it couldn't turn as fast as it needed to catch her. Its arm snaked out and tried to claw at her, close enough that Max felt the air from the movement. She stepped back to allow swinging room and her tomahawk came down with a crunch into the infected's skull.

As the second infected fell to its real death, Max turned toward the shelter opening. The hiss from behind her reminded her that the first infected was still alive. She held up her finger in a "just a second" gesture and walked backward smiling ironically at Jack. Max wanted to claim this wasn't easy for her, but she would be lying. Fighting the infected felt like second nature to her. The indiscriminate ending of their dead lives felt as if she were releasing them from a walking hell. Her tomahawk easily sliced into the skull of the infected on the ground, hissing, and growling coming to an end.

She turned back toward the shelter entrance. Jack and Blair were already at the fence just waiting for Max to catch up. As she reached the military men, she noticed a wary look in their eyes as they watched her walk. When she got to the fence entrance a man stopped the three of them from entering.

"We'll need your weapons," a large man in fatigues said.

"Yeah, don't think so, bud," Max replied, laughing out loud. Then she sobered when the seriousness of the man's face hit her.

"You're serious?" She demanded.

"Momma," Jack's voice sounded like a warning to Max, and she brushed her off.

"You have lost your damn marbles if you think I'm going to wander into this shelter without a way to defend myself and these girls," Max said, her voice rising angrily.

"No one comes in with weapons," the man replied calmly. His calm grated on Max's nerves and raised her blood pressure just a little further.

"Really? And what are all these children doing with automatic weapons then?" Max demanded. She raised her hand and waved in the direction of the party that had stopped their car.

"Those are soldiers, ma'am, and are here for your protection."

Max was sure she heard one of the boys behind her snort and say something about them needing to protect themselves against her. Max shot the dirtiest looks she could muster over her shoulder and the soldiers seemed to straighten up and wipe the grins off their faces. What they didn't realize was they weren't far from the truth. As young as the group looked, Max had been training for survival long before they had held a gun.

"We are coming in. And I'm not giving up my weapons," Max said. With that she moved forward, to move past the man. His arm shot out and grabbed her by the arm. Max stopped and looked at his hand on her arm, and then looked up at him, challenging.

"You sure you want to do this?" Max asked, venom in her tone.

"Ma'am, there are no weapons in the shelter area," the man repeated.

"I'm not deaf, bud, I heard you. And I don't care. I don't need weapons to kick your ass, so you should remove your hand from my being," she replied. She attempted to pull away, causing the solider to squeeze harder. *Hell no*.

Grabbing his hand on her arm with her free hand, she locked it in place. At the same time, she rotated the arm he held and gripped the arm he used to hold her. With a quick twist, she had his wrist and he was falling to his knees with a grunt. The pressure she had on his wrist had him gasping in pain. In the frenzy, Max could hear the soldiers behind her panic and move their weapons. She tightened the grip she had that twisted his wrist and grabbed her gun out of its holster at the same time.

"Listen, boys, do we really want this to go down like this? We have other things to be fighting, not each other," she said calmly, continuing pressure on the wrist she held.

"You're going to break my wrist," the soldier gasped from the ground.

"I did warn you, didn't I?" Max asked. The man nodded quickly, ready to agree to anything before Max did serious damage. She stood over the man and kept her gun pointed at the soldiers that were now pointing their automatic rifles at her.

"Max? Max Duncan?" A voice came from behind her. Max froze in place. She didn't drop the gun or release the man's wrist. Slowly she turned her head and looked over her shoulder.

"Yeah, hi, Griffin. Surprise," Max said lamely.

CHAPTER TWELVE

He looked the same. Max couldn't understand how that was possible. His dark hair was cropped closer to his head than when they were in high school. She guessed that was a habit he had from being in the military. He had the hint of facial hair, a face that hadn't found time for shaving since the world fell apart. His hazel eyes bore into her with shock and humor.

"Well you haven't changed a bit, have you?" He asked. He crossed his arms over his chest and stood with his feet planted apart.

"Wells? You know this woman?" The soldier on the ground choked out.

"Oh yeah, I know her. I assume you touched her?" Griffin asked, a hint of a smile showing on his face.

"She wouldn't give up her weapons."

"Yeah, she wouldn't," Griffin replied.

"Still standing here, hurting a man," Max called out.

"Could you let him go, Max?" Griffin asked.

"Depends. Do I keep my weapons?"

"What do you say, Stevenson?" Griffin asked, directing the question to the soldier on the ground. He didn't answer, just nodded his head quickly. Max shrugged her shoulders and released his wrist. The man gasped and cradled the arm against him.

"Oh, stop it," Max said, feeling her face heat with embarrassment. She wanted to slap herself for feeling that way. "You're fine. I didn't break it," she finished in a mumble.

"Jesus, Max, do you have to make an entrance? You couldn't have walked in nicely?" Griffin asked.

"I guess not," Max said, suddenly feeling uncomfortable and vulnerable.

Griffin walked further into the shelter. The place was much less chaotic than Max would have guessed. People were quiet and withdrawn, walking between tents, scurrying from place to place. They struck Max as people trying to look as small as possible, to not be noticed. *They've been through a lot*, Max thought to herself. Moving from shelter to shelter as each fell must have been horrific to see.

Griffin led them into a quiet tent, with few people in it. Looking around, he pulled Max into the corner.

"What in the hell are you doing here, Max?" He demanded.

"Jeez, what is with being manhandled today?" Max said, pulling out of his grasp. He looked at her exasperated, waiting for her to answer the question. Max just looked up at him uncomfortably. He towered over her on his 6'2" frame. She had forgotten the presence he could have when he was really close to you.

"Momma?" Jack's voice broke into the moment.

"Momma?" Griffin echoed, shock flashing across his face. Shit. Max turned around to face Jack and Blair.

"So, yeah, this is Griffin. The guy we were looking for," Max said quickly.

"You were looking for me?" Griffin asked. Max closed her eyes, taking a deep breath, and trying to steel herself for the explanation she would have to give Griffin. She immediately decided she wasn't telling him everything, not telling him about Jack now. She needed to convince him to come with her first, without using his daughter as a guilt trip.

"Yes," Max replied turning back to him. "Yes, I, well we, came here to find you. This is Blair, a girl we picked up in Charleston. And this is my daughter Jack." Max motioned behind her. Griffin awkwardly waved at them and Max almost laughed out loud at the hilarity of the situation.

"You have a daughter?" Griffin hissed at Max.

"Ummm, yes?" Max replied casually, shrugging her shoulders and not meeting his eye. He would read her mind, Max was sure of it.

"Ok, that's a conversation for another time. Why did you come to look for me, Max?" Griffin sighed, clearly irritated with her.

"I thought, well you know about the compound in Montana," Max started.

"Your family's home? Yeah? What about it?" Griffin replied. Max shot him a look.

"Don't be dense, Griffin. You know it's a fortress. It was when we were kids and Dad didn't stop there. I came to get you, to bring you there, to be safe," Max explained.

"This is a little much. How did you even know how to find me?"

"Rafe. He heard in town where you were living. Since I wasn't far, I thought I should take the chance. Maybe I made a mistake," Max said defensively. She started to turn back toward Jack and walk away. He got to walk away the first time, it was her turn she decided. She was angry. He just seemed annoyed she was even there. And all she had done was think of him and his safety. *This is what I get for caring about other people*, Max decided.

"Max, wait. Stop being all....Max-like," Griffin said, grabbing her arm lightly to stop her from turning away. This time Max did grunt out a laugh.

"Max-like? How else should I be, Griffin? I'm sorry to have upset you by my showing up. I can't imagine why it would. But I was thinking of your safety. I think, no I know, the safest place for us is my family's place."

"I have obligations here, people to take care of," he responded quietly.

"I understand, but you aren't in the military anymore, right? You can leave. The government should handle everything else," she replied.

"In times of war, the government has the right to recall any military members in the reserves, that's what I am for now."

"Did they recall you? Did you get official directives?" She demanded. She wasn't sure why, but the idea of the government trying to take Griffin and put him into harm's way with this plague enraged her.

"Not officially," Griffin trailed off, looking over her shoulder to the outside of the tent.

"Then you don't have to stay. Come with us. It's safer." Max said. She lowered her voice so only he could hear her. "You are seeing the same thing I am. It's collapsing. The government isn't going to fix this, Griffin. We should go."

"You sound like Mitch," Griffin said, with a smile. "How is the old man?"

"He's dead. Turns out a heart attack was the only thing he couldn't be prepared for." Max said briskly.

"Oh, Max, I'm..."Griffin started.

"Yeah sorry. Everyone is always sorry when someone dies. It's not something I can dwell on," she said, looking away from him again. It hurt to be near him. He looked so much the same, but age had changed some things. He was more broad, stronger. His eyes seemed aged, he had seen things.

Jack came to Max's side and took her hand. Max looked down at her daughter, Jack's eyes, the eyes of her father looking back at her. She had sensed that her mother felt nervous and came to her side to comfort. That was what her daughter did. She was comfort to Max, even when Max didn't know she needed it. Or wanted it. Jack smiled up at her and squeezed her hand at the same time.

Griffin watched the two and when Max looked back at him she saw disbelief on his face. She wondered if he suspected anything. Without knowing Jack's exact age, he could make any assumptions he wanted. When they were together as kids, they never breached the subject of having children. They were young, of course, it wasn't a thought at the time. Now that Max looked back she wondered if she hadn't accidentally gotten pregnant, would she have willingly done it?

"How about you guys stay for a while. I can set you up with cots in one of the tents. You can leave at any time of course. Let me think about this offer of yours. I'm helping here and I can't just leave without knowing things will be ok," Griffin explained softly.

Max thought about the option. It couldn't hurt to wait a day for Griffin to make his decision. Max wasn't completely opposed to being around living people for a bit before they closed themselves off in the compound. Max nodded her agreement and Griffin led them out of the tent, back into the sunlight of the day.

On their walk through the shelter, Griffin pointed out the mess tent, the medical tent, the military barracks and the communications hub. He told the story quietly of how he had been moved to two different shelters since the outbreak. Each shelter falling to the infected. Each time they moved, they had less living people to take to the next location. They had been at this shelter for two days and so far things had been quiet.

Things were quiet for two days, which gave Max a feeling of foreboding. In this environment, the likelihood of having no problems for more than a few days was extremely rare. In her mind, she considered her theory and decided that an attack of living or infected was imminent. She decided to not point that out to Griffin, who already thought she was behaving too much like her paranoid father. It wasn't paranoia that fueled Max, it was statistics.

"You guys can bunk in here." Griffin led them into a tent with cots lining both sides and one middle walkway for the occupants to make their way through. There were women in the tent, no men except young children that Max could see. Griffin didn't walk further into the tent, respecting the women's boundaries.

"There are open cots in the back, I think, but ask the ladies in here. They are in charge of this tent."

"Ok. Where do you bunk?" Max asked. Then realizing how strange the question seemed she added, "In case I need to find you." Griffin grinned at her. Her breath caught in her throat at the sight of that grin, so similar to the boy she knew.

"I'm two tents down on the left. Next to the military barracks."

With that, he left Max, Jack, and Blair alone in the tent. Blair instantly started talking to some younger women nearby. Max wondered if she should feel insulted that Blair never tried to talk to her. However, Max never made a real effort to converse with the girl, so she was probably feeling lonely. A middle-aged woman approached Max with a soft smile.

"Hello, are you new here?" The woman asked.

"Yes. We were told we could get some cots here? Where can we sleep?" Max asked. She was all about efficiency. But the woman didn't immediately respond. She smiled at Max and then focused that smile on Jack.

"Well welcome. My name is Dolores. I've somehow become the den mother for the woman's tent. What's your name?" The question was directed at Jack, not Max. Max tried again to not feel annoyed. People loved kids and Jack was a sweet child that seemed to attract everyone.

"I'm Jack. This is my momma, Max," Jack said, holding Max's hand. Max smiled at her, wondering if the kid could read her mind.

"Nice to meet you, Jack. Well, we have two cots this way that would be perfect for you," Dolores started to move down the walkway. Max hesitated, looking back at Blair.

"Blair? Do you want to sleep near us?" Max asked. The girl looked up as if she had forgotten Max and Jack were there.

"What? Oh, no. There's a cot available right here and these girls said I could sleep here," Blair responded. Max just nodded and followed Dolores. Blair was going to make her own choices. Max wasn't her mother, nor the responsible party for her.

Jack and Max were given cots that were pushed together to make room for as many beds as possible. They both had sleeping bags on them that looked to be from military stock. Max was uncomfortable leaving her bag under the cot, worried if she needed to leave fast she would have to come back there. She refused to take off her weapons unless sleeping and even then she would keep them under her pillow.

Once they had their items settled, Max decided to get the lay of the land. Jack asked to stay behind to play with some kids that were in the tent. Dolores assured Max that there were always mothers watching the children in the tent because they didn't want the kids to be underfoot with the military men. Though Max still had her reservations, she allowed Jack to stay. She gave Jack the normal instructions for finding her should anything go wrong.

Outside, Max wandered from tent to tent, seeing what kept people so busy. She saw civilians preparing food and cleaning in the mess tent. She passed by a few more sleeping tents and saw people huddled on cots, reading or talking in low tones. The sense was fear throughout the entire camp and Max didn't blame them. She supposed many of them had nowhere else to go, which astounded Max. Her entire life she had been prepared for something to happen to the world and was given the steps to complete should that happen. She struggled to understand those that didn't.

Coming upon the medical tent, Max decided to see if they had sick people inside. She would rather know ahead of time that there was a risk of an attack from within. Before entering she heard a lot of talking and yelling inside. Steeling herself for what she might find, she ducked into the large tent. There was no one wearing the white coats of doctors or the scrubs of nurses. There were people rushing from place to place. Some seemed to be in charge and knew what they were doing. Max stood watching the pandemonium from the doorway until a man across the tent saw her.

"You! You have nothing to do?" The man yelled at her. Max just shrugged.

"Do you know anything about first aid?" The man called as he began moving toward her. Max wanted to recoil. The man was covered with blood down the front of his clothes. No lab coat, no smock, just blood.

"I mean I know enough to get by, why?" Max asked warily.

"We need help and you aren't busy. Go over to that table and help," the man pointed toward a table with a woman sitting, looking dazed.

"Is she bit?" Max asked without moving.

"Bit? No. No one is bit here. Why?" The man asked.

"Are you a doctor?"

"No. I'm a mortician. Closest thing right now to a doctor I guess," the man replied ruefully.

"Ok. Well, don't treat people with bites. I mean if you do, wait for them to die, and then end them easily with a blade to the brain," Max said simply. As she spoke she saw the man's face drain of blood slightly.

"What? Why would you say that?" The man demanded.

"Haven't you seen it yet? A bite. That's all it takes. It will eventually kill the person and then they will turn. How did you not know this? Didn't the military tell you?" Max said. Her mind was whirling. Why didn't the people working in the medical tent know the risks of the plague? How had they not seen it in the previous shelters they had been in. She wanted to ask more questions, but the man just shook his head. He was about to answer but someone called his attention away and he had to deal with another situation in the tent.

Max went to the woman that was dazed. She looked her over slowly, not seeing a massive amount of blood or wounds anywhere. She didn't look up as Max stood there. Max wondered if the woman was just in some sort of shock. If that was the case there wasn't much to do for her, except cover her with a blanket and keep an eye on her.

"Hi," Max said. When the woman didn't reply, Max snapped her fingers in front of her face. The woman blinked and focused on Max, a light coming into her eyes finally.

"Hello," the woman replied.

That night Max laid with Jack and they talked in soft whispers. Jack was excited to have seen other kids and got to play all day. It was unlike her to have an entire day of play. Max expected more responsibility from the eight-year-old than other people expected from their children. Jack babbled about the other kids and the toys they had with them. The wistfulness in Jack's voice made Max feel guilty for never thinking about the girl's entertainment. Jack was always happy with a book. But it seemed that regular kid toys appealed to her too.

The conversation reminded Max of a time when all Alex could talk about was a doll that you could feed and then would poop in a diaper. They were young, maybe five and nine, but even at that young of an age Max didn't understand the need for toys. Alex was much more interested in toys and kid things. Where all Max wanted was to do what her Daddy did, which usually included camping gear or learning to garden.

By the second day of staying in the emergency shelter, Max was ready to go. Every day she went to the medical tent to help. The same man would boss her around. She could only provide the most basic of first aid to injuries. They handled contusions, cuts, skinned knees, and regular aches and pains. Though there was no doctor, the military had provided ample medical stores to handle the illnesses that might come up.

Griffin made himself scarce most of the time. They ran into each other at dinner but they both avoided any sort of complicated conversations. They had a lot of history between them and Max knew that would have to be dealt with if they would find any sort of calm existence. The uncomfortable feeling made Max sad. Life used to be so easy between the two of them. But they were children then. Adulthood changed a person.

Walking into the tent for dinner on the second night, Jack immediately saw Griffin and skipped over to his table. He smiled at her as she rambled about her day. Max was suspicious about when Jack decided they were going to be friends. Calling her daughter over the two went through the line and got their dinner trays. Jack insisted on sitting with Griffin and Max did everything possible to not groan out loud.

"Hey, Max," Griffin said as she settled across from him.

"Hi," she replied without looking up. She worked to eat quickly, but without looking like a pig at the trough. She couldn't handle idle chit-chat.

"I've been thinking about what you said, why you came here," Griffin started to say. He was rudely interrupted as a blonde woman plopped down next to him huffing as she sat down.

"Hiya, Griff," the blonde cooed. The use of his nickname gritted on Max's nerves. She'd seen the woman around the shelter but hadn't realized she and Griffin knew each other.

"Hi, Sarah," Griffin responded, flashing her one of his sparkly smiles. *Yup*, Max thought, *she's on my nerves*. The flare of jealousy in her gut surprised her. This blonde seemed to blossom in Griffin's attention. Max couldn't figure out why she even cared. It had been eight years since Griffin had left her alone in Montana, without a word like he'd promised.

"Griff, where were you today? I was looking for you. I needed help with some of the jars. They were too hard to open on my own," Sarah said. Her voice seemed to be a constant whine. The exchange made Max want to eat faster.

"I told you, hon, just smack the jar on the edges of the lid a few times with the handle of a butter knife. Then open it. It will pop open easily. You don't need me," Griffin replied smoothly.

"I always need you," Sarah replied, her hand on his arm. Max had to get out of there. She was just about to panic and just leave her dinner when shots and gunfire were heard outside. Without hesitation, she looked at Griffin who was already looking at her. The shots seemed to be continuous and Max knew that was a very bad sign. As she began to stand a soldier came in, covered in blood, his cheek missing from an infected bite.

"Shit," Max shouted. She bounded out of her seat, grabbing Jack at the same time. Jack was up and off the bench before Max could instruct her to do so.

"Jack, with me, right?" Max said, looking her daughter in the eye. Absently she noticed Griffin had come up behind Jack, bringing up the rear, his gun out. Sarah was screaming and clinging to the back of his shirt.

"Yes, Momma, with you," Jack replied, with more confidence than her little face held. Max quickly kissed her daughter's head and hugged her.

"We're going to the women's tent to get our stuff. My car keys are there. Then we're leaving," she told Griffin. He didn't argue, just nodded. *Strange*, Max thought. She had expected some sort of fight from him. But he had seen two shelters fall before. He knew how this went down.

Running for the tent opening, Max pulled Jack through the crowd to exit. People seemed panicked, not sure if they should run or hide. Griffin bellowed at people to move and hide. But his voice was lost in the chaos of fear. Once out of the mess tent the true extent of how bad things were hit Max. The soldiers were spread all around, fighting groups of the infected. As many that were standing were laying on the ground, being feasted on by the infected or left for dead. They wouldn't stay dead for long. Max knew it was time to go.

She made a beeline for the women's tent, her tomahawk out, Jack on her left side. As they went, she heard Griffin firing off rounds and the annoying sounds coming out of Sarah. An infected bent over a soldier looked up as the group approached and Max's tomahawk was there to meet it. She slowed long enough to deal with the infected and then to end the soldier to keep him from coming back. When she stood to continue moving, she found Griffin standing to her left as well, protecting Jack and Sarah, while covering her back.

They reached the women's tent and when they entered Max was shocked to find all the women cowering with their children. Two soldiers stood inside, guns at the ready. Max yelled as they walked in, to keep them from shooting them. Max headed directly to their cots and slung her pack over her shoulders. Thinking of Blair, Max started searching the faces that were still in the tent. She found the girl curled in a ball with another young woman on the floor between cots.

"Blair, come on! We need to get out of here," Max said when she reached her. Blair shook her head.

"I'm not going out there," she replied.

"Yes, you are. Come on, I can protect you. We'll get to the car and keep going," Max explained. While she spoke, she could tell the gunshots had slowed outside. She knew from the amount of infected she had seen that the slowing of shots wasn't due to the soldiers winning. The infected were taking over.

"No. I'm staying with the soldiers. They will keep us safe," Blair said in her no-nonsense tone. Max threw up her hands. She didn't have time to fight with the girl. She knew if the girl didn't want to come, she couldn't make her.

"I know you're scared, Blair, frankly so am I. But we've come this far. Keep going with us," Max cajoled.

Blair's eyes were wild with fright but set in determination at the same time. She shook her head. Jack stepped past Max and grabbed Blair in a hug. Though Max couldn't get behind her decision, she didn't begrudge the girl the option to make it. She squeezed her arm, before standing and walking back to the entrance of the tent. As she got to the soldiers that were standing guard at the entrance, she slowed.

"You really should move them from here. This isn't a fight you are going to win," Max said. Both soldiers looked at her and then to Griffin who was standing watching the outside. When Max spoke he looked in and nodded his agreement to the soldiers. Max didn't know why, but his understanding of her views gave her butterflies in her stomach. Something she would deal with later.

Back in the open area of the shelter, the infected were everywhere. People ran in all directions, with no real saving grace from the onslaught. Max took Jack's hand in her own and planned her path. Behind the fence, the infected seemed to thin. Getting there was the first goal. She looked back at Griffin, who had a distraught Sarah by the hand. She nodded at him and he nodded back. Tomahawk in hand, Max took off running for their escape.

CHAPTER THIRTEEN

Gunshots rang out from behind Max as she ran, Griffin using his sidearm to the best of its ability. With her tomahawk, Max took no prisoners while she chopped and hacked at arms, legs, and heads. As they neared the entrance of the shelter the infected bottlenecked to get through. As Max began to attack, automatic gunfire came from her right and heads exploded in front of her.

Max jumped back to avoid the spray and to not accidentally get shot. Searching she finally found a redheaded man with an automatic rifle at his shoulder. As he popped the magazine to shove another in, Griffin called out to the man.

"Turner, let's go!"

"On your six, Griff," the redheaded man called back.

"Go, Max. We're behind you," Griffin yelled forward to Max.

The ground was covered with the infected. Max had a moment of panic, imaging Jack walking by one and having it bite her in the leg. Suddenly Jack released her hand and as Max pivoted to protect her daughter, she found Griffin tugging her onto his back. Somehow, he knew exactly what had Max hesitating. The gesture had Max feeling flushed and sick, thinking that Griffin had no idea it was his own daughter on his back. A simple thing any father would have done with his child over the years of them growing up.

Shaking herself out of her own thoughts, Max turned to start picking her way through the sea of bodies. She crossed a few that still chomped at the mouth, trying to find purchase in their legs as they neared. Max chopped down with her tomahawk, making the walk safer for everyone. She led the way, with Griffin and Jack directly behind her. She assumed Sarah was still a sniveling mess behind Griffin and then the man named Turner bringing up the rear.

At the street, Max dug the keys out of her pack while she ran. She couldn't imagine someone had taken the vehicle since they parked it, but a part of her feared that their getaway would be halted by no vehicle. She hooted out a cheer when they ran down the block where she parked the SUV. The blinking lights indicated that the doors were unlocked.

As she popped the back to toss her bag in, she turned and found that Griffin had run with Jack on his back. His face was red with exertion, but he didn't put her down until he had the back door open and she could climb in. It was too sentimental for Max and she coughed to cover up her own emotions. With everyone and their items stored, Max jumped into the driver's seat, just as an infected group tripped into their street.

Hearing the engine roar the group turned toward the vehicle. Max felt done with the plague right then. She revved the engine for a moment and looked over at Griffin who had sat in the front passenger seat. He sat stoic, staring straight ahead. Max took off for the undead group, plowing the SUV grill directly into the middle of them. Bodies bounced off the bumper and hood. She didn't slow as the infected fell under the wheels and they lurched over them.

She drove as if the plague was chasing them, speeding through the streets for miles. Once they reached what seemed like the edge of Raleigh, Max pulled the truck into a quiet parking lot and shut it off. Darkness was starting to fall. She laid her head on the wheel. Only to herself would she admit she was shaken. The attack at the shelter left so many people dead and turning into the undead. She thought about Blair and hoped the girl found a safe way to escape.

Soft crying was coming from the backseat. The noise didn't register with Max at first. When she did turn around, she partially excepted to find Jack crying, though the little girl rarely did. Instead, she found Sarah, her face buried in Turner's shoulder, bawling her eyes out. The man's eyes met Max's and he looked more panicked now than he did when they were running from the undead.

"Sarah, we're fine," Griffin said softly, turning in his seat and trying to calm the woman.

"We're all alone. Oh, my god, Griff, what are we going to do," she cried out. She leaned forward to grab onto Griffin. For a split second, Max thought the bawling heap of a woman was going to crawl over the console to climb into his lap. She sighed deeply when she finally flopped back into the seat. Turning further, Max found Jack's gaze. Even the eight-year-old could see how hysterical Sarah was acting. Max had to smother a smile when Jack rolled her eyes. When she turned to look at Griffin again, he raised an eyebrow in admonishment and Max could do nothing but shrug.

"I don't want to drive at night," she told Griffin.

"I agree. We can sleep in here tonight, I think," he replied.

The decision made, Max carefully exited the SUV. She circled to look at the damage she had done by hitting the infected. Blood and black ooze covered the front of the vehicle. Surprisingly nothing was broken, making Max feel better about the impulsive decision she had made to run over the walking dead. When she got to the passenger door she found Griffin climbing out of the car as well. He closed the door and looked at Max.

"I guess you get your way," he said.

"How do you figure?" Max asked defensively. If he really thought she had wished for an infected attack to get him to go with them to Montana, he had a very low opinion of her.

"Well, I'm going with you now."

"I didn't want people to die to make that happen, Griffin. I would have left you behind eventually," she muttered. She walked to the back of the truck with Griffin following.

"I know you didn't want anyone to die, Max. But would you have left?" He asked.

"Yes. What was I gonna do? Stick around with you? Alex and Rafe are waiting for us."

"Sundown." He said casually. Max turned to look at him, leaning against the back of the car for a moment.

"You remember?"

"Of course. You talked about it all the time."

"Yeah well, even after Dad died, the three of us made sure we knew it was still our signal. Alex called and started it. Jack and I jumped in the car right away," Max explained. She popped open the back end of the truck. They worked together to fold down the third seat and arranged an area for Jack and Sarah to sleep. Turner would sleep on the second bench seat with Max and Griffin in the front seats. It would be cramped for the night, but it was safer than trying to find somewhere else to sleep in the dark. Flashlights and noise would bring any infected out of hiding.

Laying in the front seats, their heads right next to Turner in the backseat, Griffin, and Max were quiet. Max knew he wasn't sleeping. She couldn't sleep being so close to him again. Turner's breathing eventually went deep and Sarah's hiccuped crying had ceased finally. The quiet should have helped Max find comfort and sleep, but Griffin seemed to suck the air from around her.

"I can't sleep either. Today was rough," Griffin said suddenly.

"Who said I couldn't sleep?" Max shot back.

"You aren't snoring, so you aren't sleeping," Griffin said. The tone of his voice was mocking and Max knew he was smiling in the darkness.

"Ummm, I do not snore," she replied.

"Sure you don't. Jack doesn't complain about it?" Griffin asked.

"She knows better," Max said laughing quietly.

"Tough mom, huh?"

"Sometimes I guess," she replied quietly.

"I can't believe you're a mom at all, Max. I mean I should have imagined you moved on with your life, but I never imagined you as a mom," he said.

"Why not? Because I'm not soft enough?"

"Not at all. I'm not sure why it didn't occur to me. Maybe because we never talked about having kids when we were together."

"We were just kids," Max said around the lump in her throat. They never spoke about it, but it had happened. And now Max wasn't sure how Griffin would react to being a father.

"Being kids ourselves never mattered to us," he responded.

Max chose to not answer that. She saw the conversation going down a path they couldn't take, cramped in the

SUV with three other sleeping people. She could envision her anger and hurt from being left eight years ago coming out in a flood of anger. She stared at the SUV roof and thought about all the excuses he could come up with. What would be his reason for leaving her behind, after promising a life together? The more she debated the reasons he would use, the more she felt her anger already rising. She took a deep breath and let it out slowly.

"What?" Griffin asked, hearing her sigh.

"Nothing. I need to sleep," Max said, and she turned, trying to make herself comfortable in the seat.

When she fell asleep, it was deep. Her dreams swirled dark and red in her mind. She felt confused watching the images flow. She felt like she was watching a slideshow. Suddenly one of the photos came to life, arms sprung out, fingers shaped as claws with razor-like nails. Max jumped back to avoid being snagged and pulled into the image. She was sure if she was pulled in, she wouldn't escape and it would be her end.

Shaking awake, Max sat up in the SUV. The truck was full of sunlight. The rest of the group was sleeping around her. However, her dream had latched on, her breathing felt erratic and sweat dotted her brow. She wouldn't be going back to sleep. She wasn't used to sleeping in longer than the sun most of the time. Trying to be as quiet as possible, she slipped her feet into her boots and pulled a hoodie on over her T-shirt.

Max opened the driver's side door as quietly as possible. Sliding out of the truck, she grimaced at the click the door made. No one seemed to move inside, and she couldn't decide if that was good or bad. The littlest sound could indicate an attack. Everyone should be on edge. The stress of the day before had exhausted everyone. Decent night's sleep would be far and few between as they traveled to Montana. Everyone needed the sleep when they could get it.

Stretching, Max turned her face to the sun, closing her eyes for a moment. Her back was cramped from sleeping strangely in the front seat all night. She did everything she could to not turn and face Griffin. Sleeping so close to him was uncomfortable for her. His presence overwhelmed her, as he always did. It wasn't fair the effect he had on her all these years later. But once she fell asleep, it was sound, even if it was riddled with nightmares.

The sound of another door opening startled her out of her basking in the sun. Turner crawled out of his backseat bed and grinned lopsidedly at Max. She smiled slightly back, not sure how to take him.

"So, you're Max. The Max," Turner said.

"Ummm, I guess," she replied hesitantly.

"I've heard about you," he teased. Max felt uncomfortable with the playing and not knowing what Turner knew about her.

"Well, I can't say the same. Who are you?" She replied, deflecting off to him.

"Turner. Wells and I go way back. Started boot camp together and then went out overseas together twice. When we both got out, we decided to stay roommates here in Raleigh. We already knew we didn't hate each other," he finished with a laugh. Max just nodded.

"So, you know Griffin pretty well," she commented. She wasn't sure what else to say.

"I'd say that. He's saved my ass more than once in the sandbox. We've always looked out for each other," Turner said as he got somber.

"I'm glad you had each other," Max said because it seemed like the right thing to say.

"Well I think he needed me after you left him," Turner said. He seemed to immediately regret his comment, as his face heated and turned as red as his hair. "I shouldn't have said that," he said quickly.

"I left him?" Max demanded.

"I think I stepped in it. Forget I said a word," he stammered in response.

"I don't think so. What in the hell do you mean I left him? I was still in Montana, right where he left me!" Max said.

"I didn't mean anything....it was a long time ago....I don't really remember....I mean I'm dumb," Turner stammered.

Turner's face was filled with uncomfortable panic. He obviously didn't mean to say what he did and now faced with Max's wrath, he wanted to disappear. He slowly walked backward to the truck and opened the front door. Max looked at him quizzically as he opened the driver's side door, leaned in, and shoved Griffin in the shoulder. All while not taking his eyes off Max, as if she were a rabid animal ready to attack. The thought made Max smile inwardly.

"Hmmm, what, Turn?" Griffin mumbled.

"Ummm, help?" Turner's voice came out in a squeak. Griffin popped open one eye and then leaned forward to look out the door. He saw Max and her face and laid back down.

"Whatever you did, undo it. I'm not dealing with that first thing," he said.

"That? Oh, you both can just walk to wherever you want to go....I'll just leave you right here," Max said as she walked to the back of the SUV. She continued to mumble under her breath as she popped open the back to let a waking Jack out. Sarah, proving to be the prima donna Max had suspected, cried out from the cold and rolled over on her makeshift bed. Max rolled her eyes and helped Jack out.

The two of them walked around the back of the building to relieve themselves. Jack was on lookout while Max did her duty when she turned to look at her mom zipping up her pants.

"I like them," she said.

"Who?" Max asked.

"Griffin and Turner," she continued. "Sarah is alright, but man she cries a lot. She cried off and on all night. I didn't think she'd stop." Jack rolled her eyes in such a Max look, Max herself had to stare and then laugh.

"I never could say you weren't my kid. And that look right there seals the deal," Max said. She smiled as Jack giggled a little. Slinging her arm around her daughter, the two walked back to the truck where the other adults were stretching and getting ready for the drive ahead.

Max worked to move Turner's comments to the back of her mind. They were in the middle of the world falling into shambles. Worrying about what happened in her high school relationship eight years before wasn't worth the trouble. However, Turner's comment about her leaving Griffin was niggling in her mind as they decided to enter the store they had parked next to.

At the store door, Max put her thoughts to rest for the time being. She pulled her tomahawk and stretched her neck, ready for any potential attack. The store looked to have been partially looted already. Griffin, Max, and Turner agreed that they should look for additional food while they were there. While Max had a few supplies, it would only last a few days if they were careful with rationing. Sarah was no help, so they left her under the guise of watching Jack. Jack knew from the look Max gave her that she was the one watching Sarah.

The crunch of broken glass and trash seemed loud in the stale air of the store. Though it hadn't been overly hot, the inside of the store was stuffy and warm. The smell of something rotten was the first indication that they were not alone. Max touched her nose and looked at Griffin. He nodded, catching the same whiff she did. She pointed toward the front check stand first, wanting to check all the nearby hiding places. She doubted an infected could consciously hide, but it was better to be safe.

Rounding the long counter, Max sighed when she found no one to be hiding. She nodded to Griffin who waited on the other side watching for additional attacks. Turner always seemed to stand behind Griffin, watching his back. Poking around behind the counter, Max found a stack of paper bags. She handed a stack to both men and walked cautiously down the first aisle they came to.

Griffin drug his knife along the metal shelving, making Max jump. She whirled to glare at him. He just grinned at her and kept making noise, hoping to draw out what was in the store. The infected would be attracted to any loud noise. With that in mind, Max kicked an empty can across the room, causing it to bounce loudly against the far wall. Nothing moved. Whatever had come in smelling rotten was gone now.

The group bagged up some additional food that was left by the looters. Just like her apartment complex, Max found herself wondering about the intelligence of the living humans that believed taking TV's or other electronics was more important than the food they left behind in their haste. She threw beef jerky into her bag, making her think of the gas station attendant Ruth. Max began to feel frustrated with herself for feeling remorse for the people she had lost along the trip so far. This world was going to be harder than anything they knew and she was going to need to harden herself against the eventual losses.

At the truck, Max gave the food items to Jack to unpack. She handed the warmed meals ready to eat to everyone and they sat inside the truck eating. Everyone was quiet as they forked pre-made meals into their mouths. Max was used to MRE's, but by the grimace on Sarah's face in the backseat, she wasn't thrilled with the breakfast option. Max chuckled and almost choked. She sobered quickly as she saw the dirty look Griffin shot at her. *Jeez, he's gotten serious,* Max thought to herself.

Max took the time to fill the tank of the SUV with the gas they still had from the gas station. She knew they would need to scavenge more gas on the drive. As she stood pouring gas, she heard Griffin exit the car.

"You could be nicer, Max," he said as he came around her side of the car.

"Nicer to who?" Max asked, playing the innocent card.

"You know what I'm talking about. Not everyone has the same experience you do. It's like you were made for this emergency," he said.

"I'm feeling like maybe I should take that as a compliment, but then you don't sound like you mean it," she replied sarcastically. He groaned, and Max could see he was ready to set in on her when another door opened and Sarah stepped up to Griffin.

"Griff, couldn't you sit in the back with me? I know it's silly, but I'm scared out here away from the safety of the shelter," Sarah said, touching Griffin's arm in an intimate gesture.

"The shelter didn't seem so safe to me," Max interjected. She was graced with another dirty look from Griffin.

"Yeah, Sarah, I'll have Turner move to the front," Griffin said. He turned her back toward her side of the car, hand at the small of her back.

Max tapped her forehead against the side of the SUV a few times. She couldn't deal with the damsel in distress attitude Sarah was taking and how she used it to get Griffin's attention. *This is going to be the longest drive ever.*

CHAPTER FOURTEEN

"So, it's like the second day in the sandbox, I mean it's hot and sandy and we are just feeling like crap getting used to it," Turner said. "And this guy..."

"Do not tell this story, Turner," Griffin replied.

Max couldn't help but laugh. During the drive from Raleigh, Turner had talked constantly. At first, it had driven Max nuts that he wouldn't just be quiet while she drove. But during the funny stories, it was nice to hear Jack giggling in the back seat. Turner had a way with kids and he always made sure to include Jack in the conversation.

"Oh, I'm telling this story," Turner continued. "So, we are new to the desert like that, and all of us are feeling dry and miserable. Well, one day Griff decides to try some lotion he found. He covers himself, his face, his arms, and his chest. He realizes it's not soaking in and he's confused. He looks at the bottle again and realizes it's hair conditioner!"

With the last sentence Griffin groaned, and the entire car began to laugh. Max laughed along. Her laughter died as she looked in the rearview mirror and found Sarah laughing and laying her head on Griffin's shoulder. A feeling that seemed very similar to jealousy welled up in Max's chest. She fought it down, telling herself how dumb it was to care about the affection between Griffin and Sarah. Of course, he'd had a life for eight years. So had she. Except hers was very centered around their daughter.

"Didn't you read the label before putting it on?" Jack asked, her eyes watering from laughing so hard.

"Ya know, Jack, I didn't. I just figured the shape of the bottle, and what man uses conditioner on what little hair we had," Griffin replied, working hard to defend himself.

"But see it gets better," Turner cut it.

"No, no it did not," Griffin growled.

"Oh, sure it did. Don't you remember, Griff, when you decided to go take a shower to wash off the conditioner, a few of the guys figured it was sticky and decided to throw sand on you," Turner said, bending over at the waist and laughing.

"Thanks for helping me relive that shame, Turner," Griffin said, throwing his hands up and gave up trying to shut Turner up.

Max soaked up every word Turner said about their time in the Army. It was like hearing a piece of Griffin's life, a life that he lived completely separate from what he and Max had. He had grown into a man during the years apart, a process that Max at one time thought she would be a part of. The relationship between the men made Max smile to herself. Griffin had made himself a good life with the Army and the friends he made there.

As they pulled into the outskirts of a small town, the interior of the vehicle got quiet. As they drove back roads, only using the freeway when absolutely necessary, they were able to avoid a lot of the major devastation. Every time they came to a town, a place people lived, the events were clear. The small town now wasn't any different. Cars were stranded along the streets, some with doors left open. In some places bloody violence was evident, indicating the small town wasn't safe from the plague.

"We need to get gas," Max said.

"I don't see power," Griffin replied.

"No, it makes sense that it would go out eventually," she said.

"Siphon?" Griffin asked.

Max nodded her head, silently agreeing. In the time Max and Griffin had dated, he had learned a great deal from Mitch as well. He was party to much of the craziness too. Being with him during the world falling apart was like being with someone that understood her, knew her mind and how it was functioning in this survival. She had to admit that while she didn't need him to survive, it was nice to have someone to rely on. He was someone she could trust to make the right choices.

Max pulled the SUV into a parking lot that had cars that were parked. They looked to be ones that were left before the plague started. Max thought that might mean they were more likely to have enough gas to siphon. The group agreed that Max and Griffin would siphon while the rest stayed in the truck, ready if there were any issues. Turner still had his automatic rifle but was low on ammunition. She gave him an extra bowie knife she had in her bug out bag.

Approaching the first car, Griffin used his knife to pop the gas tank cover. As he progressed through the steps of getting gas Max watched the parking lot. The buildings nearby were small and local town stores. One was a deli and it caught Max's eye. For a small town full of such devastation, there didn't seem to be time for looters. She made a plan in her head of what stores they should search before they left. Her mind was full of needs that needed to be filled, thinking about items for the guys and Sarah. They had fled the shelter with no belongings. Eventually, they would want changes of clothing.

Griffin signaled that he was done. Leaning down to check, Max saw they had gotten nine gallons for the vehicle. She took that can back to the SUV and put the gas into their vehicle. She returned as Griffin worked on the second car. Out of the corner of her eye Max caught movement, causing her to spin and pull her 9mm. Watching for a moment she saw again what had caught her attention. An infected moved out of the shadow of a space between two buildings. The noise of opening and closing doors must have caught its attention, bringing it toward them.

Max tapped Griffin and pointed toward the infected. He straightened, ready to handle the undead. Max stopped him and pulled her tomahawk. He knew she was more than capable to handle one infected on her own. She walked with determination to the infected. As she approached the infected focused its dead black eyes on her. It was a young man, which made Max feel some sadness. He couldn't have been more than twenty years old.

The dance with the infected was feeling like second nature to Max. The uncoordinated body had a hard time following the movements of a living person as they moved to avoid them. One on one an infected wasn't overly dangerous if you saw them coming. Max guessed they could still sneak up on you if you weren't watching your surroundings. With the world falling to pieces she would assume watching around you would be a priority. Now that she had first-hand experience with someone like Sarah, she realized it was easier than she would have initially suspected.

Max danced to one side and as the infected boy tried to turn and grab her, she quickly cut into his head with her tomahawk. She used his shirt to clean off the blackening ooze that coated her tomahawk blade. When she stood and turned back to Griffin, she found him watching her intensely. It made her uncomfortable thinking about having an audience. She stood, shuffling from foot to foot as he just looked at her.

"Are you gonna finish the gas?" She finally asked.

"You are in your element," he said back.

"Thought you already determined that."

"Seeing you like that, handling the infected without hesitation, just reminded me of Mitch," he replied. The statement gave Max a sick feeling in her stomach. Losing her father was something she had a hard time with and she had no need to discuss him now.

"He taught me a lot, you know that. Like siphoning gas. So, I can finish if you want," Max said deflecting.

Without answering Griffin went back to finish the siphon, collecting another five gallons to add to the SUV tank. Max estimated the tank was seventeen to eighteen gallons when full. They worked through two more cars before the gas gauge indicated full on their vehicle. Then they went to work on siphoning to fill the gas cans Max had. Once they were done they were set up nice and stunk of gas. Max felt a little lightheaded from breathing the fumes for so long.

Max broke into the deli she saw. Once it was determined it was empty and relatively safe, they backed the SUV up to it. Inside Max found bottled water and soap. She went to the bathroom with her change of clothes and worked on getting the gas stink off her. She pulled her short hair up off her shoulders and tired it haphazardly on top of her head. Working the soap into a rough towel she washed her hands, arms, and chest.

She looked at herself for a moment in the mirror. Ragged, tired eyes looked back at her. Her mind was trained for the fall of society, but her body could only do so much on little sleep. While they had been safe sleeping since the start, Max found herself only sleeping partially, her mind always listening for an attack. Or she was plagued with nightmares of the things she had seen and done so far.

Once she was dressed in clean clothes, she decided to toss the dirty ones. There was no washing the gas smell out of them now. The compound would have power and running water, so she could do laundry when they were safe behind those walls. When she walked out of the bathroom she ran directly into Griffin, her face bouncing off of his chest. Max jumped back as if she had been burned.

"Was looking for the bathroom," he said gruffly, looking over her head.

"Yeah, I'm done. Did you find any clothes?" Max asked. Griffin had gone to the other stores in the complex, looking for anything to replace his gas stained clothing. He held up a plastic bag.

"Clothes for Turner, Sarah, and myself. They are from some hippie shop, but they don't smell like gas," he said.

"Gas is better than patchouli," she laughed.

"We agree on that. I made sure I picked the patchouli free items."

"Good, well I'm gonna find something for lunch," Max said as she skirted around Griffin.

The deli had no power, so anything that was in the refrigerators wasn't safe to eat. But they had bread, unopened pickles, cans of tuna and chicken salad. With an unopened mayonnaise jar, Max mixed up tuna salad and chicken salad with pickles diced inside. She slathered all of the bread with mayo and used all of the tuna and chicken in making sandwiches. Thinking that the group would appreciate something to eat that wasn't an MRE, there would be plenty of time to suffer when it came to food.

When Max brought out the sandwiches, everyone else was sitting around a large table. Bottled waters and sodas were open at each setting. Jack was in the process of putting down napkins, setting the table in a normal fashion. Max smiled at her as she brought the platter of sandwiches to place in the middle. She also brought a selection of chips from the nearby display for the meal. She noted that they would pack the rest up to take on their trip.

"What are these?" Sarah asked as she sniffed the sandwiches. Turner and Griffin had already taken large bites of their sandwiches. Jack was primly eating hers. All three of them stopped at Sarah's snobby tone. Griffin turned his eyes to Max, wariness in them, waiting for her to explode.

"Some are tuna, some are chicken," Max replied tightly.

"With mayo? Gross. I don't eat mayo," Sarah whined.

"Food options are slightly limited right now. You're welcome to see what else there is to eat in the kitchen." Max could feel a muscle jumping in her cheek. The way Turner shoved as much food in his mouth at once, she knew he could tell she was annoyed.

"Mayo is actually a decent source of fat," Griffin commented.

"Ummm, Griff, that's why I don't eat it," Sarah said, turning her blue eyes on him and smiling. She batted her lashes at him as if that would magically make him understand her.

"Healthy fat is what you need right now, Sarah. We aren't going to have a lot of normal meals," Griffin said. Max knew he was trying to head off a bad situation at the pass. And he wasn't wrong. Dealing with the woman was grating on Max's last nerve. She was not only completely obnoxious to Max, but she was a liability to the group.

"Well, maybe I'll just not eat the bread!" Sarah exclaimed as if she came up with some great idea. Max groaned audibly, and Griffin shot her a dirty look. Sarah got up from the table to retrieve a fork from the kitchen.

"Can you please just try to be civil?" Griffin whispered harshly.

"She is the one complaining about food when there are dead people walking around," Jack interjected. Griffin looked at the little girl and then to Max. He opened his mouth and then closed it again, having no idea how to argue with an eight-year-old. His look of confusion made Max laugh out loud. Then she and Jack high fived and Griffin narrowed his eyes.

"Now I have to worry about you two ganging up on me?" He asked. Turner choked on his large mouthful of food as a cackling laugh came out of him. The table was still laughing when Sarah returned, feeling victorious about finding a fork.

"What did I miss?" She asked with a smile plastered on her face.

"Oh nothing," Jack said with a small angelic smile.

Back on the road, the group fell into easy conversation. Griffin continued to sit in the back with Sarah, which left Turner entertaining Max during the drive. Both men had offered to drive, but Max had control issues. Griffin felt the need to point that out whenever she declined their help. It annoyed her the way he knew her and felt the need to call her on her tendency to take over and not let anyone else participate.

Driving along the country roads, Turner was studying the map she had brought along to find their way to Montana.

"No, I think we're going to have to hit the freeway right here," he said pointing to the lines on the freeway. "This road is going to end if we stay too long, so we need to meet the freeway and take that for a few miles."

"I hate the freeway," Max groaned.

"I don't like the idea much either, but it's our only option for us to keep going in the direction we need," Turner replied.

A few miles later they were pulling on to the freeway. Max gripped the wheel tightly and studied the road intently. All along the road cars were abandoned. Some crashed into others or into trees off the freeway completely. Max could only imagine the panic these people felt trying to flee from the populated areas. Only to find themselves trapped on the freeway in cars that couldn't go anywhere.

Slowly max maneuvered the SUV around cars. After three accidents, they found clear road and Max stepped on the gas a bit. As they flew down the freeway, sometimes they would see other vehicles moving. Griffin suggested flagging someone down, but Max wouldn't even consider it.

"We've been carjacked once. I'd rather not do that again," Max said.

"Carjacked?" Griffin exclaimed, leaning forward between the front seats. His sudden movement jolted a sleeping Sarah who yelped, as she was pushed into the window. Max had to muffle a laugh at the look of indignation on her face.

"We were carjacked in Charleston. Stuck in gridlock traffic. A guy with a shotgun decided he wanted my pickup," Max explained. Griffin looked at her in surprise.

"You let him take the truck?"

"Stop acting all shocked. I have Jack. I couldn't risk him getting off a shot and hitting her," Max said quietly. Of course, she made the right choice for her daughter.

Suddenly Max slammed on the brakes. Her whispered curse was drowned out by Griffin who almost flew into the front seat area.

"Seatbelt," Jack said in a sing-song voice from the backseat. Her smile died quickly when she saw what had stopped Max in the first place.

The freeway was blocked again by wrecked vehicles. That wasn't Max's real concern. The infected taking notice of the SUV was what made her stop suddenly. Griffin's head wasn't far from hers, studying the situation. Along with Turner, they all stared out of the front windshield. The three of them each played scenarios in their head for the best way to handle the situation.

"What is going on?" Sarah asked, trying to pull Griffin back. When she saw the infected making their way through the accidents, she cried out and shrunk back in her seat. Max just shook her head in disgust at the woman's constant panic.

"We might be able to make it around there," Turner said, pointing toward the far shoulder that fell off into trees.

"If we can't, we will be trapped by the trees," Max replied.

"Any better ideas, Max?" Griffin asked.

"Not really. I can't go fast enough to run them down because the cars are in the way," she said, thinking out loud to the men.

"So, the shoulder is the only option. If we have to fight, we get out and fight," Griffin said, leaning back into his seat now to check his gun. Turner started doing the same, though they all knew he was running low on ammo.

Max pulled the truck toward the shoulder and crept off the road onto the grass. The infected were increasingly interested in the moving target and their uncoordinated bodies made the efforts to change direction and come at the truck. Max sped up, keeping the traction on the tires in the damp grass. As they approached the edge of the last accident that fell into the shoulder, Max slowed to slide the truck through.

She let out the breath she was holding when they fit through the space with the side mirror of the crashed car scraping along the side of their truck. It wasn't enough to stop them, but the noise was loud and grating. The infected that hadn't already been interested in them now were moving faster, hoping to peel open the can of a human meal.

"You made me scrape my new stolen car," Max mumbled.

"Bill my insurance," Turner shot back.

As they rounded the accident, an infected bounced off the fender as Max pushed passed him. A slam into the back door had Jack crying out, an infected pressing its face against the glass, teeth gnashing. Max pulled away quickly only to be faced with a group of five that stood in their path back to the road. She slowed to a stop and studied them. In her mirror, she could see the two they passed coming toward the truck from there.

"What do you think? Fight?" Max asked. She put the SUV in park and looked back at Griffin. He somberly nodded his head, both of them knowing there wasn't much choice.

"Save the ammo, I think this few we can do by hand," Max commented as she pulled her tomahawk from by her leg.

"Easy for you to say, you have that thing," Turner replied.

"Then you stay in the car, dear," Max shot back.

"Not likely," he said with a snort.

The three of them exited the car at the same time, slamming doors to keep Sarah and Jack safe inside. Sarah had been told quickly that if something were to happen she was to protect Jack and drive them out of there. Secretly Max knew she would never actually trust the woman with such a task, but Griffin had started the lecture. Max figured it was one of these moments he wanted her to be nice to Sarah. So she just didn't say anything. Instead, she told herself that there was no way she was dying and leaving her daughter in the clutches of the brainless scaredy cat.

Outside, Griffin quickly took up a position as the head of the attack. Max was typically used to having that position or fighting alone, but she let it be. She took up a place to protect his one side, while Turner took up the other side. The three of them attacked the nearest infected as a group. Max chopped directly in the collarbone of an approaching infected. The male fell to one side awkwardly. Without waiting Max stabbed him directly in the temple. She pivoted just as an infected fell to the side of the one she finished, Griffin taking out its knees.

"Got it," she called, and she stabbed it while Griffin turned to the next infected that threatened them. Griffin and Turner seemed to fight in sync, something they picked up in the Army. Max didn't fit into their pair, so she took her own stance and partially watched their backs. She had just finished off the second infected on her side, when she saw the movement coming around the truck, coming up on Turner's blind spot.

"Turner," Max called, as she threw her tomahawk at the infected. The sharp blade embedded into its forehead. Turner watched as the infected fell at his feet. Max followed to retrieve her weapon quickly.

"Holy shit," Turner breathed.

"Don't let anything she does shock you," Griffin said, breathing heavily after their fight. Looking around, they realized they had ended eight infected, and cleared the path they needed to get back to the road. Both men had black ooze on them, so Max quickly took them to the back of the truck to change their clothing before getting back into the truck.

"You two aren't ruining the inside of my new car either," Max joked.

As the evening started to fall, Max began looking for a place to camp. She figured they would still sleep in the truck, but she was outvoted when they came upon a no-tell motel. Max argued she didn't want to deal with bedbugs and roaches on top of the infected. She thought she would at least have Sarah's agreement in that argument. However, she shouldn't have been shocked when she just sided with Griffin.

There were cars in some of the spots in front of rooms. They pulled into a spot, and Turner leaned over and laid on the horn. The sound was loud and echoed between buildings. Max watched closely and saw a number of upstairs curtains twitch.

"There are people here," Max said softly.

"I'm not surprised. But I'm sure there are some downstairs rooms open," Griffin said. "Turner, let's go check the office."

The two guys ran toward the office, both staying low with their weapons at their sides. Max could almost imagine them during wartime. Now they were at war again, but it wasn't against a foreign enemy. It was a very local one that could be anyone. Max watched until they entered the office, watching them clear the front room and disappear where she couldn't see any longer. Suddenly Sarah cleared her throat from the backseat.

"So, you and Griff?" Sarah asked, probing for information.

"Are old friends," Max finished.

"Just friends?"

"Well I don't call him Griff, so there's that," Max said, her attention on the office. She was almost wishing for an infected horde at the moment. Anything but the conversation she knew Sarah wanted to have right then.

"It just seems you two are more than friends. But if you say you aren't, I'll believe you," Sarah said, a note of triumph in her voice. Max forced herself not to care. Griffin wasn't hers to fawn over or fight for. She could see Jack watching her very carefully, waiting to judge her emotions Max guessed. All Max felt right then was uncomfortable.

"Here they come," Max said, in the need to change the subject. Griffin and Turner ran for the SUV, Turner holding room keys above his head with a goofy grin on his face.

Max backed the truck up to the two bottom floor rooms the guys had found keys for. They were directly next to each other, sharing a connecting door. It was a good set up for the night, Max had to finally admit to Griffin.

"Wow, the great Max was wrong about something?" He teased. Max looked at the adequately clean, if not a bit rundown, room.

"Don't need to be an ass about it," Max replied.

"Nothing about being an ass when I'm shocked that you actually admitted you were wrong."

"I admit when I'm wrong, when the occasion warrants it," Max argued.

"Really?" Griffin's voice was full of accusation.

"What? What is it you are wanting to accuse me of, Griffin? I'm not the one that walked away eight years ago," Max said the last sentence in a hissed whisper. She hadn't even really meant to bring it up. But the constant teasing and ribbing at her expense were starting to wear on the last nerves she really had. Griffin's face went red and was full of anger. It was so surprising to Max, she took a step back.

"Eight years ago? I walked away? What in the living hell are you talking about?" Griffin demanded. As his voice rose, Turner walked into the room with a bag that would make up dinner. He looked at the two of them and started to back out, but Max stopped him with an impatient wave of her hand.

Turning her back on Griffin, Max walked out of the room. She went straight to the SUV and started digging for the bottled waters they had for dinner. The crisp air of evening washed over her heated skin. She felt like the barely adult of eight years before, humiliated and angry. She breathed the air into her lungs, working to clear her mind and heart of the age-old emotions that were surfacing. Just being around Griffin again dredged up so many unanswered questions.

She stood looking up at the stars that started to appear. Why had he acted so surprised when she accused him of leaving her? It was the wrong time to bring up the past, Max knew. She wondered if they would ever work out the history between them. It was clear that Sarah wanted to start something new with Griffin. He was free to be with whoever he wished. Max wanted to clear the air before they got the compound. The last thing she needed was a big altercation in front of her family

Max returned to the room to find the group sitting on the chairs and bed in the room, eating their dinners. Jack patted the bed next to her and Max joined her. Her daughter handed her a plate with a sandwich, pickles, and a bag of chips. Max leaned over and kissed Jack on the forehead. Her daughter was always taking care of her in the small ways she could. It warmed Max's heart.

With dinner trash disposed of, the group broke up with men in one room and women in the other. Jack curled up in bed pretty quickly and fell asleep. Sarah had picked up a magazine in the deli and was leaning back on the other bed reading. Max pulled toiletries from her go bag, ready to get a little bit of a sponge bath. She took a couple of water bottles into the bathroom and set up to wash up as best as she could.

A short time later, Max exited to find Sarah gone. Her magazine was laying open on the bed she intended to take. Jack lay quietly in her bed, breathing deeply. Max set her boots on her side of the bed, slipped her knife under her pillow and had her tomahawk on the small cheap bedside table. As she climbed under the tacky orange comforter to lay next to Jack, Max turned out the lantern. She turned to breathe in the scent of her daughter as she tried to not let her mind go to Sarah sneaking into the men's hotel room to be with Griffin.

CHAPTER FIFTEEN

"Max, Max, wake up," Griffin said, as he pushed Max's shoulder. Max shot out of bed with her knife in hand. Griffin jumped to get away from the blade and fell to the hotel room floor.

"Whoa, hang on! It's just me, Max!" Griffin called from the floor. He looked up at Max in her T-shirt and panties and stared. She looked down at him, bringing her heart under control. Then she realized that Griffin was staring at her half-dressed body. Dropping her knife, she grabbed her pants from the foot of the bed and stabbed her legs through the holes.

"What the hell, Griffin? You scared the crap out of me," Max exclaimed, as he climbed to his feet. She pushed her feet into her boots as Jack climbed out of her side of the bed.

"Momma?" She inquired. Max jumping from the bed had jostled her.

"It's ok, baby. Get dressed and we'll do breakfast before we leave, ok?" Max said. She walked to her daughter and smoothed her hair slightly. Jack just smiled sleepily at her and went to brush her teeth.

"Max, where's Sarah?" Griffin asked. Max whirled to look at him. She glanced over at Sarah's bed, still made and not slept in.

"Why would I know where your bed partner was?" Max shot at him. She moved around the room, pulling items out to put on the table for breakfast.

"My bed partner? What are you talking about?" Griffin said. Just then Turner walked into the room, pulling his shirt over his head.

"I think she's implying Sarah slept with you last night. And unless I've learned to sleep much deeper in the apocalypse, I believe that's false," Turner interjected.

"What? I thought..." Max trailed off. She went to the window and looked out, relieved to see that the SUV was still there. However, she then noticed that the room key they had put on the windowsill next to the door was gone. She turned back to look at Griffin and Turner.

"I mean, I assumed she was with you. I was in the bathroom, Jack was asleep. When I came out Sarah was gone. She didn't tell me she was leaving. After the questions she asked yesterday, I assumed she went to you," Max said, feeling that her assumption now sounded foolish.

"What questions?" Griffin asked.

Max looked at the floor, bouncing from foot to foot nervously. "Well, um, she asked me about us. She wanted to know if we were a thing. I told her no. And she was happy about that."

Griffin's face looked incredulous. Max knew what he was thinking. Who was thinking about a new romance during a zombie plague? Well, Sarah did. And it had given Max a jealous feeling in her stomach, that then affected her thinking. She felt incredibly ridiculous to have let her training go so far, that she didn't check to make sure Sarah was where she assumed. With the hotel room key missing, she now had to figure Sarah went outside for a reason and took the key to get back in. But she hadn't come back all night.

"Ok, I get it. I shouldn't have just guessed. But it's what I thought. I mean why would she just leave and not tell me or you guys where she was going?"

"I don't think we should be arguing about this right now," Turner said, turning to look at both Max and Griffin. He was carefully trying to play the mediator. "Sarah is missing. We don't know if she willingly left, or if she's hurt or was attacked."

"He's right," Griffin said. He moved toward the door. "You and Jack pack up and get everything loaded. Turner and I will go looking to see if we can find any sign of her outside. We'll meet you at the SUV in twenty minutes."

Griffin walked to the door, passing Max without so much as a sideways glance. He was obviously furious with her for not being more careful about Sarah. Max huffed a sigh. *I'm not a babysitter,* she thought to herself. She was defensive, but also a part of her felt extremely guilty for not making a better decision when she noticed Sarah was gone the night before. The boys walked out and the slamming of the hotel door made Max jump and her thoughts to change to packing and finding Sarah.

Jack had already started packing up the food they had brought. Their go bags were packed and ready, as was their standard practice everywhere they went. Together they loaded the supplies back into the back of the SUV. Max, trying to get back on Griffin's good side, even went to their hotel room and retrieved the toiletries they had used and any clothing they had left behind. There wasn't much, but it was what they had.

Mother and daughter climbed into the truck and waited. There was no visible sign of Griffin or Turner. Max knew they were skilled in fighting and defending themselves. Nonetheless being apart made her nervous and anxious. She would rather be fighting alongside them, so she knew what was happening as it happened. Jack's fingers tapped the backseat window as she watched and waited. Max shook the truck with her knee bobbing up and down with nerves.

Suddenly Max saw what she wouldn't have wished upon anyone. Sarah's blonde head suddenly showed on the opposite side of the road the motel sat on. Across the street was a field of high weeds and reeds, which Max had originally assumed was some sort of marshy land. Sarah was limping, her head looking backward often. It was as if she were being pursued. Max decided quickly that she had to go get the woman.

"Jack, stay inside the truck no matter what, got it?" Max said as she readied her weapons.

"Ok. Are you going to go get her?"

"Yeah. I think she's hurt," Max responded.

"Bit?" Jack asked, her voice tinged with fear.

"Maybe, don't know. Stay here," Max said. With that, she popped open the driver's door and slammed it shut. Jack instantly hit the lock button as Max always told her. The sound of the clicking was the indication for Max that it was at least somewhat safe to leave her for the moment.

Max took off running across the parking lot to the road where Sarah was now trying to walk. As she got closer, she slowed, gauging Sarah's movements. She almost looked like an infected. As she watched her stumble across the road, the weeds on the side of the road parted in a half a dozen places. Sarah let out a scream that only seemed to call the infected to dinner. The scream wasn't the sound of an infected, causing Max to increase her speed again.

"Max," Sarah whimpered as she almost fell to the asphalt.

"Hold on, Sarah," Max said, as she threw an arm around Sarah's waist and hoisted her to her feet. The hiss of pain told Max she was right, and Sarah was injured somewhere.

"Hold onto me, we need to get you to the truck before they catch us," Max said, a little breathless. Sarah didn't answer, but her arm around Max's neck tightened.

As the women staggered their way across the street, Max could hear the hissing and growling from behind them. She knew instinctively that they weren't going to make it to the truck without a fight. They were just reaching the sign for the motel. Max moved Sarah to the pole and leaned her against it. As she released her, she realized the arm around Sarah's waist came away sticky and warm. Looking down, Max saw her arm covered with blood.

"Shit," Max exclaimed, looking closer at Sarah's waist. The woman was bleeding profusely from two large bites on her side. "Son of a bitch," Max breathed.

Without saying another word Max wheeled toward the infected. Sarah wasn't someone she particularly liked, nor did she really consider her part of her group, but she was someone Max should have tried harder to protect. And these infected killed her the moment they sunk their teeth into her flesh. *Now you are going to pay,* Max thought to herself. No longer was she thinking about how she was doing them a favor, doing the right thing by ending their ever-walking lives. Now all she felt was hate and anger. Two emotions she felt she needed to take out on someone.

Her tomahawk was in one hand and her bowie knife in the other. She had her gun in a holster on her hip, but the noise would be too great. There was no way of knowing if this group of six was part of a larger horde. Her adrenaline filled veins knew she could handle them hand to hand. The first infected reached her and she brought her tomahawk down in a swift arc, sinking it into the skull of the being. She allowed its fall to free the blade, as she turned to fight the next.

She knew that the infected didn't feel pain. Causing any injuries didn't stop them unless they couldn't use the body part any longer. Muscles and tendons still functioned the same, which meant Max could disable an infected with a slice to the hamstring. She tested this theory on the next infected that came her way. She quickly knelt and sliced deeply through the back of the thigh, continuing to move forward to avoid being grabbed by the infected. As she thought, the infected's leg buckled without the needed muscles. She swiftly turned back to the infected and thrust her bowie into its skull.

This process continued until all six of the attacking infected were down. As Max stood in the middle of the road, infected bodies everywhere, she saw movement in her peripheral vision. She spun in time to see Griffin and Turner running up to Sarah. Max waited a few more moments, to catch her breath, and ran to meet them. Griffin had knelt in front of Sarah, where she had slid to the ground by the motel sign. He had just lifted her shirt on her side and by the way his face went white, Max knew he realized Sarah's life was over.

"Max...you killed them all?" Sarah croaked as Max approached.

"Yeah, I got them, Sarah. Was the one that bit you, one of those?"

"Two of them," Sarah said.

"Well I got them for you," Max replied, trying to be as reassuring as she knew how.

Griffin stood, bringing Sarah to her feet. When she was unsteady, he bent and swept her up into his arms. They walked back to the motel and headed back into the room Max had slept in. Griffin laid Sarah out on the bed and covered her up, as she was shivering from head to toe. Max followed with Jack, joining Griffin and Turner in the connected motel room. Griffin looked pointedly at Jack as if the conversation they needed to have wouldn't be appropriate for her. But Max just shook her head slightly and had Jack sit down on one of the beds.

"The bites, they are going to kill her," Max said quietly. "Does she know?"

"I don't know. Turner and I had been at a few of the shelters. We had seen other attacks. And saw how people turned. I don't know what Sarah saw since the plague started," Griffin replied. Max felt pity for the woman.

"We should stay here, until it happens, moving her would be rough. And leaving her would be cruel," Max said.

"Do we have enough supplies for the day and night?" Turner asked.

"I have MRE's. We don't all have to stay while she sleeps. Jack and I will go and see if we can find more food and water. Maybe I can find a pharmacy that isn't already trashed. They might have some strong pain meds that will make things easier for her," Max said. She gestured to Jack that they were gonna go.

"By yourselves?" Griffin asked. Max paused at the tone of his voice. He sounded unsure, which was odd for him.

"Dude, didn't you see what she did to those walkers out there? I think she can handle herself," Turner said with a gruff laugh. The laugh was forced, his usually jovial personality dampened by the situation.

"Yeah, I just....ok, Max. You're coming back, right?" Griffin asked seriously.

"Uh, I came all the way to Raleigh to get you. Why am I going to abandon you on the side of the road now? I mean you're annoying, but not that annoying," Max said.

"Yeah ok, she's coming back," Griffin said.

"Here," Jack said, approaching Griffin. She held out a deck of cards she always had in her go bag. It was the deck of cards Max and Jack had used a number of times over the years while camping. Griffin took the cards gingerly, looking at the little girl with a smile. His smile put a vice around Max's heart. She almost felt the words "She's your daughter" spill from her mouth. She choked them down though. A no-tell motel with a dying woman in the next room wasn't the appropriate environment to tell him something this big.

"Something to do while we're gone," Jack continued as if she figured Griffin was confused. Max laughed a little and shrugged when Griffin looked at her for help.

"Thanks, Jack," Griffin said and ruffled her hair a little in thanks. Jack beamed at him.

Max and Jack drove around the small town that the motel sat outside of. It was one of those towns that sat on the outside of something larger, but people had probably loved living there. The streets were lined with trees and grass. There seemed to be one main road that cut through the town. Sadly that road told a large story of how the town was run down by the infection. Windows were busted out of businesses along the road. Cars were crashed all along the roads, some still smoldering from the fires that must have erupted. Blood smeared windows and asphalt where the infected had their way with the living.

The SUV continued to roll through the small business area. Max slowed when they came to a car crashed through the front of a small shop. She stopped completely and studied the awning that now hung at an awkward angle. It read "Docs Pharmacy".

"Well, crap. That's what we need," Max said. She pulled the SUV over toward the crashed car. She hit the horn once, twice, and then a third longer time. Then she waited. As she guessed, infected were hiding inside shops and in the small alleyways between them. She counted four that had shown themselves so far. She had her goal in mind, get into the pharmacy and see if she could find painkillers for Sarah. The infected were only a speed bump in that plan.

"Stay in the truck, with it running, until I signal. When I do, turn it off and bring the keys with you. We need to get into the pharmacy," Max said to Jack. The young girl nodded, her eyes sweeping the street as the infected approached the truck.

In the road, Max easily dispatched the few infected that showed themselves. She continued to keep her eyes moving, keeping a lookout for anything additional that might come at her. After the fourth infected fell to the concrete, no other infected showed themselves. Feeling safe, she signaled to Jack to join her. Her daughter was fast in meeting her mother in front of the pharmacy.

Max looked inside the crashed car and saw an old man lying on the steering wheel. The closed door and intact windows of the car seemed to have protected him from the infected. But the crash must have killed him on impact.

Jack's eyes misted over as she looked at the old man. Max took her chin in her hand and made her look into her eyes.

"This is the way things are now, Jack. I know it's rough, but I need you with me on this ok?" Max coached. They truly didn't have time for emotions when they were out in the open like they were now. Jack nodded at her mother and swiped at the offending tears that threatened to spill over onto her cheeks.

The pair slowly stepped into the pharmacy, walking loudly across glass spilled inside from the front windows. Max stood just inside, watching the store as well as the street for any additional attacks. None seemed to be coming. She walked slowly down the first aisle they came to. The pharmacy had some things missing, but it wasn't general looting. The items were neatly taken by people that were just trying to survive.

Behind her Jack had found plastic shopping bags and was pulling things off the shelf she felt they needed. Before they reached the back for the medications, she had 3 bags stuffed full of necessities. Since actual looters hadn't broken into the pharmacy, Max found the medical area mostly untouched. The door to the area behind the counter was locked, so Max climbed over it. On the other side she could see where people had again taken the basics, but not everything.

Sorting through medications took time, as Max didn't know the set up the pharmacist used. Eventually, she found a case that was under lock and key. She knew that had to be the place with the hard medications in it, maybe even a form of morphine. Inside the pharmaceutical area, Max couldn't find anything to pop the lock. So going back into the store area, she moved around until she found a small hardware department. She grabbed a hammer and headed back to get the meds.

Back in the truck, Jack sorted through her goods. She had made two trips to the truck with plastic bags hanging from her arms. She had all different types of snack foods that the store sold. As well as toiletries, socks, batteries, small towels, matches, and a large organization box that unfolded and fit into the back of the truck. As Max drove she sorted her items into the organization box. She had also found men's undershirts that she figured would work for Griffin and Turner. Jack's heart was gold and she always thought of others before herself.

When they finally pulled back up to the motel, Max saw it was close to noon. They had taken quite a bit longer than she had meant to. But the search for meds took time, and she didn't want to get anything wrong or leave behind what they needed. Jack had a bag of food ready for lunch and she was proud to bring her haul back to the guys.

The tone inside the rooms was somber. Griffin and Turner sat in the room with Sarah, both staring at her as if she were all of a sudden going to try to kill them. But Sarah's chest still rose and fell with breath. When Max checked her pulse, she found it be fast, but not weak. She was strong and had time yet to go. Max laid out the medications she found on the small motel table. Griffin turned to see what she had found.

"They had prescription morphine. I grabbed the liquid. I thought that might be best to get it into her," Max said, showing Griffin. He just nodded and looked back at Sarah.

Max read the dosage chart that was inside the box with the bottle of morphine. Measuring out an adult dose, Max went to Sarah's side to pour the liquid down her throat.

Before touching her mouth, Max pulled open one of her eyelids. Her eyes weren't black yet, so Max didn't feel scared. As she let her eyelid close, Sarah moaned slightly and opened both of her eyes to look at Max. She stood still, nervous about what Sarah was going to say, and unsure of how she would answer.

"Hi, Max," Sarah said softly.

"Hi, Sarah."

"I know," Sarah said.

"Know what?"

"I'm dying. I saw it happen before," she said, her voice catching. Max couldn't say anything, so she just nodded slightly. Griffin came to her side then, hearing Sarah awake. The sight of his face had Sarah's eyes brightening just a bit. Max handed the medication to Griffin and stepped away. She didn't know what the relationship was between the two of them, but Sarah had some sort of affection for Griffin. If him being close gave her comfort, Max wanted to be well out of the way.

The two of them had a whispered conversation. Max could see tears glistening on Sarah's face before Griffin softly wiped them away for her. He looked back once at Max, who looked away when she was caught watching their private moment. She saw Griffin pour the medication into Sarah's mouth. She smiled at whatever Griffin said after that. Feeling like she was spying, Max needed to get out of the room. Quickly she exited into the adjoining motel room.

Jack followed her, setting out lunch in the guys' room. Turner joined them shortly after. They all sat around the room with food, though none of them ate anything. Max couldn't seem to get the sandpaper taste out of her mouth. Jack sat across from her looking sad. And Turner sat on one of the beds looking outside as if he were searching for answers to all the unknown right now.

When Griffin entered ten minutes later, Turner jumped to his feet. Griffin shook his head at his friend and motioned for him to sit down. Turner sat and looked outside again. No one really had words for the situation. Having the need to take care of people, Jack brought food to Griffin who sat on the other bed, staring at the wall. He took the items without looking up at her. She stood for a moment and then as if she made a decision, she sat down close to Griffin.

Max watched the two of them, sitting together, staring at the wall. She wasn't aware that while she watched father and daughter, Turner watched her. He looked at Max and followed her gaze to where she watched Griffin and Jack. They sat similarly, something that only people close to them would realize. Max found herself wondering if Jack was imitating Griffin's posture on purpose, or if it was natural, and only was noticeable because she was with her father now. Turner turned back and looked at Max again. This time she felt his gaze burning into her face. He motioned toward the outside and Max's insides turned to ice.

Turner excused them, saying Max had promised him a clean shirt. He requested Max to come with him. On wooden legs, Max followed Turner out to the truck. Without saying a word he climbed into the front passenger seat and waited expectantly. Max surveyed their surroundings first. The bodies from the infected she had killed still littered the street. Sarah's blood could be seen dripping across the ground. While Max noticed these little things, she realized she almost wished there were infected to fight. She knew what Turner was going to say. And she wasn't ready to face it.

"So," Turner said.

"So," Max said, as she settled into the driver's seat. "Did you need a clean shirt? Jack picked up some..."

"She's his, isn't she," Tuner said, cutting Max off from rambling further. Max sat staring at him, trying to keep her face blank.

"I'm not sure what you mean," Max hedged. Her mind was screaming, but she kept her body and face completely still. Denial was all she had left.

"Jack. Your daughter. Griffin is her father," Turner said, spelling it out.

"I..." Max said, trailing off, wilting under the scrutiny she was under from Turner.

"The first time she looked at me, her eyes threw me off. They were so familiar. But we were racing away from the walkers, so I didn't put much thought into it. But the day or so since then, I've seen other similarities. The way they sit, their posture. They both have a quick wit, but that could be credited to you too I suppose," Turner said. He finally looked away from Max, and she sagged back into the driver's seat. The things he mentioned were just a few things Max had noticed with Griffin and Jack being in the same physical space.

"Did you tell him what you thought?" Max asked quietly.

"Why haven't you?" Turner shot back.

"Does it seem like it's been the right time at any point since we came to the shelter?"

"What about the rest of her life, Max? Where was the notification then?" Turner demanded, obviously defensive for his friend. Max didn't blame him. She had kept Griffin's daughter from him for eight years. It took the world falling apart for her to drive the short distance to find him.

"He left me. I didn't want him coming for me because I had his kid," Max replied. It was the only defense she had and it wasn't wrong.

"The story he tells is much different."

"Well for you it's a story. For me it was my life and the plan I had that disappeared as soon as he decided to leave and never look back," Max said finally. "Are you going to tell him?"

"No. That's something you need to do. I'll give you that chance. But if we make it to Montana and you haven't said anything, I will."

Max didn't say another word. She didn't react well to threats. Slamming the driver's door shut after her, she paced the parking lot. Again, she found herself wishing for something infected to fight, anything that she could kill.

CHAPTER SIXTEEN

Sarah had awoken one additional time since lunch. In the breath she had, she had explained she had meant to go to the bathroom and come back. She wanted some cover to go, so she went to the weeds across the street. Somehow in the dark, she had gotten turned around. She realized she was in trouble when she bumped into an infected that was also in the weeds. She had turned to run, but another infected had grabbed her.

Max didn't verbalize her shock, but she couldn't figure how Sarah had fought off two infected on her own. The fight, her screaming, and maybe the smell of her blood had attracted the other infected that were in the weeds. She had wandered and hidden all night, at one point falling asleep. Max almost laughed at the absurdity of falling asleep when you're being hunted. However, she stopped herself, remembering that Sarah was going to die. And she did what she could to make it back to the motel.

Griffin had administered an additional dose of morphine to help her fall back asleep. Max was sure it was too much, but they just wanted her to make it through her last hours with no pain. There was no risk of her dying of an overdose in the short time she had left. Her skin was burning to the touch. The bites on her side were still oozing blood, no clotting happening in the area. Griffin came in to watch as Max changed the makeshift bandages around the wound.

"It won't stop bleeding, will it?" He asked quietly.

"No, probably not. My theory is the illness is in the saliva. And once it makes contact with a wound on the body like this, it affects the way the blood works. That's just a guess though," Max said. She pulled the information she had from watching the same thing happen to Denise in Charleston. Sarah's symptoms were almost exact to Denise's.

"It's a decent guess. The best I've heard so far. It was strange, but there were no real military doctors at the shelters I was at," Griffin said.

Max thought about that for a moment. On one hand, it did seem strange to send out an emergency broadcast, to collect survivors in one place, but not have the faculty to handle the situation. The government had wanted people to come to them for safety. Even though Max assumed the plague wasn't curable, why wouldn't there be someone trying? On the opposite hand, Max couldn't help but think of all the things her father had feared. The government not being able to manage any issues, or even worse, being behind the apocalypse.

"Remember what my dad used to say about the world falling apart?" Max asked. She didn't look up at Griffin but continued to pack Sarah's wound and wrap a clean towel around it.

"Yeah. He was sure everything would fail," Griffin replied quietly.

"He always said that the government would be useless in a situation this widespread. His biggest fear was having to rely on them for anything," Max said. She stood and went to the bathroom to clean her hands with bottled water and soap. Griffin followed and leaned against the door jam.

"I was in the military, Max. I can't just ignore things when they are mobilizing and trying to help," Griffin said defensively.

"I understand you have seen things, I get it. It's a world you knew for a lot of years. But in the end, I don't think my dad was wrong. Which is ironic."

"Why ironic?" Griffin asked.

"Because he didn't live long enough to see his fears realized. I can't imagine how he would be right now. My sister and I strewn on opposite sides of the country, with no means of communication with the compound," Max said thoughtfully.

"Mitch would have seen this coming and had already come and gotten both you and Alex," Griffin grinned.

"Probably. Sometimes it was weird, you'd think he could see the future," Max smiled softly, remembering her father fondly.

"He sure predicted this."

"Well, I don't think he ever believed in things like the walking dead. But it wouldn't have taken much to convince him. I mean how do you deny what we're seeing all day long out there?"

"True," Griffin replied with a shrug.

"He always said you would leave and not come back. He saw that coming too," Max said. She clamped her mouth shut quickly after the sentence came out. She hadn't meant to bring up the past like that. Nonetheless, she felt under the gun with Turner figuring out Jack was Griffin's daughter. Their past grievances needed to be aired and handled before she could tell him everything.

"What? Why would Mitch have thought that? I always thought he liked me. And I didn't leave you and not come back, Max! What are you talking about?" Griffin said, rambling as he stood up straight, running his hand over his head in an aggravated motion.

"Oh, come on, Griffin. We aren't kids anymore, it's alright. You left for the Army and I was left wondering why I never heard from you again. I obviously got over it after all these years," Max lied. As she said the words it hit her how much she wasn't over it. Maybe it was because she was alone with Jack all these years, but she still held resentment for how he'd walked away from her.

"Max, I wrote you. I wrote you every day for a month after I was allowed. And then monthly, until I just stopped after a year of not hearing from you." Griffin looked her in the eye as he spoke. Max couldn't speak, the air was a dead weight in her chest.

"We weren't given access to a phone right away. But after I was, I called a number of times. Mitch said you didn't want to talk to me. I said I didn't believe him and I called again. You never answered the phone or came to the phone to tell me yourself." Griffin said. His tone said he was serious and his eyes held no misdirection.

"What are you saying? My father made sure I never heard from you?" Max asked quietly. The question wasn't really for Griffin to answer. *What does this all mean?* Max thought to herself. Her father had known she was heartbroken over Griffin leaving her. He also knew that Griffin was Jack's father. Why would he have prevented them from being together? True they had been barely out of high school, but they had plans and love that was serious.

As the facts flipped around Max's head, she stood silent. Anger began to well in her heart. Anger toward her dead father, who would never be able to answer the question of why he would do such a horrible thing to her. Was he that hellbent on keeping her on his compound, keeping Jack under his thumb, that he would lie and break her heart? Even after Jack was born, he knew that her heart was beyond repair, he never admitted to the lie.

"Max, say something," Griffin said from the doorway.

"I...don't have anything I can say I guess," she replied.

"Why didn't you call me, or my family, Max?" Griffin asked. Max looked at him and she was suddenly taken aback by the amount of emotion she could see on his face. It was too much for her. She started to feel like she was drowning but stuck in quicksand so she couldn't escape. She made a move to go around Griffin, to leave the bathroom, but he lightly grabbed her upper arm to stop her.

"Max, we need to work this out," he said, his breath tickled her ear. And that was almost her breaking point.

Suddenly Sarah shot up in bed and began to cough uncontrollably. The sound caught Max and Griffin's attention and they both ran to her side. It seemed Sarah wasn't exactly awake and able to communicate, but under the morphine's effects still. Griffin urged to back down and she curled up on her side in her sleep. Max inhaled quickly when she saw that the hands Sarah had used to cover her mouth were covered in blood.

Carefully, Max lifted one of Sarah's eyelids. With her co-worker Denise, she didn't know the signs, didn't know what to look for as the change came on. This time she was better prepared. As she lifted Sarah's eyelid, Max gasped and almost jumped back. The white of her eyes was gray, almost black in some places. Moving slowly, afraid of waking Sarah and not sure what state she would be in if she did wake, Max moved to look at her wound again. It was definitely getting darker and was also black in some places.

"It won't be much longer," Max whispered to Griffin who stood on the opposite side of the bed. "I'm sorry."

"She's a sweet girl," Griffin replied quietly.

Max didn't answer, just nodded her head. She imagined Griffin would see her in a different light. All Max saw was a sad situation where someone didn't know how to handle themselves, getting caught and killed. Sarah stomped on every nerve Max had. Nevertheless, Max would never hope for someone to die because they were annoying. And she had obviously cared for Griffin in some way. Max didn't know if those feelings were reciprocated, but she decided to tread carefully.

Leaving Griffin to sit next to Sarah and start his watch over her, Max went to the next room. Jack was prepping MREs with Turner watching in fascination. Max walked over and set out bottled waters for everyone to drink with dinner. She also fished out candy bars she had stashed, thinking everyone could use the sweet treat after the day they had gone through.

"Your daughter is quite smart," Turner said. Max turned to watch Jack prop the MRE heaters against rolled up towels.

"Yes, she is," Max replied, smiling at Jack. Jack beamed under her mother's praise.

"Momma taught me all sorts of stuff," the little girl said. She went about setting the small table with some sort of normalcy she craved.

"Griffin once told me you were raised by a doomsday prepper? Is that true?"

"Yeah. My dad was sort of off the deep end when it came to that stuff. But I learned and soaked up a ton during my childhood," Max replied.

Max was just opening her bottle of water to take a drink when the scream of a child came from outside. Max went to the window to peek out through the curtains. The scene wasn't one she wanted to see. A man, with a little girl that couldn't have been more than three-years-old, was trying to fight off infected that were clawing at them. Without even thinking about it, Max grabbed her tomahawk and ran for the hotel room door.

"Max! Wait!" Turner called after her.

Not used to having back up or waiting for help, Max ignored him and ran for the man. All she could see was a little girl that could easily die if the infected got a hold of her. The man was swinging a pipe at the infected but wasn't able to get enough power behind it to end the infected. Max saw the three that were on top of them, but from the street additional infected seemed to be coming in, reacting to the little girl screaming. Her steps quickened as she got near, to put more power behind her attack.

Her tomahawk embedded in the first infected, a woman, who had just gotten a hold of the man's shirt at the back. In the next moment, she would have sunk her teeth into him, but Max's blade ended her and the body crumpled to the ground. The father swung toward Max as if to attack, but his pipe stopped just short when he realized it was a living person.

"Behind me, get behind me," Max said quickly, and she stepped around him to attack the next infected. Putting herself in the infected's path was her plan and it worked perfectly. The remaining two were on her in a moment, making swinging the tomahawk impossible. She sidestepped the first. Snapping out her foot, she planted a kick on the midsection of the second infected, causing it to take a few stumbled steps back. That gave her enough space to run and jump at it with her tomahawk, using her momentum to crack its skull with her blade. She held tight to the handle and she stepped past the body as it fell, yanking the blade free and turning to the next infected.

The infected had tried to follow Max but instead had found its original target and was ambling toward the father and child again.

"Don't think so, asshole," Max growled and ran to chop the infected in the back of the head. It collapsed at the feet of the man and the little girl in his arms cried out again and sobbed into his neck.

"Where are you going? You need to take cover. There's more coming," Max said motioning behind her. As she did Turner and Griffin came running from the hotel room with their guns.

"You left Jack alone with Sarah???" Max demanded angrily.

"I'm not dumb, Max, I locked the middle door so if Sarah...well she can't get in there," Griffin answered cryptically before turning toward the man holding his daughter close. "Where are you going, man?"

"We better figure it out fast," Max said, as the infected started getting in range. She went straight to the nearest large infected, a beefy man, dragging a foot behind him. How he was able to move as fast as he did was incredible, his broken foot causing no delay. She quickly ended him and ran back to the group of men. The father just stared at her as if she just arrived from another planet. How could anything surprise him after the fall of the world, Max wasn't sure.

"So, what's the plan?" Max asked.

"We were, uh, running for the motel. My car ran out of gas down the road. We were walking and then they just showed up," the man rambled.

"Ok, get him a room key, Turner, and let's get them safely into a hotel room," Max instructed. Turner didn't argue, just put his gun to his shoulder and headed for the motel office.

"Move toward the motel and keep your back to the wall. That way nothing can sneak up on you," Max told the father. He did as she said quickly and Griffin looked at her.

"What are you going to do, Max?"

"I'm going to make sure nothing makes it to our door," she replied and turned back toward the infected that were coming their way. Griffin stepped up next to her, pulling his own knife and preparing to go into the fight. Warmth spread through Max. Griffin being there to support her was something she had missed. Without thinking, she knew she could depend on him.

The pair walked forward toward the approaching infected, a united front. Just as they went in for the attack, Max looked over at Griffin and nodded toward her right, indicating the direction she was attacking. He nodded back and adjusted his position to take up her blind side. Max started by severing the hamstring of the first infected, causing its leg to collapse. She moved passed the body as it fell, briefly noting the sound of Griffin's blade ending the infected as she moved to the next coming their way.

Max swung her tomahawk with her right hand and gripped her bowie in her left. She used both blades as she varied her attack, depending on the distance between the infected she fought and the next in range to reach them. Sometimes she would catch the view of Griffin on her left, his blade flashing in the sun as he danced through the infected. He was smooth and comfortable with his movement, his confidence shining through his easy movements.

Yanking her tomahawk blade free of the last skull on her side, she turned to find Griffin watching her as he cleaned his bowie off on the infected he had just killed. They were both covered in gore and Max yearned for a real shower. Griffin rubbed his hands against his jeans, trying to clean the majority of the blood off. They were surrounded by bodies. The infected fell in heaps of limbs, awkward and foreign looking. Black orbs of eyes stared up pits of infection.

"I got the family in a room down the other side of the building," Turner broke the quiet walking up, surveying the area.

"Good. Do they need supplies?" Max asked.

"He said no. He was very nervous and ready to get rid of me. I think he's afraid of you," Turner said with a wry smile.

"Me? I would think there are more things to be afraid of," Max said defensively.

"Yes, but you come across kinda strong, Max," Griffin said.

"Thanks for the support," Max said, stalking away from the men. She was determined to find water to shower with. And she needed to get away from Griffin and Turner. *Afraid of me? Why?* Max's mind was full of questions. And for her, it was strange to feel like her feelings were hurt. But that was exactly how she was feeling. Her feelings were hurt that she ran to defend the man and his child, and in the end, he was afraid of her and her strength.

Max bristled as she walked. The father had some eye-opening to do. This world needed people like Max, Mitch had always said that. People needed her strength and her bravery. She wouldn't change who she was or the actions she took to protect people. Judgement was one of the reasons she stayed away from people, even before the plague came. She rarely felt like people would understand her. But now, she was the one that knew what needed to be done.

"Max, wait up," Griffin said, jogging to catch up with her at the motel office. Max was hoping for some sort of water dispenser that might have large bottles.

"What?" Max said through gritted teeth, spinning to face him.

"Turner didn't mean anything by it," he said, his hands up in a defensive measure.

"And you?"

"I'm not wrong, but that doesn't mean coming across strong is a bad thing. You're a strong person. That's a good thing."

She entered the office, leaving Griffin behind. To her annoyance, he followed her. The office was small and cramped. One wall filled with a vending machine, that had been emptied already. On the other side of the small area, a shelf took up a wall. It was full of pamphlets about hiking, rafting, and vacation spots. *Fire starters now*, Max thought to herself, again noting how things had changed so quickly in just under a week.

Walking to the back of the room, Max found the door that led to a private office. It was another too small room, meant for the one person that worked at the office.

The desk was strewn with papers. The room smelled stale and of smoke, one worker apparently having no issues with smoking indoors. Max was surprised when she found what she had been searching for, two five-gallon bottles of water. They sat next to a water cooler that no longer had power.

"Score," she said out loud. Griffin just looked at her with one eyebrow raised.

"Looks at us, showers would be nice. Or at least a cold sponge bath," Max explained, gesturing toward the bottles.

"Gonna wash my back?" Griffin asked with a laugh.

"You're on your own, buddy," Max replied as she hefted a bottle onto her shoulder. Griffin grabbed the other.

Their light banter helped Max shake off the seriousness of the conversation they almost had. It wasn't the time to be worrying about personal relationships. It was the time to survive. If they were distracted by emotions and their history, someone could get hurt. Getting hurt was the last thing anyone needed. Max made a plan in her head, she would deal with Griffin when they got the compound. Once there, they wouldn't be worrying about their lives every moment of the day. They would be behind solid walls.

An hour later Max was drying her hair as best as she could with the cheap motel towels. She laughed as she heard Griffin cursing at the cold water. They probably could have boiled some and warmed it up, but Max figured it was more fun listening to Griffin freeze. She twisted her short hair off her neck and secured it with bobby pins. Suddenly she felt self-conscious about her appearance, something completely pointless in the middle of a plague. She found herself wondering what Griffin saw when he looked at her. Did he see someone that reminded him of the youthful girl he once knew? Or did he see her as a stranger?

Dinner was cold by the time Griffin and Max were able to sit down and eat. Both of them shoveled the food down, understanding the calories were what was important right then. Max felt like she had expended all of the energy she had in her rage against the infected throughout the day. The bodies were piling up in the parking lot. Max thought about the twitching curtains she had noticed when they arrived. Where were those people when the infected were on their doorstep?

"We need to take shifts tonight," Griffin said, pitching his voice low for only Max to hear. He glanced over to where Jack and Turner played cards on the bed across the room. Max just nodded, her mouth full.

"It will be easiest to handle Sarah right after she dies," Griffin continued.

"Agreed. There's not much of a delay. But if whoever is watching her notices that she stops breathing, they can handle it right then," Max whispered. Griffin nodded his agreement, looking down at his MRE. He poked at the food inside without eating.

"I'll take first shift," Max said. She had hopes that she could be the one to handle her when she turned. Not because she disliked the woman, but to spare Griffin the pain of having to handle it himself.

Sitting alone in a chair across from Sarah's sleeping form, Max watched carefully as her chest rose and fell. It was periodic and slow. Out of precaution, Max checked Sarah's wound again. Unsurprisingly it was still slowly oozing blood. While the heavy flow of blood had slowed, the wound continued to seep and turn black. The injured woman hadn't woken since her dose of morphine around lunch. The medication would have worn off, but she was so close to death her mind didn't allow her to wake.

All of Max's assumptions were based on what she had watched with Denise. There was no natural way to relate the plague to an illness already known to the world. Max knew there were nasty viruses and plagues that had wiped out large pieces of the human population throughout history. But reanimation was a fairy tale, it was Frankenstein's creature. Instead of one monster, there were thousands.

In her musings, Max vaguely noted the absence of a sound. She came back around to focusing on the task at hand. Staring at Sarah, Max counted seconds that her chest didn't move. *Shit,* Max thought to herself, as she unsheathed her knife. The thought had crossed her mind at one point to end Sarah before the process finished. But a small piece of her worried she was wrong on her theories about the illness. Now looking at a dead Sarah, she knew she was right. All it took was a bite.

Standing over the dead body, Max decided to just be sure. She pressed her fingers to Sarah's neck. Not finding a pulse, she moved her fingers to try again. Still nothing. Then she pulled up an eyelid and was grimly greeted by blackness. The process was done. All that was left was for Sarah to rise and feast on the living. Max couldn't allow that.

Thinking of Griffin, Jack, and even Turner next door, Max did what was necessary. Pushing her knife into Sarah's temple, Max felt tears clog her throat. Pulling a sheet over Sarah's face, Max left the room to sleep for the rest of the night.

CHAPTER SEVENTEEN

"I want to bury her," Griffin demanded. The argument was an endless circle, that had already gone on for an hour. Max had woken with the sun, even after going to bed well into the AM hours of the morning. She wanted to break the news to Griffin without him walking in and finding her dead. She had thought they would be sad, eat breakfast, and get on the road. However, Griffin had other plans.

"She doesn't know what you're doing for her, Griffin. We need to get on the road," Max said. She was packing things into her go bag. Without asking she had started loading items into the truck. Turner had gone to check on the father and child they had saved the day before but was surprised by an empty room. Max didn't see any other reason to stay around.

"But it's only right. I won't leave her body to rot in this motel."

Max groaned. She could barely handle sentimentality on a regular day. They didn't have normal days anymore. Taking time to bury a body was a normal thing to do. She looked at Griffin's face. He insisted he didn't know Sarah long, but they met at the first shelter and she had attached herself to him. Max could see he felt responsible for her and she had died while she was with them. And now Griffin thought he had failed. She took a deep breath, trying to sort through her need to follow her instincts and understand the emotional need he had.

"Ok, ok. I give up. We'll bury her. Where do you want to do this? And we will have to go back into town for shovels," Max said. Griffin touched her arm and looked into her eyes.

"Thank you."

"Yeah, well I guess we could scavenge more from town anyhow. It wasn't overly looted. I'm not sure if the town just turned fast, or if people are hiding," Max said, shrugging off the thanks. Griffin didn't answer, just nodded and went back inside the motel room to tell Turner the plan. Jack exited a few moments later and came to stand next to Max, who had frozen in her loading since they weren't leaving.

"That's a nice thing you did, Momma," Jack said.
"What did I do?"
"Agreeing to bury Sarah," she said quietly.

"Well we're a group, I'm not anyone's boss. We have to agree," Max said. And she meant that. She got her wish by having Griffin accompany them to Montana. Still, she wouldn't force him to go if he decided not to.

"I like that," the little girl smiled, a little mischief in her eyes.

"Oh, that doesn't count, little girl. You're still a child. I get your say. So, I guess I should have two votes," Max said, putting her finger to her chin as if she were thinking. Jack laughed and pushed her mom with her shoulder.

The trip into town was made as a group. The main street hadn't changed overnight. It was eerily still and silent. If they hadn't seen the car wrecks or knew that there had been plenty of infected nearby, it would seem like an abandoned town.

"It's strange nothing is really looted," Turner said from the backseat.

"Yeah. The pharmacy was basically intact when we came, except a crashed car through the front window. But the shelves were basically full. It's strange," Max replied.

"There were shovels at the pharmacy store, Momma," Jack reminded.

Entering the pharmacy together, Jack centered between the adults, they were silent except the scrape of shoes on the glass on the floor. Turner grabbed bags and started his apocalypse shopping. Max and Jack took Griffin to the hardware section, where he picked two shovels. After leaving those in the truck, he did some shopping for himself as well. Neither man had a pack, Max planned on fixing that as soon as possible. They need to be prepared for the chance they were separated.

As they walked back to the truck, the sound of a shotgun pumping stopped them all. Jack was standing just to Max's left, so Max took one step back and over, to put Jack directly in front of her. The sound had come from behind her. Max looked over at Griffin who was on the passenger side of the truck, his gun was up and aimed. Max lifted her hands in a surrender gesture and slowly turned around to face the person that seemed to be pointing a shotgun at her back.

A young man stood at the corner of the pharmacy, half hidden in the shadow of the small alley. The sun glinted off of the shotgun barrel, which was pointed directly at Max. She kept her hands in the air, using one to shield the sun slightly to get a better look at the man.

"You're stealing from Doc," the man called out.

"I don't see many people around that need the supplies," Max replied calmly. "How about you put the gun down and we talk about it."

"You are thieves. Thieves should be shot," the man called back.

"I suppose that's true. But we aren't thieves. We are surviving. Just like you are, I assume," Max said. Griffin hissed at her to be careful, as she took one small step forward. Jack knowing what her mother would expect, stepped with her, to stay hidden.

"You know about the plague? You couldn't have missed it," Max continued.

"The sick that walk and are eating people. Yeah, we know about that."

"How many are left in town? We haven't seen anyone."

"Not many. Not since the illness came," the man's voice was sad.

"How did it come here? Did the sick just wander into town?" Max asked. She continued the conversation calmly. The man's shotgun lowered little by little as they spoke. Max continued to get closer, her hands in the open so the man wouldn't feel threatened.

"Nah. Little Bud, he was out of town, looking at colleges, ya see. When he got home, he was sick. Big Bud, his dad, was the first I saw. Little Bud's mom, before she died, said Little Bud attacked them in the middle of the night. She escaped with just a bite. But Big Bud died in their bed," the man explained. As he spoke Max got within striking distance, his guard coming down as she distracted him with conversation. Suddenly he realized how close she was, and with a curse, he tried to swing the shotgun back at her. Simultaneously Max predicted his movements and grabbed the shotgun barrel and shoved it up in the air before yanking it from his hand. He lost his grip and stumbled forward into the sunlight.

A moment later, Griffin was next to Max with his gun pointed at the young man and Max had flipped the shotgun to point it as well. She checked the ammo and wasn't surprised to find it loaded. The young man couldn't have been more than nineteen. He looked at his feet, whether it was fear or shame on his face, Max wasn't sure.

"It's not nice to point guns at strangers, especially now," Max said lowly. "Especially people who have a child with them."

"Not nice at all, my man," Griffin added.

"Jack, get in the car with Turner please," Max said quietly. Without question, Jack turned and ran for the SUV. Max could hear whispered words pass between her and Turner and then the slamming of the vehicle door. Feeling more confident now that Jack was out of danger, Max lowered the gun and looked at the man. He was small, much shorter than Griffin, just eye level with Max. His hair was honey colored and sticking every direction. Part of her felt sorry for the man.

"So Big Bud attacked in town with Little Bud I suppose. Did the mother also turn and attack?" Max asked. The man didn't speak, just nodded.

"Look at me," Max demanded, tired of the pity act the man was pulling. His dark eyes met hers and they were filled with sorrow.

"You've lost a lot of people," she continued quietly. And he nodded again.

"We were staying for a few nights in the motel on the outside of town. We haven't seen much living, mostly infected. I'm guessing those are your town people. Is everyone that's alive safe?"

"Yeah, as safe as we can be. We are staying out at the old Miller place. It's been closed for a while since the bank took it. The windows are boarded, so there's about twenty of us out there now," the man spoke fast, Griffin's gun on him made him ramble. Max touched Griffin's arm softly. The man wasn't a threat to them. He was only trying to protect his town and they were strangers.

"Listen, I get that you are trying to protect your town. But you guys need to come in here, get everything useful and take it out to the Miller place. More people will come through. And they won't be as nice as we've been. We have taken very little, only what we absolutely needed. Do you hear me?" Max said sternly. The man nodded quickly.

"You have a vehicle?" She asked.

"Nah. I rode a bike."

"A bike? Like a bicycle? Are you nuts?" Max laughed. Griffin even huffed out a laugh at that.

"Well I don't have anything else," the man defended.

Max looked around the small Main Street. She focused on a small pickup. It was an older model, something perfect for this man. Taking the shotgun with her, she walked away without a word.

"Where she goin'?" The man asked Griffin.

"Your guess is as good as mine," Griffin replied.

"Ain't you with her?"

"Yeah, that doesn't mean anything to her. She could be doing anything. By the looks of that truck she's headed toward, she's gonna hot-wire it," Griffin said, following Max and motioning for the man to follow.

"Hot-wire it? Y'all are thieves, aren't you?!" The man said, his voice rising in indignation.

"What aren't you getting about the world falling apart and those rules no longer applying?" Max said over her shoulder. The man just huffed, apparently not feeling the same way.

An hour later, Max had the truck wired to start. She taught the man, who they learned was named James, how to put the wires together and how to get it started. After yanking him out of the truck once for almost shocking himself to death, Max was pretty sure she had him scared enough that he would do the right thing. While she was hotwiring the truck and showing James how to work it, Griffin and Turner loaded the bed of the truck with as many supplies as would fit. They watched as James drove carefully out of town. Max had even returned his shotgun, knowing he would need it eventually.

"That was a good thing to do, Max," Griffin said to her as they stood in the middle of Main Street.

"It wasted another hour of the day. I guess since we're still in town, we might as well get whatever else we need. I don't think James will be back to try and shoot us."

Max walked toward what looked like sporting goods shop. The windows boasted ski, hiking and rafting supplies. Max could imagine people at the motel picking up a colorful pamphlet from the office and coming into this quaint town to find the supplies they needed for their adventure. The scene in her head made her sad and angry thinking of all the things people would no longer do. There would no longer be hiking for pleasure, instead it would be a necessity to survive.

The door to the shop was locked. Max looked at it for a moment and then decided to just break out the door. She was just about to throw a large rock through it when Griffin stopped her.

"Calm down. You don't need to destroy everything in your way," he kidded.

"Do you have keys I don't know about?" She shot back.

"Maybe. Old locks like this can sometimes be jimmied with a card. Like my library card," he said holding one up in his hand.

"Were you planning on getting some light reading in?" Max asked sarcastically.

Griffin didn't answer, knowing better than to feed into her attitude. Max stood back watching as he wiggled the door a bit, then jammed his card in to push back the latch. With a push of his shoulder, the door popped open. A proud Griffin turned back to Max to hold up his library card again. He smiled at her as she just rolled her eyes and walked past him.

"Mitch didn't teach you that trick?" He said, falling into step with her.

"No. He just figured we'd break things to get in," Max replied absently. Finally finding what she was looking for, she threw two backpacks at Griffin. He caught them and nodded, realizing what she planned on doing. They walked through the store for a few moments, grabbing other items that could be useful. By the time they were done, both Griffin and Turner had bags with batteries, flashlights, lanterns, rope, multi-tools, and mess kits.

They walked together back to the pharmacy where they had parked the SUV. Turner and Jack were sitting on the back bumper with the hatch open. Jack swung her feet freely, laughing at something Turner said. As they walked Max watched Turner. His eyes were sharp, though he was talking to Jack, he was watching everything around them. His military training hadn't faded, similar to Griffin's. And he looked out for her little girl, so that put him on her good list.

During the short drive back to the motel, Jack sorted the foods they had taken from the pharmacy. She filled both of the new packs with easy to eat foods. She also loaded each with a first aid kit she had created from the products they found.

"So, the small first aid kit wasn't enough?" Turner asked her, turned in his seat to watch her work in the very back area.

"No. They don't have enough bandages, scissors, tape, or antibacterial ointments," Jack explained.

"You know a lot about first aid," he replied.

"I've paid attention to what Momma has taught me. I like first aid stuff. But I'd like to learn to help animals someday," she said, smiling her innocent little smile up to Turner. Though Jack had her Uncle Rafe in Montana, she had never had daily interaction with men that could be father figures to her. The term father figure stuck in Max's mind, and she again started thinking about telling Griffin about Jack. Turner obviously was infatuated with the little girl even more now, knowing she was the daughter of his best friend.

The group was somber when they arrived back to the motel. Griffin and Turner surveyed the area around the motel until they found a dirt location with no high weeds to hide danger. The bodies in the parking lot were a reminder of what had come out of the weeds and none of them wanted to face that again. The two men went with the shovels and Max took Jack into the room they had slept in. They kept the door shut between the two rooms, trying to ignore the fact that Sarah's dead body was still laying in a bed right next-door.

Max and Jack worked on creating something of a lunch with canned tuna, mayo packets, pickles, bread, and chips. Jack commented on being sick of tuna, but Max was lost in her own thoughts. The day had gotten away from them. The death of Sarah had distracted her from the things Griffin had said the day before. How had he written her for months, and she never saw one of the letters?

Sitting at the table, idly spinning her knife, Max searched her memories from that time. They were well burned into her brain. She had checked the mail daily for what felt like weeks. If she didn't find the mail in the box, she would find it in the house and she would search it. Had Mitch taken the letters and thrown them away before she got the chance to look? She had assigned chores that kept her from waiting for the mailman.

Now that she really thought about it, Mitch always made sure she was busy in the afternoons after his morning lessons. He would have her up and out of bed early, working around the compound. Almost daily he would take her off the compound to do wilderness training or hunting. By the time they got home, she would be exhausted. He would have always had the opportunity to check the mail before her.

The implications of this were heavy on Max. She looked at Jack who was curled up on a bed reading a book. All these years, Max had held bitterness toward Griffin for leaving her. It was that bitterness and fear that kept her from ever reaching out. She used those things as excuses for not telling him he had a daughter. Tears pricked the back of her eyes and she blinked quickly to prevent them from falling. The last eight years she had been making one of the biggest mistakes of her life.

The door opened as Griffin and Turner entered, filthy and sweaty. Max stood up and motioned for them to sit down. After cleaning up somewhat, they sat, and Max put lunch in front of them. Griffin watched her with raised eyebrows. It wasn't a typical habit of Max's to serve anyone a meal. They dug in and Max sat next to Jack.

"How's the digging going?"

"There is a lot of dense clay, so it's going slow," Turner replied around a bite of a tuna sandwich.

"I can come out and take a shift if you need," Max offered.

"To dig the grave you didn't want to take the time to dig?" Griffin asked, he again looked at her with surprise on his face.

"I'm not a complete heartless hag. I can help," Max shot back defensively.

"I think we got it. If we need you we'll let you know," Griffin replied, turning back to his lunch.

They ate the remaining time in silence. After finishing, the men left the room again without a word. Max stood and paced the room, her thoughts in turmoil. She couldn't handle being idle for so long. The heaviness of the secret she was carrying was distracting and exhausting. Deciding finally that her lack of the sleep the night before was also not helping anything, she kicked off her boots and slid into the bed Jack read in. She fell asleep with her face pressed into her daughter's hair.

Violent banging on the motel room woke Max, causing her to jump from bed half asleep. She shook her head, trying to clear the fog from her brain. She looked over at Jack who was now standing on the other side of the bed, her book still clutched in her hand. The sun had started to dip, and the motel room was getting darker. Max figured she had slept three hours at least.

Slamming on the door happened again. Max grabbed her 9mm and walked cautiously to the small window next to the door. Using the muzzle of her gun, she moved the gauzy curtain out of the way to peek at who was standing on the other side. A bloody man stood there, his eyes wide with fear and panic. Max couldn't see the source of the blood, but she noticed some of it was blacker and probably from infected bodies and not the living.

"What?" Max yelled through the door. More quietly, she turned to Jack "Go hide in the closet."

"I saw a light, please let me in," the man yelled. Max looked around and Jack held up the flashlight she had been reading by. Max nodded and motioned toward the closet.

"Go get your own room. There are keys in the motel office," Max called.

"Please. They are out here. I need to hide. I don't want to be alone," the man cried out. His voice cracked and to Max's astonishment, the man started to sob at her door. Max stood debating. She backed up, watching the door and went to get her boots. She slipped them on and then grabbed her tomahawk to slip into its holster.

"Back away from the door," Max yelled. She watched through the window and watched the man back away with his hands held high. Max pointed her gun out in front of her as she opened the door and looked at the man. She surveyed the area quickly and didn't see any immediate threats. Just then Griffin and Turner came running with their shovels, apparently hearing the man bellowing at the door.

Max stepped from the room and shut the door firmly behind her. She faced the man, who's anguish rolled off him in waves.

"What happened to you?" Max asked.

"My family, oh god, my family. We were trying to get away from a group of them. My wife tripped, we were walking, our car broke down. I had our son, so she told me to keep going. Oh god, they ate her..." the man fell to his knees and Max put her gun into its holster as well. Griffin and Turner slowed as they got closer and saw the man on the ground.

"What did you do to him, Max?" Griffin asked breathlessly. Max shot him a dirty look before looking back at the man.

"I'm so sorry. Where is your son?" She asked quietly.

"I was running, and suddenly he was yanked out of my arms. So fast. He was just gone. I killed the ones that killed him."

"Did you get bit?" Max asked. The man just shook his head, looking at the asphalt in front of him. Max just watched him for a moment. He looked down at himself and seemed to suddenly realize he was covered in blood. Panicking he started pulling his clothing off.

"Ok, ok, you're alright," Max said, stepping closer and holding her hands up to try to still his movement.

"I have to get it off. Oh Jesus, oh God...it's my son's blood. It's his."

"We have clothes that might fit. You can clean up and put those on. Come on," Max said, standing up and motioning for the man to stand. Griffin stopped her.

"Max, you don't know this man. You're gonna take him inside?"

"Do we just leave him out here to die? He's in no condition to handle himself," Max whispered.

"Turner is going to take Sarah's body. At least put him in that room. Keep him out of our room," Griffin said. Max wished she could tell him how much he was acting like a father. But she pushed that from her mind and just nodded at him.

Going to the SUV, she popped the back and led the man there. They were out of sight of the body being moved from the motel room, which Max was sure wouldn't go over well with the distraught man. She pulled clothing that they had scavenged for Griffin. Turner was too small, nothing he had would fit the man. She gave him two bottles of water to clean up before putting the clean clothes on.

Standing there watching the man just stare, Max realized he wasn't in any state to clean up. The tears were still falling from his eyes, as he looked out across the parking lot. Max was sure he was picturing his wife and son. Part of her broke for the man, even while the other part admonished anyone that wasn't ready to survive in this broken world. She tried to tap into what she thought Alex would do, her sister with all the heart.

Softly, she touched the man's arm to bring his attention to her. He looked down at her and Max was able to get a better look at his face. Max guessed he was in his 40's with salt and pepper hair. She used a cloth and water and wiped his face, cleaning the blood from it. He just stood still as she worked. As his tears fell, she wiped them away and continued to clean his skin.

"There you are," Max said, smiling softly at him, once his face was visible. He was a handsome man. His dark eyes were bloodshot from his tears, but they were surrounded by soft laugh lines that told Max he had been part of a happy life before the infected took away what made him smile.

"I'm Max," she said. She continued to clean the blood from his neck and arms.

"Cliff. My name is Cliff," he replied quietly.

"Nice to meet you, Cliff. We'll get you cleaned up and settled in a room ok?"

Cliff didn't answer her, just looked over her head at Griffin who was standing guard. Max hadn't seen him there, but she sensed they weren't alone. She had guessed Griffin was concerned and refused to leave her alone with the man. But the longer she cleaned him up, Max didn't feel anything to be afraid of with Cliff. He could have hurt her by now, grabbed her weapons from their holsters, or tried to run when he realized she wasn't alone. Instead, he stood still and let her take care of him.

"I'm not going to hurt your girl," Cliff said over her head. Max looked up at him and then looked back at Griffin who just nodded from his place against the motel wall.

"I'm not his girl," Max said, feeling like someone should correct that.

"Why not? He seems awfully protective," Cliff said. Max just laughed uncomfortably and shook her head. She reached up and pulled a shirt over Cliff's head and he put his clean arms through the holes.

"Thank you, Max. You are being very kind," Cliff said.

"Not many people accuse me of that," Max said grinning. She heard Griffin smother a laugh from behind her. She resisted the urge to flip him off. The banter would only make them seem more like a couple.

Max showed Cliff to the hotel room that Sarah had been in. The bed was stripped, but a blood stain still showed on the mattress. Cliff looked at it, then looked back at Max.

"We lost someone. We are burying her before we leave. You are welcome to stay in the other bed. Are you hungry?" Max asked.

Cliff just shook his head and sat on the bed with his head in his hands. Max hesitated, watching him from the doorway. She missed her sister. If Alex were there, she would know how to console, how to make the man feel more at ease. Max felt lost and incapable of taking on any of the painful burdens the man was feeling. She just stood, shifting from foot to foot uncomfortably.

"I'm not sure what to do now," Cliff said.

"Maybe lay down?" Max suggested. She realized after she said it, that her suggestion was lame and not at all what Cliff was getting at.

"Maybe. Yeah. I'll lay down. Maybe then I'll figure something out," he said. He was speaking more to himself than Max. He laid down, with his back to the door and was still. Max backed toward the connecting door and found Griffin on the other side waiting.

"Well?" Griffin asked.

"He lost his wife and son. They were attacked right in front of him," Max said. She walked past Griffin and found Jack still in the closet.

"You can come out. It's ok," Max said to her once she'd opened the door. The girl was completely unruffled.

She smiled at Griffin and sat back on the bed with her book and flashlight. Realizing how dark it had grown, Max closed the heavier drapes, making sure no light could get out, and turned on a lantern to illuminate the room. Griffin was still standing in the middle of the room, shovel in hand, dirt covering his clothing and skin.

"You aren't done, right?" Max said, motioning toward the shovel.

"The hole is done. Turner was going to put Sarah in. We have to cover her now."

"Ok. Need help?" Max asked. Griffin just shook his head, but he didn't make a move to leave.

"Griffin? What's the deal?" Max asked, putting her hands on her hips and staring at him.

"I'm not sure about leaving you two here with him next-door," he answered.

Max looked at him exasperated. He was the one person that was well aware of how prepared Max was to handle herself and protect her daughter. She didn't need the macho protective man routine, any more than she needed a bullet to the foot. She pushed Griffin on the shoulder and motioned for him to follow her outside. She was going to argue with him, and she didn't want to do it directly in front of Jack.

Outside Max surveyed the twilight, not seeing anything moving naturally or unnaturally. She turned to Griffin as he softly closed the door behind him.

"Ok, aren't you pretty aware that I don't need you to protect me?" Max demanded.

"Oh I know you don't think you ever need help," Griffin said casually. His demeanor just grated on Max's nerves, and the small grin he had told her he knew it.

"It's not about help, Griffin, and you know it. I can handle myself, Cliff, and protecting Jack when it comes to it. I do not need you going alpha male on me, we do not have time for it...."

"I missed you, Max," Griffin suddenly blurted, interrupting Max's tirade. It effectively shut her up. She had to remember to snap her mouth shut because it just hung open at his comment. The next thing she knew, Griffin had dropped the shovel. The loud noise distracted her for a moment, just as his hand gripped the nape of her neck and his mouth was pressed against hers.

His lips were soft and undemanding against hers. Without much thought, Max melted into him. This was no longer the high school boy she loved years ago, this was a grown man. Nevertheless, kissing him felt familiar. When his tongue slid along the seam of her lips, she sighed and allowed him entry. His arms came around her smaller frame and crushed her to him as if he needed to breathe her in. She reacted and went up to her toes to deepen the kiss and put her arms around his neck. Nothing in her adult life could compare to that kiss.

"Oh crap, uh...sorry to interrupt," Turner's voice came from behind Max. She jumped away from Griffin as if someone had set her on fire. Her hand went to her mouth, lost at what had just happened. She walked away, walking into the motel room and closing the door behind her. Leaning against the door, Max tried to get her breathing under control. She could hear Turner giving Griffin grief and then Griffin laughing gruffly. The two walked away to handle more important things, like burying a body.

CHAPTER EIGHTEEN

They gathered around the freshly covered grave. Jack held Max's hand. Max was nervous being out in the dark, not being able to see what was around them in the shadows. But Griffin had wanted to do something proper to say goodbye to Sarah. Max didn't say it, but she barely knew Sarah. What was she supposed to say? She was an airhead and was attracted to her former high school sweetheart? That's all she really knew about the woman, not that it made it less sad to see anyone die.

Jack was somber, clearly understanding this was about death. For an eight-year-old girl, she was immensely smart and calm in the face of adversity. Her heart was gold and she clearly felt that Griffin was upset at losing Sarah. The little girl reached out to touch Griffin's hand as well. When he looked down at her, she offered her hand, as if it was the most normal thing to take comfort from a little girl.

Across the grave, Max could see Turner watching her in the lantern light. Their eyes met for a moment, his look charged with his emotions about Jack and Griffin. Max had to look away from the weight of the implication. She would tell Griffin when she was damned well ready, she had already decided that. Turner couldn't pressure her into something she wasn't ready for. The time hadn't been right since they found him in North Carolina.

The time was also wrong for some passionate kiss that left Max's head spinning. For the hour it took the men to bury Sarah and come back to the motel room to clean up,

Max couldn't sit still. Jack commented on it, and Max brushed it off. Griffin had missed her. What did that mean? In eight years he never met someone, fell in love, moved on? Max had Jack, that had always been her excuse to not date. She also never wanted to be faced with the scrutiny of a man that she would probably be stronger and more equipped to handle life than him. Griffin had always been the exception to that in her life. He knew Mitch, saw her childhood, even trained with her at times.

As they stood around the grave, Max felt guilty thinking about the kiss again. Part of her so badly wanted to do it again. The other part of her was screaming at her, telling her this wasn't the right time to be thinking about a man. Griffin acted nonchalant as if it hadn't happened. Max took his cue and focused on the immediate needs. She looked down at the dark ground where Sarah would lay forever.

"I feel like we should say something, but what do we say?" Turner commented, breaking the tense silence.

"I didn't really know her," Max said quietly.

"I just met her a few days ago. But I guess I spent the most time with her. I didn't even know that much about her. So I guess I'll start. I'm sorry I didn't protect you better, Sarah. I hope you're at peace," Griffin said.

"I hope she finds Gramps in Heaven, he'll keep her safe," Jack commented. Max smiled down at her at the same time Griffin did.

"He sure would, Jack, that much I remember about your Gramps," Griffin said to her.

After a few additional moments of quiet reflection, the group slowly headed back to the motel room. Jack stayed between Griffin and Max holding their hands. The normal family feeling gripped Max's heart. She had to fight the urge to let go of Jack's hand and run for a hiding place. They arrived at their motel room before long. Turner opened the door and ushered Jack in first. He looked back at Griffin and Max and grinned before walking in after Jack. Max went to follow, but Griffin's hand fell on her arm.

"Wait, Max, we need to talk," Griffin said quietly.

"Do we have to? Like right now? I'm exhausted. I'm sure you are too. We should eat dinner and head to sleep," Max said, avoiding the subject with everything she could think of.

"Look at me, Max. You can't just ignore this," Griffin said gruffly. He reached around her and shut the motel door, making the decision for her. She turned to look at him warily. He laughed out loud, the sound echoing around the motel. She looked around and shushed him. They didn't need to attract more infected.

"You still get that caged animal look, ya know? You've always had it. Whenever something serious or emotional needed to be spoken about. You get this look," Griffin said, gesturing at her face and posture. Max purposely wiped all expression from her face and tried to loosen her stance. That only made Griffin smile again.

"I just don't think this is an appropriate time to talk about our history. It's there, we know it, but we have things to get done. We don't need the distraction," Max said firmly.

"After tonight, we'll be back on the road. And I don't know when we'll be alone again to talk about this. About the kiss."

"We don't need to talk about it. It happened, we can move on," Max said shrugging. Outwardly she fought to keep her tone light and unaffected. Waves of heat and wanting swept through her on the inside. She fought them down with everything she had.

"Move on? Did I say I wanted to do that?" Griffin said as he slowly started walking toward Max. She stepped back and bumped into the wall of the motel.

"Are you telling me you don't want me to kiss you again?" Griffin asked, his voice gruff as he closed the distance. Max could feel the heat from his body against her own. Her mind screamed at her to beg for more. However, her senses were stronger than her basic sexual needs. She just looked at him defiantly, saying nothing.

"Seeing you again has brought back so many emotions. Some that I thought I would never feel again. You have barely changed from the girl I knew in high school. The one I had planned to spend my life with until she didn't respond to my letters," Griffin grinned when he spoke, letting her know he wasn't angry, but teasing her.

"I've changed. I'm not a girl anymore," Max said, her voice squeaky.

"Oh, now see, those changes I noticed," he said, as he ran a hand from her hip, up her ribcage and ever so close to her breast, before sliding back to her hip. He lifted her chin with a finger and she registered fire in his hazel eyes before his lips found hers again. He kissed her softly then pulled back again.

"I loved you, Max. And I've never loved anyone since," he said. With that, he pulled away from her and went to the motel room door. Max stayed right where she was, her breath labored and her heart beating loudly in her ears. *What in the hell is he doing to me?* She thought to herself.

"Are you coming?" He asked from the door, innocence in his tone. Max wanted to strangle him. Without a word, she went into the motel room as he held the door open for her.

The morning seemed to come more quickly than she had expected. When the sun woke her, Jack was already awake next to her. The men were still asleep in their shared bed, overly exhausted after their digging. Quietly Max moved around the room getting herself dressed and shoes on. They had to get on the road. Her intense need to keep moving was making her impatient and snappy.

A small knock came from the door separating the two motel rooms. The noise was quiet but was enough to have both men sitting up in bed, eyes wide looking for an intruder. Max shushed them with her hands, showing them it was just Cliff in the other room. The distraught man had stayed in the room alone all night. At dinner time Max tried to bring him food, but he didn't answer the door when she knocked. Though she could have used a key to get in, she refused to impose in that way.

She swung the door open now, and Cliff stood on the other side. His eyes were red and raw looking from crying, sleep, and rubbing. His hair was in a crazy disarray and his clothes were rumpled from being slept in. He looked at Max with no emotion on his face. She smiled slightly at him.

"Good morning, Cliff."

"Morning."

"Are you hungry? We have food if you'd like to eat?" Max said.

"No. I....I don't want to impose." He sounded dejected and torn. And the emotions seemed to rip at Max's heart.

"You aren't imposing. Please come and sit. I'll get some stuff together for you," Max motioned for him to come in. Both Turner and Griffin had gotten up and dressed. They stood, waiting for Cliff to come in. The three of them nodded to each other in greeting. Jack laid in bed quiet, curled up under the blanket watching the strange man. A small smile lit Cliff's mouth as he tried to nod to her as well. Jack pulled the blanket down and smiled at him.

"Good morning," Jack said.

"Good morning," Cliff answered.

Max settled Cliff at the table and set whatever foods they had in front of him. They were in a good place with their food supplies for now and she wanted to share that while possible. However, once she put food in front of Cliff, he didn't touch anything but water. He sat and stared at the table. Max sat across from him, tapping the table in his view to bring his eyes up. The impact of the sadness was like a blow to Max. She took a deep breath and tried to decide what to say.

"We are getting ready to leave today, Cliff. What are you going to do from here?" She asked.

"We, my family, didn't have a specific place in mind. We just wanted to get away from those things. I guess I'll stay here," Cliff remarked, looking around the room as if judging its ability to be a shelter for him.

"What if you came with us?" Max asked the question before she even thought it.

"Max," Griffin said from behind her. Max cringed inwardly. She still was trying to learn how to be part of a group and play nice. Guessing she should have run this by Griffin and Turner first, she turned to Griffin. Her face was a mask of pleading. She didn't want to leave this poor man behind. Max had no doubt he'd allow himself to die however possible, to follow his family. Griffin stared at her for a moment, his face hard. But he nodded his agreement anyway.

"Go where with you?" Cliff asked.

"We are going to Montana. To somewhere safe. There will be plenty of space for anyone that wants to come," Max replied.

"Why bring me with you? You don't know me."

"No. I guess I don't. What I do know is your name is Cliff. You are a human being who has gone through a terrible loss. And I think you need people right now," Max said softly. Cliff's head fell lower still, thinking again of his family and the terrible way he had to see them die. Max covered the hand he had on the table with her own. She felt him jump at the contact, but he didn't pull back. *Alex, what would you say?* She asked her sister in her head.

"You shouldn't be alone," Max said. Cliff's hand turned and gripped her own, his grasp tight and almost painful to Max. But she let him hold on as he kept his head down with his eyes closed. Seeming to have made a decision he released her and pulled back, looking up at her and then over to Griffin who stood sentry behind her.

"Ok. I'd like to come. I don't know what else to do."

Finally, on the road, Max felt freedom sitting behind the wheel of the SUV. Griffin sat next to her, refusing to allow Cliff to sit in the front seat. In the back seat, Turner squeezed into the center keeping Cliff separate from Jack. Max knew they were being overprotective, but they would calm down after they all spent some time together. Her instincts were telling her Cliff wasn't a danger to them. Currently, the man stared out the passenger window, his forehead leaning against the glass.

For the first hour, Griffin had fiddled with the radio, checking through FM and AM stations. He couldn't understand why the government emergency signal wasn't transmitting to where they were. He tried to argue that something was wrong with the radio, but Max cheerfully reminded him the vehicle was brand spanking new. She had never actually purchased a brand new car because she wouldn't know how to do basic repairs on something with so many computer components. But she appreciated the new car smell they got to enjoy while they had it.

They stopped for lunch, making the last of the tuna and mayo sandwiches they had. Three days of tuna was a lot for anyone to eat, so Max was secretly glad they were on the last cans. Cliff even ate half of a sandwich and a couple of pickles. Max wasn't sure if he was doing it because he wanted to, or because Max put a guilt trip on him about wasting food since they didn't have any way of keeping it cold to eat later. Her patience with the man could get thin, but she would then remind herself that she was trying to be consoling and supportive.

While the group finished eating, Max studied the road atlas with the local maps she had been using. Between the two she was able to figure out the small road they were on. They had been winding through farms and thick groves of trees since they left the motel and small town behind them. It was beautiful country, but even it felt abnormal and infected. A few times they could spy infected near farmhouses or on the side of the road. Max just kept driving.

The sudden sound of growling caught Max's attention. She looked up from where she leaned against the side of the SUV. She was facing a grove of apple trees, that were just starting to blossom flowers for the fruit. The clouds in the sky gave the orchard a darkness that didn't allow clear visual. The road sat away from the trees enough that Max had felt safe stopping to eat. The cool breeze of spring was still in the air and it blew the subtle fragrance of the flowers to Max. But she also smelled something else. Something dead.

"Max. We need to go," Griffin called from the back of the SUV. He and Turner were packing everything back into their packs. Max required everything to be ready for easy transportation if needed. They didn't argue and just separated the foods and water into the four backpacks they had. Max and Jack's bags also had sleeping bags attached.

Coming around the back of the SUV, Max gasped when she saw what Griffin saw. Behind them, the road was slowly filling with the infected. They were stumbling out of the groves on either side and were headed straight toward them. As they stood watching, Max noticed how some of the infected seemed to be more coordinated, moving faster than the rest of the pack. She raised her arm and pointed at one.

"What in the hell?" She asked, of no one in particular.

"It's faster," Turner said slowly.

"Which means we need to go faster," Griffin said. He lifted Jack into the back of the SUV and she climbed into the center seat.

As Max closed the back of the SUV, she noticed more infected coming from the shadows of the trees, but not behind them. They were coming right from the trees to the sides of the SUV. She slammed the hatch shut and ran around the end of the SUV to get to her door. She stopped short when she saw an infected in her path.

"Well shit," Max said out loud. The infected heard her and turned toward her quickly. Of course, it was one of the faster infected. Max pulled her bowie and cursed a string of vile curses at herself for leaving her tomahawk inside the car.

The infected took two steps toward her, that almost seemed like a normal healthy person. Max had to admit to herself that it was slightly unnerving to see it act more human. When it reached out for her, Max grabbed the nearest wrist and pulled the infected to her, quickly embedding her knife blade into its skull. Her hand slipped from the knife handle and it went down with the infected. *Damn, Max,* she thought to herself, crouching quickly to yank the blade free. While she did, she analyzed the physical differences of this infected. The eyes were still black. It still smelled like rotten road kill. What's the difference?

"Max!" Griffin bellowed from inside the SUV. She stood up quickly and looked around and noticed they were quickly getting surrounded. She jumped into the driver's side door and turned to count heads. Everyone was accounted for. Cliff looked to be in shock, his skin a pale white, fists clenched tightly against his thighs.

Griffin had already started the SUV, so she dropped it into drive and jumped on the accelerator. The truck's tires squealed slightly as they took off. She had to avoid a group of five infected coming down the road, but she clipped one and it went flying away from the bumper.

"Where did all of these things come from?" Max asked absentmindedly, her focus on driving quickly and carefully through the curving farm roads.

"They seem to group together. Maybe that's how they find food? Like a pack?" Turner said from the backseat.

"What was with the fast ones?" Griffin added.

"The one I took down, was faster, it moved more like....a human. But I didn't see anything different on the body," Max answered.

From memory, Max knew they followed the road they were on through the curves, to a bridge that would take them over a river that ran through the countryside. Once they were over that bridge, they might have access to a larger road. She had been avoiding them for that exact reason. To see so many on a small road was enough reason to take the risk. Her goal was to put some distance between them and the large horde of infected. If they caught them, there would be no fighting them all off. They were on their last bullets. There was no fighting a horde by hand.

Coming around a corner blocked by trees, for a moment Max thought she saw smoke. With the curves in the road, it was hard to pinpoint where the smoke was coming from. Could be any of the farms, crops, or trees. They hadn't seen anyone alive since they had left the motel. Were all the inhabitants part of this infected horde?

Max slammed on the brakes as the bridge came into view. She hit the steering wheel in frustration. Sitting in the middle of the bridge was a ramshackle barrier, most likely put into place by the nearby residents. That would have been easy to move, but it looked like people didn't see it or something else violent had happened. Now there were cars crashed into it, some still smoking. In some cars, Max could see people or bodies of what were people. They didn't move, killed on impact or something worse.

"Now what?" Griffin asked, staring at the same thing Max was.

"Let's see if there's any other way across," Max said. She pulled the SUV closer to the bridge entrance. Throwing it into park, she jumped from the car immediately, this time tomahawk in hand. She walked to the side of the bridge closest to her. The river flowed quickly, full of snowmelt and rain. It was clearly deep. The embankment down to the water was steep and muddy, nothing their SUV was going to manage. She met Griffin in the middle, where he was walking back from his side of the bridge.

"Anything?" Max asked. Griffin just shook his head.

"Shit," Max muttered.

The horn of the SUV honked once, causing Max to jump. Looking back, she could see Turner signaling them. Griffin and Max ran in unison back to the truck, only to see the horde of infected coming from the trees. Max stared at them for a moment. If she didn't know any better, they took a shortcut to keep up with them, cutting through the trees instead of being on the road.

"Max, we're gonna have to run," Griffin said.

"I don't like being out in the open like that," Max replied. She continued to wrack her brain, trying to think of a solution. They hadn't seen another road in the last mile. Could the SUV make it a mile through the horde?

"No Max, we can't make it in the truck," Griffin said.

"Don't read my mind. It's annoying," Max shot back.

They ran to the back of the SUV and started pulling the go bags. As they did Turner and Jack jumped from their door. Cliff sat stone still. Max gave Jack her pack and helped her strap it in place. It was a little heavier than the girl was used to since they were trying to carry enough supplies to support five people. When they were all strapped up and ready to go, the infected's growing and snarling could be heard. Cliff had still not moved.

Max ran to his side of the car and swung open the door. He looked at her and she could see he was lost in his flashbacks, losing his wife, watching his son being eaten. Though she sympathized, she didn't have a moment to waste. She grabbed his face and forced him to look at her.

"It's time to go. NOW," she yelled at him. He didn't budge.

"Cliff, I want to help you. But I have a daughter. You know that means I will leave you here. That is NOT what your wife would want," Max said.

"Max, we HAVE to go," Griffin called to her from near the bridge, where he waited with Turner and Jack.

"One minute," Max yelled back.

"Max, you don't have a damn minute," Griffin bellowed. Max could see him from her peripheral vision, running toward her. Max decided she had to take matters into her own hands or leave the man to be eaten. She hauled off and slapped him across the face. The blow made her hand sting. His own hand flew to his cheek and color almost immediately rose from his neck into his face.

"Be angry damnit, I'm better with that than defeated. Now get your ass OUT of this car and let's go," Max screamed. Cliff started to move, but Max grabbed him by the collar and drug him out of the car at the same time. Griffin ran passed them and Max saw him sink his blade into an approaching infected. Where that one fell, five more approached.

Cliff was finally on his feet, fumbling toward the bridge. Griffin had Max by the backpack strap, practically dragging her, and looking behind them.

"I swear to God, Max, if you put yourself on the line for someone else one more time," he growled at her.

"What are you, my keeper? I had a daddy, it wasn't you," Max shot back sarcastically.

Griffin didn't say anything else, obviously not wanting to feed into her sarcastic attitude. They reached Turner and Jack right behind Cliff, who was finally getting his wits about him. Turning, Max could see some of the faster infected coming around the front of the SUV focused on their group. Getting to the other side of the accidents was their best bet. And then just keep moving.

"I'll stay here and deal with what's coming, get Jack to the other side," Max said, handing her pack to Cliff. He slung it on without question. Max palmed her knife in her left hand and tomahawk in her right. Griffin handed his pack off to Turner, squaring off with her, a look on his face daring her to argue with him. Instead, she turned to Jack.

"Follow Turner, stay where he says and stay quiet," Max instructed her. Jack flung her arms around her mother for a moment and squeezed.

"Be careful, Momma."

"I'm right behind you. Go!" Max said, pushing Jack toward Turner and Cliff. She watched only long enough to see Turner lift Jack over the concrete barrier that had been erected. She landed on the hood of a car, where she waited for Turner to join her before moving.

"Well this is fun," Max said. She checked her 9mm clip quickly, already knowing it was full. But it was the only clip she had with her, so she would use it as a last option.

"We always wanted to travel," Griffin gritted out. Even in the situation, Max found herself laughing at his joke.

Four faster infected reached them first. They stepped forward as a team, each attacking the first within their reach. Max swung her tomahawk and slammed it into the skull of the first infected, but there was a second directly behind it, hissing and grasping at her. Using the momentum from the first, Max spun and kicked out with her boot, slamming the infected in the chest. It was faster, but it still had a hard time recovering from a blow that caused it to fall. Her tomahawk free, she moved to where the infected fought to stand and quickly ended it before it could.

Griffin easily handled the two that came at him. By the time Max turned to check him, both infected were dead at his feet. He motioned for them to retreat and she agreed. The remaining slower infected were reaching the back of the SUV and they wanted to be on the other side of the mess on the bridge before they reached the concrete barriers. The movements of Griffin and Max provoked the horde, causing them to growl and hiss louder. They clamored through each other, jockeying to be the first to the meal they thought was waiting for them.

Max vaulted over the first barrier and car, landing on her feet in between the accidents. Griffin was close on her heels. The ground was littered with hundreds of bullet casings, causing Max to pause and look closely at the wreckage around them. The concrete barrier was similar to those they had seen at the shelter, but those could be obtained anywhere there was a freeway. But the casings looked to be from automatic rifles, something the military would carry. She looked at the cars and realized many of them were riddled with bullets.

"What happened here?" Max said, verbalizing her concern.

"Someone attacked these people I think, but why would they do that?" Griffin answered as he peered into a car that had a dead body at the steering wheel. The man had been shot in the head and chest. He had no visible bites and couldn't have been driving if he was infected.

"They were killed just for driving to this barrier I think. Maybe they were trying to keep this horde from crossing the bridge? But why kill healthy people?"

"I don't know, Max, but we should go," Griffin said, pointing toward the infected that were reaching the concrete barrier on the other side of the car. The dead couldn't figure how to climb over and at first, Max thought they were in the clear, but then to the side, she saw something horribly grotesque.

"Oh god, Griffin," Max moaned, and pointed. Between the concrete jersey barriers and the fence for the bridge, there was a small gap. At this gap, an infected was forcing its way through. The gap wasn't quite large enough, but the infected pushed and Max had a full view of his legs as the skin pulled away. The loss of skin or muscle as it continued to push didn't slow it down. Finally, it fell onto their side of the barrier, but it couldn't stand again. Max felt bile rise in her throat and swallowed quickly so she didn't vomit right there. The infected started to try and pull itself along on the ground, still completely focused on reaching its meal.

"Jesus, that's it, we gotta go, Max, no more investigation time," Griffin said, grabbing her hand and dragging her away. As he pulled, her gaze ran across the cars. She pulled him to a stop when she saw one with a car seat in it. She couldn't see into the seat, but as they approached her heart was in her throat, so afraid of what she'd see.

"Don't, don't do this, Max. Let's just go," Griffin said, trying to pull her away.

Max ignored him. She walked to the other side of the wrecked car. It had gunshots along the hood, that had risen to the windshield, and struck the woman that had been driving. Her body was turned as if to shield or grab her baby. But she died reaching back. Coming around the side of the car, Max noted the lack of gunshots on that side of the car. When she got to where the car seat was, the door was open. She took a deep breath, before stepping around the door to see inside. A gasp escaped her as she was relieved to see that the car seat was empty.

"Where's the baby," Max said softly. She hunched slightly to look closer at the seat. The buckle was still secured. But the actual straps had been cut. She touched the cuts, trying to make sense of the situation. The mother wasn't shielding the baby, she was trying to get the baby before whoever was there did.

"Who would cut the straps and take the baby?" Griffin asked, coming up next to Max.

"Well at least we know it couldn't have been infected," Max replied. "They don't use knives."

"Yeah. But why take the baby and kill the mother?"

"I don't know. The whole situation doesn't make sense, does it," Max said.

The sounds of the infected seemed to intensify behind them. Turning back to see what was happening, they found some of the infected were flipping over the jersey barriers and were slowly working their way to their feet. Max and Griffin looked at each other and together they ran to the other side of the bridge, dodging cars, and hopping over debris. Max could see Griffin looking at her often, keeping her in his line of sight. He would touch her or push her encouragingly when they were moving. Max wasn't sure how to react to the behavior. She was too used to being alone, that she wasn't sure how to even accept companionship.

Reaching the end of the bridge, Jack came running for Max, hefting her heavy pack as she ran. Max caught her daughter with one arm and hugged her for a moment, before turning them both toward the road and continuing at a quick pace. Turner and Cliff fell into step with them. Max reached for her pack from Cliff, who handed it back to her without looking her in the eye. Max figured they would have to have a conversation later about him shutting down and her slapping him.

"They are making it over the barrier, so we have to keep going," Griffin was telling Turner.

"I hate being out in the open like this, maybe we can find a car that can be wired," Max was saying. And as if Mother Nature just needed to be heard, the sky opened and rain began to pour down on them.

CHAPTER NINETEEN

"You have got to be kidding," Max said, holding out her arms and looking up at as rain cascaded over her face.

"We need shelter, and quick," Griffin said, his words punctuated by the first bright strike of lightning.

The group decided that there had to be farms on the opposite side of the river as well. Max knew there was a larger town coming on their route, but it wasn't for another twenty or thirty miles. They couldn't walk that in the downpour and lightning. They began trudging up the road, staying in the center on the chance of any infected in the trees on this side of the river. Max found herself imagining the infected falling off of the embankment into the river as they tried to cross. She figured they couldn't swim but doubted drowning would kill them.

Thirty minutes into their walk, the trees opened up and a field surrounded by a small barbwire fence appeared. In the distance, a large structure could be seen, but with the rain, it was difficult to pinpoint what it was. It had a roof and that was all they really needed at the moment. One by one they hopped the barbwire fence, being careful to not cause injury that would need to be handled. Once in the field, the five of them ran for the building, involuntarily hunching down when lightning would light up the sky. Being struck by lightning was not something Max could fix with a first aid kit.

When they got to the building, they realized it was an old barn. Griffin pulled the door open and shined a flashlight inside first. Nothing moved in the dark building. The clouds above them were black as night as they rained down, causing the afternoon to feel like twilight. They all rushed into the barn for protection. Inside, they all took a moment to breathe and drip on the dusty ground.

Max, Griffin, and Turner did a full assessment of the building. The only entrance was the large door they came in through. There were large windows that had probably been for animals, but they were all shuttered and latched closed. There was some hay in the building, maybe stored there for the farm to use as needed. But beyond that, it seemed safe enough.

"We need to dry out," Max said, wringing her T-shirt at the bottom.

"Last thing we need is someone coming down with trench foot," Turner commented. Max glanced at him impressed. "Served in more than just the desert, ya know," he said defensively. Max just smiled.

Jack was Max's first priority. She took her behind some hay and had her strip out of all her wet clothing. She dressed in dry clothes from her pack, lucking out that not all of it was soaked in her pack as well. Her boots stayed off and she walked around in socks until everything dried out. Max pulled out a semi-dry shirt from her bag. It was better than what she had been wearing, so she pulled off the sopping wet shirt. As she laid it next to Jack's on a wood divider she heard a throat clear behind her.

Spinning, Max found Griffin standing behind the hay she was using as cover. He was shirtless and clearly watching her change. Instantly self-conscience, Max grabbed her dry shirt and pulled it over her head quickly.

"Eight years turned you into a perv, huh?" Max said, sidestepping him to grab dry socks.

"Eight years ago, you wouldn't have acted like it was a big deal," Griffin remarked back. "Did you have someone in South Carolina?"

"What? No! Why are you asking me that?" Max asked in disbelief. Why did he continue to want to have these awkward conversations?

"You're skittish, Max."

"Uh, no I'm not," Max replied in a voice that didn't even convince her. He stepped forward and she took a step back.

"You're always running. That's not the Max I knew," he said in a low voice.

"Well the Griffin I knew wasn't always acting like he was hunting me," Max shot back.

"I'm not the one that waltzed in and upended your life, Max. You showed up in mine," he said as he crossed his arms over his bare chest. She couldn't help but notice how he'd changed over the years. He was obviously an adult now, but the same things she found attractive then he still had. His smile was the same, his eyes still looked like the eighteen-year-old boy that said goodbye on his way to boot camp. But he had filled out. Now he was impressive with no shirt on, thicker with defined muscles.

He grinned at her as she stood silent and she realized she'd been caught checking him out. She huffed out an indignant sigh and turned back to her go bag to sort through dry clothes. He closed the distance and crouched down next to her.

"I was only coming to ask if you had any shirts that would fit me. All of mine got wet in the rain," he whispered near her ear. His breath caused the hair on her neck to stand up and goosebumps to raise down her arms. Noticing, he wrapped his arms around her from behind and rubbed his hands up and down her arms.

"Cold?" He asked.

"Yes, no, I mean yeah but I'm fine," Max stuttered. *What is happening to me?* She thought. She was acting like a stupid school girl, falling head over heels for the popular boy in class. Well, they were no longer high school students. They were adults. And Max was holding a gigantic secret from him that would blow up in her face eventually. She stiffened as she thought about Griffin rejecting her when he found out that Jack was his daughter. All of the flirty advances would stop, he would never be able to forgive her for keeping his daughter for him for eight years.

"So, a shirt?" Griffin asked.

"I don't have any more shirts your size. But here, take this blanket," Max handed him a microfleece blanket over her shoulder. "What about Turner? He need something?" Max asked, avoiding any additional uncomfortable conversation.

"Nah, somehow his stuff stayed dry. Cliff is insisting on not changing, though we convinced him to take off his boots and put on dry socks. We'll need to get more clothes for him eventually," Griffin said and stood up as he wrapped the blanket around his shoulders. Max stood as well and turned to face him.

"Listen, I'm sorry," Max said.

"Wait, what? Max Duncan is sorry? For what, may I ask?" Griffin said, giving her his boyish grin that she could barely resist.

"Shut it, or I will take it back," Max said. Griffin held up a hand to indicate she should continue. "I should have asked about Cliff joining us. I'm not used to this," she said motioning between them.

"This? You'll need to be more specific."

"You're a jackass, ya know? I'm not used to having a group, people around that might have an opinion on things. I've been on my own for a long time now," Max explained. Griffin grew serious and nodded, understanding.

"I get it."

"My gut is telling me this guy isn't dangerous. And after what he went through. I knew leaving him would be like killing him," Max continued softly.

"You're all heart, Max Duncan," Griffin replied, as he stepped closer to her again. This time she didn't back away, refused to seem like she was running.

"Momma?" Jack called from the other side of the hay pile. Griffin chuckled quietly as his pursuit was effectively cut off by an eight-year-old.

"Yeah, Jack?" Max called back, smiling slyly at Griffin as they stood close together.

"We were going to turn on a lantern in the center where we could set up a sleeping area. Turner is going to go outside and see how much light you can see. Is that alright?" Jack called.

"If Turner wants to do it, you don't have to ask, sweetie," Max replied. Jack was also not used to anyone else being in charge of what was happening with her. She solely knew to rely on her mother's judgment and none other. Though the little girl loved being around people, she also referred back to her mother always.

She could be heard speaking to Turner, their voices floating over to Max and Griffin in their private corner. They just watched each other, at a bypass. A much deeper conversation was needed, but privacy behind a stack of hay wasn't going to work. They still hadn't addressed the situation of the letters. Did she believe him? All these years later, why would he concoct such a lie? And it was a story he had told Turner before she ever came to North Carolina to find him.

"I believe you," Max said suddenly. *Damn me and my big mouth,* she thought to herself. She didn't have much of a filter, and it seemed to be obliterated with Griffin around. He didn't say anything, just raised an eyebrow.

"I believe you about the letters. I don't know why Mitch did what he did, but I believe you wrote and called."

Griffin's stance seemed to relax as if he had been holding on to that for eight long years. Carrying the burden of wondering whatever happened to them. That was something Max could definitely relate to. For the first time, she reached out to him first. She touched his face softly before raising up on her toes to press a kiss to his lips. She made it quick, but it was clearly a sign that she was feeling whatever he was too. But she pulled back quickly, remembering there was a lot of baggage to clear up still.

"But, Griffin, there are things. We have things to discuss when it all calms down a bit," she said. Thinking, she then added, "I never loved anyone else either."

After some checks and balances, the lantern was finally on its medium setting, and couldn't be seen from the outside. Max pulled the sleeping bags she and Jack had from their water coverings, thankful they hadn't unpacked from their camping trip before the plague hit. Max always wrapped their sleeping gear in waterproof bags to keep them from sleeping soggy. Turner and Griffin used the small fleece blankets Max and Jack carried. Jack and Max huddled beneath a sleeping bag with hay at their backs. Cliff laid further away, under the other sleeping bag, his back to the group.

They had eaten a dinner of MREs and pickles. Cliff had finally eaten like he was actually hungry, but he didn't say much. Max kept looking at him over their meals, hoping he'd say something. But he kept his eyes on his meal and only conversed with Jack about the food. Max looked at his back now and wished she knew what to say to the man. He'd lost everything and Max was trying to force him into caring enough to keep going on.

Griffin turned the lantern down once they all decided they were ready for sleep. The sound of the rain pelted the wood of the barn and Max found it hard to shut out the noise and fall asleep. Jack curled warmly against her side and was like her own personal heater. Her breathing fell deep and regular as she fell asleep quickly, exhausted from the running and chaos of the day. Max soon found her own eyes growing heavy, her body functions letting her know she had pushed too far and hard.

Gunshots were their alarm before the sun fully rose from the horizon. Max sat up straight from her hay bed, the cool morning air a shock to her warm body. Griffin was by her side in a moment, hand on her shoulder to stop her from reacting. She looked at him and nodded, she was awake and knew to stay quiet. She pulled on a jacket before standing and walking to a wall where she could peer through the cracks of the wood.

The adults all peered through different areas of the barn walls, trying to detect where the shooting was coming from. Max whistled low and motioned toward her wall as another volley of gunfire could be heard. She couldn't see anyone in the low light of dawn, but the sounds were definitely coming from her viewpoint. They all gathered on that side of the barn, waiting to see if the shooter would reveal themselves.

"There," Turner whispered, pointing. Max squinted seeing a few dark shadows and tried to distinguish which were infected and which were healthy.

"I count two, maybe three non-infected," Griffin whispered.

"Do we help?" Cliff said the first words he had spoken since Max had slapped him.

"No, we know what's out there. We would all end up dead," Max said matter-of-factly. She continued to watch, to see how the situation would unfold. Her first concern was if these shots would draw the infected to their barn

"I wonder how many made it over the barrier," Turner said.

"Not all of them were figuring it out, but plenty were," Griffin replied.

They waited another fifteen minutes, listening for any sign of infected or living coming their way. When nothing happened they all slowly moved back into the center of the barn where they had made their makeshift camp. The sun was starting to brighten the interior, giving them some time to prepare breakfast. They sat together to eat granola bars and fruit cups. In the silence they could hear the breeze through the wood panels, giving the indication of a cool day. However, the clouds and rain had disappeared for the time being.

Damp boots were strapped back on, and partially dry clothing was packed away. As they strapped on their packs, Max reviewed the map trying to determine where they were. She thought she knew where the bridge was they crossed. From there she estimated where the farm was. Her best guess was they were fifteen miles from the nearest town. With Jack that could take a day, if not longer. Walking at night would be a death trap, so they would have to find somewhere to sleep on their way.

The countryside was quiet as they walked through the fields back to the road they had come from. The group was tense, wondering where the infected went that were in pursuit that morning. They walked along the barbwire fence for a while, keeping their eyes out for anything out of sorts. The light glinted off of the shell casings that had fallen in the road. There were no other signs of a fight, no infected bodies, no large amounts of blood to indicate a healthy person was caught. Both parties seemed to be on their feet and ready for another fight somewhere.

Midday came with little talk among the members of the group. Jack stuck with her mother for most of the walk. When she started to get really weary, they decided stopping for lunch was a decent idea. A meal of beef jerky and chips was lunch, with bottled water. Max could see their supply of water wouldn't last more than a day, maybe two.

"We need to get back over to the river at some point, we need to fill up on water," Max said out loud. She didn't really expect an answer, but she couldn't handle the uncomfortable silence any longer. Typically she was one to avoid conversation when they came along. But when you were the only living humans in the area, it felt strange to not hear each other's voices.

"Going into the trees again could be a risk," Griffin replied.

"Worth it, we can't run out of water," Max said around a mouthful of jerky. Griffin just nodded and looked down at his own half-full bottle of water. They hadn't been able to take all of the water they had in the SUV before fleeing. Each bag only had four regular sized bottles. With Cliff, that amount stretched thin for four adults and one small child.

Getting to the river was easy. The road they walked seemed to follow the river's path for the most part. The five of them quietly entered the sparse tree line, looking around for anything that moved. Reaching the water line, Max quickly collected water to boil. She started a small fire on a dry spot near the water and set up to watch for any attack. Everyone sat with their backs to the water, knowing an attack couldn't come from that direction.

Snapping branches and the fall of rock against rock pulled Max's attention to the other side of the river. Standing directly across from them was a wild looking woman, her long hair flew in all directions. It was hard to tell her skin color from their distance due to the muck that seemed to cover her face. She stood watching Max and her group quietly. Max slowly raised her hand in greeting, but the woman just looked back the way she came and took off in the opposite direction.

"Strange," Max murmured.

"People are going to react differently to things I guess," Turner replied, shrugging his shoulders while he watched in the direction the woman ran.

A few moments later the moans of the infected could be heard. Max and Griffin stood quickly, looking around to find the sound. As the sounds grew louder, the infected appeared on the opposite side of the river exactly where the woman had been standing. The infected seemed confused about where their prey went. Max stood stock still and everyone on their side of the river was silent, waiting for something to happen.

Suddenly one of the infected looked their way and it's black eyes seemed to widen, almost like an expression of surprise. The look felt creepy to Max. Each time of these things acted human it made her skin crawl. Its attention now on Max's group, the infected broke off and started to try to make it to the river. The remaining infected looked over as the noise was made. Noticing the one infected had found food, the group followed.

"They can't swim," Max said matter-of-factly. She couldn't be sure of that, but they had no coordination to get across a river. Especially one that was moving as fast as the current between them now.

"Are you sure?" Cliff asked.

"Well, I mean I'm mostly sure," Max replied.

"I want to see this. It's good to know what they can do," Griffin said, standing square with his gun in his hand. Turner nodded his agreement and took up a post next to Griffin. Max stood slightly behind them trying to keep eyes on both sides of the river. She was interested in what would happen when the infected hit the water, but she was also concerned about an attack from the trees behind them. She looked down at the water that was just getting to a rolling boil in her small pot. That needed to boil for at least twenty minutes for her to feel good about it.

The group of infected seemed to stumble down the river embankment, one tumbling when it got to a pretty steep section. The body flipped over itself and for a moment it looked dead. But suddenly the head raised and its jaws continued to snap at the air while it seemed to move each limb individually to get back on its feet. The others continued down the easier path they seemed to have found. Their eyes were on the group of healthy humans across the river, not the water in between them.

The first to step into the river stepped down heavily, and it's foot found purchase. It took three more steps, wading deeper into the water. Max started feeling nervous as the others followed suit. Then one of the group seemed to slip, one leg going out from under it. The current caught it off balance and the infected went down into the water. The body bobbed and floated into the center of the river and it was carried off before they knew what had happened.

The loss of one from their group didn't slow down the rest of the infected. They weren't deterred by the rolling water between them and their prey. A second infected fell to its knees in deeper water and as the current took it, it knocked two additional dead over. The three could be seen rolling and turning through the water as it rushed them away. The last two infected pushed into the deeper water in the middle of their crossing. The water was pulling at the tatters of their remaining clothing.

Max slipped off her still damp boots in preparation. She was realizing she had been wrong. The infected couldn't swim. But when push came to shove, they were able to walk across a river when it wasn't over their heads. They couldn't select their footing the way a healthy person could. However, they could get lucky.

She pulled her knife and waded into the water waiting for the infected to reach her. Griffin and Turner came up behind her, Griffin letting his annoyance be known.

"Relax. Why waste ammo when I can just handle them here," Max said.

"Because it's not exactly safe to fight while you're standing in a cold river, balancing on slick rocks," Griffin said.

"I can handle this," Max replied.

Without more argument, Max took a few more steps toward the infected. The first came within an arm's reach of Max and she grabbed its outstretched arm and yanked it forward. The pull threw it off balance and it fell into the river. Max quickly bent and slammed her blade into the base of its skull. As she stood to fight the next walker, her foot came down on a sharp rock. Crying out she quickly tried to find her balance on a flat surface. Instead, she fell backward into the shallow water.

Before she could think, the infected was falling on her, trying to grab her legs. She quickly kicked out and landed a kick on the side of its head as she used her arms to pull herself backward. Her hands were grabbed from behind and she was hauled out of the river by Griffin and Turner. They unceremoniously dropped her on her rear in the dirt. Griffin turned and immediately shot the infected through the forehead.

Whirling to face Max, Griffin's face was painted in a mask of fury. Jack was at her side, pulling dry clothes from her pack. Max sat shivering and looking up at Griffin, waiting for the onslaught.

"Why do you insist on always putting yourself in danger?" He demanded.

"I slipped," Max replied. Her face heated with embarrassment. She hadn't thought twice about wading into the river. Dealing with the infected before it posed a true threat to them seemed the only solution. The noise of a shot could bring more walkers, but also they didn't really have the ammo to spare.

"I told you it wasn't safe. We are a group. We work together. I realize that's a foreign thing for you," he said angrily, throwing up his arms in irritation.

"Relax. We got it handled," Max responded. She didn't really know what else to say. Was she supposed to apologize for not listening to him? That wasn't going to happen.

"Because we pulled your ass from the river before that zombie bit into you," Griffin said through gritted teeth.

"That's what a team does, right?" Max said, blinking up at Griffin. His face flushed with anger. He knew she was being flippant. But continuing the argument wasn't going to change anything.

Max stood, ending the conversation. She took the clothing from Jack and went behind a few trees to change out of her soaking wet pants and shirt. Even without Griffin's admonishments, Max knew she was being risky with the river. But she made choices that were for the benefit of the group. She wasn't just throwing her welfare to the wind because it was fun. She yanked her shirt over her head and huffed out a breath. Having other people making judgments about her behavior wasn't something she was used to, nor did she think she wanted to get used to it.

"Momma?" Jack's voice came from the other side of the tree Max was behind. She walked around to face Max. Her face was pale and she looked scared.

"What's wrong, Jack?" Max asked. She looked around, searching for an attack. But she didn't see anything except trees. She could hear the murmur of talking between the men back at the river's edge.

"Are you ok?"

"Yeah. Why?"

"Griffin was really mad. Was he right? You put yourself in danger?" Jack asked quietly.

Max studied her daughter for a moment. In eight years Max had worked to never show Jack weakness. She always wanted the girl to know how to fight, be strong, be prepared and take care of herself. Max had always kept a strong face on around Jack. That's not to say Max hadn't felt pain or sadness over the years. She just kept her emotions private. Even from her daughter. Now Jack was seeing emotions from another adult. And she wasn't sure how to handle them.

"Everything out here is dangerous now, Jack. Sometimes I have to make decisions that are dangerous. But no, Griffin is wrong, I don't put myself in danger just to do it. I do it to protect you and the group," Max said. She bent to brush off her feet before pulling on dry socks and pushing her feet back into her partially damp boots.

"You'll be careful, right? I'm not sure what to do without you." Jack's lip trembled slightly as she talked. It was a look Max could remember from years before. The first time she fell off her bike after taking off the training wheels. She had scraped her knee. She had tried so hard to not cry, and her lip had trembled before the dam broke.

"Hey, you don't need to worry about that," Max said. She reached out to Jack and pulled her into her chest for a hug. Jack put her little arms around her mother's waist and squeezed tight. "I'm not leaving you, Jack. We will get to Montana and be safe."

The water had boiled and been cooled. Max carefully filled everyone's bottles that were low on water. Once they were all filled again, they made their way back to the open road. The sun was moving toward the middle of the sky. The rain had left the countryside damp. The smell of wet asphalt and dirt was in the humid air. The end of winter seemed to be holding on to spring, with a chill in the air even with the sun high in the sky.

An hour later they found a mostly dry place on the side of the road. They sat in a circle and made a snack of the random foods they had in their packs. Beef jerky, chips, canned peaches, and everyone got a can of soda that Max had packed. They ate in silence, watching the area for movement. Max studied Cliff who was sitting across from her. The man had still not spoken to her and she was starting to think she was going to need to start the conversation with the man.

"Cliff?" Max said to get him to look at her. He didn't say anything, just stared at her.

"Ummm, I'm sorry I hit you yesterday," Max said quietly. His face didn't change, he just stared at her, making her feel uncomfortable. He probably knew that deep down she wasn't actually sorry. She did what she needed to. She couldn't leave him to give up and die.

"I'm not," he finally replied.

"You're not? Then why the silent treatment?" When Max asked the question, the man's head fell and his shoulders slumped.

"Shame. I'm ashamed of myself," he whispered without looking back up. Griffin and Turner looked at Max and back at Cliff. Griffin's face seemed to tell Max to fix things. She just looked at him, helpless to console or even know what words she needed to say to make Cliff feel better. Griffin just looked at her pointedly and then gestured to Cliff. Max sighed inwardly. She felt completely inept.

Getting up from her spot, Max switched seats with Jack so she could sit next to Cliff. When she settled on the ground next to him, he looked over at her. Sadness washed his face, making Max think about his laugh lines again. When would he ever think about laughing or smiling again?

"Cliff, you shouldn't feel shame. You lost your family. That is the hardest thing anyone can go through. We just don't want you to lose yourself now too. Your family wouldn't want that for you," Max said softly. She could see Griffin watching them out of the corner of her eye. There was a small smile on his face.

"I know. That's what I thought when you hit me and made me think about it. My wife would never want me to give up. But I miss them so much," he said, finishing his sentence with a quiet sob. Max could feel her heart break for him. She reached behind and softly patted his back. Feeling awkward she almost pulled back, but Cliff leaned into her, his head on her shoulder as he cried. Max started to panic, not knowing how to handle the physical interaction. But as she listened to Cliff cry, she realized being there for him to lean on was all he really needed from her. She wrapped her arm around him then, and held him to her, allowing him to share the burden of his sorrow.

CHAPTER TWENTY

"Of course, I can still ride," Max said indignantly.

"Calm down. It was just a question. How do I know what you've been doing the last eight years," Griffin shot back.

"Can the two lovebirds keep their arguing to a minimum? We do still need to worry about the infected," Turner said from the other end of the alley they were all standing in.

The group had come to a small town that seemed to consist of a truck stop, convenience store, trailer park and one biker bar. Outside of the bar, a row of bikes sat. At the end, there were five bikes laid over on their sides and piled onto one another. Something or someone had crashed into them and caused a domino effect. The ones standing looked to be in perfect condition. Griffin came up with the idea that riding would get them to where they needed to go faster. They would be able to navigate smaller areas easier. Max couldn't disagree, though they would need to avoid any infected.

"We don't even know if there are keys," Max said.

"It's a small biker bar. I would bet the keys are on the bikes, or inside the bar somewhere," Griffin replied.

"I see helmets too," Turner said, peering around the building they were hiding behind. So far they hadn't seen any infected. They also hadn't seen any living people, which led them to believe the people that belonged to the motorcycles were somewhere, walking infected. To be safe, they had stayed hidden between the store and truck stop that sat across the street from the bar.

"Ok, who's going to check?" Max asked. The question was her way of showing she was trying to work on being part of the group. She didn't just assume she was going and start running across the street. Her first inclination had been to do exactly that. But she had taken a moment to think about what Griffin had said. Not only that but also the fear she had seen on Jack's little face. She didn't want her daughter to be scared any more than she needed to be.

"You and I will go. Turner will stay here with the bags, Jack, and Cliff," Griffin said. He dropped his backpack near the wall, followed by Max's. They each held their knives in their hands, guns on their hips.

"I can't ride one of those," Cliff said.

"It's ok. We can double up," Max said.

A few minutes later Griffin and Max stepped into the open and waited for any immediate threats. Nothing moved, the only sound was the light breeze through the trees along the sides of the main road. Together they ran to the row of bikes. Max quietly checked the first few and found no keys nearby. Griffin started on the other end and held up a pair of keys in triumph. The keys belonged to a large cruiser. Perfect for two adults.

It only took about three minutes to check the rest of the bikes and find no keys. They stood together looking at the door of the bar. There were no windows and the door was solid wood. Max felt apprehension crawl up her back at going in blind. Griffin looked at her for a moment and she nodded her head, prepared for whatever may lay ahead of them. They decided to fling open the door and wait to see if anything attacked, before entering into the dark abyss.

Max pulled a small penlight she had in her back pocket. Griffin stood to one side of the door and Max posted on the other side. Griffin counted down silently and grabbed the door, pulling it back toward him. They both waited. The sounds of scraping against the ground were immediately heard, followed by the smell of death wafting out into the open. Max covered her nose and stepped back slightly. With no windows and no power, the bar had just been sitting with the infected rotting away inside.

Suddenly a body appeared in the doorway opening, an infected drawn to the movement and light of the outside. As it stepped forward, Max didn't hesitate, slamming her knife into the temple of the large body. The infected fell in a pile on the sidewalk, leather chaps and vest boasting his bike affiliations. The sight of a healthy person enraged the infected still inside the bar, and growls rose from the darkness.

Max raised her light for a moment, illuminating the entrance area of the bar. She jumped back quickly from a pair of arms that thrust through the door toward her. A broken body followed, reaching out for Max. Before she reacted, Griffin was stepping up to take the infected down. Max moved to the side of the body allowing it to fall and looked back up into the entrance of the bar. She could hear more infected inside, but they weren't at the entrance yet.

"We're gonna have to go in," Max said. Griffin nodded and joined her at the entrance, peering into the dark with the small illumination from her penlight. They moved together into the bar, Griffin slightly behind and to her left. They moved as a team, the memory of training as children coming back to them. Griffin tapped Max's shoulder, moving them together to the left, staying along the inside wall.

With the door propped open and Max's small light, they could make out vague shapes as they moved through the room. There was bar furniture, plain wood tables and chairs around the room. Max imagined they were once arranged in some sort of organized style, but now the items were busted and thrown around the bar. The ground was sticky under their boots, whether from years of filth or the blood from the battle that ensued, Max couldn't guess.

They reached the first corner of the bar and were turning a dark corner when Griffin let out a low curse. He disappeared from view and Max panicked for a moment, turning to point her light. As she swung the beam his head popped back up from where he had bent. At their feet an infected lay, now truly dead. His legs were trapped beneath a jukebox that had been tipped over. He wore leathers similar to the biker she had killed outside. Bending down, Max found a chain attached to his belt, keys dangling on the end. She held them up to show Griffin, who nodded.

Two down. One set left to find.

They moved around the room, running into the bar. Bar stools littered the ground around the bar area, some looking to have been used as weapons. Behind the bar, growling could be heard from the ground. Griffin and Max moved to the opening, finding an infected on the ground, one leg bent at an unnatural angle. The break explained why the infected man didn't come running the moment they entered the bar. Carefully Max stepped around the mess behind the bar and embedded her knife blade into its head. She searched the belt of the body but assumed it was the actual bartender who may not own a bike at all.

Shuffling from the opposite side of the bar drew their attention. The pair stood behind the bar, waiting to see what the darkness held. Two infected stumbled forward. One glance at Max and Griffin, and the two fought to get through the sea of furniture and debris on the bar floor. Griffin grabbed a nearby barstool and gripped it by the legs. Taking a step into the swing he smashed the stool against the head of the first infected. The body flew off its feet, crashing into the bar before slumping to the ground.

Max rushed toward it, slicing into its temple before it could get it's bearings again. She ran her hand along where the belt should have been, but her hand encountered stickiness and warm. She yanked her hand back and cried out. She pointed her penlight at the infected and realized her hand had been touching the intestines that were hanging from its stomach. Max started to retch, not able to hold back the bile that was rising in her throat. She turned to her hands and knees and emptied her stomach contents at the feet of the infected.

"Max!" Griffin cried out when he heard her being sick.

"I'm ok, I'm ok," she said weakly as she stood. She used a clean piece of her shirt to wipe her mouth. Looking around, she realized Griffin had handled the last infected while she was puking. He stood next to her now, staring at her in the dim light trying to determine what was going on.

"I, uh, his guts were where his belt should have been. So yeah, I touched more than I wanted to. Just caught me off guard," Max rambled. Griffin pushed her hair away from her face, looking her over. She pushed his hands away, turning toward the last infected to search for keys. This time she used her penlight to make sure she didn't get any unpleasant surprises. The second body also proved to be unsuccessful for keys. Frustrated Max spun away, looking around to see if somehow either of the infected had dropped them.

"None here either," Max said to Griffin as he followed her and her small light deeper into the bar. The further they moved from the open door, the deeper the darkness became. In the back of the bar, a pool table sat. Pieces of pool sticks were littered across the table, dark spots stained the felt top. Signs of a massive attack were all throughout the bar.

Max shined her small light across the ground, looking for anything that shined. As they walked their boots made sickly noises, sticking to the fluids that had been spilled during whatever attack happened. Max could picture that the news of the plague hitting the more populated areas reached the small town, but because they weren't seeing it, it didn't feel possible. These bikers came to the bar like they normally did, but someone sick showed up as well.

Near the back wall, two bodies were piled. Griffin and Max approached them slowly, watching them closely for any movement. When they were close enough that the small light provided some illumination, they could see both of them had gunshot wounds to the head. Max feeling relieved that they wouldn't be waking up to attack, crouched down and checked their belts. The sound of a chain indicated she had found her prize.

"Let's get out of here," Max said. The dark bar was making her skin crawl. She was ready to be back out in the cool sunshine.

They ran back to the hiding spot where they left Turner, Cliff, and Jack, holding the keys they had found. They were able to match them to the three bikes they would need. It was decided that Jack would ride with Griffin, Max would ride alone and Turner would double with Cliff on the larger cruiser they found. Max hadn't argued when Griffin suggested Jack ride with him. She knew he wouldn't have suggested it if he wasn't sure it was safe for Jack. Max also hadn't ridden double with someone in years, so she didn't want to risk Jack on the back of her bike.

"We should check the store," Max said. They were strapping their packs to the bikes, making sure everything was tied down tightly. Jack was wearing a small helmet that must have belonged to a woman riding with someone that had come to the bar before the plague hit. Max had tightened the strap on it a few times, checking and rechecking that her head would be safe in the event of an accident.

"We're running a little light on provisions. Better to check now while we can," Max added, motioning toward the store. The windows in the front were busted out, the place looking to have been looted. But there was truly no way of knowing what was left without entering the store and picking through what was inside.

Agreeing with her, Griffin accompanied Max into the store, leaving Turner to protect Jack and Cliff if necessary. The inside of the store was dark and dank. The smell of blood seemed to be heavy on the air, but with the mess of spilled milk spoiling on the ground, it was hard to pinpoint. Griffin and Max worked together to search the remaining canned goods. There weren't many, the store resembling a small gas station market. They took everything that was there, as well as crackers and ramen soups.

Back at the bikes, they packed the food into saddlebags on the bike Max would ride. Everyone began to climb onto their bikes. Max stood with Jack as Griffin got his bike started. It had an electric start which made it catch quickly.

The gas tank looked to be three fourths full, which was a blessing that would get them to the next large city at least. Once there they planned to hot-wire a vehicle large enough for them.

Jack climbed onto the back of the bike with Griffin easily. They had found keys to a Harley with a passenger backrest on the back. Jack settled in as Griffin kicked up the kickstand. Max leaned close to Jack, yelling over the louder than necessary exhaust.

"Hold on tight, you hear me, Jack?" Max yelled. She was more than a little nervous about Jack riding with someone other than her. Common sense told her it was the right thing to do. Jack nodded her little helmet and leaned forward to wrap her arms around Griffin's waist. He patted her arm before looking over at Max and nodding his understanding to her.

Max went to her own bike and put on her helmet. She mounted her bike and kicked up the kickstand. Her bike was a kickstart and with one foot planted strongly on the ground, she used all of her weight to kick down on the kickstand. The bike immediately caught, an obviously well taken care of bike to be a one-kicker start. The smell of exhaust reached her nose as she moved her bike slowly up behind Griffin's. They turned on their seats to watch Turner starting his with electric start, Cliff behind him attempting to figure out how to be comfortable for their ride.

As they took off, Griffin headed toward the train track they had agreed on using until they had to move up to the freeway. They wanted to stay as concealed as they could. As long as the track was clear, they should be able to ride there for a few miles. Max quickly got the feel for the unknown machine under her. It was hard for her to not feel glee at the freedom she felt, with the cool air whipping around her.

Looking forward, she felt that glee slip away as she thought about the scene she was seeing. Griffin riding, with their daughter behind him. Keeping her safe and making decisions about what was the best for her. And him having no idea that she was his daughter. Max also felt fear for how Jack would react once Max told her the truth as well. Would she feel cheated, angry, understanding? Would her daughter understand how she ended up at a place where she didn't tell Griffin that he had a daughter?

Jack's hair flew behind her, loose under her helmet. Her dark hair was all Max. Her attitude and what she had learned from Max made her more and more like her mother. Her heart, her sense of humor, those were Griffin. Max loved her daughter, Jack always knew that. But it was well known that Max wasn't the most emotionally involved mother. She tried to always provide what her daughter needed but being around Griffin had made Max question so much about the years that had passed.

Guilt flooded her. Her heart believed Griffin, he had written her. If she had just tried harder, reached out to his family, he would have known about Jack. And Max wouldn't have grown into the bitter woman she had become. Jack wouldn't have been cheated out of the years of Griffin in her life. On the heels of the guilt, resolve followed. Turner knew the truth, and it would soon be the time to tell Griffin.

Thirty minutes into their rough ride along the railroad, Griffin turned into the woods, following a slim path. Max slowed and turned sharply to follow. She checked her side mirrors and found Turner to not be far behind them. They road as fast as they could through the trees, feeling unsafe and vulnerable on the bikes. When Max burst into the open, she watched as Griffin and Jack turned down the freeway and headed down the clear road. Max found herself grinning as she was able to increase her speed and fly down the open space.

Rooftops could be seen on either side of the freeway as the sun dipped low in the sky. As they entered the city limits, cars were littering the freeway. Max planted a foot on the bumper of one as she maneuvered her bike through one wreck. Slowing, she pulled up next to Griffin, who sat idling looking at the city. It was getting late, none of them wanted to be out during the night. Entering the city had risks of its own.

Turner pulled up next to them and they all switched off their motors. Riding was exhausting, and they hadn't taken many breaks on their way, wanting to cover as much ground as possible. Max kicked out her kickstand and swung her leg over the seat. Her legs felt like jelly and pain radiated through her hips. Cliff looked as bad as Max was feeling, the man limping in a circle trying to work the needles out of his body. Griffin helped Jack get off the back of his bike, the little girl showing no ill effects from riding, youth being a beautiful thing.

"What do you think, Max?" Griffin asked.

"I'm not sure. We need shelter for the night. Tomorrow we can find a car," Max replied.

"Let's stay on the outskirts," Turner suggested, motioning toward the first exit they saw. "Better to stay where fewer people were when the plague hit. Downtown is going to be a real nightmare."

"Maybe an abandoned house. I've had luck with that before," Max mused out loud.

"I'm sure there's plenty of those around here," Turner said.

Casting her eyes around the freeway, the shadows began to deepen as the sun moved lower in the sky. Those shadows played with her mind, creating scenes of moving creatures watching them from a distance. She stared into some of them for a moment, proving to herself that nothing hid or waited for them. The infected didn't wait. They came for their meals directly.

They stretched and forced their bodies back onto the bikes. Slowly they exited the freeway and turned into one of the first neighborhoods they saw. The scene was similar to those Max had seen since society began to break apart. Debris was strewn along the street, anything from random trash to clothing, shoes, and toys. There were suitcases sitting next to a van in one driveway. *A family that never had the chance to escape,* Max thought to herself sadly.

Max chose a house that didn't seem as disturbed as the others. Her gut told her that no one was home at the start of the plague, making it less likely to be filled with the infected now. Even with the gut feeling, when they cut off their engines, they sat and waited for movement or noise. When nothing came, Griffin went to the front door with Turner covering his back. When they returned to the bikes, they confirmed the house was empty.

Carrying their supplies in, they found a softly colored home with mint walls in the kitchen. Max walked down the hallway slowly, looking at the family photos hanging on the walls. She tried to imagine what type of people lived in such a pretty home. The photos boasted of an old love, between two people that had been together most of their lives.

Photos of grandchildren were hung in abundance, the sign of a life full of family and love.

"It's sad, isn't it?" Griffin said, walking up behind her.

"I wonder what it was like to live this life," Max said quietly, running her finger along a frame that held the older couple surrounded by adults who were probably their children and grandchildren at their feet. "This is what normal life should look like. Love, marriage, children, a life built together. I never saw that."

"I did. Everyone is different though, Max. What works for some, doesn't work for everyone. These people had a life full of love in these photos. At least when the plague hit, they already had a chance to have it."

"Would we have had this? If I had gotten your letters?" Max asked, her voice almost a whisper. At first, she wasn't sure Griffin had heard her. He didn't answer, didn't move his gaze from the family photo on the wall.

"Maybe. Why didn't you have it with someone else?" Griffin asked.

Suddenly a realization came over Max. They were safe for the moment in this house. The secret was laying heavy on her mind. If she didn't tell him while she had a quiet moment, she would end up blurting it out ungracefully during an inappropriate time. She knew that much about herself. Without really knowing the words she would use, she turned to him in the hall.

"We need to talk. I have some things I need to say," Max told him. He looked at her and nodded. Together they made their way deeper into the house until they came to a room. It was a guest room and office, with a small twin bed and large working area. The room was littered with yarn and fabric, boasting of an artistic hand that enjoyed a lot of time in the space. Max turned in the room, looking at all of the details. She felt like an intruder, even though she knew the likelihood that the people were alive was slim.

"What's up, Max?" Griffin asked. She looked at him. Her hands were shaking, so she gripped them together in front of her. However, that just made her knuckles go white with the strain, so she started fiddling with items in the room.

"You should probably sit down," she started. Griffin looked at her strangely but then took a seat across the room on the small bed.

"You said you wrote. I didn't know that. When you left, I was heartbroken. My dad knew it. But he must have made sure I never found your letters," she said.

"We've already been through this, you said you believe me," he replied. But Max didn't stop talking.

"After my sadness passed, or maybe it never passed, I just pushed it away. I got angry. I was so mad at you for leaving me. I was mad at you for not following through with the promises and plans we had," Max said, her voice shaking. She could feel tears prick in her eyes, and she squeezed them shut trying to prevent any from falling. One thing Max didn't do was cry. She paused. Not sure what her next words should be, even though she knew what needed to be said. Her throat was sandpaper and she debated running from the room.

"Ok..." Griffin said, urging her to continue.

"The anger was worse I think, because of Jack," Max finally said. Before he could say anything, she kept talking. Her back was to him as she spoke, she couldn't bear looking into his eyes, to see the hatred he would have to feel for her.

"It was only a few weeks after you had left. Before you were able to write I'm guessing. When I found out," she whispered.

"Found out what? Say it, Max," Griffin said, his voice eerily calm. It made her spin to look at him. His hands were balled into fists on the mattress as if he were waiting to hit something.

"Found out I was pregnant," Max confessed finally.

Griffin sat stone still, his face a blank mask. His eyes seemed unfocused as his mind worked through the information that Max had given him. She was debating going to him, sitting next to him, trying to make him understand why she made the choice she had. But she imagined there was no way to see this through her eyes. In his mind, she had left him, he had written and she never responded.

"How old is Jack? I don't know why I never asked," Griffin asked suddenly.

"She's eight."

"Damn it, Mitch," Griffin suddenly said, exploding up off the bed to pace the room. Max stood still in her spot watching him walk. "He knew. He knew what he was doing keeping us apart. I mean sure we were too young to have a baby. But we would have done the right thing," Griffin was saying more to himself then Max. Suddenly he whirled to face her, with the anger she expected finally on his face. His eyes blazed with it as his gaze bore into hers.

"Why didn't you try to get in touch with me? You could have called my parents if you really thought I had left you with no contact. They would have told me about Jack," he demanded.

"Keep your voice down, please," Max said in a low voice.

"She doesn't know either, does she?"

Max just shook her head. Jack had always accepted the story of her father being gone as truth, never questioning further into it. Max assumed she was just too young to really understand the concept of not having two parents.

"I didn't call. I didn't look for you. I was wrong to do that. But I was in pain. The last thing I wanted was you coming back to me, just because I was pregnant. You didn't want me, so we didn't need you," Max said, trying to explain.

"Eight years, Max, eight years! You could have picked up a phone, found me. I missed out on eight years. With her, with my daughter," Griffin said, his voice gruff with emotion. Max's guilt seemed to settle in her stomach, making her ill with it. She stepped toward Griffin, laying a hand on his arm. He didn't pull away, so she moved closer. She pulled his face to look at hers, so he could see the sincerity in her words.

"I am truly sorry. I was wrong. I think I've always known that. That's why I came to get you when everything went to shit. Part of me always thought I'd find you someday, and we'd hash this out. But then everything started ending. All I could think was what if something happened to you, or me and no one ever knew the truth."

"She doesn't know. She doesn't know I'm her father," Griffin said quietly.

"No. But I know we have to tell her. Maybe I should talk to her first?" Max suggested. Griffin just nodded at her and pulled away finally.

"You have every right to hate me for this, Griffin. And I won't blame you if that's what you decide," she said, her eyes full of sadness. She had known telling him this truth would ruin whatever road they may have found to lead them to what was meant to be all those years ago. Nonetheless, she had to tell him, Jack having her father in her life was more important than Max having a romantic relationship.

"I don't hate you, Max. I'm so damn mad at you right now though. And I need to figure that out."

"Ok." She couldn't say anything else.

"After you talk to Jack, can I have some time alone with her?"

"Of course. I'll let her know you want that."

Griffin walked out of the room without another word. Max followed behind him slowly. She watched him walk into the room where everyone was getting comfortable and thinking about dinner plans. The inside of the house was starting to get dim with no power for lights. Griffin walked up to Jack, running his hand over her head for a moment. She looked at him quizzically but smiled at the affection. He couldn't seem to take his eyes off of her. Max just stood in the doorway watching him while he watched Jack pull out items they needed for the night and discussing dinner with Turner. Suddenly Griffin stepped back and scrubbed at his eyes and Max knew he was hiding his tears.

"Jack, can you come with me for a minute? Bring a lantern." Max said from her perch in the hallway.

Jack didn't question, just grabbed a light from her pack and followed her mother down the hall. Max took her into the same room she had been in with Griffin. Before they turned the light on, they worked together to secure the shades tightly with fabric tape. Then for extra security, Max hung an additional piece of fabric from the curtain rod. The lantern emitted a soft white glow, lighting up the craft room for them.

Max sat on the bed and patted the seat next to her. Jack sat down and looked at her mother, curiosity in her eyes. Max smiled at her and touched the end of her hair that hung over her shoulder.

"Jack, I've never minced words with you before. What I have to tell you is going to be really hard," Max started. She watched Jack's eyes cloud with concern as she watched her mother speak.

"You've never asked much about your father," Max said.

"You said he was gone. I thought that was the story," Jack replied slowly, not yet understanding where the conversation was headed.

"That is what I said," Max said, trying hard to pick her words. "But if I'm telling the truth, I lied about that."

"You lied?" Jack repeated.

"Yes. I mean technically, yes, your father was gone. He was never around. He never met you. Because if he had, I know now, he would not have been without you."

"You know now? How do you know that?" Jack asked. Max knew her mind must have been racing with the implications. She wondered if she let her think about it long enough, would she put it all together.

"When I was young, I was very much so in love with my high school sweetheart. He and I had promises and plans. He left for the Army and he was supposed to write once he was allowed to in boot camp. Just after he left, I found out I was pregnant. With you. He never knew about you, because I never heard from him after he left for boot camp."

"So, he didn't want you, why would he want me?" Jack lifted her chin in defiance, wanting to defend her mother's actions, even though Max knew how wrong they were.

"It wasn't true though, Jack. He did write. For over a year. But I never knew," Max said, hedging around the fact of how she'd found out. Jack just looked at her, a question on her face.

"I know this now, and I just found out, because my high school sweetheart was Griffin."

Max waited, much like she did with Griffin. She was waiting for anger, disbelief, tears. But Jack sat still, staring at Max. The look reminded Max so much of Griffin's reaction, that she wanted to laugh out loud. However, she realized how wrong that would be at the moment, so she refrained. She touched Jack's cheek softly, trying to urge a response from her.

"Griffin?" She finally asked.

"Yes, honey. That's why it was so important we find him. I couldn't let him die, without...I don't know....knowing you, finding out he was a father. I couldn't find out he was dead, and you never know who your father was," Max said softly.

"I rode a motorcycle with my father today?" Jack asked, her voice a mere whisper that Max barely heard. She nodded her head in response. "Does he know now?"

"I just told him. I'm sure he'd like to talk to you. Would you like that?"

Jack didn't answer, only nodded her head slightly. Max squeezed her hand and left the room to find Griffin. He was at the end of the hall, waiting impatiently. Turner stood off to his side as if he was waiting for Griffin to bolt and do something reckless. He may have judged Griffin right, the man looked like he was ready to sprint down the hallway before Max even reached the end. He was nervous and fidgeting, but his eyes were on the door down the hall.

"I told her," Max said.

"And?"

"She'd like to talk to you," Max replied. Griffin turned his eyes to hers then. Max was sad, though not surprised, to see less warmth there than before. She knew it would take time for him to forgive her deceit. She didn't blame him.

"What do I say?" He asked.

"I'm not sure any of us know at this point. Just go in and talk to her. She'll probably let you know what she wants you to talk about," Max said with a small smile.

Griffin walked woodenly down the hall. When he got to the door, Max could see him take a physical moment to breathe and get himself together. When he disappeared into the room Max felt her heart crack, thinking of all the time she had wasted for them.

"You did the right thing, Max," Turner said, laying his hand comfortingly on Max's shoulder.

"Only took eight years."

CHAPTER TWENTY-ONE

Max finished dinner. Then because that didn't take her mind off of things, she unpacked her bags and inventoried her supplies. She counted and recounted food, making meal plans in her mind with what they had left. Going through the kitchen, she was able to replenish some of what they had used the last few days. She packed additional supplies in each pack so everyone had food on them for emergencies.

An hour later, the house was dark. Turner worked with Max to secure the windows, ensuring that they could use lanterns without letting anyone know they were hiding inside the house. They placed a few lanterns in the living room where they were all sitting. Cliff played solitaire with Jack's cards, keeping to himself. He didn't know what was going on, but he could sense something very personal was happening and he wanted to stay out of it.

When the door down the hall opened, Max hopped to her feet. Jack led the way, holding the lantern low to show their way to the living room. Max tried to judge her daughter's emotions, but her face was a smooth mask of nothing. The lack of an evidence of her first talk with her father made Max feel nervous and uncomfortable. A part of her wanted to protect her from any of this. Nonetheless, Max was certain once the initial awkwardness settled away, Jack would find a relationship with her father.

Griffin avoided looking at Max, heading straight for Turner when they came out. Feeling she deserved to know how their talk went, Max followed the men into the kitchen. Griffin whirled on her the moment she entered.

"So she just thought I was gone. No hero story about me being dead?" His voice was laced with sarcasm.

"I wasn't sure what else to tell her when she asked," Max replied.

"Wells, man, you two have things to talk about. I'm gonna go..." Turner started to say.

"No!" Griffin and Max snapped at the same time.

"Ok..." Turner said, stepping back from them and sitting at the small kitchen table.

"What did she want to talk about?" Max asked finally. Griffin just stared at her and she waited.

"She had questions. I answered what I could. She defended you," Griffin said with a wry laugh.

"This is hard on her. It's always been just her and I," she replied.

"It didn't have to be, Max. You cheated her of so much," he accused.

"I know. And I will have to ask her to forgive me, and hope that she does."

"She'll never stay angry at you. She loves you too much. I could have had that too with her," Griffin said sadly. The fight was seeping out of him, grief over what he missed filling in.

"There's still time. She's such a good girl. Her heart is real and pure. She loves everyone she meets," Max explained, a smile on her face. "All of that was in spite of being raised by me. So it must have been in the DNA you gave her. I have something for you to see."

Max pulled a small book from her back pocket. When she left their home in South Carolina, Max left everything behind, except this small book. The book held photos of the last eight years, at least one from each year of the life of Jack. She couldn't leave without it. She had hoped someday she would show Griffin. But even if she didn't find him, she wanted to always have those memories with her.

His hands held the book gingerly as if he was afraid of ruining it. When he opened to the first photo, he found Max, barely an adult, laying in a hospital bed with their baby on her chest. Max smiled slightly at the camera, exhausted from labor but so very enthralled with her baby. Griffin's hand covered his mouth, as he squinted in the darkness. Max pulled out her small penlight and gave it to him.

Sitting at the kitchen table next to Turner, Griffin used the light so he could see each photo in detail. Turner commented in all the right ways, saying how she was a beautiful baby and pointing out things that looked like Griffin. Max stood watching as Griffin tried to absorb each photo into his memory. When he reached the end, he went back to the beginning to look again. He traced her chubby baby cheeks with his finger, a soft smile on his lips.

Max left the kitchen to check on Jack and to get dinner ready for everyone. She found Jack sitting alone staring into space. She had a lantern next to her, shadows playing across her face making it hard for Max to determine her thoughts. She sat next to her and was just quiet for a few moments.

"He said he would have wanted me. And that he wants me now," Jack finally said into the space she was staring at.

"I'm not surprised. Who wouldn't want a daughter like you," Max replied quietly. Jack's small hand found hers and gripped her fingers tightly.

"I still love you the best, Momma. I'm not mad at you," Jack said.

"You don't have to love me best, Jack. You can love Griffin, your dad, as much as you want," Max said, squeezing her hand back.

"Will I love him? Will he feel like my dad?"

"It'll come. I'm sure of it, honey. He's shocked, just like you. But I can already see how much he cares about you," Max reassured.

"I like him. He's funny. And he doesn't treat me like a baby." That comment made Max smile. Jack the eight-year-old going on eighteen.

"You aren't a baby, but you still need your parents. And you know what, we need you," Max said quietly.

"You do?" Jack asked, looking at her mother incredulously. She never thought Max needed anything.

"Of course! Who would make sure we all were fed well? And who would make sure I was wearing dry clothes?" Max teased, bumping her shoulder into Jack's.

That was how Griffin found them when he came out of the kitchen. He walked over to hand Max back her book, which he did carefully, still acting like the book was the most precious thing he had ever seen. The thought made Max smile wider. He looked at Jack and smiled down at her.

"You were a very beautiful baby, Jack," he said.

"Oh, thank you," Jack replied shyly.

"I hope you know I wish I had been there for that," Griffin added.

"I know you do. Now that I know you, I kinda wish it too," Jack replied.

"We have a lot to do before we get to Montana, but once we're there, I hope I get the chance to know you a little better," Griffin hedged.

"Ok. I'd like that."

Setting up sleeping areas was tense. Cliff easily went off on his own, sleeping in the formal dining room, instead of in the living room with them. It was decided that Jack would sleep on the couch. Griffin was determined to never be far from the little girl. He and Max had to come to a compromise where they both had their heads near Jack on the couch. However, this set up put them sleeping right next to each other. While they argued over things, Turner set up his bed with a comforter he found in a bedroom. He stood watching them bicker with a huge smile on his face.

"Wipe that crap look off your face," Griffin shot over his shoulder at him.

"I don't know what you mean, Wells," Turner replied, feigning innocence.

"Nothing is funny about this," Griffin said.

"Well it's a little funny," Max interjected. Griffin just glared at her, which made her choke on a laugh. Jack watched them both in astonishment. She couldn't figure out the situation for herself, but her mother and father couldn't seem to figure it out either.

"You are going to be great at this co-parenting thing," Turner added, as he laid down on his makeshift bed.

"Yes, I've become a professional in the last few hours since I found out I even had a kid," Griffin said gruffly.

"I'm sure you'll do fine. It's not like I know what a father should be like anyway," Jack suddenly said. All of the adults in the room stopped and looked at her. Just like that, the tension left the room and they were all laughing. Jack smiled, her joke doing exactly what she had hoped. Though it was a joke, it wasn't untrue either, Max realized. Jack had no idea how a father should act. She had only seen Gramps with her momma and she was old enough now to know that wasn't a normal father, daughter relationship.

With the lanterns turned off the house was pitch black. Max still couldn't get used to no street lights or business signs lighting up windows even after you'd gone to bed. The neighborhood was eerily quiet as well, the lack of sound almost worse than a street full of traffic and people. Right then Max would have done anything for living people yelling and shouting throughout the houses. The silence grated on her nerves making it very difficult to think about sleeping.

Jack's soft snores behind her on the couch indicated her daughter didn't have the same problem.

"She fell asleep fast," Griffin whispered. Max turned in her sleeping bag to face him. Though she couldn't see him clearly, she knew he was close to her.

"She can fall asleep anywhere really, she's been like that since she was a baby," Max answered.

"Tell me what it was like with her as a baby."

Max sighed. There was so much to say. "She was quiet. Sometimes it made me nervous. I knew nothing about being a mother, and here I was with a brand new baby and no one but my dad around to help me."

"Mitch must have hated me."

"I don't know if it was hate, to be honest. He never said he disliked you. Just that he believed you weren't coming back. But he said that knowing you were writing and he was hiding it from me. I think it was more about keeping Jack and I on the compound."

"How did you end up on the East Coast?" He asked in a whispered tone.

"After a year or so, I realized that Mitch was worse than he was when I was a kid. He was horribly paranoid about everything. He used to try every jar of baby food or bottle of formula before she could eat it. He was convinced that someone would try to kill out a whole generation of babies to start a fall of the human race."

"Jesus," Griffin breathed.

"Yeah," Max agreed. She continued, "So after I realized it wasn't going to do Jack any good to stay on the compound, I decided to move as far away as possible. We had family in South Carolina, they let us live with them for a while before I got on my feet."

"Did Jack like it there?" He asked.

"I think so. She had lots of friends at school. And we were able to go camping whenever we wanted. The thing about Jack is, she's better with people than I am," she said with a quiet laugh. When Griffin replied she could hear the smile in his voice.

"Well, she definitely got her snarky humor from you."

"That's probably true. She's been dealing with me for eight years. She doesn't know any better."

"I just don't understand it, Max. You were alone with a baby. Why wouldn't you have wanted my help?" He reached out in the dark, looking for Max's hand. She met him halfway and let him squeeze her fingers. She felt like he was giving her a signal that they would work it out, talk it to death, and figure it out together.

"I was young. I was determined to not crawl back to someone who I thought had left me. It was as simple as that. I grew up with one parent, so I didn't even really think that would hurt Jack in the long run."

"But you didn't have a choice to know your mother because she died. I was alive," Griffin replied, his voice a little louder now. Max shushed him. She didn't want his anger to wake Jack and upset her.

"I know. But never knowing her, didn't leave me with any pain from that. I mean sure I wondered, but it wasn't hurtful to me. I figured Jack would just be the same." She didn't have any other explanations for him. It was more a choice made by a bitter girl left alone to give birth to her child alone. And that bitterness carried with her for years. Once she wasn't angry, she then felt it was too late to change her choice.

"I was overseas a lot in those years with the Army. But I would have tried."

"I know."

They went silent after that and Max felt emotionally drained from the day. Griffin seemed to sense that and he didn't ask any more questions. As she started to fall asleep, she was awoken by Griffin shifting and getting out of his bed. She could see his outline, crouching over Jack's sleeping form. She watched as he fixed her sleeping bag that she had tried to kick out of. He tucked her in and just looked at her. Max knew he couldn't see her clearly, but he was still trying to comprehend the fact that the little girl was his.

The sun disappeared from them the next day. The sky was angry and black with clouds rolling in. A wind whipped through the neighborhood, moving debris and making noises all around them. Max stood next to a window that pointed out to the street. She had lifted a side of the covering and was watching to see if anything was more than wind and debris.

The sounds of the wind against the window and the sounds of the house creaking prevented her from hearing anyone approach. She almost dropped the covering to step back when she saw them, afraid of being spotted. Quickly she realized they were living, not the infected wandering the neighborhood. They were methodically checking the driveways with cars, opening doors that were unlocked, pulling out suitcases that were packed for an escape. Max just stood, watching them, understanding their organized need to scavenge whatever they could.

They turned toward the house they were in and Max slid more to the side to watch them from the shadows. They weren't trying to enter houses, but if they saw movement, she wasn't sure what they would do. They checked the saddlebags on the bikes first. They would find nothing there, Max knew because she had insisted on bringing all of their supplies in when they stopped. She didn't begrudge others for trying to survive, but she had already been carjacked. She wasn't offering her supplies to thieves willingly.

At first, she thought they must have seen her standing at the window, they all turned toward the house at the same time. Max stood completely stone still while shushing the group inside the house. They were all talking quietly, there was no way the sound carried to the group of scavengers. But something about the house attracted their attention and they moved toward the door.

Max slowly put the cover down and moved to the door. Griffin and Turner had pushed a large bookcase against the door for this situation, as they broke off the lock to get into the house. Griffin turned to her now, realizing something was going on and met her at the bookcase. She pressed her ear near where the bookcase met the door, hoping to hear something from the group outside.

"What's up?" Griffin whispered, standing close to her.

"Group of living. The house caught their attention. They're at the door," Max quietly said back.

From behind the bookcase, Max heard the doorknob be tested. She moved and pressed herself against the front of the furniture, adding weight to the door. She knew the doorknob would give because there was no lock on it. Griffin followed her lead and they both pressed against the door, waiting for the group outside to make their move.

Griffin's eyes darted to Max and then over to Jack, who stood against the far wall with Turner. They both watched the door waiting for what was coming. Griffin's gaze landed on Jack and stayed there, his eyebrows drawing together. Max recognized the worry on his face. It was the worry a parent had when they thought about protecting their child. That worry only intensified when there was so much unknown to protect them from.

She knew that there was no proof these scavengers were bad people. If she were more like her sister Alex, she may have asked them in, fed them a meal and sent them nicely on their way. Max didn't trust the way Alex did. She was suspicious of everyone's actions. The plague had only intensified that feeling. Being carjacked on day one hadn't helped her predisposition to her untrusting behavior.

The bookcase bumped forward slightly, before pushing back against the door and wall. Max held her breath, wondering what the group would do when they realized they couldn't get in. The second attempt was more violent, the bookcase coming an inch away from the wall. Max knew it was enough space for them to see inside if someone pressed their eye to the opening. The bookcase leaned back with a loud thud, giving away the fact that something was actually against the door.

"Get the packs ready. We're gonna have to go out the back," Max whispered harshly. Jack immediately was in gear packing up the last few things that they had out still. Turner and Cliff threw their bags over their shoulders, waiting for Griffin and Max to make their move.

"Go to the back. Get the door open. We will run for it as soon as we can," Max said. When they had chosen the house to stay in, Max had investigated all exit options. This neighborhood didn't have fenced yards, all of the small green space running together behind the buildings. They could run out and down the row to the road easily, the scavengers never the wiser.

Once Max and Griffin were alone, Max turned so she was pressing her hands against the bookcase. She listened intently to see if she could determine what the group was going to do. Once more the bookcase bent toward them and thudded back to the wall. That was the moment, Max and Griffin both knew it. Together, they turned and ran for the backdoor. The sliding glass was left open with the rest of the group waiting for them to run.

In a fluid motion, Max had her pack in her hand and was running down the grass along the houses. She used the bags momentum to swing it up onto her back while she ran. Without looking she could feel the rest of the group with her, Jack to her left like always. Out of the corner of her eye, she noticed what changed. Griffin was running to the left and slightly behind Jack. A defensive position and a way to keep her in his line of sight.

Reaching the asphalt road, Max stopped and looked both ways. In the distance she could see a car exit the neighborhood, the driver never noticed the group bursting into the street. She quickly spied an older four-door sedan and she ran straight for it. She knew she could easily hot-wire the vehicle if given the time. No one asked but just followed her direction at a quick pace. They all wanted to put space between them and the other group getting into the house they were in.

Turner reached the car first, realizing quickly what Max planned to do. He tried the driver's door, and as everyone arrived at the car they all tried handles. The car was locked up tight. Turner looked at Max and she nodded. She didn't want to wait and try to jimmy the door open, the butt of Turner's rifle doing the job of busting out the window easily. Reaching in, he opened the driver's door and stepped back for Max to see in. She dropped her pack and sat on her knees near the steering column.

Unlocking the rest of the doors, the group popped open the doors and the trunk. They loaded the extra supplies into the trunk, keeping their bug out bags with them on the inside. By the time everyone was getting settled, Max had stripped the appropriate wires and was touching them together to get a spark. The car sputtered to life. As soon as it caught, she twisted the wires together and jumped into the car. It was then she heard the yell from behind them.

She didn't wait but threw the car into reverse and lurched into the street. In her rearview, she could see the group that had been scavenging coming out of the same backyard area they had come. Apparently, they had entered the house and realized someone had just escaped. Now they were yelling and motioning toward the car, but no one fired any shots. Max didn't feel like they needed to know what the yelling was about and quickly got the sedan moving forward.

The broken window allowed a cold damp air to flood the car. Before long Max could feel her body cooling and her teeth chattering. Griffin pulled one of the sleeping bags open to cover Jack in the back seat where she curled up next to Turner to stay warm. The clouds were black and covering any hopes of sunshine to warm the day. The moment between winter and spring seeming to blur, leaving them with a chill.

Max sped out of the neighborhood, heading back to the freeway they had exited on the motorcycles. Once they swung onto the freeway, Griffin pulled out the roadmap and started giving guidance. They all settled into a tense silence as they drove through the congested city. Max originally wanted to take small roads around the freeway, but she wasn't sure they would be any clearer.

As they had seen before, there was some signs of military presence. Barricades could be seen on some freeway exits, cars pushed all the way up to the barricades on both sides. Some people trying to flee to the freeway, while others wanted to go the other way. Max could picture people pulling off at the barricades, hoping the military servicemen had answers for them. Many of the cars had doors propped open, windows were broken out, and trash was strewn about. Between some of the tires, she could see bodies on the ground, lying haphazardly wherever they fell.

"There are bullet holes in the cars," Griffin said quietly. He was staring out of the open window on the passenger side. Max slowed more so they could study the scene.

She realized quickly that he was right. There had been some sort of shootout at the barricade, with the occupants of the cars being the target.

"But why would they be shooting into cars? Those would have been healthy people," Max said, more to herself than anyone else. The question was rhetorical for her, as she didn't expect even the military to know how to protect people from the plague. The scene in front of them was too similar to the one they had come across two days earlier on the country bridge.

"Maybe the infected was mixed in?" Turner suggested from the backseat. But there was a tone in his voice that said he didn't really believe that.

Max couldn't handle staring at the gruesome scene anymore. She could see Jack keeping her face turned away, looking out the opposite window until they pulled away. Max carefully maneuvered around stopped and piled up cars. For the number of cars, there were not enough bodies, which gave Max a foreboding feeling in her gut. Those bodies went somewhere, and likely they were walking dead now.

As they approached the downtown area of the city, Max slowed the vehicle again. She hit her hand on the steering wheel, looking at the scene in front of them. The downtown corridor of the freeway was completely blocked with bumper to bumper cars. Some were stuck in some sort of accident, while others must have been stopped when traffic just couldn't move any further.

Max threw the car into reverse and carefully backed to the last exit they had passed. It was one that didn't have a barricade and only a few cars were on it. Max easily left the freeway and they were suddenly surrounded by tall corporate buildings. Some were smoldering wreckage at the bottoms, that once held coffee shops and shopping. Others had broken out windows, cars crashed into them and even some were boarded up. Max suddenly stopped, looking at a hotel that stood looming in front of them.

"Oh my god," she breathed. Looking up, Griffin was able to see what Max was staring at. From the higher levels of the hotel, sheets were strewn together, the words "We're Alive" written in some sort of black substance. Next to the sign was the beginning of a makeshift rope, also made of sheets. Max stared at the rope for a long moment. It was nowhere near the ground, seeming to not be done. But she was left to wonder if someone had been in such a panic, a fall to their death was better than what waited for them in the hotel.

"Do you think they are still in there?" Griffin asked.

"Even if they were, what can we do?" Max replied.

Griffin didn't say anything. There was nothing they could say. People at the top of a hotel, alive or not, would be close to impossible to get to. If they were searching for help from the top, then Max assumed they couldn't make their way downstairs on their own. She was fairly sure that the reason for that would be the infected that were probably teeming through the hotel hallways. There was no way of knowing when the plague had hit this city, and how long the people had been trapped. The conclusion stood, there was nothing they could do.

Max made quick work of the downtown congestion, working her way through to the next freeway onramp. When they approached it, they could see the freeway was still full, so she bypassed it and continued to work her way north. Five exits later, the congestion started to thin and by the seventh they were able to pull back on the larger road and speed up to cover more ground.

Leaving the city in their rearview gave Max some comfort. They hadn't seen any hordes of infected which was her greatest fear, driving the sedan. The road was easy to navigate once they left the city limits. People either didn't make it that far or they had done the same as Max was now, pedal down to get far away from the city full of people and dead.

A few hours later they ate a lunch of canned peas, beef jerky, and Starburst candies that Jack had in her bug out bag. Max ate in the driver's seat, keeping her eyes on the road. The sun was high in the sky hidden behind gray clouds, making her feel confident that they could get a large number of miles out of the way. She glanced down at the fuel gauge noting they were at three-fourths a tank. The sedan would get better gas mileage than the SUV, which was a positive. The negative was they didn't have a fuel reserve, as they had to leave theirs behind with the SUV.

A piece of beef jerky was put near her face, bringing her out of her concerns around fuel. She looked over at Griffin who was still in the passenger seat next to her. He motioned for her to take the jerky and she did, chewing quickly.

"You need to eat more," Griffin said.

"I'm eating plenty."

"You don't. You eat less than Jack. We have the food now. You should eat it. And we will worry about provisions later," Griffin insisted, hanging another piece of jerky near her mouth. She took it with her teeth and chewed thoughtfully. She always made sure Jack had enough to eat. No one had ever really paid attention to her needs, beside herself. Max knew her limits, knew what she really needed, and what she didn't. Mitch had sent her out camping or to do survival training with very little to eat. Sometimes she wouldn't want to hunt or forage, so she would just stretch the little food for as long as she could.

"Thanks," Max finally said quietly. Griffin didn't respond but grinned widely. Max was sure he had some smartass comment to make, but she was glad he kept it to himself.

As the car was getting ready to run on fumes, they pulled into a small rest stop right off the interstate. Max slowed to a crawl, eyeing the cars parked and crowded into the rest stop. If they hadn't known there was a plague going on, it would just seem that a large number of cars had stopped, and people were all taking a bathroom break. It was eerie, with no alive bodies moving around the rest stop like you would typically see on an afternoon drive. No children running and calling to their parents. No one at the vending machines getting snacks for the road. No line from the bathroom doors.

"We need fuel. But where do we think the people went?" Max asked the group.

"I'm guessing if they were alive, they fled. The cars were left behind by those that were no longer alive," Turner said from the backseat.

"Thanks, captain obvious," Griffin replied.

"I don't see any infected outside, not to say there aren't any inside. We need to be quick and quiet," Max said, ignoring the men's joking.

"We don't have a gas can to fill," Griffin reminded her.

"Yeah, I know. I have tools in my bag, but we need to search for some sort of larger container."

They started with the larger vehicles. The first one they approached was a van. Max slowly approached, checking the windows for any sign of infected bodies. She was saddened to see the toys inside the van, indicating there were children there at one point. Pressing her face to the windows, she couldn't see any containers that would work for them and she moved on. No reason to be sad about something she couldn't help now.

The third truck Griffin checked was a construction vehicle, piled with tools in the bed. Strapped down inside was a ten-gallon gas can, and it was full. He signaled to Max and Turner with a low whistle, which was the sign to return to the sedan. They met up just as Griffin was filling the car with the gas he already found. From there it was an easy process to fill the car and then fill the gas can to be prepared to continue their drive.

While the three of them worked outside the car, Jack sat inside with Cliff. Max was at first weirded out by Cliff's attention to Jack. But it didn't take her long to realize that after losing his own child, he was protective of Jack. She wasn't his blood or his responsibility, but he wanted to help keep her safe. Something he couldn't do with his own family. While they drove, Max could see Cliff's eyes fill with unshed tears while he stared out of the car window. She could almost read his thoughts filled with his wife and child.

The day's drive was uneventful, just as Max liked it. They had driven close to six hours for the day. Twilight was hinting, as the sun began to dip below the horizon. They were debating on a location for camp during the night. If push came to shove, they would all sleep inside the locked sedan. Though uncomfortable, it would be relatively safe from any infected.

According to the map they were getting near a medium sized city. Max mentioned to the group that the outskirt of a city was sure to have some sort of shelter they could take. As they spoke, Max's eye was caught by a flashing light sitting near the freeway, ahead of them. She took her foot off the gas, worried what may be causing the light. As they crept closer, she realized it was a road sign, which she assumed was solar powered because nothing else in the city was lit.

"What is that?" Cliff asked, his voice again causing Max to jump because she could forget what he sounded like over the span of time he was silent.

The sign lit up with orange letters again. It read "Government Safe Zone. All vehicles will be searched." The sign flashed dark again, and then another message came up. "Safety Here," was all it said. It then flashed to the first message again. Max watched it for a moment, wondering if there would be anything else, but it just continued to flash the two lines. The sign sat alone on the side of the road, no sign of government or anything living.

"I wonder what this safe zone is," Griffin said.

"Well if it's anything like the ones you had in North Carolina, it probably doesn't exist any longer," Max replied. Griffin just shrugged a shoulder in her direction, as he continued to look out his window, searching the area for any clues.

Max continued down the freeway, keeping her headlights off. She was determined to only turn them on at the last moment, afraid to attract any unwanted attention with the bright lights. With no street lights or other car lights, the city was eerie and dark. Shadows seemed to be deep pits in the ground, with no ambient light to illuminate the frightening areas. Max's eyes were growing accustomed to the dark as it gradually took over the day.

Suddenly many small lights seemed to appear out of nowhere down an exit they were approaching. The lights bobbed and grew as they got closer to the car. Max's hands tightened on her steering wheel, trying to see what was happening. Gradually she increased the car's speed, determined to avoid whoever or whatever was bringing the lights toward them. As she began to pass the exit, the lights bobbled in front of them.

"Max, stop!" Griffin exclaimed, just as Max realized she was going to mow down living people. She slammed on the breaks, and Griffin caught himself on the dashboard, his face just a few inches from the windshield. He stared out, silently watching the scene unfold.

In front of the sedan, two lines of men appeared, wearing fatigues which seemed to indicate they were military of some sort. They all held their rifles out and pointed directly at the car. No one said anything, they just waited. Max didn't turn off the car, just sat watching the men as they watched the car. Griffin's hand went to the door handle, and Max hissed at him to stay inside. If she had to make a quick getaway, she needed all people in her party inside the car.

"This is the United States Government. Exit your vehicle immediately." The demand came loudly, from a bullhorn.

"Well that's one thing we aren't doing," Max said aloud.

"They seem pretty serious," Griffin replied, hand still on the door.

"Yeah, so am I."

"Max, probably not the best time to see who can stare without blinking here," Turner piped up from the backseat.

As they sat, not complying with the order, a man with silver hair stepped through the lines of men and walked directly to the car. He stopped when he was an arm's length from the front grill, his face now visible in the waning light of day. Deliberately, the man unholstered his sidearm and raised the gun to point directly at Max's face.

"I said I am the United States Government. And I'm ordering you to exit your vehicle NOW."

CHAPTER TWENTY-TWO

The man claiming to be the United States Government carried himself as if he alone ran the country. His gray hair seemed to glint in the light that spilled from the headlights. His eyes seemed to bore into the car, staring at each of them until they were fighting the need to squirm in their seats. Max could see Griffin sit a little straighter and alert in his seat, the command of the man reaching into his Army training.

Max had no such training. Her mind was set the moment the man started to order them around. She didn't like him and he couldn't tell her what to do. Her stubbornness rose up her spine, causing her to tighten her hands on the steering wheel as she stared at the man with the gun aimed at her face. She eyed him expectantly, waiting for him to make a move, but he just looked at her, meeting her defiant gaze. And then, to Max's utter shock, he smirked at her.

"I think he's a Major," Griffin muttered. Max glanced at him quickly, shooting him a look like he was crazy. That didn't mean anything to her, and it wouldn't change how she felt about someone telling her to get out of her own vehicle.

"That means, Max, he probably leads this group, or is the leader of this government area," Turner explained from the backseat, apparently picking up on her annoyance with Griffin.

Without a word, Griffin opened the door and stepped out of the car. Max had to bite back a number of curses she wanted to hurl at him, knowing now she couldn't just drive away like she had partially planned. Griffin held his hands up where they could be seen, but the Major didn't look away from Max. He seemed to be reading her, and immediately realized she was probably the one that was the most trouble inside the vehicle. She knew he wouldn't be wrong about that assumption. Her general distrust of the military at that time was only going to make it harder for her to do anything the man said.

"Name is Griffin Wells, retired Army, Sir," Griffin said loudly. His voice rose and carried into the car and over to the ears of the men holding their rifles on their car still. The moment was tense and threatening but hearing that one of the men in the car was retired Army, Max could see some of the flashlights waver slightly.

"Rank?" The Major asked.

"Sergeant First Class Wells, Sir,' Griffin replied tightly.

"Well this is going to get interesting," Turner mumbled from behind Max. He was now leaning forward watching Griffin and the Major.

"Why?" Max asked.

"Well, if this guy is a Major, which I think he is, he can press Griff and I into service if he wants to. Now that he knows Griff's rank, he'll likely be thinking of how he can use him," Turner explained.

The additional information seemed to change the way Max perceived the interaction happening in front of their car. The Major was cool, calm, and collected. He held the gun almost passively at Max while watching her with sharp eyes. At the same time, he seemed to see Griffin and was able to weigh his choices. The wheels in the man's head were moving and it could almost be heard in the car.

"Your group needs to exit the vehicle, Sergeant Wells," the man said. He lowered the gun finally from Max and seemed to dismiss her as he turned to Griffin, who stood at attention. "I'm Major Callahan, the top ranking officer in this government safe zone. We will be searching your vehicle before you enter the city."

"I'll speak with them, Sir," Griffin replied and turned to walk back to the door he left open.

"You do that, Sergeant, and you let them know there is no choice."

Climbing back into the car, Griffin turned to Max. His face was set in determined lines, realizing he had a fight on his hands. Her face looked back at him, impassive and blank to hide her true feelings.

"Max, we should stop here for the night. It'll be safe and there's probably food," Griffin started.

"I don't like that guy."

"Because he pointed a gun at you? I guess I can understand that," Griffin replied hesitantly.

"Can't we just go around the city? I'll just drive at night," Max continued.

"We need to stop, Max. We don't have enough gas to get us through the night. We can't look for gas in the dark. This isn't a bad time to stop. There are other living people here."

"Is this some need to be loyal to your military brothers or something?" Max demanded. "I'm not putting my daughter in an unsafe situation because you have some unnecessary need to obey orders."

"Your daughter? How about OUR daughter," Griffin bit out. His words stung, and Max sat back slightly. "I wouldn't put her in danger knowingly, Max."

"Guys, we need to make a decision. That Major Callahan doesn't look to be someone with much patience," Turner cut in from the backseat.

Max turned to look out the windshield again. She saw that Callahan had not called off the troops that were still pointing rifles at their car. She found the whole scene to be absurd. Five living people in a small sedan. To this military establishment that seemed to be the biggest threat to them currently. Callahan hadn't moved from his spot near the front of the car as if he was daring Max to run him down. Her hand itched to grab the steering wheel and do just that.

"Max, let's go. We don't have anything to hide. Let them search the car," Griffin said.

Deciding it was easier to just agree with him, Max opened her door. It signaled the rest of the group that they were staying. Griffin got out of the car again and went to the back with Max to get their bags. As soon as they popped open the trunk men came around the car and started taking their bags and pushing Max and Griffin out of the way.

"Momma!" Jack called as she was pulled from the car and pushed in a different direction. Turner was climbing out of the opposite side of the car, and his head swung wildly when he heard Jack yell. Cliff had been pushed against the side of the car and was being frisked, but his eyes followed Jack's movements, his jaw tight, fists balled on the top of the sedan. Max noticed none of this, seeing only her daughter being pulled and maneuvered away from the car.

"Hey, jackass! Get your hands off my daughter!" Max exclaimed as she went toward Jack. She was stopped by an arm to her chest. She stopped and looked over at the man that had stopped her. The sneer on her face gave Griffin warning of what she was about to do. He yelled her name and tried to make a grab for her, but he was too late. Max had already dipped low and threw a straight punch at the soldier's groin. As he bent with a groan, she raised her knee and pulled his head to meet it. The crunch she heard was satisfying, as she pushed him back, blood coming from his now broken nose.

She advanced toward her daughter, who was being detained by two soldiers. Max's vision was red seeing the men holding her back. Her attack on the first soldier had seemed so sudden it took a moment for any of the additional soldiers to react. She easily evaded the next that tried to grab her. It took less than 10 seconds for Max to reach the men that were holding onto her daughter.

"I said, jackass," Max said as she shoved the first soldier. "Get your damn hands off my daughter!"

Her shouts drew more attention from the men surrounding the car and searching it. Max absently noted how they searched the car as if there could be a bomb attached, not just an infected person. The second soldier that was holding Jack, released her and stepped toward Max, who stepped to her left, letting his arm pass her shoulder. She pushed his arm further across his body and with her left, and her less strong arm, she swung a fist directly at his jaw.

The soldier stepped back dazed. Griffin arrived just in time to catch him before he tripped and fell on his ass. Max stood in front of Jack, her hand on her arm, the look on her face pure savage mother. Griffin stepped to her side and tried to calm the frenzy that was happening. Max Duncan was usually a surprise to most people, especially those that thought they could easily take her. She had trained for years as an adult to fight hand to hand, which only added to the survival lessons her father had given her.

"What in the living hell is going on here?" Major Callahan broke into the circle that was beginning to form around Max, Jack, and Griffin. His demand was loud and booming, causing the soldiers to immediately fall in line and back up slightly until they were given orders.

"Sir, my companion," Griffin started but Max cut him off.

"His companion can speak for herself," she said, shooting Griffin a look that said she didn't need his help.

"So, you have a smart mouth, we can remedy that," Callahan said.

"Really? Well, the one thing you can do to remedy that is tell your goons to keep their paws off my daughter," Max said defiantly. Callahan stood over a head taller than her. He was broad, a man who had taken great pride in his physical appearance for many years. And Max could care less. She raised her chin, her gaze meeting Callahan's filled with bold contempt.

"No one would manhandle a child here. They were keeping her safe," Callahan said. His gaze was cold and calculating as if he were weighing his vegetables at the grocery store. Nothing to worry about, just going about his normal business. Max wasn't sure if she should be offended or not.

"I beg to differ. She's safe with me. So, if we can just be shown to where we can sleep, we'll be out of your hair first thing tomorrow," Max said. Her hand tightened on Jack, keeping her close to her body, in the chance someone tried to grab her again.

"Private Smith!" Callahan suddenly bellowed, the loud noise causing even Max to jump a little. The quick smirk on Callahan's face said he saw her reaction to his yell, and that he didn't think she was a problem at all. *I'll show him a problem if someone touches my daughter again*, Max thought to herself as she just sneered back at the Major.

A young man came running to Callahan's side, his face red from exertion. He huffed out his breath, trying to look capable in front of the officer. Max looked at him with raised eyebrows, judging the boy to only be around eighteen or nineteen-years-old. She glanced over at Griffin, who was standing near Jack, straight-backed and at attention. He was also looking at the young boy with surprise on his face. He couldn't have been a day out of boot camp if that.

"Yes, Sir," Private Smith said, standing at attention to await his orders.

"Take the newcomers to be processed at the welcome tent," Callahan said. "Any guns will have to be turned over, but you can keep your other things, like your ax." He gestured absently at Max's hip.

"It's a tactical tomahawk, thanks," Max replied sweetly, sarcasm dripping from her words. She could hear the barely audible groan from Griffin. It reminded her of old times, getting in trouble at school. Max could never keep her mouth shut, while Griffin always just wanted to avoid getting into deeper.

"Yes, well, you can keep it on you. I assume you aren't planning on using it on any of the living people inside?" The Major said as he started to turn away. Callahan's question was rhetorical, and Max knew it. However, she could rarely stop herself.

"Depends I suppose," she replied.

Callahan stopped and turned back to Max. He looked down his nose at her, which only irritated her further. His eyes studied her again, but as before he judged her as no concern and moved on with his men following him. Watching as he went, Max was reminded of sharks with the little shark suckers that follow them. Callahan was cunning and quick like a shark, while his little minions were busy trying to suck off him to earn their place at his table.

Private Smith led the group to an entrance gate. There were towers on either side, manned with men and guns. Looking along the fencing, Max spotted a few additional towers that were most likely manned as well. The defenses were prepared at this facility, unlike those in North Carolina. The fencing wasn't much more than chainlink and cement barriers, but there were many more armed military personnel to protect against an oncoming threat.

They walked through the gate and Max was taken aback by the number of people inside. Beyond the first tent, the shelter bustled like a busy Main Street. People were carrying buckets, baskets, and bags from tent to tent. The people doing the manual labor were dressed in civilian clothes, Max noted, pressed into service by the Major. There were smiles on some faces, which also caught Max off guard. What was there really to smile about?

The first tent near the gate was the welcome tent, and Private Smith led them through unceremoniously. There were long tables facing the entrance, with file cabinets lined up behind. The tables were manned by a few in military fatigues. When Max and her group walked in, there was no one else being checked in at the time, so the tent was quiet compared to the outside. Private Smith stood off to one side and pointed toward the tables, as if it was all the most normal in the world.

Approaching a table, Max looked down at the seated man, Quick according to his name tag.

"We don't really need to register," Max began.

"Everyone that enters and stays here has to register, ma'am," Quick replied.

"We aren't really staying. Just trying to pass through."

"Your car is out on the freeway beyond the gate, correct?" Quick asked the question and poised with a pen over a form he was ready to fill out.

"Sure. And if we can just move through the city in that car, we will be on our way," Max replied. Griffin nudged her with his shoulder for a moment and gave her a knowing look. She looked away before they argued in front of the strangers. She had no trust in the military. Major Callahan had rubbed her wrong the moment he pointed a gun at her face. She didn't want to stay. Given the choice, she would rather sleep in the sedan on the side of the freeway.

"We only need to stay one night," Griffin interjected, clearly ignoring Max and her feelings. Jack pressed to Max's left side, unnerved by the tension.

"Registration then will need to happen," Quick replied. With that, he began to run through the questions with Griffin and fill out his paperwork. Max listened casually but she was busy studying the movements within the tent. There was a lot of paperwork for a shelter like this. It was really well organized for something that had come together just a week ago. The preparedness made Max wonder. Why was this group so ready, and yet multiple centers in North

Carolina were understaffed and unable to withstand the infected?

Max's attention was pulled back to Griffin and his conversation with the registration man Quick. They were speaking about Jack now. The little girl was pushing into Max, even more, making herself look small to the side and behind Max. The fear coming from her, made Max tune into the conversation.

"So, she's your daughter?" Quick was asking.

"Yes."

"All children are being taken to a safe facility," Quick began.

"She is safe with us," Griffin cut him off, his tone brokering no debate on the matter.

"You said you are military, so you understand how the government works. We need to protect our people, the survival of humans lies with the children of the world right now," Quick was saying, reciting something he had clearly said a number of times before.

"Being military doesn't make it ok in my mind for you to take my daughter from our care. If she were alone, I could understand transporting her. But she's not. She's with us," Griffin motioned to the group of adults that were standing around Jack. Cliff stood behind Max now, his face a stone wall, watching over her head to see what was about to unfold. Turner moved from foot to foot, swinging his gaze between Quick and Griffin. Max could imagine his loyalties were torn and he was trying to take his cues from Griffin in the situation.

"The government has decreed that the children are to be transported to the facilities that have been created for their protection," Quick replied, relentless in his message.

"Listen, as her father just told you, you are not taking our daughter from us. I am her mother. He's her father. There is no legal right for you to touch a hair on her head," Max said, stepping up closer to the table, to stand next to Griffin.

"Actually, we do," a voice boomed from behind them. Without turning Max knew that Major Callahan had decided to join the tent and add to the argument.

"Has the government fallen so far that they are separating children from their parents now? Their legal guardians no longer hold sway?" Griffin said, turning toward the Major. He was quickly forgetting his military training and caring much less than the man deserved his respect.

"The United States Government is doing what it can to not only protect its citizens but also ensure we will not be wiped from its lands," Callahan replied. He casually walked around the group and behind the long tables. He stood behind Quick, who had quickly jumped to attention when the Major had entered.

"Well then, we no longer recognize that government entity, and we will be leaving the way we came in," Max said. She turned and took Jack's hand in hers. Cliff turned to walk toward the entrance and Max was hot on his heels with Jack. Suddenly two men stepped between Cliff and Max, cutting off her exit. She stood for a moment evaluating, and then went to step around them as if they weren't there. She was yanked back by the arm she was holding Jack with, and Jack was yanked from her grip.

Griffin was at her side a moment later, arguing with the man that had grabbed Jack. Callahan stood calmly behind the table he was at, motioning men with flicks of his hands. Max was roughly grabbed from behind and yanked backward. Her arms were pinned to her side as she could do nothing but watch Griffin yell at the soldiers trying to take Jack. Turner was with him, trying to mediate but trying to get Jack back. At the same time, he was preventing Cliff from attacking the soldiers, realizing that wouldn't help anything,

Max wasn't of the same mind. She didn't like being manhandled. And the last thing she could handle was someone trying to take her daughter. Jack's screams rung in her ears, calling for Max, begging her to help her. Max tested the arms that were holding her and found them strong. Looking over at Callahan she felt rage rise as she found him just watching the scene with no emotion on his face.

"I warned you," Max called out to him. Once his eyes met hers she continued, "I told you to keep your minions' grubby hands off my daughter." With that, she swung her head back and collided with the nose of the man holding her. She didn't have enough space for much momentum, the blow wasn't hard enough to break the bone. However, it was hard enough to bring tears to the soldier's eyes and make him hesitate in his hold. That hesitation was all she needed.

Pivoting, Max was able to position her leg between the soldier's legs and bring it up with a quick shot to his inner thigh. He released her as his leg buckled under his weight and he had to shift. As soon as her arms were free Max stepped back from the soldier's, whose eyes were now on her and full of aggression. Max just smirked at him, goading him to come at her. That was all it took for him to attack.

Bouncing on her toes, her training came back into her body with no effort. It was well trained in attack scenarios, that she had never had to use in real-world situations until now. As the soldier came at her with his fists raised, he didn't anticipate the rear kick she delivered to his lower right side. The wind knocked out of him he faltered to the left. Max took a swinging step forward and hopped to land a superman punch to the side of the soldier's head. He fell to the ground with a thud.

She didn't wait to see if he was getting back up, she turned and ran straight for the group of men arguing with a crying Jack. Max didn't stop by Griffin, instead, she attacked. She had no patience for men who thought they could tell her what to do, or try and take her baby girl. Jack saw her mother coming and her eyes grew wide with fear as she watched her land a solid jab into the kidney of the first soldier. The man swung toward her, surprised by the blow but not down by any means.

The first blow Max felt was a punch to her gut as another soldier joined the fray. She couldn't stop her body from folding in on itself, as her breath left in a rush. Quickly Max took a few steps back and protected her head with her hands. When she straightened she realized it was Private Smith that had struck her. The young boy she had been sympathizing with looked at her now with raw fear on his face. Max took a deep breath and glared at him, he had started something he couldn't finish.

No preamble this time, Max walked straight to Smith and backhanded him across the face. His stunned look was all she needed as he passed him and approached the soldiers again that held her daughter.

"Let her go," Max growled.

"Max, calm down," Griffin started to say.

"Stay out of this, Griffin, or I'll take you down too," Max said without looking at him. Words weren't going to save their daughter, and she was all out of words.

"We can just take her and go," Griffin said, turning back to the soldiers.

Max stepped forward and made a grab for Jack, but the soldier that had her swung her away and caused the girl to fall to the ground. A scream erupted from Max's throat before she flew at the soldier, throwing two fast punches at his face, before lowering to strike at the body. The man didn't realize Max's abilities and wasn't prepared. He tried to grab her, to stop her but she evaded. He tried to strike out at her with his fists, but she blocked all but two of his blows. The two that did land were on her shoulder and ribs. Max didn't feel any pain, only adrenaline as it flooded her blood, to fuel her fight to protect her child.

All the while, Max continued to move, until she was between the soldiers and Jack on the ground. Jack realizing what her mother was doing, jumped up and started to move toward the door. It was her scream that alerted Max to something coming. She didn't turn fast enough though, as the Major walked up calmly behind her, a rifle in his hand. The butt of the weapon struck Max solidly in the back of the head. The last thing she saw before the world went black was Griffin's anger filled face.

CHAPTER TWENTY-THREE

The world came back to her in a blaze of pain. A fierce pounding in her head seemed to vibrate through her whole body, beating in time with her thudding heart. After the pain, the next sensation Max became aware of was the cold feeling of concrete beneath her cheek. Without moving or opening her eyes she took stock of her body and what she was aware of. She was glad to not feel any other injuries beyond the one to her head.

Her head, what happened to her head? Max slowly blinked her eyelids, without moving another muscle. She was afraid to move her head, to cause more pain in addition to what was already sharp and stabbing into her skull. The first thing she noticed with her eyes open was she was in a room, alone. The floor and walls were dull gray concrete. In the middle of the room was a drain. A room used by a butcher maybe, but Max couldn't be sure.

Lifting her arm felt like she was lifting a twenty-pound dumbbell. She reached her fingers into her hair and encountered a sticky bump on the back of her head. She concentrated, trying to remember what had happened to her. Remembering the fight, Jack's cry when she realized someone was coming to get Max and Griffin's face. She clearly remembered Griffin's face, angry and contorted like he was ready to fly into battle against whatever enemy came at them.

Looking around the room now, she worried about the conclusion of that fight. Where was Jack? Griffin? If the fight had gone their way, why was she in a concrete room? Max slowly lifted herself into a sitting position. She waited a minute with her eyes closed as her stomach tried to revolt against her movements, the pain intensifying as she moved around. Once she could manage it, she opened her eyes into squinted slits and slowly stood up.

Stumbling to the door Max was equally shocked and not surprised that the door was firmly locked. There were no windows, no way to see out. She had no concept of how much time had passed since she had been knocked unconscious The unknowns were starting to cause panic and despite her pain, Max began to bang on the door. After a few minutes, when no one came to the door, she rested her fist and began to kick the door with her booted foot.

After what seemed to be an eternity, she heard movement on the opposite side of the door. She stepped back, worried about an attack. When the door swung open, Griffin was thrust inside and the door was closed and locked again. He looked at her for a moment, before going to her and hugging her close. Max wrapped her arms around him, breathing in the familiar scent of his skin. She gave herself a moment to be calm and at peace with him holding onto her.

"I was so worried when they dragged you away," he said into her hair. He stepped back then, searching her head for the wound. When his hands found it, she hissed in pain and stepped back.

"Is it bad?" Griffin asked, stepping close to her again. She just shook her head, but then grimaced when that hurt too.

"Where's Jack?" Max demanded.

"With Turner."

"They didn't take her?"

"No. I convinced Callahan that she should stay with us until they move kids to the safe location. They aren't moving anyone for a week or so because there aren't many kids here right now," Griffin explained.

"They can't have our daughter, Griffin, you can't let them take her," Max said, a tone of pleading lacing her voice.

"I won't. I'm working on getting them to agree to not take her. Turner and I have been assigned posts, so she will stay with Cliff when we're working."

"Posts? We aren't staying here."

"I know that. We are reserves and can be pressed into service. The Major knows that and he's pushing the line with us."

"Where in the hell am I?" Max asked, gesturing around her cement box.

"You're in holding. You can't solve everything by violence, Max," Griffin replied. Max's eyes narrowed at him, but he stood his ground. "This is the government, you can't just start swinging your fists and think you're going to win. They've arrested you."

"Arrested me? For trying to protect my daughter? What happened to being able to protect what's yours?" Max couldn't believe it. Arrested? She'd never had a run-in with law enforcement in her whole life. Now there she was having to deal with irrational demands of a Major claiming to be the voice of the United States Government.

"They don't see it that way. You broke the laws in place by not letting them complete their duties. Things have changed, Max. We need to change with it."

"You agree with them." Max felt betrayed. She took another step away from him, distance to help her think more clearly.

"I didn't say that," Griffin said.

"How long are they keeping me in here? Why did they let you in?" Max had a million questions running through her mind. Most importantly how did she get out of the cell, and how did she get Jack the hell out of this shelter?

"I don't know how long. They thought if I explained things, you might calm down and stop fighting," Griffin looked at her with a small smile. "I told them that was highly unlikely."

"Unlikely is correct. I will continue to fight if I have a reason to fight. And protecting Jack is my job."

"A job you share now," Griffin reminded.

"I'm aware. But for eight years that's been my job alone. And I'm not about to fail it now."

"You aren't going to fail. You just need to stop fighting."

"Where's my tomahawk? My knife? My bag?" Max asked her questions in rapid succession. The fog from her head was starting to clear and she wanted to make some sort of plan to get back on the road and to Montana.

"I have all of your things," Griffin replied with a sigh.

"Get me out of here, Griffin," Max said, leaning into him with her shoulder.

"There's something else, Max," Griffin said hesitantly.

"Great, more good news?"

"Not news per se, something strange that I think might mean something," Griffin said. He stood back so he could look Max in the eye while he continued. "After they hauled you off, the Major started asking some strange questions. They had all of our names on the registration list and he wanted to know where we were going. I told him, Montana. His face changed when I said that, though he thought I didn't notice." He stopped, scrubbing the back of his neck with his hand. He paced away from Max, taking a few steps, before pivoting and looking at her again.

"He then started asking specifics about you, and I thought it was because you were arrested. But then the questions got really specific. He wanted to know if you had siblings. Asked specifically about a brother that may live in Montana."

An icy chill shivered up Max's spine. The Duncans were well known in their small area of Montana. How could they not be? The three kids raised by the crazy dad. But outside of there, they were nobody. They were still two states away from Montana. How would a Major in the United States Army know anything about Rafe Duncan who lived near Kalispell, Montana?

"What did you say?" Max asked.

"I hedged around it. Said you had family all around. No way of knowing where they were now. I think he knew I was lying though."

Max opened her mouth to ask another question, but the door was suddenly unlocked and a soldier motioned for Griffin to get out. He hugged Max again, whispering to her to cooperate and then he was gone. The door was again slammed shut and locked. Max stood and stared at the locked door for a long moment. The queasy feeling in her stomach seemed to intensify, not from pain, but the unknown.

Without windows, she couldn't be sure of the time that passed. She eventually chose a spot on the far wall, so she would have enough time to jump up if someone entered the room. She pressed her back against the wall and let her legs sit straight out in front of her. The room had nothing in it, no mattress, no blankets, no place to go to the bathroom. She had to assume they weren't planning on keeping her there long.

However, time continued to pass. She was stiff from sitting on the hard ground, her bladder was ready to burst, and she was feeling tired as if it was getting later and later. She was sure it was well near the middle of the night at that point. She paced the room, trying to loosen the muscles in her back and legs and to keep from peeing her pants. To keep her mind occupied she counted steps.

It was twelve steps across the room. By the time she reached three hundred and fifty-five, the door swung open. Her temper was flaring as she was hungry, sore, tired and badly in need of a bathroom break. When the Major entered the room, looking as if he was still wide awake and fresh as a brand new morning, Max wanted to punch him in his square jaw.

Instead, she was hauled out of the room, with no one saying a word. Two men grabbed her by the arms, yanking them roughly behind her and pushed her down a dark hallway. She tried to repeat Griffin's words in her head to keep herself from lashing out. She couldn't fix this with violence he had said. Well, she would play along for now, but if that didn't work, violence was the very next step.

At the end of the hall, a door was sitting open and she was shoved into the darkness before another door was slammed on her. Fumbling on the walls, hoping for a light, she found a switch and flipped it. The shelter ran off of some sort of generator and had limited electricity in the building she was in. A soft white glow came from the one lightbulb in the room.

It was a one-room bathroom. Seeing the toilet, Max rushed to rip off her pants and sit hastily on the seat. As she allowed her body to do its business, she tried not to think about how unsanitary the bathroom probably was. At that point, she would have been happy with a hole in the ground. Once she was done, she physically felt lighter, but her mood didn't improve.

Pushing down the handle on the toilet, the water evacuated, but nothing filled the bowl again. She wondered what the point was to not just use the outside as a bathroom. As she stood with her musings, the door was opened with no hesitation. The soldiers grabbed her again in their arm holds and led her back to the room she had originally been in. She again counted steps to calm herself and control her reaction to being handled by the two men.

When she was returned to her cell, there were two chairs in the room now. Major Callahan sat in one, and the other faced him. She was pushed into the chair and then the soldiers began to secure her arms to the chair itself. However the Major stopped them.

"That won't be necessary. I'm sure Ms. Duncan will be cooperative," the Major said, dismissing her as a threat. Max didn't say anything, just folded her free arms across her chest and glared at the Major.

"So, Ms. Duncan, Max. Can I call you Max?"

"That's my name," Max said.

"Right. Max, you've been arrested for not complying with the evacuate order for children. Do you have anything to say in your defense on that?"

"Is this a trial?" Max asked.

"No. Of course not. We still have our laws in place, Max. You will be given a true trial, with a jury of your peers," the Major said. It was then Max noticed he was holding a file folder on his lap. He drummed his fingers on it as he studied her.

"So, I'm not going to be released?" Max asked.

"Are you going to allow your daughter to be evacuated with the children as necessary?"

"Absolutely not," Max replied with no hesitation. "You have no right to just take my daughter. She is safer with me then she would be with any of you."

"And that's because of your family compound in Montana," the Major said, as he now opened the file folder and studied the contents. He kept it angled away so Max couldn't see any of the words, but he flipped a page up as if reading additional pages. Max could see a map on the first page, and though she couldn't see the names of roads, she immediately recognized Flathead Lake, which wasn't far from her family home.

"That's where you're going, right, Max?"

His use of her name was now grating on her nerves. She realized he was probably using it often to personalize their conversation. However part of her believed he was trying to put her on edge, throw her off somehow. She just sat still and studied him. Griffin had told her he had informed them that they were going to Montana. He didn't tell Max he was specific about the compound. The information churned in Max's mind, but she continued to keep her face impassive, giving away nothing.

"We are headed to Montana for safety," she finally said, once it was clear the Major wasn't going to move on without her reply.

"Ah, to meet with your siblings? Alexandria and Rafe?"

It was then Max knew that Griffin had not given the Major the information he was using. Griffin would never have called Alex by her full first name. Hell, she was pretty sure he didn't even know what Alex actually stood for since they never referred to her by it. She hoped she had kept the surprise hidden from her face. Her mind was running a mile a minute. What did this man care about her family? How did he know her siblings?

She didn't answer him, just stared. Her body felt rigid, but she forced it into a relaxed slouch as if nothing he was saying to her mattered a bit. The adjustment she made was noted by the Major, as his eyes watched her for any signs of emotion. Max felt like she was a part of a standoff, staring back at him waiting for him to give. Instead of conveying anything he wanted, she worked on making herself seem bored.

In the next instant, she was sprawled across the concrete floor. With little warning, the Major reached across the open space and backhanded Max out of the chair, causing her body and the chair to fly to the floor. Her elbow hit the concrete and Max screamed in pain. She rolled onto her stomach and was climbing up from all fours when she realized her two guards were standing over her with guns, challenging her to fight back. She glared at them through the stars she was seeing in her vision.

"Max, I really thought we were clear on how this was going to work. Maybe I need to explain further," Callahan started. He sat calmly in his chair, looking at her nonchalantly, his hands folded primly over the folder in his lap.

"You are in my custody. You will answer my questions and abide by the rules of this shelter, which are the rules of the United States Government. If you do not comply with the requests given to you, you will be punished."

"Funny, I thought the government didn't torture their own citizens. I must have missed that memo," Max replied sarcastically. She began to stand, but the Major nodded to one of the soldiers. The kick to her stomach left her on the floor gasping for air. As she gasped and coughed the soldiers picked her and her chair up, setting her back in front of Callahan.

"Your sarcasm has no place here, Max. If we can't speak civilly, I worry that your health will be in jeopardy," Callahan said as he studied her face. She just coughed and looked at him, saying nothing.

"Should we start over? I think that's a good idea. So again, you are headed to meet with your siblings?" Callahan posed it as a question, but Max knew she didn't need to answer. His folder held more information than she knew, she wasn't about to give him any more.

"I don't know where my family is," she finally said. That wasn't completely a lie. She knew Rafe should be in Montana, as he lived on the compound. And Alex had started Sundown, so she would have left Las Vegas as soon as possible to head there. But Max didn't have any confirmation that either of them was where they should be.

"Max, I believe that's a lie," Callahan said. He stood with his folder. He again nodded to one of the soldiers, who moved in front of Max. She looked up at him defiantly, waiting to see what would happen. His fist curled and struck Max on the cheek with no hesitation. She again was knocked off the flimsy chair, her cheek radiated pain throughout her face and head. She laid still for a moment as she decided if she was going to be ill. Behind her, the door opened, and the men filed out, taking the chairs with them.

She fell asleep laying against the back wall. Still having no idea what the time was, her body just told her it was time to shut down. It was difficult to sleep in any position for a length of time. The room was cold, so she didn't want to remove her sweater for a pillow. Curling an arm under her head worked for a bit, but her arm fell asleep, along with her hip that was pressed into the concrete. Her cheek was tender and she had to be careful if she laid on that side, not putting too much pressure on it and her arm.

When the door opened again, Max was groggy and startled awake. A tray was set inside, and the door was slapped shut again. She stayed where she was, waiting, not trusting anything that came from the soldiers. She counted in her head, and when she had counted to sixty enough times to probably be five minutes, she approached the tray. It held bread, cheese, jerky, and a cardboard carton of orange juice. She took it back to the far wall and ate quickly, her stomach reminding her how long it had been since she last ate.

After the food was gone, she studied the tray. It was plastic and they made sure to not include anything that could be used as a weapon. Of course, they weren't that stupid. She tossed the tray aside and leaned back against the wall. She tried to evaluate her internal clock to figure out how long she had been locked in the room. One meal, two bathroom breaks, and one visit from Callahan. She assumed it had only been about twelve hours.

She closed her eyes as she leaned her head back. Her cheek still smarted from the punch, but it was manageable now. Her mind wandered through the day since they arrived at the safe zone. The freeway had led them straight to the shelter, not giving them the option of entering the city without entering the shelter. Max wondered if the whole city was controlled by the military. How were they controlling the number of citizens that must have lived and worked there?

The most pressing issue for her was why Callahan was interested in her family. How had he known about her siblings, their names, and their relation to her? She had only given her first and last name at the registration, no additional information. Nonetheless, somehow Callahan was able to tie her to the Duncans of Montana without question. The violent reaction to her not giving information gave her the indication that whatever he wanted was important enough to him to violate all of her rights.

Rights, were there any of those left at this point? This all went down this path because she wouldn't just give up her daughter. But if Callahan had realized who she was before she was arrested, she had to assume he would have found any reason to arrest her. Her family being on the radar of the military had her concerned, wondering what her brother and sister had been doing since the plague started.

These deliberations were cut off when soldiers entered her room again. She stood up quickly, waiting to see what they would do. She was first led out of the room again to the bathroom. She quickly relieved herself and found a glass of water on the sink, so she dunked her finger in it and used it to clean her teeth hastily. Again, she was yanked from the bathroom and led back to the concrete cell. However, that time, the soldiers didn't shove her in and close the door, but followed her in.

Callahan leaned against the back wall of the cell, similar to the position Max had taken when they entered. She glanced around, wondering if they had a camera watching her at all times. When she was brought in, he pushed off the wall and gave her a sharp smile. It was like looking into the eyes of a snake, waiting for it to strike out as it approached you. His fatigues were ironed with crisp lines, clean and respectable. Looking at him you wouldn't believe there was a plague ravaging the country.

"Hello, Max."

She stood still and didn't answer. Her arms were still being held by the soldiers and a third man, Private Smith, stood off the side with his rifle. If the Major wasn't worried about her, why bring so many men? She just stared at him waiting for him to start his questions. She knew they were coming, he had the folder in his hands again.

"I thought maybe we could try talking again," he said.

"I've told you all I know," Max replied, trying to shrug her shoulders, but found that to be impossible with her arms trapped.

"And I don't believe you. I think we established that," he said testily. Max was actually pleased to see she could make his facade slip just a little.

"I don't know what you'd like me to say to that. You either believe me or get your info somewhere else."

"I think we can still get some needed information from you, Max, or I wouldn't be here," he said, as he motioned to the soldier standing off to the side. The man nodded and stepped up to Max. She just raised an eyebrow at him. Private Smith had a blooming bruise appearing on his cheek where Max had struck him. His eyes were on hers, full of dread, but still following orders. His fist flew and struck Max in the stomach, causing her to suck in air and cough. He threw three more punches into her belly before Callahan called to him to stop.

"This can all stop, Max. Just answer the questions. Where are Alexandria and Rafe?"

"Don't...know," Max replied, choking as she tried to get air into her lungs.

"Tsk, Tsk," Callahan said before he motioned to the men holding onto her arms. She was roughly shoved to her knees and then thrown to the ground. On her hands and knees, Private Smith stepped back to her and kicked her in the ribs. She fell to her side, curling into a ball to protect her head. The kicks continued from all three soldiers, striking her ribs, arms, and legs. Her body was protesting the pain that was being inflicted, and Max couldn't help stop herself from crying out.

That stopped the attack. Max laid on the ground, trying to breathe. Her ribs hurt badly, making her wonder if they didn't break something in their onslaught. The boots in the room shuffled around as the door was opened again, and chairs were brought in. Max was lifted roughly and shoved into the chair, where she sat slumped to her side, favoring the ribs that hurt the most.

"We don't like to hurt you, Max," Callahan said. He sat across from her, with a lack of any emotion on his face. He had the folder open again but was watching Max in her chair.

"Could have fooled me," Max shot back.

"Well, beating women isn't exactly a favorite pastime of mine. I doubt for these men either," Callahan motioned to the three men that stood in the cell with them. None of them made eye contact with Max when she looked around at them.

"No? Let me guess, torturing animals is more your thing?"

"Has anyone ever told you that your mouth is going to get you into trouble?"

"Every day," Max replied without hesitation.

"And you just can't seem to learn," Callahan said as he shook his head in mock disbelief.

"Guess I'm a slow student."

"Let's try this again. You are headed to Montana, this has been established. What do you know of the whereabouts of your siblings?"

"I don't know anything about where they are right now. Seems my cellphone stopped working, weird."

Sighing, Callahan motioned to one of the men to come over. Young Private Smith stood in front of her, fists balled at his side. Max didn't acknowledge him, just stared through him to the far wall. Instead of the punch, she was expecting, he slapped her with his open hand. When she brought her head back to face center, he struck her again, harder this time. This blow caused her lip to split and blood to run down her chin. She looked back, and Private Smith stepped away again.

"Your father created the compound your brother lives on, you were raised on it. How are the defenses set up?" Callahan continued.

"Defenses? It's not a military base. It's a home," Max replied, wiping the blood from her face.

"A home with a large stone wall surrounding it, like a fortress," Callahan stated. His detailed knowledge of the compound made Max uncomfortable. How would he know about the fence unless someone had been there? And if they had been there, Alex and Rafe weren't, because he was still looking for them.

"What do you want with my family?" Max asked, turning the questions back to the Major.

"That's not your concern."

"The hell it isn't. That's my family and I'm not going to just answer your questions without knowing what you want with them."

"Then we are at another impasse," he said to Max. Then he turned to the soldiers and continued, "Move her to the new room."

Max wondered what this new room could be, as the soldiers advanced on her. Violence was just below the surface on Max. But the soldiers and the Major had guns. Even if she could take one or two down, that would leave time for the others to draw their weapons and shoot her. That outcome wouldn't get her to Jack faster. She didn't fight when the soldiers pinned her arms and lifted her from her seat. Her body wanted to protest, but Max forced one foot in front of the other.

Callahan followed as they walked down the hallway. The hall was full of doors, though Max never saw inside of any except her cell and the bathroom. Private Smith hurried ahead of them to a door near the bathroom. Unlocking it, he stood to the side to allow them to enter. Max was led into the room, which was more dimly lit than the one she had been in before. It was just as sparse, with no real furniture inside.

There were boxes stacked against one wall and a chair against the opposite wall of the door.

What caught Max's attention immediately was the large hook hanging from the center of the ceiling. It looked like something a butcher would hang a slab of meat from. Handcuffs were produced from one of the soldiers and her hands were secured in front of her. Suddenly Max realized what was happening, and she tried to pull away. The soldier just yanked her to the center of the room as she tried to fight. She kicked out and landed a solid blow to the man's thigh. He yelped in pain and the other soldier hit the back of Max's head, almost knocking her to the ground.

Her head swam as she tried to gather her senses. Her arms were lifted above her head and one soldier lifted her by her waist, securing the handcuffs over the hook. Then Private Smith, who stood off to the side, watching with the light of fear in his eyes, used a remote to lower the hook until just Max's toes touched the ground. She scraped her feet along the concrete floor. Trying to find purchase, she wanted to take the tension off of her shoulders, but they didn't lower her any further.

Callahan had stood outside of the door watching the entire scene. Once Max was secured on the hook he walked into the room and grabbed the chair that sat in front of her now. He moved it until he was happy with the positioning, and sat with his folder.

"Now, let's try this again," he started, staring at the hanging Max.

CHAPTER TWENTY-FOUR

She had lost all idea of time. Hanging from the meat hook, Max tried to judge how long she had been in the room. Her position had been alternated three times so far, with the hanging times feeling like hours. She counted, and when that started to drive her crazy she tried to think of all the ways she would make Callahan pay for what he was doing to her. Those daydreams sometimes took her mind off of the painful ache that would build in her shoulders from hanging without feet to support her.

The door banged open, startling her. The same soldiers filed in ahead of Callahan. Max had begun to name the two she didn't know Tweedle Dum and Tweedle Dumber. It made her feel better inside to laugh at them, even though they had no idea she was doing so. She, of course, had met Private Smith before, and the boy always seemed to be scared and unsure of what was happening. Besides the fear, he still followed the orders given by the Major. Military loyalty winning out over his human sensibilities.

"Good morning, Max," Callahan said, as he moved his chair to the front row seat to her interrogation today.

"Morning? Could have fooled me," Max replied, her voice a weak whisper.

The soldiers lifted her and disconnected her hands from the hook above her head. She gritted her teeth against crying out at the agonizing pain from rotating her shoulders, letting her arms fall. Tears pricked the backs of her eyes, but she refused to show that type of weakness in front of the Major.

"Well I'm hoping this morning you will be more accommodating," Callahan said, picking an invisible piece of lint off of his pants and then looking at Max. She was shoved into a chair across from him.

"Speaking of accommodations," Max said, slouching in the chair as relaxed as possible, "The accommodations of my room seem to be lacking. I didn't even get a pillow chocolate."

Her wise crack seemed to dig at the Major slightly, a fire lighting his dark eyes for a moment. He stared at her, saying nothing. Then he just shook his head in disgust. The soldiers stepped forward. It was then that Max realized they had brought other items into the room with them. She took in the buckets of water, washcloth and the large bin. Then she looked back at Callahan.

"Waterboarding? Really? Now I really know you're off your meds. The US Government doesn't waterboard their citizens."

"What about this situation seems normal to you, Max? Do you believe you are being detained in a normal lawful manner? Do you believe that all normal laws still stand after the country began to fall apart to a plague?"

"So, what you're saying is you don't actually represent any government," Max said. This was the most information she had received from Callahan since the questioning started. She knew well enough that the behavior and treatment she was on the receiving end of were not legal. However, what she didn't know was why Callahan wanted her or her siblings.

"I represent what is left of the US Government," Callahan replied stiffly.

"What's left? Like is the President left?"

"There is a President in power. Just not the one you know of."

"What happened to the President?"

"What's happened to everyone? The plague hit DC the same as everywhere else," Callahan shrugged as if he wasn't concerned with the happening of it.

"So, the new President, the new government, is ok with torturing United States citizens?" Max asked.

"That's enough questions from you. I've given you information, so I think I'm due to some answers as well, Max. Where is your brother?"

"My brother? Only my brother?" Max asked. She had carefully filed away all of the questions Callahan had asked her during their little sessions the last few days.

"Max, what did I say about the questions?"

Before Max could react, her body was hit with an electric shock and she fell to the side off the chair, her muscles involuntarily convulsing. Tweedle Dum held a baton stun gun against her side and Max began to scream as her body twitched and her skin itched. Callahan waved off the soldier and he stepped back.

"You will need to behave, Max," the Major said, bending slightly to the side to look Max in the face. With her hands still bound, she had struck her chin when she fell and she could taste the coppery bite of blood in her mouth. She was hoisted back into the chair and she could barely sit without falling over again. Her energy was depleted from having no real meals. Dehydration was setting in, her lips cracked and bleeding from a lack of water and from the numerous blows to her face.

"Where is your brother Rafe?" Callahan asked again.

"I don't know," Max replied.

"That isn't the answer I'm looking for, Max."

"It's the only one I'm giving you," Max said, defiance trying to rise up in her.

Suddenly she was yanked back and her chair was tilted at an angle over the tub. She tried to fight the hands that held her still, but she was tied to the chair by a rope that they looped around her waist. A washcloth was held over her face and before she could get a deep breath, water began to pour over the washcloth. The water was ice cold, causing her to flinch and gasp in reaction. That only created a worse problem, drowning. Water invaded her mouth, her nose, her throat. Dehydration was no longer on her mind, drowning was.

For Max the moment felt like an eternity, she couldn't breathe, her mind felt like it was going to start short-circuiting. Just as she was sure she wouldn't survive, she was yanked into a vertical position and sat in front of Callahan again. She gasped for breath, choking and sputtering on the water that had slipped down her throat. Her hair, already dirty and hanging in ratted clumps, was drenched and soaking her thin T-shirt. Her sweater had long ago been disposed of, leaving her cold and shivering now that she was wet.

"Where is Rafe, Max?" Callahan asked again.

"Thanks for the drink, I was feeling parched," Max replied, spitting at his feet.

"What does Rafe know about the plague?" Callahan asked another question that had surprised Max the first time he had asked it.

"I'm sure he knows it kills people," Max responded with the same answer she had provided before.

Callahan sighed, clearly exasperated with her lack of response to his questions. With a nod of his head, she was again hit with a blast of electricity from the baton stun gun. This time the current touched her abdomen. A soldier stood behind her, keeping her from flipping out of her chair. She tried to keep her teeth clenched, but the burning pain was more than she could handle, and a brutal scream ripped from her throat.

The baton was pulled away from her body, but the burning didn't stop immediately. Her muscles twitched painfully. She was able to clench her jaw to keep herself from crying out further. Her eyes watered, but she refused to allow tears to fall. Forcing her eyes to focus on Callahan, she could feel pure hatred. The man sat in his perfect uniform, his perfect haircut and stared at her with no concern on his face.

"I don't know what you want from me. I don't know anything," Max said.

"You know much more than you are willing to let on. Why would a family live on a compound?"

"My dad was crazy. Not much more to it," Max replied.

"What would you be trying to keep out?"

"Everything?" Max answered. She rolled her shoulders slightly trying to work the stiffness out. Everything hurt, she had to be sure not to wince and give away how bad she really was feeling.

"Where is Rafe?" Callahan asked.

"You seem to know a lot about my family. Shouldn't you know where Rafe is?" Max responded.

Her answer was not what Callahan wanted. Again she was yanked back and positioned over the tub. She didn't fight this time, didn't say anything. Struggling wouldn't make a difference. The soldiers were going to follow their orders. Max wasn't going to answer any questions. She made eye contact with Private Smith before they covered her face with the washcloth. The young man was pale, his eyes wide with fear and shock. Max stared at him until they covered her eyes.

The water was a shock, even though she was expecting it. She held her breath, but her body began to panic. She tried to turn her head to get away from the flow of water, but the washcloth was tight across her airways. She gagged and choked, visions of drowning and never seeing Jack again filled her mind. She tried to spit water out but it just kept flowing.

"That's enough," Callahan's voice reached Max's oxygen-starved brain just before the men flipped her back forward. They angled her slightly toward the ground, allowing the water to flow from her nostrils and mouth. She retched water and her stomach contents with no hesitation. The bile burned her abused throat. She could see Callahan pull his feet back slightly as the fluids splashed toward him.

"Feed her and hang her back up," Callahan said, standing and walking toward the door.

"Thanks...for the....visit," Max croaked out, her smart-ass attitude still intact. Callahan stopped at the door and came back to where Max slumped in the chair. Max tried to lean back to look up at him as he stood in front of her. Quick as a striking snake, Callahan slapped Max across the face, reopening the split lip she had. Max's head was slung to the side and she left it there letting the sting fade slowly.

"We will cure you of that mouth eventually," Callahan said and exited the cell.

After her sparse meal and glass of water, that she could barely choke down after the waterboarding, she was lifted and left to hang by her wrists again. The water dripping from her body puddled below her feet. Max lost count of the sound of the drips. As she began to float between awake and unconsciousness she found herself again trying to think through how her older brother was involved with Callahan. Involved was probably too far, as Callahan obviously had no idea where Rafe was.

His line of questioning insinuated that her brother was somehow involved with the plague, further than the fight for survival everyone was dealing with. She remembered how she couldn't reach Rafe before the cell network fell. Where was her brother when he should have been at the compound, preparing for their arrival and their lives behind the walls? Callahan knew what their home looked like, at least the wall that her father had worked on for years.

As her vision dimmed and she gave over to sleep, she tried to not think of all of the things that could have gone wrong since she spoke with Alex last. The faces of her niece and nephew floated in her brain and she allowed a tear to slip from the corner of her eye before she sucked them back. She didn't have the luxury of crying right now. She let herself drift, no longer able to fight the exhaustion her body was feeling.

Max tried to count the number of times Callahan referred to the morning when he came into her cell. If she based it on that, she had been alternating between hanging and laying on the floor for five days. Five long days where despair tried to seep into her mind, pulling her down. Five days of her not seeing Griffin, Jack, or anyone besides Callahan and his minions. Sparse meals and soaking wet clothing from the torture and wake up calls of ice cold water being thrown on her.

On day five, or maybe six, Max wasn't sure, she sat unbound across from Callahan. She shivered from the water and the cold that seemed to trickle into the concrete room. She wrapped her arms around her stomach to try and hold in some of the warmth of her body, the fear of hypothermia setting in. Callahan was in a talkative mood, though Max had mainly ignored him with the same drivel he spouted every visit. However, he changed up his approach suddenly.

"I have always enjoyed Flathead Lake, Max. Do you fish? I love to fish. It's quiet. There's solitude. I used to catch some of the largest rainbow trout in that lake. There's no solitude like that anymore," Callahan said.

"Ok..." Max replied, confused.

"I know you have probably wondered why I'm asking these questions," he suddenly said, changing subjects. Max stared at him as if his head had fallen right off his shoulders and was rolling around the room. She had asked him time after time why he was asking her about her brother and sister. He had refused to acknowledge her inquiries. She knew he heard her, but she wasn't allowed to ask questions. So he pretended they didn't happen.

"No, what? Really? Why would I be wondering that?" Max replied, annoyance lacing her voice. Callahan raised his eyebrow at her, annoyed by her flippant attitude. Her face held the bruises, gashes, and split lips from the number of times he informed her he didn't appreciate her attitude. Those instances didn't stop Max. Deep inside she felt the only way she could continue to fight back was to keep mouthing off. If she could keep pushing his buttons and give him no information, she was still fighting back.

"We have a problem with this plague, Max. We don't have a cure."

"No? I thought maybe you were just keeping it for yourself."

"As we do not have a cure, we have to find out where the illness started, how it spread and then maybe we can find a way to fight it. Wouldn't you agree, Max?" Callahan asked the question, ignoring her remark. She just stared at him. Of course, she agreed they needed a solution to the plague, but she was still lost to how that related to her family.

"There is reason to believe that your brother Rafe has something to do with the cure to this plague." Callahan carefully dropped his bomb on Max and sat back waiting.

"Rafe? Have something to do with this plague? That's kinda insane. Which fits, since it's you I'm talking to," Max replied.

"What does your brother do for work Max?"

"Your pretty file doesn't tell you that?"

"Of course, it does. But I thought we were having a conversation. Your brother works in security. Contract work to be specific. And he was recently contracted for a job at a government subsidiary. You, I assume, were aware of that."

Actually, she wasn't. Max thought back to the last time she and Rafe had a long conversation on the phone. It wasn't that they didn't talk, but typically they had quick calls just checking in. She knew he was working security because it was what he was good at. However they never really talked about his specific jobs. Some of them were confidential and she just didn't ask.

"He acquired information from that facility that was confidential. He has been, how should I say it, avoiding capture since then."

"Capture? What in the hell are you trying to do to my brother?" Max sat up straighter, anger flaring and flushing her pale face.

"Where is Rafe, Max? Where is your brother?" Callahan asked for the hundredth time.

"I've told you, I don't know. And you said he's been avoiding capture. So you're looking. You would know better than me," Max huffed out, annoyed that they were back to the same line of questioning.

"We know he's not home, in Montana. Do you want to know why we know that?"

Max again didn't answer. It was mostly fear that kept her from saying anything. She wasn't sure she wanted to know the answer to that question. But Callahan didn't really care what she wanted to hear. He partially smirked at her. That evil filled look told Max that the answer wasn't going to be good.

"When my men went there, he fled with his information. They tried to burn the house with him in it, but they were unsuccessful," Callahan said, his voice nonchalant.

Max was on him before he could blink and before she could think of all the reasons it was bad for her to attack him. The surprise of the attack was the only way she got as far as she did. Callahan and the soldiers looked at her as if she was a broken little girl. Her body screamed in protest as she forced it to do as she wanted. Yet, the fury she felt fueled her muscles, her movements were smooth and strong.

Callahan flew backward as Max barreled into him, tackling him to the ground. She was smaller than him and easily rolled and was sitting on his chest before he could react. She began throwing punches into his face. She landed two solid strikes and was pulling back for a third before she was jolted by electricity shocking her back. Falling forward, she rolled off of Callahan and rolled into a ball to stop her body from the tremors.

Furious, Callahan jumped to his feet. He pushed back the soldier that was holding the baton stun gun to her body and the electricity stopped. The burning pain resumed and Max had to gasp to get air into her lungs. It was a futile action though, as Callahan booted her in the stomach. Max coughed and struggled to breathe. The Major was in control now, angry and smarting from being bested by a small woman.

His kicks were timed perfectly. Just as Max thought she was getting her breath back, he would steal it again. She tried to roll away but he just followed. Planting her hands on the ground, Max tried to fight to her feet, but Callahan stomped on her fingers, causing her to scream in pain. She fell back to the ground, holding her injured hand to her chest.

"That's right, Max. You can't win here," Callahan said to her, his voice low and menacing. He pulled back his arm and snapped a punch into her cheek. Pain exploded behind her eyes, blackness threatening to consume her.

"What makes you angry, Max? That your brother can't get away forever? We will find him. Or that we burned your little house to the ground?" Callahan said, taunting her, hitting her again in the face. Her head snapped back, hitting the concrete floor. Her body began to go limp, giving in to the unconsciousness that called her away from the pain.

"And your daughter? You'll never see her again. Now that we know who you are, she's perfect bait to get your brother. Thank you for bringing me the perfect plan, Max," Callahan spat on her face before standing straight again.

"NOOOO!" Max screamed, her voice sounding strangled and weak. Callahan turned to her for a moment again, and laughed, before leaving the room.

She was left on the ground that time, curled in a ball full of pain, panting, trying to get breath flowing. Her home, burned? That couldn't be true. Her mind refused to believe her home was gone. Callahan hadn't mentioned any of the outbuildings or the bunker in all of his questioning. Did he not know about those? Was all of this a lie to get her to fight? She was left wondering if she would ever get out of the room to find out.

What felt like hours later, the soldiers came back in. This time they had a woman with them. She looked scared, but she came straight to Max with a black bag. She looked into her eyes with a light, causing Max to hiss and try to pull away. The woman held onto her face and checked her cheeks and chin with gentle probing fingers. Max still tried to pull away, feeling pain and fear from being touched by anyone.

"Shhhh it's ok," the woman whispered. "I'm a doctor. I just want to check your injuries."

Something in the woman's soft voice made Max relax, feeling more at ease now with the exam. When she got to Max's shirt, she asked for permission to check her ribs and Max nodded. The doctor lifted the shirt slightly and touched her ribs. When she exposed Max's stomach, she gasped quietly at the bruising that lined her middle, as well as the burn points where the baton had been held against her body for too long. Max grimaced at the look on the doctor's face, not wanting to look at her own body and see whatever had made the doctor look at her like that.

"I don't think your ribs are broken, possible hairline fractures in some places. Without X-rays, I can't tell for sure. You need to be really careful," the doctor said to her after she pulled her shirt back down. She then leaned over Max's face and applied butterfly bandages to the gashes that were still bleeding from her cheeks and forehead.

"My hand," Max said, holding out the injured digits.

"My god. What happened?" The doctor whispered.

"No talking!" Tweedle Dumber yelled from the entrance to the cell.

"To evaluate her injuries, I need to know how they feel, so I have to talk," the doctor calmly replied and rolled her eyes where only Max could see.

"Stomped on, it hurts," Max continued, gesturing to her hand.

The doctor took her hand gingerly, softly running her fingers along the bones, causing Max to wince in pain at certain points. The doctor's forehead furrowed as she tried to determine if the fingers were broken. Reaching into her bag she pulled out a bag of tape and gauze. As she taped the ring finger and middle fingers together she explained that it didn't seem any of them were broken completely. But those two were swelling so far, and could possibly have fractures. The splint and mobilization should keep her from any permanent damage.

"That is of course if you don't move it," the doctor whispered, as she looked around the room. She took in the chains, the hook in the ceiling, the overturned chairs, the waterboarding items and looked back at Max.

"Whatever they want, just give it to them," she whispered. She packed up her bag, moving slowly so she could talk to Max a moment longer.

"I can't. My daughter. Jack is with her father Griffin. Do you know them?"

"The little girl that has dark hair like yours? Yes, I've seen her."

"Please tell her, I love her. But I can't give Callahan what he wants," Max pleaded, looking into the doctor's eyes. The doctor didn't reply, but she nodded quickly.

With a squeeze to Max's uninjured hand, the doctor stood to leave the room. Max started to roll onto her side to find a comfortable position, but Tweedle Dumb and Dumber hoisted her off the ground. They roughly hooked her wrists together again and lifted her to hang her by the hook. Max screamed as they raised her arms above her head, causing her ribs to protest violently. The soldiers ignored her and left her scraping her toes against the concrete.

Her body was exhausted. Her mind couldn't comprehend everything Callahan had given her in their conversation. Rafe knew about the plague, maybe the cure. But he was on the run. Why would he run if that's what he had? Max pictured her home in her mind, perfect and strong, as her father had built it for them. Trying to picture it burned was impossible and Max stopped trying. Instead, she allowed images of home, Rafe, Alex, Jack, and even Griffin to invade her mind. She passed out hanging from the hook, her family comforting her.

"Jesus Christ, what did they do to her?"

The voice didn't register with Max enough to wake her up. Her mind was too cloudy and exhausted to wake up when the door opened and someone entered. When hands touched her near her ribs she hissed and tried to pull back, but she couldn't maneuver much hanging from the meat hook.

"Be careful, she's in pain," another voice said.

"Shhhh, baby, it's ok. It's me, it's Griffin. Can you wake up?"

Griffin. The name floated through Max's brain. Griffin, the boy she had loved as a girl and probably still loved now. What was Griffin doing there? In her mind she willed her body to react, her eyes to open. But nothing responded. She continued to hang limply as Griffin brought a chair over to her. He stepped up and grabbed her securely around her waist. She cried out as she was lifted, and Griffin shushed her in her ear.

"Babe, you gotta be quiet. I know it hurts. I'm sorry."

Slowly Griffin stepped off the chair with Max over his shoulder. The pain in her ribs jolting caused pain to radiate through her body, stealing her breath. Nevertheless, something inside her told her she had to stay quiet. Griffin laid Max on the cold ground and knelt beside her. She immediately curled into a ball on her side, trying to fend off some of the pain, but no matter where she went, everything hurt.

"Max, come on, honey, you gotta wake up. We have to get out of here. I can't carry you out and fight if we have to," Griffin was saying, as he rolled her back toward him.

Taking all of her remaining willpower, Max summoned the energy she needed to open her eyes. She blinked in the darkness and flinched when a flashlight crossed over her face. Then Griffin pointed the flashlight at his own face and she was overwhelmed with the emotions that hit her. He smiled at her and leaned down to kiss her softly.

"Howdy, stranger," she said in a scratchy voice.

"Howdy to you. Ready to blow this party? Just doesn't seem like it's fun anymore," he replied. She didn't answer, just nodded and held up her uninjured hand. He stood and pulled her to her feet carefully. She leaned heavily on him before she could get the circulation moving throughout her body again. Her ribs ached and as the blood rushed back to her injured hand, needles of hot white agony ran down each of her injured fingers. She cradled it against her chest and stumbled before standing on her own.

"How did you get in here?" Max asked.

"With that key." Griffin motioned over to the other side of the room. By the door stood Turner, with a gun to Private Smith's head. Smith was in a white undershirt and white boxers, obviously taken from his bed. He stood trembling with tears on his face. Turner pressed the gun against Smith's temple.

"Yes, this key has been very helpful. Though to be fair, he wasn't given much a choice," Turner said.

"We grabbed him when he was on his way back to bed from the latrine. Didn't take much to convince him to bring us to where they were holding you. Weak piece of trash," Griffin punctuated his sentence with a well-aimed spit toward Smith's feet.

"Jack! Where's Jack?" Max felt panic bubble as she turned around in a circle and didn't find her daughter with them.

"Calm down, Max, she's ok."

"Where is she?"

"We got her and Cliff outside of the shelter first. They found the car we drove in. Callahan's men drove it off one of the exits inside the shelter. We hot-wired it, and Cliff took it deeper into the city. We have a planned meet up." Griffin explained. He then motioned to Turner, who pushed Private Smith into the room.

"The Major won't forget this. He'll find you," Smith stammered.

"He can try," Griffin replied.

Turner and Griffin strung Private Smith up the same way they had left Max. He was taller than Max, allowing him to touch the ground with his feet. Griffin and Turner securely tied him to the hook and then circled the rope with duct tape. Lastly, Smith's mouth was covered with tape. Turner smacked him on the cheek.

"In case you get the crazy idea to scream, kid."

Griffin walked to Smith and looked him in the eye for a moment. His face was angry and stark.

"You helped do that to her? You beat a defenseless woman while in the custody of the government? Nod your head," Griffin said in a low menacing voice.

"I'm not exactly defenseless," Max mumbled.

Smith's eyes were wild with fear. He looked from Griffin to Turner, whose face didn't hold a better expression. He then looked at Max. His eyes pleaded with her to vouch for him, she supposed. She thought back to the multiple tortures, the pain, the humiliation, all at Callahan's orders. Smith never hesitated to follow those orders, whether it meant to hurt Max or not.

She turned her back on him. That was all Griffin needed. Max listened as fists struck flesh. Smith grunted and his cries for help were muffled by the tape. She couldn't help but grimace at the noises, feeling like they were a reminder of her time in the cell. Her mind was torn as she wanted Callahan and his minions to get what was coming to them.

But also, Smith was young and probably scared and doing whatever he needed to save his own skin.

Finally, Griffin stepped back from Smith. The soldier was bleeding from the cheek. Griffin had avoided his nose, not wanting to completely suffocate him by breaking his nose and leaving his mouth covered with tape. Breathing hard, Griffin flexed his red knuckles and looked over at Max. He went to her and put his arms gingerly around her.

"I'm sorry. I needed to do something," he murmured into her hair. She just nodded her understanding.

"Can we get out of here?"

"Yes. We figured out a weak spot where we can sneak into the city beyond the controlled zone. That's the direction Cliff and Jack are waiting."

Turner led the small rebellion group. Max was in the middle and Griffin brought up the rear, keeping an eye out for anyone that might sneak up on them. They got to the entrance of the building and slowed for Turner to check and make sure the coast was clear. He checked his watch before stepping out. Griffin quietly explained while they stood still that they had timed the watches since they had arrived, learning how the shelter worked. It was like a predictable machine and they knew exactly when they could sneak out.

A hand stuck back into the door and motioned them forward. Stepping into the crisp clean air was like life entering into Max's body again. She breathed deeply, bringing the oxygen deep into her lungs. She hadn't smelled anything fresh for days and the feeling was wonderful. The cool air caressed her bare skin, causing her to shiver. She could smell the trees and vegetation nearby. As well as the smells of gas and food being cooked. Not all of the smells were pleasant, but every one of them brought Max joy.

Griffin squeezed her arm, encouraging her to move faster. She grinned like a loon at him, so happy to be stepping foot outside again. Griffin just grinned back but pushed her forward. Turner was following a slim path between the gate and the building they were leaving. The cell seemed to be in a large concrete structure at the edge of the shelter. Of course, Callahan would do that, he wouldn't want anyone to hear or know what he was doing. Max had made enough noise to wake the dead, but it didn't seem like anyone passed close enough to ever hear.

Following Turner, Max squeezed between the wall and fence and stepped carefully. Her coordination felt off, possibly from hanging for so long, or from dehydration. Turner had just reached a corner when he stopped and crouched down. Max looked through the chain link and realized that the other side of the fence was a steep grassed hill. At the bottom, concrete jersey barriers were lined and stacked. Max assumed it was to fend off the infected, though from that distance she couldn't see any.

The sound of metal being moved caught Max's attention and she looked down to see what Turner was doing. Slowly he pulled apart two sections of the fence that had been cut open. He quickly slipped through and held it open for Max. She tried to crouch down, but the pain lancing through her body caused her to fall to the side. Griffin was with her immediately helping her up. Between the two men, they were able to move Max through the open fencing. Griffin followed quickly after.

Immediately after all three of them were on the other side of the fence a soft beeping sounded, and Turner hit the grass. Griffin followed and pulled Max with him. Getting to the ground quickly took the breath from Max and she began to hyperventilate trying to get air back into her body. Turner turned off the alarm on his watch and they waited. Max laid her head on the grass and closed her eyes for a moment, thinking if she just rested she would be ok to move again. She hadn't meant for the blackness of exhaustion to suck her down again.

CHAPTER TWENTY-FIVE

Her head jostled around, waking her from sleep. The feeling of floating gave her a queasy feeling in her stomach for a moment. Max opened her eyes to see Griffin's determined face above her. She was cradled in his arms as he walked quickly away from the shelter. She cursed in her head realizing she had passed out again.

"Griffin," she said quietly. He stopped abruptly in surprise and looked down at her.

"Damn, Max, you gotta stop doing that. It scares the crap outta me."

"Sorry."

"Don't be sorry. I'm sorry. We pushed you too hard too fast. You are probably feeling like hell."

"Hell is one way to put it," she replied, grimacing as she felt her injured ribs pressed against his body.

"This is hurting you?" He asked. She nodded slightly.

They were in the city, away from the shelter. The shine of the lights from the camp could still be seen, so they hadn't gone far. Griffin stepped closer to the building they were walking by and placed Max's feet on the ground carefully. He held her waist softly as she got her bearings and found her balance again. Her head was still spinning and for a moment she was afraid she was going to pass out again. She placed her uninjured hand against the nearby wall and leaned in, taking deep breaths to calm her body.

"We can't stay here long, Max. They will figure out you are missing soon," Turner whispered.

"I know. I'm sorry. I just can't seem....to....focus," Max mumbled her reply as she started to fall again. Griffin was there, holding her up, before scooping her back into his arms.

"I'm sorry this hurts, but you can't walk. We have to get you to the car," he said as Max cried out softly from the movement. She nodded her understanding and buried her face in his shoulder to try and deal with the pain. Now that she wanted to pass out, the pain seemed to keep the black at bay.

"How long? How long was I kept in there?"

"It's been six days since I visited you when you were first taken there."

"What made you come for me?" Max asked. Six days. The pain she felt and the condition her body was in made her feel like it had been weeks, not just six days.

"The doctor," Griffin started to say but was stopped by Turner. They had come to a small alley. Turner stood at the corner of the entrance, and Griffin leaned against the wall behind him. Taking out a flashlight, Turner flashed down the alley two short shots, then one long, then two short again. A car started up and headlights illuminated the alley.

"Momma?" Jack's voice came from the car.

"Jack!" Max called back to her.

Griffin walked down to the car and opened the back door.

"Jack, honey, move over a bit. Your mom isn't feeling so great, need to give her a little room." He smiled fondly at the girl as she immediately obeyed his request. Max wondered how they had been together while she had been locked up. He carefully placed Max in the seat before sliding her into the center and climbing in next to her.

As soon as they were all in Cliff pulled out of the alley and headed the opposite direction of the shelter. The city was pitch black around them, night swallowing the buildings in places giving Max a surreal feeling. The headlights were the only light beside the moon, which wasn't full enough to help illuminate things. The darkness made Max nervous, but they had no choice but to run in the night. If they had waited until the sun rose, Callahan would have been in Max's cell for his daily conversations.

Max turned back to Griffin, "The doctor?"

"Oh right. The doctor came to us yesterday. She was really upset and wanted to speak with me. Once we found a chance to talk alone, she told me about your injuries, and what she thought was happening to you in there."

"We had already decided it was time to go," Turner added from the front seat. "Things were...off...there. And they wouldn't stop mentioning taking Jack."

"Right. So, we had prepared, cut the fence. Snuck out once at night to find the car. Moved it to the alley. Made sure our supplies were loaded up. We had been planning on coming to get you in a few days. But the doctor came and she didn't think you would make it," Griffin said. Then in a smaller voice, he added, "She was afraid you were giving up."

"I told her that I wouldn't give Callahan what he wanted, and to make sure you knew that," Max replied.

"She told us that. So, we moved up our timeline and came to get you as soon as night fell. What was it that Callahan wanted so badly?"

"Rafe. He wants my brother."

"Why would he want your brother?" Turner asked.

"Callahan said Rafe knows about the plague. He even claimed that Rafe knew how to cure it," Max replied.

"How could that be possible?" Griffin asked.

"I don't know. Callahan spun a good story about how it could have happened. But no matter what he said, I know my brother. He would never keep the cure hidden. Rafe is a good man. He would want to help people."

"What proof did Callahan have?"

"He didn't give me proof. But he knew things. Things about Montana, about Rafe and Alex, about our home."

"And when you didn't answer him?"

"Take your pick," Max said, weakly gesturing to her body.

"I'm so sorry, Max. I should have been there sooner. I asked daily to see you, but they always had excuses for why it wasn't a good time. I would never have guessed it would have gone so far," Griffin said. He took her injured hand in his and looked down at the brace.

"Doctor said she thinks it's broken. She did what she could for it," Max said softly. "Tell me, what else did you see that was weird at the shelter?"

"They had scouting parties in and out every day, but they never brought anyone back. We assumed they were looking for living people. You also weren't the only one Callahan was questioning. We saw people drug away to the same building you were in. A lot of the soldiers were rough and inappropriate with the survivors. Something that would typically never be allowed in a military installment," Griffin explained.

"They aren't looking for the living. I think they are looking for my brother. And anyone associated with the place he was working. Callahan claimed they had been at my home," Max grimaced and looked away for a moment.

"What is it, Max?"

"He claims they burned my home down," she replied quietly.

"What?!" Griffin exclaimed, pulling back to look at her.

"Ouch," Max muttered as she caught herself from sliding sideways.

"Sorry...sorry," Griffin said as he propped her back up next to him. "What do you mean he burned down your home?"

"He knew things about the way the house on the compound looked. Said they were after Rafe. But that he escaped when they burned the house," Max's voice was flat and emotionless. She couldn't bring herself to believe that her home was gone. Or to imagine her brother running from a fire.

"You don't really believe that, do you? Why would they attack Rafe if he had something they wanted?"

"None of it makes sense, Griffin. My family, we aren't important in the world beyond our compound. The whole thing is so confusing."

"Do we still go to Montana?" Cliff asked from the driver's seat. He didn't take his eyes off the dark road, the headlights slicing a path through the upended cars and debris littering the streets. Max thought for a moment, gazing out of the windshield. If the walls were still around the compound, it would still be a safe place to stay. They would have to rebuild. It would take time, but it was worth it if they could survive the plague there. And her sister, Alex, would be going there.

"Yes. It's still the safest place I know," Max replied finally.

They drove through the night. Getting away from the city had been easy after they put distance between the shelter and themselves. When dawn started to break, the car was running on fumes. Griffin and Turner worked together to siphon a few cars that were stopped or crashed along the freeway. By midmorning, everyone was exhausted and the car reeked of gas fumes. Max slept through most of the stopping and the morning. Jack curled up against her mother carefully and slept peacefully.

Deciding they were far enough away now to get rest, Cliff pulled the sedan behind a small farm store that stood on the outskirts of a small town. They hid among bobcats and tractors. Nothing moved around the area, alive or infected. Using jackets in the windows, they blocked out some of the light and sleep came easily, despite the tight conditions of the sedan.

Max came awake with a start. Her face was pressed into Griffin's chest, his arm carefully draped around her. He was breathing deeply, a soft snore coming from his open mouth. She laid still for a moment, evaluating the pains she felt, trying to determine what had awoken her so suddenly. The loud sound of an engine near the sedan answered her unspoken question.

"Cliff," Max said, her voice hoarse at first. She cleared her throat and pushed herself into a painful sitting position. "Cliff!" She said to the front seat, louder this time.

"Max, what is it?" Griffin asked, awake now that she was talking and moving. She tried to lean forward to shake

Cliff, but her ribs protested and she fell back against the seat gasping. As she sat the sound of the engine came louder now, and Griffin shot forward to shake Cliff. The man sat up quickly, eyes wild and unfocused.

"There's someone here," Griffin said quietly. Turner was already pulling the jackets from the windows to get a view from the outside. He cursed out loud when a military-style Hummer appeared on the other side of the equipment they were hiding behind. As if they immediately spotted the movement, the Hummer took off for the end of the row and started to turn in their direction.

"Cliff, let's get the hell out of here," Turner said as he grabbed his rifle and checked the safety. In a panic, Cliff reached under the steering column to work with the wires. Max tried to sit forward to see what he was doing. She could hear the electric sound of the wires touching but it took a few tries before the car turned over and stayed on. The Hummer had rounded the building and was barreling toward the front of their car.

Cliff threw the sedan into reverse and looked behind him. Max ducked out the way, air escaping her mouth in a rush as the pain in her ribs tore through her. She laid into Jack, who took her uninjured hand in her little hands. Max turned her face into her daughter's and kissed her cheek quickly. Then they were both thrown into Griffin's side as Cliff performed a crazy turn to get the sedan facing the other way.

Looking over her shoulder, Max could see the Hummer was on their bumper. It was hard to see into the vehicle, but she could see at least the driver, one soldier in the passenger seat and another that was leaning forward yelling at the driver. No Callahan. But of course, he would send his minions after her. He'd never lower himself and come after her himself. Staring at the soldiers, she wondered what their orders were. Obtain her and bring her back. Or kill her so she couldn't tell others what was happening under Callahan's command.

"We need to go faster," Max said to Cliff, as they slid onto the small road the equipment company sat on. He pressed his foot further on the gas, but their little car wasn't going to be a match for the Hummer's powerful engine.

Coming to a four-way stop, Cliff didn't slow the car, he just sped straight through it. The road was surrounded by woods on either side, their direction taking them more into the mountains and forest. They came upon the small town they were planning on coming into and scavenging. There was no time for that now. The Hummer just followed them through the small streets and buildings.

"Maybe I can lose them in town?" Cliff said uncertainly.

"Maybe we should pull over, I'll give myself up. Then you could go to Montana. Keep Jack safe," Max said in a quiet voice to Griffin.

"No, absolutely not. Plus, do you really think if we pull over, they will let any of us go at that point?"

"We aren't going to outrun them," Max said.

Griffin looked over his shoulder now, and his face was set in grim lines. He turned back around and grabbed his rifle as well, checking the safety and preparing himself for a fight. Max felt useless. She could probably shoot with her uninjured hand, but supporting a gun with her broken hand was going to be hard. Her tomahawk was in the trunk with the rest of their weapons, because not everything would fit into the small sedan cab.

Cliff took a sudden turn, and then another, winding them through some of the small city streets. Max prayed that they didn't find a dead end street in their wild race to get away from the Hummer. The large vehicle had to turn slower, each turn gave them a little breathing room. But once they were turned the soldiers could speed up and come after them again.

They came to the end of the small town and Cliff took the remaining street that seemed to lead them back to the main street they had entered on. The gas pedal was pushed to the floor but the sedan just couldn't go any faster in the small amount of time. Suddenly they were bumped forward. The soldiers were done playing cat and mouse. The Hummer bumper connected with the sedan again, pushing them forward. Cliff struggled to keep the car under control.

When they reached the main road, the soldier timed their strike for the perfect moment. Cliff took the turn to get back onto the main road and the Hummer solidly connected with the rear of the car, sending them sliding across the asphalt. The car went off the other side of the road, and into the trees.

"HOLD ON," Cliff shouted.

The momentum from the Hummer's assault threw the car into the woods, with incredible force. Max threw her arms around Jack, bracing them both as she watched the car head straight for a large tree. The squeal of tires and brakes could be heard as Cliff tried to control the car and stop the inevitable impact they were heading toward. The last noise before the crunch of the car against wood was Jack screaming.

As the car finally came to a halt, they all flew forward in their seats. Seatbelts saved them from any major injuries, but the car was wrecked beyond driving. The pain in Max's already abused body caused her to see stars as she tried to unwrap her arms from around Jack and check her daughter for injuries. Griffin was also reaching across, touching Jack's face and head, making sure she didn't have any major wounds.

"I'm ok," Jack sniffed, tears rolling down her face.

"Are you sure?" Griffin asked. Jack nodded.

"You're bleeding," Max said. She reached over to touch a cut on Griffin's forehead. "It's not bad."

"I think I hit my head on the window when we spun."

"Where are the soldiers?" Turner asked suddenly from the front seat.

Panic flared in Max. They were sitting ducks in the car, crashed in the woods. She turned to look out the back window and realized she couldn't clearly see the road. The embankment they went down was steep, and the Hummer hadn't followed. *Where were they?* Max thought to herself, knowing whatever the orders were, the soldiers wouldn't stop until they had completed their mission.

"We need to get out of this car. Maybe go into the woods to hide," Max said. Griffin agreed and popped open his door slowly. He got out and crouched with his rifle at the ready, waiting to see if an attack was imminent. When nothing seemed to be coming from the road, Turner and Cliff also exited. Cliff ran to the back of the car and lifted the trunk, pulling out their packs. It was then that they heard the yells from the soldiers.

Max slid from the car and reached in to pull Jack behind her. Once out, Jack grabbed her pack and Turner led the group into the woods. Max carefully strapped her tomahawk to her waist, not feeling comfortable without a weapon and followed her daughter into the trees. The pop, pop, pop sound of gunfire sounded behind her, and she bent slightly and started to run. The hollow sound of bullets striking trees nearby made her move faster, despite her body protesting.

Griffin was behind her returning fire as Cliff ran by them to get to Jack and Turner. With Turner in the lead, they wove through the trees, trying to put something between them and soldiers. They had come down the embankment after them and were pursuing them into the woods. In total there were five soldiers, more than Max guessed. They were all in dark fatigues, carrying rifles pressed to their shoulders. Every few trees, Griffin would press himself behind a trunk and return fire to slow the group down.

A surprised bellow caught Max's attention and she whirled to look back at the soldiers. She had assumed that Griffin's shots had found their mark, but instead, she watched as an infected fell upon the soldier, biting into his exposed neck, spilling blood down his fatigues. Griffin turned to Max, his eyes wide with surprise and they both surveyed the woods. Together in sick realization, they found they had missed one thing in the woods as they ran in. It was full of the infected. And they were drawn by the noise of the gunfire.

Max pulled her tomahawk with her uninjured hand and spun to catch up with Jack. Griffin easily passed her as they ran, both wanting to get to Jack and protect her. Max slid to a stop, breathing heavily when she caught up. Jack was tucked against Cliff protectively and Turner was moving slower now through the trees, picking off infected as he could while they moved forward.

The cracking of brush had Max turning to look behind them to find a group of five infected lumbering toward them. Griffin stepped up with his rifle and began to take single shots, he quickly took care of those following and Max fell into step with him as they followed the group deeper into the trees.

"Where did the soldiers go?" Max asked suddenly, realizing it didn't seem like they were pursuing them any longer.

"I think they decided facing the infected wasn't worth it," Griffin replied.

"Probably figure the infected will finish the job on me."

"Execution by infected."

They walked as quietly as they could, trying to not draw attention to themselves if possible. Infected would stumble into their path and they would be quickly dispatched. When it felt safe from the soldiers, they turned back toward the road and what would lead them to town. They walked a large arc, hoping that if the soldiers were still looking for them, they wouldn't be looking so far from where they started.

Abruptly Turner stopped and pulled his rifle back to his shoulder. Cliff pulled Jack closer into the middle of the group. When Max and Griffin caught up, they realized they were walking directly into a horde of infected. And if their path was any indication, they knew the living were in the woods. Turner began to shoot at the nearest ones, trying to make a path, with Griffin shooting off to one side and Max standing guard on the other.

"I'm out!" Turner's shout came from the front of the group. He slung the rifle across his back and pulled a knife from his hip. Griffin soon had to do the same, running out of ammo and having no safe time to reload.

"We have to run for the road," Griffin yelled.

With Jack between the adults, they began to jog toward the nearest exit of the trees. As they ran, Max struggled to keep up, her breathing labored. When the group of them burst onto the road, the Hummer could be seen down the road. The doors all stood open, none of the soldiers nearby. Max turned to look back at the road and found the infected rambling out of the shadows, chasing the living group. She stepped toward the trees and chopped down the first one with her tomahawk. The handle was ripped from her hand, her strength not able to hold tight.

"Damn it," she muttered.

"I'll get it," Griffin said as he walked by her to the infected body on the ground. He yanked the tomahawk free and used it on the next infected that was within reach. He then cleaned the blade on the infected's clothing and brought it back to Max.

"You should only fight when it's absolutely necessary," Griffin said to her quietly.

"Does that sound like me?"

"No. But you aren't at one hundred percent. That's not a bad thing, Max. Just means you're mortal like the rest of us."

Max didn't answer, just jogged to catch up to Turner, Jack, and Cliff. They were making their way back toward the small town. Finding a vehicle was their top priority. Then put as much distance between them and the soldiers as possible. They reached the first building that looked like a small log house but was really a real estate office. The signs outside boasted they sold land and pre-made wood houses to put on them. The group ducked behind the building quickly, concealing themselves from any nearby eyes.

They made their way through small alleys that split old red brick walls. The areas were littered with debris, from the lack of trash pick-up and people fleeing the plague. The town felt like a ghost town, with no living moving except the group of five looking for a car. They came to an old pickup and decided it would be decent even if two adults had to camp out in the bed of the truck. It was only until they got to Montana, which Max only thought would take another day at most.

Max took the job of hot-wiring the truck since she was feeling woozy and sick from all the movement. Turner took Cliff and Jack and decided to scavenge a nearby store. Max settled into the driver's seat of the truck for a moment, and let her head fall back against the glass window behind her.

"Are you alright?" Griffin asked, watching her with concern on his face.

"Just in pain, ya know, every time I breathe." She shifted a little, trying to give her ribs a rest but then another part of her body would hurt. She got back out of the truck, to find her tools for the hot-wire. Two pills and a bottle of water were shoved into her face. She looked up at Griffin, one eyebrow raised in question.

"Tylenol with Codeine. It was the only pain reliever they didn't take when they went through our stuff I guess. We'll try to find something stronger for you before we go. But take this. It should take the edge off."

Max didn't want to feel foggy in the environment they were in. Living in the plague-filled world meant being top of your game at all times. You didn't have time for mistakes or laziness. On the other hand, Max couldn't keep functioning with the pain she was feeling in her side. Her hip was also a nasty shade of black and purple from the constant kicking. After much internal debate, she finally took the pills from Griffin's hand and swallowed them with water.

She was just going back to find her tools when a scream ripped through the small town. Max froze, listening for the direction of the scream. However, she was in motion a moment later, following a sprinting Griffin. Max's brain felt frozen, thinking of Jack and feeling dread. The scream, it couldn't be her. She had let Jack out of her sight. Since she was going with Turner, Max hadn't questioned it. She had actually relaxed a bit having other adults around to help keep her safe. Now she found herself wondering if she had been wrong for letting her go.

Griffin found the store Turner had entered with Jack and Cliff. He ran inside, without slowing. Max surveyed the outside, before tentatively stepping into the darker interior. She found herself in a small grocery store. Products and trash were strewn around the room. Shopping carts were piled against the sliding doors, but Turner had broken out a wall of windows to enter the building instead.

"Momma!" Jack shrieked and ran straight for Max. Her daughter was covered in blood and Max fell to her knees when she got close.

"What happened? Oh my god, Jack, are you hurt? Where?" Max was spitting out the questions while running her hands over Jack's body. Not finding any wounds showing, Max looked up at her face.

"It's not me, the blood isn't from me," Jack stuttered.
"Who's?"

"Turner." Jack began to sob and wrapped herself around Max. Carefully without making them both fall, Max stood with Jack in her arms. She walked deeper into the store, looking for Griffin. When she found a trail of blood on the ground, she followed it. First, she found two truly dead infected, collapsed onto each other in the row. The large one had once been a man, an employee of the store, judging by the red apron he was wearing over a polo shirt. His face was stained with fresh blood, giving Max a sick feeling in her stomach. The other was a smaller man and a knife handle was sticking out of his temple. Putting Jack down, Max reached down and pulled out the knife.

"Griffin?" Max called quietly.

"Here." His muffled voice came from further into the store.

Max picked Jack back up and followed where she though Griffin was. When they got close, Cliff came out of the darkness, startling Max. She stepped back and began to raise the knife in her hand before she realized he wasn't infected.

"I'll take her," he said solemnly. Leaning closer to Max's ear he whispered, "She doesn't need to see this any more than she already has."

Max nodded and let Jack go into Cliff's arms. She sniffled into his neck. Max realized for Jack to be covered in Turner's blood, she must have seen what had happened to him. Her heart broke a little thinking about what her daughter had to endure in this world. Max came upon Griffin, on his knees next to Turner who was laying on his back. Max immediately went to Griffin's side and gasped at what she saw. Turner's shoulder had a large bite, blood pooling beneath his body.

"Oh god, what happened?" Max asked.

"The infected were in the row over from us. I don't know why I didn't hear them, smell them," Turner said in a small voice. He winced in his pain. "When we started moving around, it caught their attention. We got to the end of this row and they came around at the same time. Jack....Jack was too close. I pushed her back, but the big one got me."

"You saved Jack. She's alive because of you," Griffin said. His voice cracked, and Max laid her hand on his back, wishing she had the strength to give him.

"Good. That's good. You're a dad now, Griff. That's just crazy."

"Right. Who would have guessed," Griffin said with a sad smile.

"So you gotta make the right choice here. You need to go and get your daughter to safety."

"We will."

"I mean now. Leave me here, Griff. We know my trip is over."

"We'll stay with you. I can't just leave you like this, Turner. You're my brother," Griffin said, his voice almost pleading.

"You can, you will. You have your family to take care of now. Get away from here, before more men show up to take them back to the facility." Turner pushed Griffin's hand away from his wound. He had been doing what he could to slow the bleeding, but as Max knew, the wound would never heal. The blood began to flow with more force. Turner reached for his hip and pulled his gun from its holster.

"I will take care of this on my own. You will not carry that burden, do you hear me, brother?" Turner said, his voice coming with more force and certainty now. Griffin just looked at him stricken, unable to speak. Turner instead turned to look at Max.

"You'll take care of him, right?"

"Of course, I will," she answered immediately.

"Get him out of here. I would have loved to see your beautiful Montana," he paused, his face contorting in pain. "It's strange. I know it's done, but my brain wants to fight it. You guys need to go. Max, get him out of here!"

Max leaned down quickly and placed a soft kiss on Turner's forehead.

"Thank you, for saving my baby."

She stood then, grabbing Griffin's hand in hers. He didn't respond but she yanked at him until he stood woodenly next to her.

"Damn it, go, Griffin," Turner pleaded from the ground. He pushed his pack toward Max and she picked it up, now heavy with the foods they had packed from the store.

"Thank you, Turner," Griffin said quietly. Turner nodded slightly and gave him a mock salute.

"Come on, Griffin, let's go. We need to get Jack away from here," Max spoke quietly, trying to soothe him and reach him with her words.

Griffin didn't speak as they walked back through the store. His hand squeezed Max's tightly and it was that lifeline she held onto as she led him through the broken window into the sunlight. Cliff had taken Jack back to the truck they were taking, both of them closed inside the cab for safety.

Max slung the bag of food into the bed of the truck, just as a gunshot rang out from behind them. Griffin's body tensed, and Max could see he was going to bolt back to the store. She jumped in front of him and put her hands on his chest. His face was full of agony, the pain of losing his brother in arms. He pushed against her, his eyes not focused on her, but on where she knew he was picturing Turner's dead body.

"Griffin, there's nothing to do for him. He knew that. He sent you away to save us all."

"I left him."

"You didn't leave him, he made you go." She pushed him harder, to get him to look at her. "Honey, look at me."

He finally looked down at Max, his hands came up and covered hers, squeezing. Max held in the squeak of pain she wanted to let out from the pressure on her broken hand. Griffin needed her strength right then, not her broken pieces.

"I know, it has to hurt like hell. I didn't know Turner long, and it's hurting me. There was nothing to be done. And now we need to protect Jack, just like Turner did."

Sitting in the running truck, Griffin's knuckles were white on the steering wheel. Max sat in the middle and Cliff was crammed into the passenger side. Jack sat half on Max and half on Cliff. Losing Turner made the group want to stay close together. Max put her hand on Griffin's shoulder, squeezing reassuringly.

"Let's get home."

CHAPTER TWENTY-SIX

The beauty of Montana was unbeatable for Max. As they crossed into the state, still driving their single cab pick up, Max soaked in the breathtaking sights of mountains and green trees. They drove the last road to the turnoff for the compound, a winding road that climbed into the forest. The turnoff was hidden by the growth of trees, but Max knew it well and found it without thinking.

They bumped down the road, noting what looked like piles of burned infected in one of the clearings off to the side. Max's heart gave a little jump. If there was someone cleaning up the infected outside of the walls, then someone was inside. She slowed the truck to round a corner that she knew would lead them to the gate. Looking into the woods, she didn't see any infected nearby.

She immediately jumped out of the truck when they reached the large metal rolling gate. Punching the code into the keypad the door moved back, allowing the truck to be driven in by Griffin. Once the truck cleared the tracks, Max stepped in and closed the door. Once secure, she turned and took in her home.

The stone fence was intact all the way around from what she could see and the gate already proved it worked and was secure. The house was over the first hill on the property, and part of Max was afraid to climb the hill and find the house burned to the ground. Gazing that direction, she noticed people emerging at the top of the hill. The woman, in the middle, holding a hammer in one hand and a Bowie knife in the other was all Max needed to see.

Leaving her group in the truck, Max ran for the people on the hill. As soon as she ran, the woman from the top came running down to meet her. The two collided at the bottom, hugging each other tightly.

"Maxy," Alex, Max's older sister said. "I was losing faith, I thought you would never make it."

"Alex, oh god, Alex."

In that moment, being home, the closest thing to safe since the plague started, Max began to cry. Her tears fell onto her sister's shirt, and she gripped her harder. When Alex squeezed Max tighter against her, Max let out a little yelp of pain. Alex released her and stepped back to look at her. She took in the tear-streaked face, the filthy clothes, the bandages.

"Max, what in the hell happened to you?"

"I have so much to tell you," Max said, slowly sitting on the ground, realizing her head was getting fuzzy and the pain in her ribs was increasing. Alex knelt with her, and let Max continue to cry into her chest, as she did when she was a little girl with a skinned knee. She rocked Max slightly, holding her lightly, as to not press on any unknown injuries.

"Auntie Alex," Jack cried as she ran up to them. The little girl collapsed next to her mother and Alex pulled her in for a hug and kiss as well.

"Billie and Henry are up the hill if you want to go find them," Alex said smiling at her niece. Jack's face beamed, happier than she had been in weeks. She dropped her pack and took off running for the group of people still waiting at the top of the hill.

"Blake?" Max asked. Alex just shook her head slightly, her eyes taking on a haunted look. "Oh god, Alex I'm so sorry." Max wrapped her arms around her sister. Behind her, she could hear Cliff and Griffin talking quietly. Max released Alex so she could stand up carefully. She wavered a little and Griffin was at her elbow quickly.

"Hi, Alex," Griffin said.

"Griffin?" Alex was clearly confused, and a little shocked to see Jack's father standing next to Max.

"It's a long story," Max said. She then motioned to the man standing still behind them. "This is Cliff. He lost his family and has come with us. I told him there was room for him."

"Of course. There's room for everyone. It's so nice to meet you, Cliff." Alex, the sweet one of their family, walked right up to Cliff and hugged him. He looked slightly taken aback, but he returned her hug.

Alex then turned to lead them up the path to the top of the hill. Max wanted to call out to her sister, tell her what Callahan had told her. She wanted her sister to prepare her for their home to be burned down. But she didn't say anything, just followed up the hill with Griffin's assistance. She could feel the adrenaline and strength leaving her body and she was nothing but weary now.

They reached the top of the hill and Max fell into Griffin as she slumped in relief. The house, the home her father had built and she grew up in, was still standing. Tears fell on her cheeks again and she scrubbed them away before anyone saw. Griffin, of course, noticed everything and he held her tightly, supporting her with the strength he had to share. They had both been through hell to get there, and now that they were, it was hard to comprehend.

"He lied," Max finally said.

"Of course, he did," Griffin replied.

Alex turned away from where she was introducing Cliff to the other adults in the group. Max noticed Alex also found people that needed her help and brought them home with her. Alex came to Max and stood by her while they looked at the house.

"Who lied?" Alex asked. Max smirked. Her sister heard everything and was so damn perceptive.

"It's part of all I have to tell you. Introduce us to your friends."

Alex led Max and Griffin over to two teenagers that were listening to the quick chatter between Jack and Alex's children Billie and Henry. The tall boy looked up when they approached and he smiled easily. The girl next to him was clearly his sister, their coloring so similar. And when she smiled, her face looked just like her brother's.

"This is Easton and Candace. Kids, this is my sister Max. And her...uh...friend? Griffin," Alex said. Griffin covered up a laugh and Max shot him a death look.

"Looks like you have stories for me too, Alex," Max said, smiling at the older kids. She could see the pride on her sister's face when she looked at them. Knowing her the way she did, Max was sure she had taken these children and cared for them as her own. It was just in her sister's heart to love all that came to her.

"This is Margaret," Alex motioned to an older woman, with gray spiked hair. She was a grandmotherly type Max figured, but she was tough too. The woman smiled and walked over to Max.

"Your sister has been worried about you," she said as she offered her hand to Max. Max took it with her uninjured hand and shook.

"I've been worried about her too. I'm happy to meet you."

"And this is Marcus, just a stray I seemed to have picked up," Alex said sarcastically, nodding her head toward an attractive man standing slightly off to the side. Max noted the fact that he looked uncomfortable in the situation and Alex seemed to enjoy giving him a hard time. She raised her eyebrow at her sister and Alex just rolled her eyes and turned back to the kids. She bent to hug and kiss Jack again.

"Nice to meet you, Marcus," Max said, waving slightly. He waved back and smiled. Max felt like she had to smile back because the man's face was so genuinely friendly. She could tell Alex had quite a lot she needed to share.

"Max, come up to the house. We need to talk. Margaret, would you mind getting Griffin and Cliff settled? We'll put them in the bunkhouse," Alex said. Max walked with Alex toward the house and she noted the damage to the front and the work being done.

"Was it a fire?" Max asked in a small voice.

"Yes. You seemed to think something worse was happening."

They entered the house through the side door. The house was clean, except for the work being done to repair the broken windows and burned wall portion. Max ran her hand along the kitchen counter, memories flooding her of a time when life was simple. No matter how strange it was to be raised by her father, their lives on the compound were clear and simple. They had one main goal, being prepared to survive. Everything else wasn't necessary.

Alex brought Max to the sofa and after working to get comfortable, Max started from the beginning. She told Alex about how they got stuck in the mall after being carjacked and the weather. When she got the part about saving Griffin and the fact that Jack knew the truth now, Alex was stunned. She didn't say a word, just listened as Max poured it all out. Max also told her about how their father had made sure she never heard from Griffin. That part seemed to make Alex quite angry. When Max got to the part about Callahan, Alex finally stopped her.

"Wait, this Major Callahan is looking for Rafe?"

"That's what he said. It's why he kept me locked up."

"And tortured you for information, that you clearly didn't have?" Alex's beautiful face was flushing with anger. She stood up and began to pace the room.

"He told me the house burned down. I'm not sure now if that was a lie, or whoever set the fire didn't wait to see how far it got," Max said.

"So, it was the military that came here, ransacked the house, and tried to burn it to the ground. I can't understand any of this," Alex said.

"I guess so. Did you know where Rafe was working? There was no sign of him when you got here?"

"No. He was gone when we got here. The last time I talked to him he just talked about the compound, nothing about work. He didn't act like there was anything important going on."

"That's not like him, Alex. If something big, like knowing about this plague, was happening, wouldn't he tell us?" Max asked.

"I want to think so. But he was living out here alone, or I think he was."

"What do you mean you think he was?"

"When I was cleaning up and trying to determine what was being looked for, I found some things. Women's things in the bathroom, some socks under his bed. I'm not sure he was sleeping in his room, but maybe in Dad's."

"You think he had a woman here and didn't tell us?"

"Maybe we teased him too much about having a woman in his life, so he just didn't include us in that part of his life," Alex replied.

"I'm worried. Where is he?" Max said.

"I am too," Alex admitted. "I've been wracking my brain on it. I've been to a few of the smaller towns in the area, thinking maybe he got stranded or hurt. I haven't found any sign of him."

Max stood then and headed to the hallway that led to her bedroom. She stepped into the room and noted it was clean. The bed was made, but not recently slept in. The closet door was open and the hangers were hanging neatly at one end. She left her room and went to Rafe's then, trying to visualize what Alex had told her.

"Margaret has been on a cleaning spree. After I searched everything, she insisted on getting the house ready for you and Rafe. She's convinced he will come back."

"He got out of here before Callahan's men could get him. Or he fought his way out. But he got away. If he hadn't, Callahan wouldn't have done all of this to me," Max said, holding up her broken hand.

"You need to rest, Max," Alex said, falling into mothering mode now that Max was with her.

"You're probably right. The house is safe to sleep in, right?"

"Yeah definitely. Marcus has proved a little bit useful, after working construction at some point. We determined the burned wall isn't load bearing because Dad added onto the back of the house when he built the second floor. We're working on replacing that wall somehow. The house is sound."

"I'm going to bunk in my room then," Max said, heading back to that door.

"Max?" Alex called to her as she reached her door. Max looked back at her. "I'm so glad you made it. I couldn't do this without you."

"Me either, Alex."

Rest turned into almost twelve solid hours of sleep. Max was only awake once when Griffin and Alex came in and forced her awake to eat. She sat against her headboard and ate the soup Alex was feeding her since she couldn't hold the bowl and work the spoon at the same time. One thing Max hated was feeling like a patient. Her body had other ideas, pulling her back to sleep easily after her stomach was full. She curled to one side, finding Griffin with her, his hand playing with her hair as she slept. She sighed in contentment and fell deeper into the abyss.

The next day, feeling antsy to be out of bed, she emerged into the Montana sunshine. She found Jack with the other kids, pulling weeds in the garden. Her daughter was happy and waved at her mother but continued her chore. Easton and Marcus were working together on the outdoor shower that Rafe had started. She found her sister in the root cellar her father had built years before. Alex was cataloging what was in the stores and Max was sure she was planning for the year.

"Hey," Max said when she stepped in.

"Hey, sleepyhead. Feeling a little better?" Alex scrutinized Max's face, making her want to look away. She knew the bruises would take time to fade.

"The sleep helped. Where's Griffin?"

"Last I heard, he and Cliff were washing the clothes you brought with you. Jack mentioned a Turner. What happened to him?"

"He didn't make it. Lost him the day before we got here. He saved Jack when some infected surprised them. He and Griffin went through boot camp together. They were really tight," Max explained. Alex sighed and let her head hang down for a moment before looking at Max again.

"It's the story of this world. Losing those we care about. We are lucky to be behind these walls with those that made it here."

"Always the positive one, aren't you, Alex?" Max said sarcastically.

"It's the only way I can be right now."

"What's with Easton and Candace?"

"I found them outside of Las Vegas. Their mother was killed by an infected. Before she died, she asked me to take them. Protect them. So I have. They have made themselves part of the family," Alex explained.

"That was good of you."

"It's the same I would hope someone would do for Billie and Henry if I were to die," Alex said, shrugging and turning back to the canned goods she was counting.

Max stepped down to stand next to her. The root cellar was a room their father had dug into the ground himself with an excavator. Once he had it to the depth he wanted he built the cellar out of cinder blocks, plywood, and concrete. When Max was young, her father taught her how to can and how to make things like jelly from the produce they had on the compound. The root cellar was always full of goods they could eat, especially in winter when fresh fruits and vegetables weren't always available. Later, once Max was older, her father built a temperature controlled greenhouse, giving them the ability to grow some things year around.

"How was Dad so right about all of this?" Max asked.

"Don't you wish you could ask him? I've been thinking that since this all began. I can almost see his face. The one when he knew he was right and I was wrong. Almost as if I was still a child," Alex replied.

"He never prepared me for torture," Max said softly. Alex stopped her writing and looked over at Max with warm eyes.

"No, he never prepared us for that. But you survived, Max. And that's all he would have wanted," Alex said.

"What are we going to do about Rafe? We can't just wait for him to come back. Something more is going on here," Max said.

"I know. I've been thinking about it. My only other guess is he went into the mountains somewhere. A place he knew he could hide, where the Major and his men wouldn't know to look," Alex replied thoughtfully.

"It would need to be easily defendable. He wouldn't put himself somewhere he couldn't see what was coming at him before it made it to him. Especially since he's on the run from the military."

"Where does that leave us? You two camped and did things together more after I left. Is there somewhere you can think of?" Alex asked.

Max tried to rack her brain. When they were teenagers, their father would tell them to go camping. He wouldn't help them or tell them where to go. Rafe and Max had created some special places they enjoyed going. Places where water was plentiful, fishing was easy, or the small game was easy to catch. There were a handful of locations she could think of. Only two though, that she would call defensible and safe.

"Two that really stand out in my mind for what he would be looking for. Do we go for him? See if he's there?"

"We'll have to take a team, maybe four of us. The woods are full of the infected. I think at first the ones we were dealing with had been drawn by the military coming here. Now they follow the sounds we make. The walls keep them out, but we still have to clean it up every once in a while."

"So we will be faced with the infected in the woods, as well as possibly the military looking for Rafe, or me. Awesome. Sounds like a day at the beach," Max replied, rolling her eyes.

"Your sarcasm wasn't hurt apparently," Alex said laughing.

"You wouldn't know me if it wasn't working," Max replied, joining in the laughter.

"What is that strange sound I hear down there?" A voice came from the entrance of the cellar. Max looked over at Alex, just in time to see her roll her eyes in annoyance.

"What's with Marcus?" Max whispered.

"He's obnoxious."

"He's attractive." Max pointed out.

"Yeah. Well, I just lost my husband, I'm not really noticing that right now."

"I'm sorry, Alex, I wasn't trying to imply you weren't sad about Blake. I'm so sorry about him not making it," Max said, laying her hand on her sister's arm.

"I know. I don't really have time for mourning anyway. I loved Blake. He's gone. I'm heartbroken. But I have to be one hundred percent in the moment to handle all that we need to do."

Max climbed out of the cellar back into the sunshine, greeting Marcus at the top of the steps. Deciding to get herself cleaned up, Max headed into the house. Once inside, a thought struck her, and she climbed the stairs to her father's room. Pushing open the door she stood on the threshold just looking at the familiar surroundings.

Alex had been right to assume Rafe had been sleeping in the room. It was lived in, things were moved around. Items that were obviously Rafe's were also in the room. Max went to the closet, finding her father's footlocker where it always was at the bottom. The lock that used to keep the kids out of it, hung open on the latch now. Taking a deep breath, she pulled open the box.

Sitting back on her heels, Max realized she wasn't sure what she expected. Maybe Rafe's things to be taking the place of their father's. Instead, when she looked into the footlocker it looked so similar to the way she remembered it from before. The kids were never allowed into their father's personal items, but Max had seen him open it enough times to remember how organized he was.

She first lifted the top shelf that held small things, none of which were emotional items. Mitch had stored his spare pocket knife, flint, and a package of waterproof matches, among other survival items stored on the top. The items on the bottom were what interested Max. Setting the shelf to the side, she reached in to pull a pile of photos out. Flipping through them quickly, Max remembered looking through them numerous times when she was growing up. They were the only photos of their mother that existed in the house. Mitch stored them in the footlocker. Sometimes, if he was feeling sentimental, he would bring the photos out and let the kids look at them.

The locker was packed with other random items. At the bottom, Max finally found what she hoped would be in there. Taking the bundle to the bed, she sat down heavily. At least fifty envelopes were strung together with a piece of twine. Flipping through them, Max could see her name repeated over and over in Griffin's handwriting. She unwrapped the bundle and let the letters spill out onto the bed. She rifled through until she figured out which one had the oldest postmark, a date that made her heart squeeze a little. It was around the same time she realized she was pregnant with Jack.

Max wasn't sure how long she sat there, ripping open envelopes, reading the letters and then finding the next one. She tried to absorb the words of love being written to her by a young boy who was full of ambition and dreams. As the letters went on, and he didn't receive a response from Max, the letters became more urgent. He went through being sad, begging for any word from her. And near the end, the letters were angry and bitter.

"He kept them?" Griffin's voice came from the doorway. Max's head snapped up and she had to blink a little in the sudden light when he switched on a lamp. It had gotten darker outside, but she had been so distracted by the letters she hadn't realized.

"I thought, guessed really, that if he were to keep them he would have had them in the one place we weren't allowed to go," Max replied. Suddenly she felt very self-conscious and not sure of herself. The words had been written years before, but to Max, they were brand new. She knew they weren't for Griffin.

"Now do you believe me?"

"I always believed you. I wanted to read them if they were here."

"And?"

"And what?" Max asked. She turned and straightened up the letters, keeping them organized in their envelopes so she would always know the order they arrived in. In her mind, someday, no matter what happened with Griffin and Max, she would be able to show their daughter that there had been love there.

"What did you think of the letters, Max?" Griffin asked, his voice taking on a gruff tone. Max stood and faced him. She couldn't seem to stop playing with her fingers, so she grabbed the hem of her shirt to stop the fidgeting. She looked up into Griffin's eyes, who had stepped within reach now.

"I think I'm sorry you thought I didn't love you. I'm sorry you had to go through boot camp thinking I had abandoned you. I wish..." Max trailed off. The intensity in Griffin's eyes made her stomach flutter. She felt ill-equipped to deal with the feelings she had and she suddenly felt like a teenager all over again.

"You wish?"

"I wish I had known you had written. I wish my father hadn't hurt me, hurt us, the way he did. I wish we were still those kids. Crazy in love with grand plans."

"Do we have to be kids to be in love?" Griffin reached out, touching a stray curl that had found its way across her cheek. Pushing it back, his finger ran along the shell of her ear, causing goosebumps to rise on her arms.

"What are you saying, Griffin?" Max asked. Her ability to handle emotional situations felt limited. A part of her was screaming to just tell Griffin how she felt. However, a larger part of her told her to shut her mouth and hear him first, so she didn't humiliate herself.

"Max, you have never been good with signals, have you?" Griffin laughed quietly. Max just weakly shrugged. He knew her better than any other man ever had in her life. She hadn't changed a great deal in eight years, at the core she was the same girl that Griffin had loved. Their survival across the country had shown Max that her heart still yearned for Griffin.

"I love you, Max," Griffin finally said, looking her directly in the eye, almost challenging her to argue.

"I love you too," Max said immediately.

"Was that so hard?" Griffin said with a grin. He closed the distance between them quickly and pressed his lips against hers. Max didn't hesitate to kiss him back and to wrap her arms around him. After a moment she pulled back breathless. She was pleased to hear Griffin breathing just as erratically. He pressed his lips against her forehead and stayed there for a moment.

"This is crazy. There are literally zombies at the gates. And we're talking about love?" Max said, pulling back to look up at him. He kissed her again, rough and full of desire.

"There's not a better time to find love," he whispered against her mouth.

The makeshift family gathered in the dining room and kitchen to eat dinner together that night. The laughter from the kids' table flowed over Max, giving her a second reason that day to smile a genuine smile. Griffin's hand squeezed her knee under the table and she flashed her smile at him. Alex sat across from Max, watching the interactions between the couple. She couldn't hide her smile either.

The kids were sent to play in the living room, while the adults stayed gathered around the table. Max and Alex laid out all of the information they knew. When Max talked about her torture and Callahan, the room was silent except for her softly spoken words. She gathered strength by holding Griffin's hand between both of her in her lap.

"Rafe is out there. We know it," Max finished.

"We have two spots we believe he could be in the mountains. Neither is completely reachable by vehicle. Our father didn't make it easy on us when we were in the wild," Alex explained.

"What are you wanting to do?" Marcus asked, leaning his elbows on the table.

"We need to find our brother, before Callahan and his men do," Max said.

"We are under the assumption that they are looking for him daily," Griffin explained. "While at the shelter where Callahan is headquartered, daily search parties went out. I timed one group between leaving and returning. They were gone three days. That's enough time to get to Montana, search for a day or so, and head back."

"Do you girls know how your brother would be mixed up in this plague?" Margaret asked. Alex and Max both shook their heads.

"Our brother is a good man. If he knew how to solve this, cure it, he wouldn't be hiding in the mountains," Alex replied.

"But he must know something. Or Callahan wouldn't be going to these lengths to find him," Max added and Alex nodded her agreement.

"As soon as Max has healed up, we are going to find him," Alex announced.

"I'm going," Easton spoke up. While Candace went with the kids into the living room, Easton insisted on staying with the adults. Max watched the way Alex treated him kindly and with affection.

"East..." Alex started.

"I want to help. And you know I can," he replied.

"We'll talk about it later," Alex suggested. Easton didn't argue. He just nodded his head at Alex.

"I'm definitely not letting you out of my sight, Max, I'm going," Griffin said. Max just rolled her eyes, but she didn't argue. The moment caused Alex to laugh out loud. Max shot her a glare but then smiled. Despite the plague, death, and horror they had been living through, being with her sister and Griffin made Max feel lighter.

Alex and Max took a walk around the property after the dinner talk. They walked in silence for awhile. Max ran her hand along the rock of the wall, the scrape of it reminding her of being a young child and running the same path around the compound. That was before the wall was finished, but some of it was all the same. Now this place that she had run from was the place that would keep them all safe.

"We have a lot to get ready for this trip to find Rafe," Alex said breaking into Max's thoughts. Max just nodded her agreement, though her sister wasn't looking at her.

"You can stay behind if you want to, Max."

"Why would I do that?" Max asked incredulously.

"You have a lot to live for here."

"So, do you, Alex! And we aren't dying. We are better together than apart," Max replied. She put her arm around her sister's waist.

Max believed that completely. The Duncans were a force to be reckoned with when they were whole. They had picked up some valuable additions along the way. They were a strong team when they were together, watching each other's backs. They were only missing Rafe. Determination welled in Max. They would find Rafe and make their family complete behind the walls. They would work to keep the compound viable. As a team, a family, they would survive.

EPILOGUE

Dear Max,

Hey, babe. I'm not sure I'm supposed to be writing, but I found a pen and paper and couldn't wait. I'm writing by flashlight right now. We're on a pretty rigorous schedule. Lights out means lights out. All the guys in my dorm are passed out from being so tired.

I couldn't sleep so I thought I'd write you a bit of a letter. I'm hoping to be able to mail this to you this week. I'm working hard and staying in line. I know you thought I would have a hard time listening and following orders. They don't give you much of a choice around here. Ha Ha. But I'm doing what my dad told me to do, keep my nose clean.

I've been thinking a lot about you since I got here. It's only been a few weeks, but I miss you. And it's hard to not be able to talk to you or see you. Will you send me some photos of you? Maybe some of us from camping or something? This will be the longest we've not talked since we got together. I know you thought the time would be good for us, so I just keep telling myself that.

Well, babe, I'm doing this for us. I don't mean to sound defeated, I'm not. I'm just homesick. But I'm going to do my absolute best because this is the way for us to start our life on the right foot. And once I get assigned a base, we'll move you there and we can be together. I love you, Max. I don't know if I tell you that enough. But just don't forget, that even though I'm here, I love you. And I'm thinking about you all the time.

>Love You,
>Griffin

Dear Max,

So, I missed you with my phone call today. Your dad said you were camping with Rafe for the week. I guess I'll have to try again next week. I'm dying to talk to you and actually hear your voice. Are you getting my letters? I haven't heard anything from you, so I'm including my address in this letter again, just in case you aren't writing it right or something.

I've been hoping every day when they do mail call that I'll get something from you. I've gotten letters from my parents. They said they haven't seen you lately. I had hoped you would visit them while I was gone, so they wouldn't be lonely. But I understand your dad probably keeps you busy, especially now that you aren't in school.

Well, I'm still working my ass off here. We run daily. And then sit-ups, push-ups, and pull-ups. We all have rotating duties too. Some of them really suck and then some are just boring. But just like most things around here, you don't really have a choice. You do the job, or you leave. And quitting isn't an option for me.

I also have learned how to eat an entire meal in four minutes or less. Crazy, right? You always complained that I ate too fast, and now I'm only getting faster. They don't give you a lot of time for chow, so you choke down what you can without tasting anything. Just need it for fuel to face whatever is coming next.

Babe, I really miss you. What is that saying about distance making the heart grow fonder? That's not to say I didn't love you before. But now, being away for so long, makes me realize how much I need you around. We are a great team. And I miss that team. Someday, Max, when I make you my wife, we'll be a team that faces the world together. Us against everything else!

I hope I hear from you soon. I'm going crazy not knowing how you are.

Love you,
Griff

Max,

Why aren't you writing, Max? Have I done something to upset you? When I left, we talked and you said you understood and agreed with what I needed to do. I knew you weren't super happy about it. But I thought we agreed that our love could battle anything. And it wasn't going to be too long. You said you'd write and we would make this work together.

I've tried to call you like ten times now. Every time your dad answers or there's no answer. And for some reason, your answering machine isn't picking up. Your dad isn't telling me why you aren't coming to the phone. Somehow, you're just never home when I call. How is that possible?

Max, I love you more than anything. If I could just come home now and get you I would. But how do I ruin everything I'm working toward? And I'm working toward it for us, for you and me to have the life we've always talked about. Please, Max, I miss you. Even when you're being difficult, I even miss that. Write, please.

>I love you,
>Griffin

Max,

This is going to be the last letter I send, Max. It's been a year. I came home after boot camp. Did you know that? Even if you did, I guess you didn't care. I was at my house. I came to the compound, but the gate was closed and locked and no one answered when I hit the buzzer. I stayed out there longer than I should have. I feel stupid.

I can't lie, Max, I feel like I'm adrift without you. Everything I planned in my life was because you would be by my side. I never loved anyone before you. I've never known what it is to have my heart crushed. I guess this is what it is. My guys from boot camp give me crap for acting like a woman. I try to not show them how badly I'm hurting. Someday, I guess it won't matter anymore.

I thought when I met you, you were made for me, and I was made for you. Something changed your mind about us. And I wish I knew what that was. Whatever it was, it couldn't have been important enough to just cut me off without an explanation. I don't know if I could ever forgive you for this, Max.

I don't even know why I'm writing this letter. I need closure. I need to say goodbye. Even if you will never read this, even if you just burn it. I know you won't reply. I think I lost all hope for that a while ago. I need to feel like I said my piece and I said goodbye.

I left Montana believing I had your love, your faith. I believed I had you. I know we are just kids, Max, like your dad liked to remind us all the time. But what we had, our love, it wasn't just for kids. We would have made it for the long haul. I would have loved you every day of your life if you had let me. I guess I might still love you forever, but you'll never know it.

Goodbye, Max. I hope whatever you found makes you happier than I did.

Griffin

<<<◇>>>

Acknowledgements

Thank you so much for joining Max Duncan on her escape to Montana. I hope you enjoyed her journey through the infected landscape of the country. The Duncan women hold a true place in my heart, with their strength and courage. To keep up with more of their stories, be sure to follow along on my website courtneykonstantin.com. I also post updates on my Facebook page at https://www.facebook.com/AuthorCKonstantin.

A huge thank you again to NoLine Designs (https://www.facebook.com/NoLineDesign) for a wonderful cover for SURVIVE. It's always nice to work with someone that can take my rambling ideas and create something that represents the story so well. The cover is the first thing a reader sees when they look at a book. I wanted Max to look all the strong woman she is, and NoLine Designs got it done for me!

As always my brainstorming bestie was by my side during the writing of SURVIVE. Thank you for reading every message I sent, no matter how long and all over the board it may have been. You always know when to rein me in when necessary, and push me further when I need it.

It's good that I have a great editor, since I have issues with commas apparently. Pam Ebeler from Undivided Editing keeps me on track with those evil little things, making sure I am able to concentrate on the bigger picture. Thanks for all your hard work Pam, I appreciate you!

The Sundown Series is far from over. Be sure to tune in as the story continues with the search for Rafe Duncan!

Made in the USA
Columbia, SC
25 November 2023